# Dark Horses

## Susan Mihalic

WELBECK

Published in 2021 by Welbeck Fiction Limited, part of Welbeck Publishing Group,
20 Mortimer Street London W1T 3JW

Cover design by Alexandra Allden
Cover photograph © Jitka Saniova / Arcangel Images

The moral right of the author has been asserted.

A CIP catalogue record for this book is available from the British Library

Paperback ISBN: 978-1-78739-518-3
E-book ISBN: 978-1-78739-517-6

Printed and bound by CPI Group (UK) Ltd., Croydon, CR0 4YY

10 9 8 7 6 5 4 3 2 1

For Penny and Janet
Wish you were here

# - One -

THE PILLS WEREN'T working yet.

My shoes echoed in the corridor as I hurried to the girls' room and pushed open the door. Cherry-scented antiseptic stung my throat as I ran into the first stall, pinned my knees together, and shot the bolt in the door. I hadn't had a bladder infection in ages. I'd hoped it would go away on its own, but yesterday I'd been forced to tell Mama about it when I passed blood. Without comment, she'd given me one of her old prescriptions of antibiotics. The pills were expired, but they were helping. Still, I was way below peak performance level, with Daddy picking me up in five minutes to take me to a three-day competition.

I willed myself to pee. Not a trickle. Not a drop. Just the urge to urinate and the inability to do so.

The restroom door opened and sighed shut with a soft bump.

"Seniors can't even go off campus for lunch anymore and that horsey little eleventh-grader leaves every day at one? What is it now, eleven-thirty, and she's out of here? We *earned* this."

"I know."

I didn't have to see the dimes in the penny loafers to recognize Sass Stewart and Annabelle Hardy.

Lots of people wanted to be Sass's friend, a preemptive move to avoid being a target, but we'd been at odds since elementary school. I was the horsey little eleventh-grader.

"Why does she get special privileges?" Annabelle said.

Sass expelled a sustained fart from a stall down the way.

"Gross," Annabelle said.

"No, gross is Horse Girl's mother with her legs wrapped around Mr. Dashwood at the overlook."

She hadn't even finished the sentence before my face prickled and sound became more acute. Annabelle squealed.

Down the row, toilet paper twirled on the spindle.

"Leda's mother saw them in the back of his station wagon, and her legs were in the air. Can you imagine?"

"Sick."

"She was probably drunk. But it explains why Roan"—Sass flushed the toilet—"gets special privileges. Her mother's screwing the headmaster. Shoot. I broke a nail."

"I have a file," Annabelle said.

The door to Sass's stall banged open and her navy loafers clopped past, dimes glittering.

In Daddy's words, the only way to take a ball-busting fence was head-on.

I pulled my panties up, jerked my kilt down, and yanked open my door. "Excuse me."

Annabelle's eyes popped. Sass's smile died. I was taller than they were, my back ramrod straight from years of riding.

I approached the sinks and turned on the tap. "First, you're both stupid cunts."

They gasped as if I'd slapped them. The *C* word was all-powerful, a line they'd never dare cross.

"Second, my mother didn't want me on this schedule, so there goes your narrative about special favors." I soaped my hands. "Third, she'd never fuck a man who wears a toupee."

I rinsed and dried my hands, tossed the paper towel in the trash, and went out into the corridor, anger and adrenaline propelling me down the hall to my locker. Had Mama lost her mind?

The door of the girls' room opened and closed. Footsteps came toward me. I reached for the fattest book I could put my hands on, ready to hit Sass upside the head if she said another word.

As they passed behind me, Sass stage-whispered, "A whore for a mother and a horse for a daughter."

I heaved my biology book at her, but she dodged and the book hit the floor with an ungodly loud smack.

They ran down the hall to the computer lab. From the door, Annabelle flipped me off. Sass made a hole with one hand and poked the index finger of her other hand in and out of it a few times. Then they returned to class.

Cunts.

As I retrieved my book, Mr. Griffin stuck his head out of the chemistry classroom, frowning.

"I dropped it."

He regarded me skeptically and ducked back into his room.

Outside, in the thin November sunshine, I sat on one of the marble benches to wait for Daddy. If he hadn't heard, did I warn Mama? No, never side against Daddy. He always won. Should I warn him? No, he'd be in a foul mood all weekend. Best to feign ignorance.

Plan of inaction in place, I settled enough to think beyond a strategy. My parents didn't have a happy marriage. Mama's infidelity surprised me less than her carelessness. The overlook sat on a ridge at the side of the narrow, winding road to our house. It was a known make-out place for kids but too public a spot for legs in the air, and Mama and Mr. Dashwood weren't kids. What was she thinking? She baited Daddy all the time, but this went beyond baiting.

I couldn't let Mama distract me. I had to focus. The Middleton Cup was a small but prestigious invitational show. I'd be sixteen next month, but at fifteen, I was the youngest competitor ever invited to participate.

Daddy regularly led me through exercises in which I visualized success. I imagined each problem as a horse, and one by one I led them into stalls in a barn. Mama was having an affair. Daddy would find out and might know already. Gossip was raging. My bladder was twanging and stabbing and burning. I rolled the stall doors shut.

By the time Daddy turned the Land Cruiser through the filigreed iron gates, I was confident I was conveying the keen anticipation of competition and not my desire for a slug of bourbon.

"Ready to ride?" he asked as I got in.

"Ready."

"You feeling better?"

"Yes, sir." I searched for something to stretch my answer into an acceptable length. Daddy perceived short answers as rude. "The antibiotics are working."

"Good. I told your mother you were well enough to ride. Right?"

"Yes, sir. I feel much better." Not true, but it didn't matter. He'd mentioned Mama without sounding as if he were fixing to kill her, which meant he didn't know yet. He sounded condescending and superior—one hundred percent himself. He'd been conditioned to superiority since conception. Montgomerys were exceptional. He'd grown up hearing that from his own father, and I heard it from him all the time.

He navigated through the heavy traffic in town. With Thanksgiving one week away, Sheridan was especially crowded, catering to leaf peepers here to take in the fall color in the Shenandoah Valley. Indian corn wreaths hung on the doors of the antiques shops lining the square. In the windows, avalanches of pumpkins spilled around scarecrows.

Daddy threaded the Land Cruiser around a man who was loading an old milk-painted table into a van.

When we were on the parkway that led to the interstate, he said, "You really feel better, darlin'? You're pretty quiet."

"Just thinking about the dressage test." That was what I should have been thinking about, but my mind kept straying to Mama.

"What comes after the lengthening trot across the diagonal?"

I answered with relief. Dressage made sense. "Ten-meter half circle returning to track at B."

"What comes before the flying lead change over the centerline?"

"Twenty-meter half circle."

Jasper and I had practiced the individual movements, including the transitions, but we'd ridden the complete test only a couple of times so he wouldn't anticipate what was coming. Also, I'd imagined our entrance hall as a scaled-down arena, and I'd walked, trotted, and cantered my way through the test on my own two feet a dozen times.

"Last show of the year for you," Daddy said.

"I wish I were competing this winter."

"The horses need the break." He glanced over his shoulder and merged onto the interstate.

Middleton was only ninety minutes south of Sheridan, near enough to make the trip easily but far enough to merit staying the night. I spent the rest of the drive riding the dressage test stride for stride in my mind, turning in a perfect performance each time.

At the show park, we drove through the competitors' gate and trundled slowly past rows of stalls.

Competitive riding was a small world. I had ongoing and serious rivalries with a number of the riders unloading their horses and milling around. I waved at Michael Elliot, who ignored me, nodded at Daddy, and led Charlatan, his rangy gray Thoroughbred, across the path in front of us.

We parked behind Barn H. Daddy pointed at our trailer, parked nearby in a row of similar high-dollar rigs, and handed me his keys. "Get changed and meet me back here. Jasper's in H-6."

I took my duffel from the back and walked across the grass to the trailer.

The first thing I did was use the toilet. The urge to pee was less critical than it had been earlier, but a weak stream of urine came out, which was an improvement. I shed my school uniform, put on jodhpurs and boots, pulled my hair into a ponytail, and pinned it into a bun. When I was ready, I checked the mirror on the back of the bathroom door. Look like a winner, feel like a winner, Daddy said. I looked professional, competent, and as capable of winning as anyone else.

My head was where it should be as I crossed the soft, spongy grass to the barn, where Daddy stood under the shed row talking to Frank Falconetti.

"He's turning into a hell of a horse," Frank said. "Should've kept him."

"He has a lot of promise—right, darlin'?" Daddy raised an eyebrow at me.

"He's more than promising," I said.

A throaty nicker came from inside H-6.

Frank smiled. "Don't suppose you want to sell him back to me."

I didn't smile. "Not funny."

He laughed. "All right. Well, go get 'em, kid. Best of luck to you."

"You, too," Daddy said.

I slipped into the stall and put my arms around Jasper's neck. Daddy always warned me not to get attached to my horses, because they came and went, but Jasper was special. I inhaled his clean, horsey smell and rubbed his ears. He stretched his head toward me. He was ridiculous about his ears.

"You're not going anywhere," I whispered.

Daddy interrupted our lovefest. "You drew number one." He held up a round white disc with *1* on it.

Riding first was a disadvantage. Dressage was the only subjective phase of eventing, and judges graded the early riders more harshly to leave themselves room for higher marks as the competition continued.

He read my expression. "You'll be fine. Orientation is in ten minutes. We need to get going. Let's head over to—where is it, Ed?"

Eddie's voice came from the neighboring stall, which we'd commandeered as a tack room. "The meeting room under the stadium."

At home I mucked stalls and groomed and tacked my own horses, but at shows, Eddie and Mateo took care of that. Eddie had been at Rosemont a lot longer than I had. He'd never competed, but he'd been by Daddy's side forever. Both of them understood horses in a way I was still trying to learn.

I finished rubbing Jasper's ears and joined Daddy outside the stall as Eddie emerged from the tack room, a program in his hands. He pointed to a map on one of the pages. "There."

"Thanks," Daddy said. "Do you have the measuring wheel?"

Eddie disappeared briefly and returned with the wheel.

"We'll be back for the jog, and then Roan can hack him around one of the warm-up fields."

Eddie nodded and ran a hand through his short, thinning gray hair. "Y'all will do good here. I feel it in my bones."

Eddie's bones were always optimistic.

Other riders and trainers were filtering into the meeting room when Daddy and I arrived. Jamie Benedict, who had trained with Daddy for years before moving to Frank's barn, sat beside me. One of us often came in second to the other's first, but I'd rather lose to Jamie than to someone else. Even though he was older than I was, he'd always treated me like an equal. Other riders tried to intimidate me because I was young.

"You riding Psycho Pony?" he whispered.

"Jasper. You?"

"Luna. Hi, Monty." He reached across me to shake Daddy's hand.

The show park officials joined us, and the meeting started with announcements. Daddy jotted down notes in the margins of the program.

"How'd you do in the draw?" Jamie asked.

"One."

"Ouch."

"Someone has to go first." I never admitted to nervousness.

After the meeting, we headed to the cross-country course for the official walk. We started off in a large group, but gradually we spread out. Daddy used the wheel to measure the exact distance between jumps. The course covered three miles, but because it was shaped like a horseshoe, the finish was only about a hundred yards from the start.

He dug his heel into the turf by a jump at the edge of the woods. "Good ground. But watch out here. You'll take off in sunlight and land in shadow."

I wrote *sunlight/shadow* on the course map.

We returned to the barn in time for the jog. I put on my jacket and buttoned it. Daddy brushed nonexistent lint from the lapel.

The jog took place on an asphalt path lined with pots of flowers; spectators were kept at a distance by ropes strung between stanchions. A panel of officials, including a veterinarian, assessed Jasper's soundness as I trotted him away from them, toward them, and back and forth in front of them. My legs were long but his were longer, and I had to run to keep up with him. He shone with good health and excellent care, and he was passed with smiles and nods from the panel.

Back at the barn, Mateo saddled him while I shed the jacket and downed a bottle of water from the cooler in the tack room.

I might have been running a fever, but the late afternoon felt more like midsummer than fall. Sheridan was still warm, too, but at our altitude we'd been getting frost. The leaves hadn't even begun to change here.

When Jasper was ready, Daddy boosted me into the saddle. I gathered the reins and tried to compartmentalize my discomfort. He walked alongside us on a path to one of the warm-up fields bordering the parking area. The field had a circus-like atmosphere, with different riders in various stages of exercising their horses. In the center, some riders were practicing the movements for tomorrow's test.

"Walk-trot-canter around the field," Daddy said. "Both directions."

Jasper and I stuck to the perimeter fence, walking around it once, then trotting, then cantering, and then reversing and doing it all over again in the opposite direction, and at some point I became so absorbed in riding that I forgot about my UTI pain.

Daddy and Eddie waited at the edge of the field, watching us intently.

"That's good," Daddy called. "He's stretched his legs and had a look around." He glanced at his watch. "We'd better check into the hotel."

Mateo and I groomed Jasper and bedded him down while Daddy and Eddie went over tomorrow's schedule. I took a carrot from the cooler, broke it into pieces, and dropped them into the feed bucket. Jasper vacuumed them up, frothing pale orange around his lips, his black eyes luminous. One of the old books in Daddy's study maintained that the first consideration in choosing a horse was a kind eye. There were more important things to look for, but I always remembered that phrase when I looked into Jasper's eyes.

On the drive to the hotel, I reclined my seat back. I'd hardly slept the past two nights because I'd been so uncomfortable, but I dozed now, rousing only when we stopped and the engine shut off. I sat up and blinked in the sallow light under the awning.

"Wait here," Daddy said.

The hotel was a couple of miles from the park, so a lot of other horse people were staying here, too. I waved at a group of them and tried not to look tired. Good thing I was only competing on one horse. In the summer, I sometimes rode two or three horses at a single event. I didn't have the energy for that this weekend, especially with midterms next week. School always overlapped the beginning and end of the season.

The thought of school was more unwelcome than usual, and after a moment I remembered why. Sass. Mama.

*Compartmentalize*, I told myself in Daddy's voice. All that could wait. I was in Middleton, and I had a job to do.


THE NEXT MORNING Daddy called me before dawn. I showered, slicked my hair into a bun, and dressed in my dressage attire: white riding pants, shirt, stock tie, black dress boots, blunt silver spurs. I had just put on the shadbelly, the special cutaway black jacket, when there was a knock on my door. I peeked through the peephole and opened it.

"You look like a winner, darlin'," Daddy said. "How do you feel?"

"Like a winner."

The sun rose as we drove to the park. I loved early mornings, and on competition days I could have taken on the world.

Eddie had left coffee brewing in the trailer, where he and Mateo had stayed the night. Daddy poured a mug for himself, black as tar and twice as strong, and half a mug for me. I added cream from the tiny refrigerator, and we walked together to the barn.

Eddie had braided Jasper's thick black mane and sewn the braids into perfect rosettes. I drank my coffee and wolfed down an energy bar as he tacked my horse. Daddy checked the girth and the bridle. Jasper's ears were alert, and he mouthed the bit, but there was no eye-rolling or head-tossing. Horses had more than a dozen facial expressions, and Jasper's was bright, interested. He was practically smiling. I grinned myself.

Competition was an hour away, but as soon as he was ready, I put on my black dress helmet and white kid gloves. Daddy gave me a leg up—the saddle was more comfortable today than it had been yesterday—and led us to the same field we'd ridden in yesterday. It was almost deserted.

"He's always quiet in the barn," Daddy said, "but you know he lights up under saddle."

As if to verify that, Jasper danced sideways with his hind-quarters. I took him through some figure eights to get his attention and bend his body, and when his back was soft and round and the stiffness in his hindquarters was gone, I moved him into the trot.

"Hands," Daddy said as we passed him.

I corrected my hand position. I tended to carry my left hand higher than my right.

We went into a canter, and Jasper bucked, a major fault.

"Let him get it out of his system," Daddy called.

Jasper relaxed into the canter, and after a while Daddy had me put him through some lateral work and lead changes.

When he said, "Let's take him over to the practice arena," my nerve endings trilled. We would enter the dressage arena directly from the practice arena.

Outside the ring, Mateo went over Jasper's glossy dark bay coat one more time with a spotless white hand towel. Daddy straightened the tails of my jacket. While they tidied us up, I observed the other riders. Jamie and Luna looked fit. So did Bree Reardon and Bingo. Charlatan slung his head as he entered the arena; Michael's face was taut.

"Somebody's nervous," I said.

Michael scowled. "Who asked you?"

I shrugged. Psyching out one's opponent was a time-honored technique.

"Roan," Daddy said. "They're fixing to call your class in about ten minutes. Jasper's listening to you. Maintain that connection, and you'll ride a good test."

"Yes, sir."

"Take a deep breath and let it out. . . . Another one. . . . One more. . . . Good. Stay relaxed. Stay focused. And smile."

Riders weren't judged on demeanor, but a grim expression created a negative impression. Daddy even made me smile during lessons so I'd be in the habit.

"Knock 'em dead, darlin'." He slapped me lightly on the thigh.

I kept Jasper moving around the warm-up arena in a slow trot. A general announcement came over the loudspeaker welcoming everyone to the invitational. Then the announcer said,

"Now entering the arena, number one, Emerald Jazz Dancer, owned by Rosemont Farms and ridden by Roan Montgomery."

The bell signaled the beginning of the test.

As we cantered into the competition arena, everything receded except the horse under me, the stretch of soft dirt ahead of us, and the sun gleaming on the white paint and shiny black letters.

At X, dead center of the arena, we stopped in a solid four-square halt so impeccable that I almost laughed. I saluted the judges and proceeded into a collected trot, tracking left at C. I rode H to K in a medium trot, resuming a collected trot at K.

Over the next five minutes, we covered the entire arena, executing prescribed movements at particular letters, Jasper gathering tremendous power and releasing it with precision and ease. His strides were even and level, and his back and haunches moved with a relaxed swing. It seemed like we'd barely begun when we halted again at the invisible X.

I held the reins in my left hand, dropped my right hand by my side, and nodded my final salute to the judges. The world rushed back amid applause and cheers and whistles. I patted Jasper's sweat-damp shoulder. "Good job. *Great* job."

Daddy and Mateo met us by the in-gate. Outside the practice arena, we passed Michael, who was up next. If I'd liked him better, I'd have felt sorry for him.

"Hard act to follow," I said.

He shot me a dirty look.

I swung my right leg over Jasper's neck and dropped to the ground. Mateo draped a cooling sheet over him.

Daddy handed me a bottle of water. "Beautiful, darlin'."

"Pure class," Mateo said.

"Thank you," I said to Mateo. It was impossible to offer sufficient thanks to my show team. They always made me look good. They were well compensated—Daddy was an exacting but generous employer—but I never wanted them to think I took them for granted.

Mateo acknowledged my thanks with a nod and led Jasper away while Daddy and I waited for my score. I was high as a kite.

"That was Emerald Jazz Dancer, ridden by Roan Montgomery, with a score of 54.8."

Subdued applause from the stands reflected disapproval of the judges' scoring.

Daddy was philosophical. "Luck of the draw. If you'd ridden later, you'd have scored better. You were damned near perfect."

When he said something as extravagant as "damned near perfect," he meant it.

At the barn, Mateo was hosing Jasper off in the wash rack. Jasper curled back his upper lip as Mateo sprayed him in the face.

"Go back to the trailer and change." Daddy held out the key.

We watched another two hours of the competition, had sandwiches with Eddie and Mateo, and walked the course twice more. By dusk, the dressage results were in. I'd placed tenth, which worried me, but standings could change completely by this time tomorrow. Cross-country was where Jasper and I excelled.

As we drove back to the hotel, I started thinking about a bath. I smelled like a barnyard—which I didn't mind. The combination of horse and sweat and leather was my aromatherapy.

The lobby was packed and noisy with horse-show people. Vic Embry from Sports News Network kissed my cheek. "I've been trying to catch up with you two all day. You rode a phenomenal test."

"Thanks."

"How about a drink?" Daddy said to Vic. He handed me a plastic key card. "Go on up, darlin'. I won't be long."

I exchanged greetings with other riders and trainers as I squeezed onto an almost-full elevator. Jamie, wedged in the back but a head taller than everyone else, said, "Well done."

I pressed the button for the third floor. "You, too. Congratulations." He was in first place.

"I mean it. You were robbed on your score."

"Luck of the draw."

In my room, I took my hair down and rooted around in my duffel while the tub filled. I had packed a jar of lavender bath salts, made by Gertrude, who had different ideas about aromatherapy.

"Lavender's supposed to help you relax," she'd said.

"Do you think I need to relax?"

"You put a lot of pressure on yourself."

I found the jar with its pretty hand-lettered label. Gertrude was tireless, keeping two houses, cooking for us as well as for herself and Eddie—and she still did stuff like this.

Mindful of the fact that I still had a bladder infection, which felt worse now than it had at the show park, I poured a shallow handful of the lavender salt into the tub. It smelled sweet, but I didn't have a lot of faith in its relaxation properties. Something from Mama's medicine chest would work better, but I didn't dare raid her pills. She kept a close inventory.

I stepped into the tub and settled back against the cold white porcelain. Hot water closed over me. Bliss.

I sank lower and let my arms float. Water filled my ears and muffled the noisy flow from the tap.

A hot bath was better than a pill. At least, it felt better. Judging from Mama's ability to sleep like the dead, a pill was more effective. Or lots of pills. I could eat handfuls of them, like she did.

That, and not Mama's accounting system, was the real danger. I returned to my original conclusion: A hot bath was better than a pill. I was less likely to kill myself this way, unless I dozed off and drowned.

What kind of idiot fell asleep and drowned in the bathtub? I snorted and sat up, wiping water from my eyes. Then I jolted upright. Daddy leaned against the doorway, his arms folded as casually as if he were in line at the bank, but his eyes were gluttonous.

I drew my legs to my chest and hugged my knees. "We're at a show."

He rarely bothered me at shows. I counted on that. But he didn't budge.

I leaned forward and shut off the water. "I'm in the bath."

"Vic and I ran into Frank and decided to have dinner," he said. "Shall I bring you something?"

"No."

His eyebrow went up.

"Sir. No, sir."

He came in and sat on the side of the tub. I tried to make myself into something small, with a shell, as he unwrapped a miniature soap and dipped his hand into the water. I was rigid as he sluiced hot soapy water across my shoulders.

"It's all right. I've bathed you since you were little. You used to bathe me, too."

I remembered. "Daddy, please."

Soap-slick fingers trailed down my spine and up again.

Gooseflesh rose all over me, even underwater. I stared at the dripping faucet.

"Look at me," he said.

The water beaded into another droplet, swelling until its weight pulled it free. Drip.

He pushed his fingers into my hair, made a fist, pulled my head back. "Look at me."

I did.

He kissed me, his mouth gentle and persuasive. When I didn't resist, he loosened his grip and disentangled his fingers. Then he tugged my earlobe and arranged a strand of hair over my shoulder.

"Order something from room service. I'll give you a wake-up call in the morning." He kissed my forehead. "Don't stay up too late. Love you, darlin'."

"Love you, too, Daddy," I whispered.

# - Two -

DRESSAGE AND STADIUM jumping took place in arenas, but cross-country was spread out over acres of fields, hills, valleys, and woods, and negotiating obstacles at speed was all that mattered.

I'd studied the course map last night while I picked the turkey off a club sandwich in my room and again over an early breakfast with Daddy in the hotel restaurant, where he and the competition exchanged quick smiles and firm handshakes and best-of-lucks for the day while I concentrated on the map. I was riding first again. The order of go wouldn't be reshuffled until the day's results were in.

As I had with the dressage test, I visualized my ride, associating the obstacles on the map with the obstacles on the course. I'd noted every landmark, turn, takeoff, and landing, and I'd written target times on the map; I knew exactly where I needed to be and when I needed to be there. Strategy was important, but it was theory. I was ready to get on my horse and ride.

The show park was a postcard come to life: cloudless pastel sunrise, emerald grass, tidy white rail fences, immaculate flower beds with masses of chrysanthemums in autumn colors. It was a perfect day to kick ass.

We went straight to the barn, where Jasper dozed, one hind foot cocked, ears at half-mast. As regal and imposing as he looked when we were working, he was downright goofy in the barn.

"He was awake for breakfast," Eddie said. "He's just relaxed."

Daddy opened the door to the stall, and Jasper woke up and shook his head vigorously, as if shaking off his silly barn persona.

"Okay, darlin'," Daddy said. "Here we go."

While he and Mateo saddled Jasper, I went into the tack room and finished dressing. I was already in a black polo shirt, jodhpurs, and boots, and to this I added a protective vest, my oversized Clox sports watch, and my crash hat. Eddie strapped the required medical armband around my upper arm. I put my number on over the safety vest and pulled on well-worn black gloves.

We warmed up in an almost empty arena, where Jasper took flight over practice fences as if he had wings. Bree Reardon was wearing a leopard-print shirt that matched Bingo's headstall and saddle pad. Daddy said black and white made a cleaner, more classic line, but it would have been fun to match my horse's tack wearing something besides black.

"Good job," Daddy said as we walked briskly toward the course. "Watch your balance and keep coming into eighteen. You hesitate in the least, he'll hesitate, too."

Hesitation mattered to the degree of one-hundredth of a second, less time than it took to blink.

Eddie led us in a big circle behind the starting box.

"Press on where you can," Daddy said. "Be aware of your time. Ride it the way we planned. Aim to finish in about seven-five, seven-ten."

The seconds ticked off on the big Swiss timer by the box. I adjusted the fit of my helmet and the Velcro fasteners on my body protector.

"You listening?" Daddy said.

"Seven-five, seven-ten."

His eyes narrowed. I returned his gaze mildly, and he decided I wasn't talking back.

"One," called an official, and Eddie led us into the starting box.

Jasper quivered with anticipation.

"You're awake now, aren't you?" I murmured.

The timekeeper began counting down from ten.

"Nine . . . eight . . . seven . . ."

At "zero"—eight o'clock precisely—we lunged forward in a gallop.

The first three jumps were fly fences, wide but not much of a vertical challenge, and Jasper took them with ease.

We approached the fourth fence, a brush pile, and he telegraphed a microsecond of doubt.

"Jump!" I yelled, and he cleared the pile.

On landing, I squeezed him with my legs, asking him to open up his stride, and we streaked across the field. I rode low and flat to decrease wind resistance, but coming to the stone wall, I sat up and used every natural aid I had: seat, legs, hands, and voice.

"Jump!"

We sailed over the wall.

At the coffin jump, three fences set in a dip, Jasper rounded himself in and out of the combination. We raced uphill. At the top, we leaped onto and off the bank jump.

The clock ticking in my head was second nature, but as we approached one of the novelty jumps, an obstacle constructed to resemble a giant horseshoe, I consulted my watch. We were going faster than we needed to, but we were in tenth place. With all the other riders yet to go and stadium jumping tomorrow, I needed to finish well within the allotted seven minutes, thirty seconds. Daddy had said so himself: "Seven-five, seven-ten." At this pace we would beat that by at least fifteen seconds, but Jasper wasn't showing any signs of fatigue. I decided not to check his speed.

Twenty-eight jumps, and he soared over every one of them. I whooped as we blew past the timer.

I slowed to a jog. Friction from the reins had lathered Jasper's neck with frothy white sweat, but he was prancing as we met Daddy, accompanied by Eddie. I hopped down, winded.

"You see your time?" Daddy nodded toward the timer at the edge of the field.

My mouth dropped open. 6:37.02. I turned back to Daddy. The coldness in his eyes sucked the exhilaration out of me.

There was such a thing as going too fast. Jasper was huffing but not exhausted or wind-broken.

Eddie caught my eye and patted Jasper's neck, right where the reins had worked the sweat into foam, patting it into invisibility.

"He's okay." I sounded more certain than I felt. Riding too fast could earn me a yellow card. I'd received one last year for failing to have my chinstrap fastened during a warm-up.

One of the course veterinarians approached for the mandatory vet check.

My heart was beating as hard as Jasper's as I led him around while the vet—and Daddy—observed him. The vet placed his stethoscope to Jasper's side and felt his legs.

"Good to go," he said.

I longed to go with Eddie as he started back to the barn with Jasper, but Daddy put a firm hand on my elbow. "Vic wants to talk to us."

He led me to a flower bed bordered by a white rail fence. The green hills of the cross-country course rose beyond it, a pretty backdrop for an interview.

Vic stood in the foreground, illuminated by lights on tall stands and silvered umbrella reflectors. His producer, Laura, held an arm out to Daddy and me, indicating that we should step nearer to the talent. Then she joined the camera operator, the red light on the camera came on, and she said, "When you're ready, Vic."

"Ready?" he asked Daddy and me. "Three, two, one." He looked straight into the camera. "I'm here with Roan Montgomery, who has just completed the cross-country in blistering time here at Middleton, and her father and coach, three-time Olympic gold medalist Monty Montgomery. Roan, that was a tremendous athletic effort."

I tried to project the elation I'd felt at the finish. "Thank you."

"You came in nearly a full minute faster than the optimum time for the course. Are you concerned that might have taken too much out of your horse?"

Since I hadn't earned a yellow card or harmed Jasper, that was the remaining problem. If I'd fatigued him, he could be sluggish or sore for tomorrow's stadium jumping.

I kept smiling. "Daddy puts a lot of emphasis on conditioning. Jasper's in phenomenal shape. He'll be ready tomorrow."

Vic stuck the microphone in Daddy's face. "Monty?"

"I won't say she rode exactly to orders, but it's easy to second-guess when you're not the one on the horse. Considering his form, I think they have as fair a chance as anyone else tomorrow."

"You've consistently jumped clean cross-country rounds all season," Vic said to me. "That qualifies you to ride in two-star events next year. How do you feel about that?"

Vic always asked, "How do you feel about that?" I liked to imagine someone who'd lost saying, "Like shit." Also, it was conceivable that someone who'd come in first could feel bad, as I did now.

"Awesome. We've been working hard, and we were ready for this. But there are a lot of great horses here and a lot of riders who've worked hard all season."

"Don't you have an advantage? No one else is training with Monty Montgomery."

Daddy gave my shoulders a fond squeeze, and I flashed a smile up at him, our trademark Daddy's girl gesture.

"I'm very lucky," I said.

BETWEEN TIME PENALTIES and falls, cross-country proved a nightmare for the other riders. Luna went down at the water jump. She was uninjured, but Jamie was taken away in an ambulance, drenched, dazed, and holding his left arm against his chest.

I expected Daddy to light into me as soon as we were alone, but he was tight-lipped on the drive back to the hotel. What I'd done wasn't the worst thing in the world. He'd have been more pissed if I'd failed to move up in the standings.

The voice in my head whined with justification.

In the lobby, again mobbed with show people, we accepted congratulations on my new first-place standing. Daddy smoothly fulfilled his role as proud father-trainer-coach, but every comment on my time was another bullet in his arsenal.

We endured an uncomfortable elevator ride. The doors parted, and Daddy strode toward our rooms, somehow taking up the whole width of the hall so I was forced to tag along behind him.

He unlocked the door to my room. "Get cleaned up and changed."

"Are we going to the party?" There was always a big party the night of the cross-country phase. Usually it was fun, even though Daddy never let me stay long.

"No. We have reservations in an hour."

"Who are we having dinner with?" At shows, we often dined with executives from the companies whose products I endorsed, Romolo Madrid Saddlery and Clox Sports and Fitness Watches.

"No one," Daddy said.

Great. Dinner for two with Daddy.

I showered, dried my hair, and put on a black skirt and soft white cashmere sweater. Mostly I wore riding clothes or my school uniform, but Mama shopped all the time, and she often came home with something for me. I thanked her, but I couldn't have cared less about clothes.

Daddy knocked on my door, freshly showered himself, every inch the athlete he'd been before I was born, the rider who had single-handedly generated popular interest in the rarefied sport of three-day eventing. He'd been introduced so often as the face of eventing that his teammates had taken to calling him "The Face."

I followed him through the parking lot to the Land Cruiser. At six o'clock, the sky was dark and the streetlamps had come on. I fastened my seat belt. He did not. He never wore a seat belt, and after he retired he'd stopped wearing a helmet when he rode. Daddy the Invincible.

The restaurant was dimly lit, elegant. Tiny lamps glowed on the tables.

He ordered a bourbon and branch for himself, milk for me, and Chateaubriand and Caesar salad for both of us. When the waiter left, he said, "What time did I tell you to turn in?"

Here it came. At least we were in public. He would never display a bad temper or poor manners in public. Even in private he seldom yelled. Sometimes I wished he would—until he did, and then I was reminded that his persistent icy-calm logic was preferable.

"Seven-five, seven-ten."

"What time did you turn in?"

"Six thirty-seven." I didn't bother with the fractions.

"Why did you not follow my instructions?"

"I wasn't thinking." Not true. I *had* been thinking. My mistake.

"Nor were you looking at your watch or listening to me. Nor did you grasp that seven-ten was more than fast enough. You won today, but you may lose tomorrow because of it."

"It's a twenty-five-second difference." My argument was weak. Half a minute didn't mean much in everyday life, but it meant a lot in cross-country.

"Twenty-eight, to be precise. Or thirty-three, if you'd ridden it in seven-ten. The effort it took leaves Jasper with less for tomorrow. It was irresponsible. It shows immaturity and lack of judgment. All you had to do was ride the way I told you to."

"I'm sorry. But the way cross-country used to be run—"

"Long form requires different training. No one else rode like you rode today. Their horses are going to be fresher tomorrow because they weren't misused today."

"I didn't—" I'd been about to say I hadn't misused my horse, but I had. There was no excuse for the way I'd ridden. "I'm sorry."

He lifted two fingers to get the waiter's attention and signaled for another drink.

"Frank regrets selling him," he said.

The seemingly casual comment deflated my lungs. He was threatening me. In my lap, I clasped my hands in a bone-crunching handshake. "It won't happen again."

When the food came, I downed a few bites of meat and drank my milk. I wasn't the equestrian Daddy was, but I was a better rider with better judgment than I'd exhibited today. Daddy, having made his point, didn't rub it in, but neither did he recant his threat or try to make me feel better, although he was the one person who could have.

As we walked down the hotel hallway—side by side this time—he said, "I'm fixing to call your mother. You want to talk to her?"

The last thing I wanted was a strained conversation with Mama.

"No, sir."

He kissed my forehead. "I'll wake you up in the morning. Love you, darlin'."

"Love you, too, Daddy."

In my room, I crawled into bed fully dressed. He didn't often make threats, but his coaching style wasn't all positive affirmations, either. He reserved his charm for the public. It drove me crazy sometimes, the man I knew versus the man everyone else saw.

What had me wound up at the moment was the threat of losing Jasper. I had other horses. Their talent equaled his, and I won on them, too, but I'd fallen in love with Jasper; we'd had an instant chemical attraction, a perfect connection. He was magic, and when we were together, I was magic, too.

Daddy had no patience for romanticizing. I was a professional. I was expected to act like one.

I glanced at the minibar but had enough sense not to raid it. Unable to take the edge off, I faced facts. I'd stupidly disregarded Daddy's instructions today. He had an almost supernatural understanding of horses and riding, not to mention more experience and talent than anyone else I'd ever met. He'd literally written *The Book on Eventing*.

He hadn't actually *said* he was on the verge of selling Jasper; the threat was more subtle. Still valid, but Jasper and I weren't in immediate danger. All I had to do was ride the way he told me. I could do that.

I led his threat into a stall in my mind. The barn was getting crowded.

I changed into my nightgown and got back into bed with my lit book. Midterms were next week. Excellence was expected on all fronts.

I'd read a few pages when I became aware of Daddy's television from next door. No, not his TV. His voice.

I got up and pressed my ear to the wall between our rooms.

"By the way, she moved into first place today."

His tone suggested Mama should have asked but hadn't. The conversation was like every other conversation they had, Daddy full of heavy-handed implications, Mama responding with a complete lack of engagement, regardless of the topic.

Their unhappiness was my fault. Some parents might have told a little white lie about their child's date of conception, but Mama had made it clear that Daddy married her only because she was pregnant. She'd been more than willing to have an abortion.

She'd told the same stories so many times they'd lost their power to hurt me, except for one, the story about her moving my crib from the small nursery adjoining the master bedroom to a room at the opposite end of the house.

"But we won't be able to hear the baby cry," Daddy had objected.

"Exactly," Mama had replied.

Had the things that were wrong with my family started there, with a screaming baby who needed to be silenced? My first nursery had been converted into a closet, the second nursery had become the same bedroom I'd slept in all my life, and I still couldn't be heard at the other end of the hall.

The hotel walls were much thinner than the walls at Rosemont.

"You keep combining pills and bourbon, and I'm going to come home and find you dead."

That would be inconvenient—police, medical examiner, unfavorable publicity, the embarrassment of an overdose. People asking why.

I took the TV remote from the dresser and climbed back into bed.

"You're out of your mind," Daddy said.

I switched on the TV and turned the volume loud enough to drown out his voice—too loud for me to keep reading. I closed my book and turned off the lamp and channel-surfed until I landed on an old black-and-white movie, and the strange too-fast cadences of the actors' speech, their not-quite-British accents, lulled me to sleep.


SINCE I WAS in first place overall, I would ride last in Sunday's stadium jumping, but we were at the park early because Daddy wanted to see what Jasper's energy level was like and how he was moving after yesterday's ride. I had some concern about that myself.

Eddie led Jasper around the stable yard and reported he had eaten his usual hearty breakfast. Daddy checked his legs and satisfied himself that they were cool. There was another vet inspection by the same panel who had evaluated the horses on Thursday. Jasper was sound, eager, and energetic.

About half an hour before show jumping was to start, the course was posted on a bulletin board outside the open-air arena.

Daddy took it in at a glance and moved aside to allow me to study it and to make room for other riders, who were jostling to see it. Bree stepped on my foot and didn't apologize.

It took me maybe thirty seconds to memorize the pattern of the course, subject to the striding and turns Daddy would advise. I'd follow his instructions to the letter.

"Riders, you may walk the course," came over the loudspeaker.

I turned away from the bulletin board and found myself eye to eye with Bree.

She smirked. "Nice job yesterday."

"Thanks. Sorry you had such a poor finish. It's a terrible way to go into today."

That unsettled her. I saw it in her eyes.

"Good luck," I said cheerfully, and I joined Daddy by the gate, where coaches and riders were already streaming onto the course.

The brightly painted fences and pots of flowers flanking them were festive in the early-morning sun. More than half the bleacher seats were taken, and people were still getting settled.

"Roan," Daddy said.

"Just checking out the crowd."

"Check out the course. You have to anticipate what might be a problem for him."

Tight turns could save time and ground but you risked leaving your horse unbalanced coming into a jump, which could result in downed rails. I sized up the trouble spots: short distances between fences at the start of the course; the seventh fence right by the in-gate could tempt Jasper to duck out; tall bushes after eleven might make him think we'd taken the last jump, which could cause him to jump flat, but around the bushes was one final obstacle, a black-and-yellow wall oxer.

At each fence, Daddy gave me his advice, and I was pleased that it echoed my own solutions, but even if it hadn't, I'd have done what he said. All I had to do was ride the way he told me.

We sat in the stands and watched the competition. Rails came down. Riders were disqualified. Bree's round went badly. Sophie Archuleta rode brilliantly until her horse shied at the wall oxer and she came off.

Daddy stood up. "Let's go warm up."

I was already dressed except for my tie, hunt jacket, and helmet. I put them on while Daddy saddled Jasper. He walked us over to a warm-up arena, where he stood with one foot propped on the lowest rail of the fence and Jasper stepped out smartly in an extended walk. Under me, he felt good—not tired, not misused. My spirits rose, and after a couple of circuits I nudged him into a trot and then into a canter.

In the adjacent arena, Frank Falconetti raised his voice. "Don't sit against him, Mike. He'll flip his head and not see the fence."

I looked over. Michael shortened Charlatan's reins.

"No," Frank yelled, "you're making it worse. Try again."

Jasper and I took some practice fences, Daddy occasionally prompting from the sidelines but mostly just watching. Finally he inclined his head toward the gate. Michael and Frank were gone. The warm-up arenas were empty. It was time.


THE ARENA WAS quiet as we entered.

The opening circle, taken at a lope, allowed Jasper to see the fences and the judges to see us. All the horses still competing had passed this morning's vet check, but the judges wanted to observe each horse's fitness for themselves.

We triggered the timer as we approached the first jump. I aimed Jasper at the middle of the fence.

We were still in the air when I sighted the second fence. One stride into the landing, I took him into the curve that would give him more distance, two more good strides before taking off.

I knew before his front hoofs touched the ground that we had to take seven strides to the brick wall. An eighth would throw him off. I squeezed with my calves.

Jasper's takeoffs were strong, he cleared the fences with inches to spare, and he landed without breaking the rhythm of his canter. We finished the course with no faults in a respectable sixty-eight seconds, tying with Michael and Charlatan—and thanks to our cross-country results, that meant I was not only the youngest rider ever to compete at the invitational but also the youngest winner.

We lined up with Michael and the third- and fourth-place competitors in the middle of the arena for the awards presentation. The president of the show park handed me a heavy silver cup and clipped a big blue ribbon to Jasper's bridle, and we took the traditional victory canter around the arena.

I patted Jasper's neck as we trotted out the in-gate, grateful beyond words to him.

Daddy took the silver cup. I dismounted and rubbed Jasper's ears and pressed a kiss between his eyes. "Thank you," I whispered. I thanked Mateo and Eddie, too, before they led him off. Daddy walked with them for a few paces, giving Eddie instructions for the ride home while I accepted a congratulatory kiss on the cheek from Frank, who looked happy for me and pleased for Michael, who had placed second. I tried not to imagine Michael winning on Jasper.

"How's Jamie?"

"Back home. Doped up, so he's not in too much pain."

Daddy returned empty-handed. He'd passed off my trophy to Eddie or Mateo. I'd have liked to hold on to it, but the important thing was the win, not the cup.

"Think you'll make it Thursday?" Daddy said to Frank.

Thursday? Oh. Thanksgiving.

"Planning to."

"Great. Ready, darlin'?"

"Monty." Vic approached us. "A word for the camera?"

We gave another interview to Vic, and now that I'd made up for my cross-country sins, it was easy to smile, to be gracious and generous, to be with Daddy. Afterward I autographed programs for a gaggle of preteen girls made giddy by the very idea of horses and posed for pictures with them.

Eventually we started for home. Middleton was thirty miles behind us when Daddy said, "You lucked out, darlin'."

The glow of winning dimmed. I recognized the truth, and behind it the veiled reminder that my future with Jasper wasn't a given. I'd have to work to keep my horse.

# - Three -

WHEN WE GOT home, I found Mama passed out on the living room sofa. The lights and the television were on. She got spooked when she was alone. Once upon a time, I'd kept her company when Daddy traveled, but then I got older, and her drinking got worse but still didn't create enough of a buffer between her and her family, so she'd added pills. After that I'd begun accompanying Daddy when he taught his clinics.

Tonight he'd driven down to the barn to do the walk-through. I left my bags in the entrance hall and checked on Mama.

Unconscious, when she couldn't say things that hurt, she was beautiful. She lay on her back, one hand thrown over her head, her long, shiny black hair tumbling around her shoulders.

I touched her shoulder. "We're home."

No response.

"Do you want supper?"

"You back already?" She turned away, snuggling into the cushions.

I turned off the television and most of the lights and took her highball glass and the bottle of Maker's Mark from the coffee table. I left the bottle by Daddy's place in the dining room.

I put the casserole Gertrude had left us in the oven and took my bags up to my room. Mama wouldn't be at the table, so I didn't bother to change clothes, but I washed my hands and face before I went back downstairs.

The warming casserole smelled rich with Cajun spices and andouille sausage. At least once a month Gertrude prepared a dish from her native New Orleans. Daddy disliked heat, so she went lightly on the cayenne, but the andouille would have a bite.

He came in from the back porch. "Where's your mother?"

"Living room."

After he passed through the dining room, I went to the kitchen door and cracked it open to listen: labored sigh, receding footsteps.

I was tossing the salad when I heard him again.

"Kit, you need to eat something."

Food was one of many battlegrounds they fought on. Mama was thin, like a coat hanger, and determined to stay that way. She watched what I ate, too, to Daddy's annoyance. And mine. In eventing, strength was more important than thinness.

Mama's speech slurred.

"Fine," Daddy said.

I checked the casserole. I was ravenous, but Gertrude didn't believe in microwaves. She said they robbed food of nutrients and changed its texture.

Daddy pushed open the kitchen door. "Supper ready yet?"

"It would be if we had a microwave."

He smiled briefly.

"I'll serve the salad," I said.

Polite conversation was encouraged at meals, so as he made his drink, I said, "Midterms are this week. My lit exam is tomorrow."

A groan came from the living room. I was disturbing Mama's coma.

Daddy didn't even blink. "You study this weekend?"

"Some. I need to review everything."

When we finished the salad, I took away the plates and salad forks. In the oven, the casserole bubbled at the edges, but the middle was cool. Good enough. I scooped Daddy's portion from around the outside and mine from the middle.

"What other tests do you have?" he asked as we ate.

"Biology, French, and history."

"But you'll be done on Wednesday. And you're feeling better."

"Sir?"

"Your bladder infection."

From the living room, Mama snored lightly.

I planned to finish the antibiotics, but the pain and burning had disappeared. "Yes, sir."

"That's good."

I finished eating before he did, my mind compartmentalizing with shocking facility. I didn't have to think about Wednesday night yet. Time to be a student.

"May I be excused?"

"Sure. Leave the dishes for Gertrude. I'll clear up after myself."

I took the back stairs up to the second floor. They were original to the house's 1690 construction, and more than three centuries later the stone steps, grooved with use, canted to one side, but they came out right by my room.

Moonlight shone through my window, bathing the room in light and shadow. I closed my door and wished I could lock it, but since Daddy didn't take my grades lightly, I was safe tonight.

THE NEXT MORNING I was at the barn by five to muck stalls. The grooms were already at work. Daddy was supervising the feeding.

"Good morning. Ready for your test?"

"Yes, sir." I yawned, covering my mouth with my hand. "Sorry. I didn't go to bed until after midnight. Morning."

He didn't offer me the option of returning to the house for another hour or two of sleep. I hadn't expected him to. I liked barn chores and enjoyed a semiformal camaraderie with the grooms. They liked that Daddy required me to understand stable management from the ground up, and they especially liked that if I completed my own work with time to spare, I helped them with theirs.

I rolled open the door of Jasper's stall and went inside.

"How are you, beauty?" I laid my cheek against his neck and inhaled. Horses always smelled good, but they had an extra tang in the fall. It smelled like childhood, countless early mornings, long days, and late nights at home and at shows—grooming, mucking, riding, and loving every minute.

Jasper, none the worse for the weekend, shambled along beside me as I led him to his paddock. It wasn't good for the horses to inhale the dust stirred up by cleaning.

I went back for Vigo, who stalked down the aisle as if he were king of the barn. Beneath his haughty demeanor, he was a teddy bear. I liked riding him.

Psycho Pony, not so much. Her real name was Diva. The nickname was a joke I had with Jamie. She glared and turned her hindquarters toward me when I opened her stall door.

"You'd better not kick me, you cow." I swung her halter toward her flank. She shifted her rump away from me and allowed me to put her halter on. The halter was okay. The lead rope was suspicious but acceptable so long as I kept it short. A longe line or hose was cause for an epic freak-out.

Diva and I made a good story on paper. She had been sired by Lord Byron, Daddy's favorite horse. The media never tired of pointing out that both Diva and I were descended from Olympic gold medalists, though Diva was second generation and I was fourth. But both of us were roans, which led to the endlessly fascinating fact that I'd been named after a horse. Luckily, I didn't bear Byron's actual name. Daddy had named me after his color. He was a blue roan, his sleek black coat shot through with white.

Diva had inherited Byron's coloring, talent, and temperament—beautiful, brilliant, and a total head case. Every show we took her to made special provisions for her. She had private warm-up times so no one else would be in the arena. Stalls on either side of her remained empty. She bit, she kicked, she pulled faces at people and other horses. She was a nightmare except when she was under saddle, when she was a dream. Even so, I disliked her. I didn't mind a challenge, but Diva was dangerous.

I finished mucking, fluffed the fresh straw bedding, and returned the horses to their stalls. Jasper and Vigo put their muzzles in their buckets and began eating their grain. Diva once again spun her big butt toward me. She would literally rather kick me than eat.

The sun was up and the morning had warmed by the time I returned to the house. I peeked in the living room. Mama was no longer sprawled on the sofa, so I assumed she'd gotten to bed somehow.

I showered, dressed for school, and met Daddy in the dining room shortly before seven. He was reading the newspaper, which excused me from making conversation. Mama didn't eat breakfast. That usually made it the best meal of the day.

Daddy and I didn't talk much on the way to school. I opened my lit book and gazed down at it, occasionally turning pages, so he wouldn't bother me.

He let me out in front of the building. "Do a good job on your test. See you at one."

The first bell rang as I walked up the steps to the portico. Inside, the hall was crowded, which was odd. Sheridan Academy prided itself on a combination of rigorous academics and strict discipline. We had to be in our seats ready to work before the second bell.

Harold Moon, a thin, serious senior whose locker was next to mine, gave me a sickly "Hello" when I greeted him. Then he mumbled something about his physics exam and headed down the hall.

That explained why people were still milling around. Test days started with a confusing change in schedule. There was no homeroom.

"Hey, Roan, you ready for the test?"

I closed my locker. Chelsea Yost was in homeroom and American lit with me.

"I think so. What about you?"

"I studied all weekend, but if I don't pull an A, I won't have the GPA to stay in Accelerated Studies next semester."

I hoped that wasn't true. I liked Chelsea. We'd been best friends in elementary school, complete with playdates at my house and sleepovers at her house, but she was afraid of horses and I'd never cared for Barbies, and we'd grown apart. We were still friendly, though, and until our schedules had diverged this year, we'd sat together at lunch.

We walked down the hall together.

"Did you win this weekend?" Chelsea was asking out of politeness, not because she was really interested. She thought the modeling stuff was cool, but when I went into too much detail about something that had happened at a show, her entire face glazed like a doughnut.

"I did," I said.

She smiled, happy for me but probably happier about the short answer. "That's great!" At least she sounded sincere.

Mrs. Kenyon wasn't in the classroom yet. I took my seat at the back of the room.

A muffled sputter made me look up. A pack of senior girls had crowded into the doorway, Sass and Annabelle in the middle. Sass cut her eyes at the chalkboard that stretched across the front of the room.

A crude cartoon covered half of it, a man with an evangelical pompadour and a woman with long hair and long legs that were in the air. He loomed over her, aiming an enormous, weirdly shaped penis at her.

*Dickwood you're hung like a horse* was printed in the speech bubble coming from her mouth.

Sass had captured Mr. Dashwood's toupee, and to dispel any doubt the woman was Mama, the man was saying, *Pussy-Kit I love you.*

"Oh, my God," Chelsea said from the next row over.

I was cold to the point of being frozen except for my face, which burned hot.

*Do something. Say something.*

I stood up. My legs felt disconnected from the rest of me, but I started up the aisle, my eyes fixed on the cartoon. Nerves almost made me laugh. That penis looked like a baseball bat. Sass had dated that big dumb baseball player from Sheridan High. What was his name? . . . Lee Herman.

With short, fast strokes of the eraser, I eradicated first Mama and then the speech bubbles. With a stick of chalk, I transformed Mr. Dashwood's toupee into a baseball cap.

I gestured toward the penis. "Hey, Sass, is this what you remember from sucking Lee Herman's dick?"

Chelsea hooted and then clapped her hands over her mouth. A couple of people applauded.

Sass's face turned pink. "I'd never do that!"

"No shit" came from the back of the room.

The voice belonged to Will Howard. He'd never acknowledged my existence, but I knew him. He and two of his buddies had been kicked off the track team earlier this fall when they'd tested positive for drugs. The school had tried to keep it quiet, but through the same rumor mill that was grinding out the news about Mama and Mr. Dashwood, word had gotten out.

Laughter broke across the room. Sass had dated Will when I was a freshman. He'd know what she would or wouldn't do.

"You prick." Sass pushed herself away from the door, back into the hall.

Annabelle and the rest of the minions broke away. I turned back to the board and had just finished erasing the cartoon when the second bell rang and Mrs. Kenyon came in.

She didn't even glance my way. "Roan, sit down. People, we have ninety minutes for this test, and y'all are going to need every one of them."

I returned to my seat, flushed as much with victory as embarrassment—until I saw Mrs. Kenyon standing motionless with her back to the class.

A ghostly impression of the drawing remained.

She'd been in the classroom too long to be shocked. She went to the board and covered up the ghost of the cartoon in her neat schoolteacher script: *Up to 5 extra points for an essay comparing and contrasting the concepts of transcendentalism and anti-transcendentalism.*

Her face was severe when she turned around and began to distribute the exam, a packet of legal-length pages.

She did a half-halt by my desk. "You will see me after class."

She thought I'd drawn that. The instinct to protest was so strong that I opened my mouth, but she put the exam facedown on my desk and continued down the row.

I closed my mouth.

Will Howard, looking at me from his seat across the aisle, shrugged slightly. Getting into trouble hadn't fazed him. The school hadn't even suspended him. His family was Howard Construction. I was protected by the same privilege. I was a Montgomery. I wouldn't get suspendedeven if I had drawn the cartoon, but I needed to head off Mrs. Kenyon before she called Daddy.

"Turn over your papers and begin," she said.

Feeling sick, I turned my paper over. Two questions per page allowed ample room to write mini-essays in reply, but the words blurred. I couldn't make them out.

I glanced around to see if anyone else was having this problem. Everyone was scribbling away—except Will. He winked at me.

I looked down at my paper and forced myself to focus on the letters until they sharpened into words and then sentences, and I began to write the answers.


MRS. KENYON SAT on top of the desk in front of me, her feet in the seat. "What's going on?"

"I didn't draw that."

"Who did?"

I'd have ratted on Sass in a heartbeat if it hadn't meant explaining the drawing.

"It was already on the board when I got to class."

Mrs. Kenyon regarded me with her usual expression, something like that of a bulldog, but even now not an unfriendly bulldog.

I started to pick at the desktop, but anxious behavior was a giveaway. I stopped.

"Those senior girls give you a hard time, don't they, Sass and Annabelle?"

I cracked a hard smile. "I give it back to them."

"Did they have anything to do with this?"

"You'd have to ask them."

She seemed to weigh her next question. "Are things all right at home?"

"Yes, ma'am." I took a rule from Daddy's playbook: The best defense was a good offense. "Why do you ask?"

"No reason. But if something were wrong, you could tell me."

What went on in my family was private.

Well, some of it. Mama's relationship with Mr. Dashwood was rapidly becoming public.

"I'm going to be late for French."

She didn't seem satisfied, but she said, "You can go."

During my French review, Sass was called to the office over the PA. I couldn't gloat because I expected to hear myself summoned, too, but the remainder of the class was uneventful.

At lunchtime, I spent a few minutes fiddling with pencils and notebooks in my locker, waiting for the hall to empty so I could slip into the cafeteria unnoticed, but I wasn't up to the stares and whispers.

I didn't have many alternatives for a hideout. Students weren't allowed to roam the halls unsupervised, even a student with as many privileges as I had. In the end, I went to the biology lab, took my seat, and planned my escape. When the review was over, I'd collect my books from my locker, avoid eye contact, and go outside and wait for Daddy.

That was almost what happened—only when I pushed open the heavy glass door to the portico, Mama's forest green Jaguar waited at the base of the steps.

# - Four -

THE PASSENGER WINDOW glided down. Oversized sunglasses obscured half her face, her eyes hidden by the dark lenses.

"Get in."

I did. The window slid up, and the tires spun on the gravel as we roared through the gates. She turned left, toward home, but then went around the town square and picked up the parkway, heading toward the interstate.

"Daddy's expecting me."

"Not today. We're going shopping."

"I have plenty of clothes."

"I'm taking you shopping." She ground out the words, her jaw tight.

Of the unlimited ways to piss Mama off or hurt her feelings, not showing appreciation ranked high on the list.

"Thanks," I said.

She glanced my way. She knew I was appeasing her. I considered dredging up some enthusiasm, but then she'd accuse me of being condescending, which would have been true.

When I thought we'd been quiet long enough to diffuse hurt feelings, I twisted sideways to put my books in the backseat.

As I did, I saw Mama's profile. The vertical lines on either side of her mouth were filled every few months, but her lips turned down in permanent unhappiness.

"You," she said. "You and your father. The whole world watches you, applauds you, tells you how wonderful you are. It's all about you."

We careened onto the frontage road, sped through a stop sign, and shot onto the interstate. She wasn't a good driver, but she'd never been this reckless. Mr. Dashwood had called her, I thought. Her secret was in the open, and she wanted to get me alone and find out what had happened. Also, she might have been drunk.

She turned the big dark lenses in my direction. "Do you have any idea how lonely I am?"

Against my will, sympathy for her began to tinge my caution.

She didn't slow down when we exited the interstate for the two-lane road that dropped down into Leesburg, and only through a miracle did we arrive at Wickham Centre an hour later.

Mama double-parked the Jag near the entrance to Collier's Department Store. She had a long history with Collier's. When she'd worked at their Fifth Avenue flagship store, she'd appeared in an employee modeling campaign in their catalogue; she still referred to those days as her modeling career, but the only thing that had come of it was she'd met Daddy at a party.

She eyed me as we went inside to the smells of competing perfumes and pricey leather handbags.

"Let's get you something your father will appreciate."

She swept ahead of me, navigating a maze of departments, sailing straight through juniors and up the escalator to a quiet carpeted enclave with *After Five* painted in script on one wall.

A tall, slender woman with short bleached white hair floated over to us. "Mrs. Montgomery, how lovely to see you. This can't be Roan!"

"I'm afraid so," Mama said. "Roan, you remember Ulla."

I did. Ulla was her personal shopper, as if Mama needed any help in that department.

Ulla held out her hand and I shook it, feeling delicate bones underneath thin skin. Mama had the same hollow-boned delicacy.

"We need a special-occasion dress for her," Mama said.

"Wonderful," Ulla said. "Shall we go down to the teen department? They have—"

"No," Mama said. "I want to see her in something grown-up. She's not a little girl anymore."

Ulla never stopped smiling. She just appraised me with a practiced eye. "Size six?"

"Sometimes an eight," Mama said.

Ulla led us to a dressing room the size of Jasper's stall, scooping up dresses along the way as Mama pointed them out.

"This one is very sophisticated for someone her age." Ulla hung a black lace sheath on a hook. It wasn't something I'd ever have chosen for myself. None of them were. "But with her height she'll carry it well. This one—"

"Roan, you need to try these on." Mama settled on a chair with gold-and-white-striped upholstery. Beside it a small marble-topped table held a vase of fresh white roses.

"I will."

"What are you waiting for?"

"Some privacy?"

Ulla put her hand on the doorknob. "I'll be outside."

"Ulla, stay. Roan, she sees dozens of ladies without their clothes every day. You're not special." Her tone implied she was joking, but Mama often covered her hostility with humor that wasn't funny. When she said I wasn't special, she meant it.

Ulla smiled. "You have a lovely figure."

I had to choose my battles. I turned away from them, unbuttoned my blouse, took off my kilt, and hugged myself.

Mama held out a long green gown with a plunging V-neck. "Try this one."

She had taken off the sunglasses. The jade green of her eyes looked almost festive against the bloodshot whites. She had been drinking. They lacked the puffiness tears would have caused.

Abruptly furious at her for having an affair with John Dashwood, for getting caught, for not loving me or caring what happened to me, I snatched the dress from her.

She looked startled. This wasn't the behavior she expected of me, and maybe my body wasn't what she expected, either. When was the last time Mama had seen me naked? When was the last time she'd seen me at all?

I dropped the dress over my head. It fell down the length of my body.

"A good color," Ulla said.

Mama recovered. "Come here." She adjusted the skirt.

"It's too much dress for her," Ulla said softly.

"Because it's meant for someone twice my age," I told her. What did Mama hope to accomplish by making me look provocative—and saying she was doing it for Daddy? They were both crazy.

She shook her head as I tried on each dress, a strapless pink princess gown, the black lace sheath, a black chiffon off-the-shoulder cocktail dress. I looked like a kid playing dress-up.

She studied me. "Not any of the black ones. Have the shoe department bring up something dressy. Call lingerie, too. She needs a bra."

Ulla carried away the rejects, and I was alone with Mama.

I didn't take off the black chiffon because there was nothing left to try on, and I wasn't going to stand there nearly naked. I twirled. The chiffon floated away from my legs and drifted back into place. Very Ginger Rogers. I liked those old musicals.

Mama's eyes met mine in the mirror and flitted away. She studied the roses on the table. "Did you really accuse Sass Stewart of sucking some baseball player's dick?"

"I did, but there's more."

"John told me."

John. Instantly I had a sense of the intimacy between them.

"Mama . . . Daddy will find out. Wouldn't it be better if you told him?"

"I don't care what's best for your father."

"I meant better for you."

Frown lines appeared between her eyebrows despite whatever had been injected there. "I'm tired of other people deciding what's best for me. Your father's done it for so long I wasn't sure I *could* make my own decisions anymore. He takes small bites, but before you realize it, he's eaten you alive." She paused. "You get to make a lot of decisions, but this isn't one of them."

"What decisions do I get to make?" I asked, incredulous.

"You chose him. That was a big decision."

"When did I do that?"

"You choose him every day in a hundred little ways."

"It isn't a choice when you're too young to understand." My voice was like dust.

"You're old enough to understand now. You were old enough to understand when he killed Bailey. You *still* chose him."

Bailey had been Mama's attempt at buying my love. He was the best thing she'd ever done—half springer, half golden, they'd said at the shelter, with soulful gold eyes and silky toffee-colored fur.

I ignored her attempt to leverage Bailey's death against me. "You could make him stop," I whispered.

She looked at me as if she didn't know me, as if I didn't know her, and snorted softly. "Like I said, it's all about you."

THE RIDE HOME was long and painful. Her driving was less erratic, which verified she had indeed been drinking when she'd picked me up, but it had a fixed quality, both hands on the steering wheel, eyes on the road, like I wasn't there.

Tightness and pressure had settled in my forehead and the back of my neck by the time she let me out in front of the house with my books and shopping bags and drove the Jag around to the garage.

As I closed the door, Daddy called to me from his study. I could not catch a break.

The study, his domain, even smelled like him, leather and bourbon and citrus and horses. Trophies, including my Middleton cup, gleamed on the shelves. His medals shone like pirate's treasure on a cushion of dark blue velvet under a glass case. The case was also home to a special leather-bound edition of *The Book on Eventing*, Daddy's bestselling memoir, open to a photo spread of him on Byron—dressage, cross-country, stadium jumping—culminating naturally with Daddy in gold-medal position on the Olympic podium. When I was little, I'd defaced that photo in a regular copy of the book, tearing out the page and cutting my head out of a school photo and pasting it over Daddy's. I still had the page tucked away in a desk drawer. One day, I'd stand on that podium.

Daddy sat behind his big rosewood desk, his smile only slightly less bright than his megawatt victory smile. "Your new blog post is racking up comments."

My new post wasn't mine any more than my Facebook and Instagram and YouTube accounts were. My sponsors wanted me to have a social media presence, but I didn't even know the passwords. Daddy posted as me. The voice he'd developed to fit my image even sounded like me, more or less, and since I didn't have to write anything myself, I limited my objections. I thought *Love and hugs, Roan* at the end of every post, be it blog, Facebook, or Instagram, was over the top, but he said it made me sound friendly and outgoing.

"Did you have a good time with your mother?"

"I got a dress and some other things."

"I'm glad you enjoyed yourself."

He knew shopping, not to mention spending time with Mama, was anything but enjoyable for me, but it was a harmless pretense compared to some others.

"Supper's on in about five minutes," he said.

I took everything up to my room, left the shopping bags on my bed, hung the gold-and-white Collier's dress bag in the closet—and then reached into the far back corner, put my hand inside an old riding boot, and closed my fingers around the neck of a bottle.

It had been in my closet since July and was nearly full. If I really had a problem, it would have been empty. I uncapped it, and the familiar aroma of bourbon drifted up. It smelled like Daddy. I put the bottle to my lips and sipped, barely wetting my tongue.

Tasted like Daddy, too.

With that thought, I took a regular-sized drink.

I savored the sweetness and warmth for a moment before capping the bottle and returning it to the boot. I made myself presentable for supper, starting with brushing my teeth. My parents were usually so awash in bourbon themselves that I doubted they'd have smelled it on me, but there was a difference between being careless and taking risks. I was a risk-taker, like Daddy. I understood the chances I took. Mama had been careless, and she'd been caught.

They were already seated, Mama at the foot of the table, Daddy at the head. Mama's usual disengagement had been replaced by irritation. Daddy seemed mellow, a pleasant façade while it lasted.

Gertrude came through the kitchen door with a platter of something savory and fragrant—lamb tenderloin, my favorite. She gave me a covert wink.

My second wink today.

She served Mama first, then Daddy, then me. She set the platter on the sideboard and brought the side dishes around.

"Will there be anything else, Mrs. Montgomery?"

Mama dismissed her with a wave.

Gertrude was unfazed. "Good night. I'll see you in the morning."

"Good night," I said.

Mama picked at her food, using her fork to move it around but rarely raising a bite to her lips. Tonight she might have been helped along by nerves. We had that in common. Nervousness killed my appetite.

I hadn't eaten since breakfast, though. I'd counted on grabbing a snack before afternoon lessons.

My knife scraped against the plate as it sliced through the tender meat.

"God, Roan, you weren't *actually* raised in a barn." Mama bared her teeth in a smile. "Stop cramming food in your mouth."

I put down my fork, swallowed the food that was in my mouth, and blotted my lips with my napkin.

"Some of us," Daddy said, "don't weigh ourselves in ounces. It's possible to enjoy a meal. Try it sometime. *Vogue*'s not calling."

He'd gone for Mama's most vulnerable spot. Being thin and beautiful and rich didn't compensate for her sham modeling career.

"I gave up any chance I ever had at happiness for you." She was looking at me. "He didn't want me. He wanted *you*." Her lips curved. "He still wants you."

I stared down at my plate. She made it sound like bad things were all there was to Daddy and me, but it wasn't all bad; *he* wasn't all bad—was he?

"Kit," Daddy said.

"You think it's a secret?"

Not a secret, but the thing we never talked about. I wanted her to make him stop, not ruin everything. Just fix the broken parts.

"I've been disposable since she was born. You got what you wanted. The hell with me."

Disappointment and relief and a peculiar hurt tugged against one another inside me.

"That's right. I want a wife who spends half her life unconscious."

I folded my napkin. "May I be excused?"

"No," Mama said. "We'll sit here like a family."

I appealed silently to Daddy. He replied with a nod. I stood up and picked up my plate.

Mama grabbed my wrist as I started past her. "I said no."

"Let her go." Daddy's tone—clipped, steely—made me go cold, and I was the one he was trying to protect.

She released me. White marks from her fingers striped my wrist. She rose and pushed past me. "I'm so goddamned sick of both of you, I could slit my fucking throat."

DADDY REMAINED IN his chair, working on his drink while I cleared the table. Mama's venom coursed through me, but no matter what she said or how awful she was, I deserved worse.

He left to do his evening walk-through. I went upstairs and began putting away the things Mama had bought me. Bras, the fitting of which had been excruciatingly embarrassing. Red satin pumps with heels so high and skinny that they pitched me forward. Cosmetics. I wore makeup when I was doing a commercial or a photo shoot, but I disliked the feel of it, as if my face had been dipped in plastic. I dumped it in a drawer in my bathroom.

I changed into my nightgown before settling down at my desk to concentrate on blue-eyed parents and brown-eyed children.

In today's review, Mr. Hanlon had more or less told us what the exam would cover, so I skimmed my notes and had turned my attention to the conjugation of irregular French verbs when a knock came at my door and Daddy stuck his head in.

"Just want to say good night." He hesitated. "Your mother doesn't mean everything she says."

For all his hardness, he did possess a glimmer of empathy.

"She means it," I said.

He lingered. "Maybe Wednesday night you can give me a sneak peek at what was in those shopping bags."

"Clothes. Nothing special."

"I'll be the judge of that."

Not all bad—but far from all good.

"I'd better get back to studying."

"Good night, darlin'," he said. "Love you."

And then, so help me God, he winked.

# - Five -

THE NEXT MORNING, Chelsea waited by my locker. "Guess what."

"You're staying in Accelerated Studies?"

"Yeah, I did okay on the test. But this is even better. Sass and Annabelle got suspended."

So that's what it took to get suspended. Good to know where the line between discipline and privilege lay: no dick pics of the headmaster.

"For how long?"

"Only until Monday, but they won't be allowed to make up their midterms. They're getting big fat zeroes on four tests."

I put my books away and closed my locker door. "How do you know?"

"It's all over school."

"Is the reason they were suspended all over school, too?"

"Yeah, because of that drawing." She faltered. "Look, don't worry. Nobody believes it. Your mom wouldn't do that. Your dad's hot."

I cringed at her assessment of Daddy.

"Sass just knows how to get to you. She always has."

True enough. We'd argued over Barbies at a sleepover at Chelsea's back in fifth grade. Well, Chelsea and I had been in fifth. Sass had been in sixth, but she and Chelsea were neighbors, so Mrs. Yost made Chelsea invite her.

Chelsea blinked at me. "Are you wearing makeup?"

"Mascara. I have to get to French. What do you have now?"

"Spanish."

"Good luck."

I breezed through my French test and was on my way to biology when I saw Will Howard coming down the hall with Rico and Wedge, his fellow drug users and former teammates. Rico spotted me and nudged Will and said something I couldn't hear.

"Knock it off," Will said. "Y'all go ahead. I'll catch up."

Rico looked sufficiently chastened. Will stopped in front of me. He might be a burnout, but he was a cute one. His eyes were a deep true cobalt fringed by dark lashes.

"Hey. How's it going?"

"Okay," I said. "Thanks for what you said yesterday."

He smiled. His teeth were straight and white. "Sass is a piece of work."

*A non-fellatio-performing piece of work.* That would have been more entertaining than what I said. "I'm going to biology. You?"

"Trig."

"Is it hard?" What kind of idiotic question was that? I was good at math.

"Practical. You have to know math to build things."

He built things? Oh—Howard Construction, the family business.

"Like biology for me," I said. "We've been studying genetics. It's what we do at the farm. The breeding program. With the horses."

"Sounds interesting."

"No, it doesn't. It is, but it doesn't sound interesting."

"I'm interested," he said.

*Since when?* I almost asked, but he was saying, "Good luck on your test. Not that you need it. Slam dunk, right?"

"Probably."

He smiled again. "See you later."

I needed the entire ninety minutes to complete my exam, triple-checking my answers to make up for the fact that Will Howard had distracted me. Interested in genetics—or interested in me? He'd never spoken to me until today. Yesterday's bon mot, "No shit," had been directed at Sass.

At lunchtime I took my tray and my history notebook to an unoccupied corner table near a janitorial closet. On a later lunch shift, the custodians in fact sat there, but at eleven-thirty, it was mine. I took my position in gunslinger's corner, my back to the wall, and surveyed the cafeteria.

Harold sat with some kids from his church. I'd sat with them before, but except for Harold, the church clique was as closed as any other. Chelsea was on a different shift. So was Will, who probably ate with Rico and Wedge. I wouldn't fit in with them, either. What drugs did they use? Not meth, I hoped. It would be a shame if Will's pretty white teeth fell out.

I ate the icing off my cake while I reviewed my notes. When I looked up, John Dashwood was getting in line for lunch. Most teachers skipped ahead of the students, but Mr. Dashwood never did. He chatted with the ninth-grader in front of him as they moved down the line—and then, tray in hand, he made straight for my sanctuary.

Fight or flight? Fleeing would give credence to the gossip. Freeze? Tonic immobility was a valid biological response.

He put his tray down across from mine and smiled. "Roan." He pulled out his chair. "How's exam week going for you?"

"Fine. How's it going for you?"

It was a smart-ass remark said in a smart-ass way, and it would have meant big trouble if I'd said it to Daddy.

He poked at his spaghetti with his fork. "Suspensions are never a happy occasion. Parents get upset."

I understood he meant parents got upset with him, not their children.

"Sorry," I said. I wasn't.

"You don't owe anyone an apology."

Behind the ugly aviator-frame glasses and the roadkill toupee—which, granted, was hard to see past—he seemed marginally less ridiculous.

"What happens now?" I asked.

"That depends on the board of trustees. This isn't the exemplary behavior expected of a headmaster."

He'd lose his job. He'd have to leave Sheridan. Would he take Mama with him? I envisioned Mr. Dashwood as my stepfather, the three of us eating at a cheap table in a cheap apartment.

"What happens to you and Mama? What does that depend on?"

His eyebrows almost vanished under his artificially low hairline. "I have a wife."

"You could leave her."

"No, I couldn't. This time she may leave me, but I'm not leaving her."

This time?

"You've done this before." My voice was low and furious. "You don't care about Mama."

"I won't make excuses for what I've done. I'm sorry it's made things difficult for you."

"Then you shouldn't have done it." I pushed back from the table and rose so quickly that my chair started to tip. I grabbed it before it hit the floor. The last thing I wanted was to draw attention to me and my lunch companion. He'd sat with me to demonstrate he had nothing to feel guilty about. He was crazy if he thought I'd let him use me.

"You shouldn't have done it." I swiped my notebook from the table. "And you deserve whatever happens."


AFTER SCHOOL, GERTRUDE picked me up. The back of her Subaru was filled with bulging canvas grocery bags—green for us, blue for her and Eddie—and her hair had been trimmed. Tuesdays were for errands.

"Hey, sugar. I told your daddy we need to run by the florist. We have a decorating emergency. Your mother thought I was ordering the centerpieces, and I thought she was, and neither of us did."

Exactly like Mama to say she'd do something and not follow through. When she should have been ordering flowers, she'd probably been screwing Mr. Dashwood.

The florist was behind the square in a squat brick building. Inside, coolers of flowers lined the walls. I examined blown-glass angels and porcelain hearts on display tables while Gertrude went to the counter.

She returned after a few minutes. "We didn't order early enough, and now they're slammed. Help me pick out some flowers. I'll try to do something with them."

Shopping with Gertrude was more fun than shopping with Mama. The florist gave us tall galvanized tin buckets to transport the flowers in—rust-colored lilies, amber and gold roses, bronze chrysanthemums.

"Want ice cream from the drive-through?" Gertrude asked when we'd wedged the buckets among the groceries.

"Daddy's waiting."

I was on a light training schedule until January, but that didn't mean lessons came to a standstill. After I rode Vigo, it was time for chores. I barely had time to shower before supper, but I couldn't come to the table smelling of horse—Mama's rule, but Daddy and I went along with it.

We needn't have bothered. She wasn't at the table.

Gertrude served Daddy's plate with salmon. "Should I make a tray for Mrs. Montgomery?"

"She's not feeling well," Daddy said. "She's resting."

Translation: She was drunk, hung over, on a hunger strike, had knocked herself out with pills, or some combination thereof.

"How was school?" he asked.

Lunch with Mr. Dashwood, French and biology tests—and Will Howard: *I'm interested.*

"Good. I aced my tests. I have history tomorrow. I'll be through by ten."

"Let's ride out when you get home."

"Cool." Riding out was one of our normal times.

Also normal: washing dishes after supper, studying, Daddy stopping by my room later to say good night.

But no matter how tightly I held on to normal, abnormal was always there.

"Don't stay up too late." With the tips of his fingers, he tilted my face up to his.

He was going to kiss me. I parted my lips slightly.

He kissed my forehead. "Good night. Love you."

"Love you, too," I said thinly.

I had parted my lips.

AFTER MY HISTORY exam, I waited for Daddy on the bench in front of the school. He was late. Undoubtedly that meant he wasn't picking me up. He might send Eddie or Gertrude, but I wasn't that lucky. It would be Mama. I hadn't seen her since she'd threatened to slit her throat, but since Daddy hadn't said she was dead, I figured she hadn't done herself in. If she ever did, it would be via overdose, but that wouldn't have been a sufficiently brutal declaration: "I'm so goddamned sick of both of you, I could take a lot of pills."

Despite the forecast for rain, the morning was warm, the sky glazed yellow. I peeled off my sweater and wished Daddy would let me have a cell phone. I considered calling him from the office, but I didn't want to encounter Mr. Dashwood. He was keeping a low profile, but I'd glimpsed him earlier in the hall.

I was still waiting when the bell rang at eleven-thirty. Seconds later, students poured through the doors.

A shadow blocked the sun. I looked up.

"Figured you were long gone," Will Howard said.

"Guess my ride stood me up."

"You going home?"

I nodded.

"I'll take you."

I didn't move.

"I don't bite," he said.

*That's too bad*, I thought.

"Okay. Thanks."

I trailed after him to the student parking lot. Sheridan Academy had several buses, but most of the students who were old enough to drive had their own cars.

Will's ride was a big white pickup with a pile of lumber in the bed and the Howard Construction logo on both doors. He opened the passenger door for me, which seemed uncharacteristically well mannered.

The cab was clean but stifling with heat and the odor of cigarettes. He started the engine and let it idle while he flicked a switch on the dashboard. The air conditioner blew away the ashy odor.

"My house is about five miles past the overlook," I said.

"I know."

"You do?"

"Hard not to know about Rosemont if you live in Sheridan. Anyway, I run by there all the time."

"Is it on your way home?"

"Nope."

"Oh. I can call Daddy. You don't have to—"

"Said it's not on my way. Didn't say I mind." He loosened his necktie, took off his blazer, and rolled up his shirtsleeves. I checked for track marks, but his forearms were normal. Nice muscle definition, too. I had a thing about forearms.

He reversed out of his parking space and crept forward in the line of cars exiting the lot.

"Doing anything special tomorrow?" he asked.

"Yeah, a big dinner, about twenty people."

"You have a big family."

"No, only Mama and Daddy and me."

"Who are all those other people?"

"Horse people."

We pulled out of the parking lot, and then we were through the school gates and on the road.

"What about you?" I said. "Is it only you and your parents?"

"I have a little sister, and my brother and his wife and their kids are coming. So it'll be a crowd. Not compared to your house, though."

What would a big, rowdy family holiday be like, with little kids running around a cozy dining room, and everybody talking at once?

Will adjusted the rearview mirror. "What else do you have planned?"

"Training and riding out up in the hills."

"You get to do much of that?"

"Most of my riding time is spent in lessons."

"That blows. Or does it?"

"No. I love it."

He wove his way through the holiday traffic on the square. "It's pretty this time of year. The town."

I looked at him without turning my head. *The town looks pretty?* Who was this guy, and what had he done with Will Howard?

Traffic thinned as we entered the North Street neighborhood. We passed Chelsea's sprawling brick ranch house and the Stewarts' imitation Tudor mini-mansion.

North Street gave way to open space—pastures where horses and cows grazed and farmhouses dotted the hills. They reminded me of Gertrude and Eddie's house. We started uphill into the twists and turns. Will nodded toward two low walls of stacked white stones flanking a narrow road to the right. "That's our driveway."

I didn't see a house, only trees, thick with fall color.

"So," he said. "Tomorrow you'll eat too much turkey and pumpkin pie, and you'll—what did you call that, riding on?"

"Out."

"Out. What else?"

"Nothing. What about you?"

"I'm working on a dollhouse for my sister."

"You're building your sister a dollhouse?"

"Yeah. For Christmas. Why? You find that hard to believe?"

"Well . . . yes."

He grinned. "I'm a man of many talents."

"Apparently."

He concentrated for a minute on the steep curves. "Would you like to go to a movie?"

I hadn't seen that coming.

"You mean like a date?"

"No."

I calculated the odds of survival if I flung myself out of the truck; we weren't going very fast.

"It's not *like* a date. It *is* a date. I pick you up, take you to some rom-com, we eat pizza, I take you home."

My embarrassment receded. A date sounded like fun. Except for the rom-com, it sounded like something I wanted to do.

Will was watching the road, but he glanced at me.

"My parents won't allow me to date until I'm eighteen." I doubted Daddy would allow it then.

"How old are you?"

"Fifteen."

"You're kidding."

"I'll be sixteen next month," I said helpfully.

"When's your birthday?"

"Twenty-ninth. When's yours?"

"October third. You're telling me I have to wait more than two years before I can take you on a date? I mean, assuming you say yes."

Was he flirting?

"Your parents might reconsider if I met them and they saw I'm an upstanding young citizen."

"You?"

"Yeah. Don't believe everything you hear."

"So you weren't kicked off the track team for failing a drug test?"

"There was more to it."

"Like the test gave a false positive? For all three of you?" My doubt came through loud and clear.

He shook his head. "No."

"Then I don't think my parents are going to buy the upstanding citizen thing."

"Fair enough, I reckon."

He didn't seem exactly offended, but the mood had changed. The conversation had become more real than rom-coms and pizza.

"It doesn't bother you?" I said. "Not being on the team?"

"I love running, not competition. I like being in the zone."

I knew what he meant by being in the zone, but running had never gotten me there.

"I hate running," I said, "but I love competition."

"You run? If your parents won't let you go on a date, maybe we can go for a run."

"No." My disappointment surprised me; for a second, I'd imagined us running together. "There's no point in asking."

We took the curve before the overlook. I caught my breath sharply as I registered first a polished black Land Cruiser, then Daddy at the wheel—and his expression, when he recognized me in the pickup, morphed from surprised to murderous.

"Stop. That was Daddy. *Pull over*," I added urgently when Will seemed to think I was kidding. He slowed the truck and pulled into the overlook.

Through the back window of the pickup, Daddy had disappeared around the curve, but he would turn around at the first opportunity—the road with the stacked stone walls. I hadn't realized how serious my transgression was until I saw The Face. Permission was required for any deviation in schedule, even though he was the one who'd been late.

"Why are you so freaked?" Will asked.

"You don't know Daddy."

"If I've gotten you in trouble, I'm sorry."

"It's not your fault." I fumbled with my seat belt. "I should have known better."

"You should have known better than to catch a ride?"

"I told you, I can't date until I'm eighteen."

"This wasn't a date."

"It doesn't matter. He has expectations."

"You always do what he expects?"

"Yes," I said.

Daddy's expression had smoothed into blandness in the time it took him to return to the overlook, get out of the SUV, and open my door. "Care to introduce me to your friend?"

"Daddy, this is Will Howard—from lit class. Will, this is my father."

"Nice to meet you." Will leaned across me and extended his right hand.

Daddy shook it briefly. "Well, Will Howard from lit class, thank you for getting her this far. Roan, let's go."

I slid out of the truck. "Thanks."

"Anytime."

Daddy shepherded me into the Land Cruiser. Ahead of us, Will turned left onto the road. He didn't peel off; he was perfectly casual about it, as if Daddy's picking me up here had been prearranged. He even lifted a hand in a wave I didn't dare return.

I stole a look at Daddy's face and didn't defend my decision to accept a lift home or point out that if I had a phone like everyone else, it wouldn't have happened. He was on fire, and I hadn't gotten this far by throwing gasoline on the flames. The heat analogy was subconscious; the car was freezing, the AC at full blast—and I'd left my sweater in Will's truck. I hoped it wouldn't smell like cigarettes when I got it back.

# - Six -

DADDY'S AGITATION ABATED on the drive home. Maybe he'd decided my catching a ride with a classmate wasn't a big deal—although a thrill ran through me every time I remembered Will had asked me out. Like it would ever happen. Like I wanted to date a burnout.

Daddy dropped me at the house. "I'll be at the barn. Sadie's colicking. Glenn's been out twice already."

It must have been serious for him to call the vet. Daddy and Eddie could handle almost any medical situation, but colic could kill.

"We're trying to avoid surgery," he said.

"Do you need me at the barn?"

"No, ride out without me, darlin'."

Riding out on my own was infinitely better than riding out with him. He drove down the hill and parked outside the foaling barn. I didn't know all the mares, but if Sadie was in foal, her condition might be more complicated.

Savory smells greeted me when I opened the front door, and I detoured into the kitchen, where Gertrude sat at the table crumbling cornbread into a mixing bowl and humming along to

Cajun music streaming on her phone. Sometimes she'd grab my hand and send me spinning and we'd dance around the kitchen, but this afternoon she had work to do. Whole rounds of cornbread were stacked on a platter beside the bowl.

Her brown eyes had gold flecks that always shone when she smiled. "Hey, sugar. Cornbread's hot."

Nothing was finer than Gertrude's cornbread, with its crispy crust and slightly sticky middle.

I took a plate from the cabinet and a knife and fork from the drawer.

"How was your day?" she asked.

"Great." That was a little too enthusiastic. School never made me that happy. "How about yours?"

"Getting things ready for tomorrow. Dressing tastes better if it sets overnight so the flavors can blend."

I cut a wedge of cornbread, slit it in half, and slathered the inside with butter.

"You ready for company tomorrow?" she asked.

"I'd rather eat with you and Eddie." Butter oozed down the outside of my cornbread. Hence the need for the fork.

"You're welcome to join us," she said.

I'd have loved to slip away to Gertrude and Eddie's, but I could hardly have two turkey dinners. I'd have to settle for visiting them on Friday for leftovers.

"Save me a piece of black-bottom pie. Why are you making the dressing? Aren't the caterers coming?"

"Your daddy asked me to make it."

I savored the first bite of cornbread—sweet butter, sharp buttermilk. "This is amazing."

"I don't know where you put it, sugar."

"She's gotten curvier in the past year," Mama said.

*She lives.*

I opened my eyes. She held a highball glass, the bourbon minimally diluted. Her black pants, cut low on the hip, and white silk blouse were more appropriate for a magazine spread than a horse farm, but Mama never set foot in the barn.

"Did you know," she said to Gertrude, "Roan wears a bra now?"

"She's growing up," Gertrude said.

"And she's got a hot little body to prove it."

Gertrude kept crumbling cornbread.

"Gertrude knows I wear a bra," I said. "Who do you think bought me all those sports bras this summer?"

"I assumed Daddy took you shopping."

It was an innocent-enough comment if you didn't know what Mama and I knew.

"Gertrude, can you turn that *down*?" Mama asked.

"Sure." Gertrude tapped her phone, and the bouncy eight-beat music went silent.

"You didn't have to turn it *off*." Mama took a drink. "The centerpieces and the arrangement for the foyer look good. Are you leaving them on the porch all night?"

"The flowers will keep fresher if they stay cool."

"But you won't be here in the morning to put them out."

"I can put them in place after supper if you want, but the house is warm."

Mama nodded. "They'll be fresher if they stay on the porch tonight, but tomorrow—"

"I'll put them out," I said.

"Sugar, it's no trouble."

"You're off tomorrow. Daddy said you and Eddie are off until Sunday afternoon. It's silly for you to come up here to put flowers on the table. I'll do it."

Mama smiled, her lips pinched. "So thoughtful of you."

"I'm happy to do it."

We were facing off again, Mama reminding Gertrude of her place, and me reminding Mama of the same thing. Gertrude was family—more of a mother to me than she'd ever been. It was Gertrude who'd made me feel like I had a family, Gertrude who'd comforted me when Bailey died.

Mama tilted her head, acknowledging my point, and turned and let the door swing shut behind her.

"Mama." I followed her through the dining room and living room. She started up the stairs. "Mama."

She didn't turn around.

I'd hurt her feelings. I always did. Running after her, trying to talk to her, would only result in her lashing out and me crying. I watched her head to the second floor. She had remarkably good footing for a drunk in heels on marble stairs.

In the kitchen, Gertrude wouldn't meet my eyes—embarrassed for Mama or me or maybe all of us, though she was no stranger to Mama's pettiness.

"You all right, sugar?"

"Yeah. She's just had too much to drink."

"Eat up while it's hot," Gertrude said, but the cornbread wasn't appealing anymore. The melted butter on the plate had started to congeal.

"I'll take it with me."

In my bathroom, I flushed it down the toilet. Just once, it would be nice to enjoy a meal, or even a snack, without Mama ruining it.

I WALKED DOWN the wide brick aisle of the training barn to an earthy potpourri—the pungency of horse, the dried-grassiness of alfalfa and timothy, heavy molasses-laced feed, and vitamin-rich horse urine.

I ignored Diva, greeted Vigo with lumps of sugar, and crossed the aisle to Jasper's stall, taking the halter and lead rope from the hook on the door.

"Hey, you." I rolled open the stall door. "We're riding out."

Jasper dipped his head to place it in the noseband of the halter, and I buckled the strap.

I removed his stall blanket, led him to the crossties, clipped a rope to either side of his halter, and went to the tack room. On two walls, saddles perched on saddle trees, protected from dust by canvas covers. Rows of bridles lined the space above them. On the third wall, the heavy winter blankets hung ready; it hadn't been cold enough to use them yet. On the fourth wall, shelves held grooming kits, each labeled with the name of a horse. I took Jasper's kit and swiped a handful of sweet grain from the feed room.

His lips skimmed it from my palm.

"Your daddy sees you hand-feeding that horse, he'll have your hide," Eddie said. He had a leg wrap in one hand and a bottle of liniment in the other.

"I always hand-feed him. Anyway, Daddy's not here."

"He's in the foaling barn. I always say you got more guts than brains."

"Thanks."

"It's not a compliment," Eddie said.

I laughed. "How's Sadie?"

"Drugged up on muscle relaxants. She may lose the foal. We'll know more in the next few hours." Eddie continued on his way, turning toward the stud barn.

As I groomed Jasper, I spoke softly to him. Daddy believed communication with horses should consist of commands and signals and the occasional soothing "Easy, boy," or "Good girl," because they couldn't understand anything more, but I told Jasper everything. Almost.

He was in good flesh despite the hard competition at Middleton. Some horses came off a three-day event up to thirty pounds lighter, but Daddy and Eddie took equine nutrition and hydration seriously.

I took his bridle and hunt saddle from the tack room.

"We're going into the hills. What do you say? Good boy."

For an hour, I rode him up and down the hills that rose above rolling meadows carpeted with winter rye. From the crest of the hills, Rosemont looked like the toy farm I'd had when I was a kid. Our house sat at the top of a hill, Gertrude and Eddie's farmhouse lay below it in the curve of the driveway, and beyond their place stood the employee apartments, built to match the character of the original structures. The pastures were dotted with horses. Fences, dark brown rails dipped in creosote, raced across the fields at right angles.

Regardless of Mama's attempts at manipulation and the trouble brewing between her and Daddy, I felt good. I was doing what I loved best in the place I loved most—and alone with Jasper, I had room to think about this afternoon: A boy had asked me on a date.

"I can't go," I told Jasper. One ear swiveled toward me, indicating he was listening. What would a date with Will be like? What would we talk about? Would he kiss me, and would it be hard or soft, with tongue or without? Given his remark about Sass, he might expect more than kissing.

My fantasy of pizza and a movie and a gentle good-night kiss—okay, with tongue—dissolved. He was a total burnout, and he knew nothing about horses. *Ride on*, for God's sake.

Jasper turned his head to look at me, and I became aware that I'd stopped riding. I was simply sitting there, stock-still, halfway up the hill.

"You're right," I said. "It doesn't matter. I'm not going on a date with anyone anytime soon."

Except the memory echoing in the back of my mind made my guts coil like I was the one colicking, not Sadie. Sunday night supper, Gertrude's casserole, and Daddy.

I did have a date. And it was tonight.


THE TEMPERATURE PLUMMETED in the night. I woke up shivering and clutching the quilts. A cold draft blew over me. When I'd gone to bed I'd left the windows open because my room had been stuffy. Now the wind was rising, and the thick, heavy drapes filled like sails.

Reluctantly I left the bed, sucking air between my teeth when my bare feet touched the floorboards.

As I pulled down my windows, blue-white lightning flashed and a bass crash of thunder made the windowpanes vibrate. The branches of the oak trees in the backyard and along the road to the barn waved, shedding leaves that whirled through the air.

"Wild night."

I spun.

Daddy stood in my doorway wearing jeans and a heavy jacket. "Get back in bed, darlin'."

He crossed the room, put one hand at the small of my back, and guided me to bed, where he held back the covers.

"Lie down. I'll tuck you in."

Was that what he was calling it now?

He drew the quilts all the way to my chin and brushed my hair back from my face. My scalp tingled. His hand was cool. He smelled of horses.

"Sadie's okay, but we had to take the foal. Three months early . . . she didn't have a chance. She was a pretty little roan, just like you." He stroked my hair. "You know you're the most important thing in the world to me, right?"

"Okay."

"No, tell me you believe you're the most important thing in my life."

"I believe you." I did. He was telling the truth.

He leaned over and kissed me the way I'd thought he would last night.

"It's late," he said.

It had been late before. Late didn't stop him. Mama didn't stop him. I couldn't stop him.

Sadie and her dead baby stopped him.

"I'm beat. I've been working with that mare—" He glanced at my clock—"eighteen hours. I need some sleep. Love you, darlin'."

"Love you, too, Daddy."

He left, closing the door behind him.

Lightning lit up my room again, and a clap of thunder made the house shake. I rubbed my mouth, trying to get rid of the feeling of his lips on mine. Not good enough. Once more, I braved the cold floor, went into my bathroom, and brushed my teeth and tongue until my mouth felt clean again.

THE NEXT MORNING we were short-staffed because of the holiday, so I cleaned my three stalls and had done two more in the stud barn when Daddy sent me back to the house.

The rain came down in cold glassy sheets that billowed in the heavy wind. Thunder rumbled steadily, punctuated by an occasional deafening crash, and the lightning looked as if it flashed underwater. Wet leaves lay thick on the ground, and small limbs had fallen.

Despite rain-repellant pants and a hooded jacket, I was drenched by the time I reached the house. I left my wet boots and jacket on the screened porch off the kitchen and went inside in my socks. Water had gotten in my boots, and my feet were freezing.

The kitchen was as hot and humid as a steam room, and caterers in white tunics swarmed everywhere. Mama was nowhere to be seen. She left the cooking to the professionals. These particular professionals showed up every Thanksgiving and every Christmas Eve, like distant relatives. The head chef, Albert, smiled at me.

The doorway to the back stairs was blocked with a rolling rack that held catering paraphernalia. In the dining room, Gertrude and Daddy had inserted extensions into the table after supper last night. Place settings gleamed. Gertrude's floral arrangements, lined up down the center of the table, were works of art. Putting them out had taken me all of five minutes.

I thawed in the shower. Bits of hay that had found their way inside my clothes swirled down the drain.

I dried my hair and started applying makeup. I'd learned a few things from makeup artists over the years, and I used a light hand.

Without enthusiasm, I removed the protective plastic bag from my new dress. It was beautiful. I slipped into it. The hem fell about two inches above my knees, so it showed some leg but wasn't too short. The problem was the neckline, which was nowhere near my neck. Held up only by a couple of skinny straps, it plunged between my breasts.

I twisted my arms behind my back to zip up the bodice, but when the zipper was maybe three-quarters up, it caught the fabric. I contorted and stretched, but every position I tried was too awkward for me to work it free, and it was done up too far for me to wriggle out of the dress. If I tore it, Mama would accuse me of doing it on purpose—which wasn't a bad idea, but the threat of another meltdown made me dismiss the temptation.

I went down the hall to the master bedroom and knocked. "Mama, it's me."

No response.

"It's me—Roan."

She opened the door. "I know your name."

Her makeup and hair were done, but her loosely belted blue wrapper was falling off her shoulders, and from the waist down it was more or less open, showing the stretch marks and the Cesarean scar. I'd been a big baby. Fumes of bourbon rolled off her breath. She hadn't taken one nice, steadying drink. She was either drunk or in the process of getting that way.

"Your father send you?"

"My zipper's stuck." I followed her into the bedroom.

She turned me around and tugged at the sides of the bodice, as if that would loosen the zipper.

On her dressing table I spied a bottle of Maker's Mark. Beside it, a glass was half-empty. So was the bottle, which could be good since her consumption would be limited or bad depending on how much she'd had. A Stonehenge of pill bottles was arranged around the bourbon. Perhaps she'd taken a miracle combination that would render her less antagonistic.

"How did you manage to do this?" Her fingers were like icicles.

The telephone rang.

"Goddammit." The wrapper swirled around her legs as she went to Daddy's nightstand. "Gertrude is never here when I need her. I don't know what we pay her for. Hello." That last word was said into the handset with the breathless charm Mama could turn on and off like a light switch. She listened. "One second." She extended the handset toward me. "For you."

"Who is it?"

"Walt something." She shook the phone at me. "Do you want to talk to him or not? I'm not your secretary."

I took the phone. "Hello."

"It's not Walt something. It's Will something," Will Howard said. "You should replace that lady who's not your secretary. She can't get anything right."

Warmth rushed through me. "Happy Thanksgiving." I turned my back to Mama so she could continue to work on my zipper. Also, I didn't want her eyes scouring my face.

"Was that your mom?"

"I'm afraid so."

"Is she still there?"

She tugged at the zipper.

"Yes. How did you get this number?"

"Internet. I take it you don't get a lot of calls."

"Some." More like none.

"You've got to get out more. Speaking of which, did you ask about going to a movie or for a run or something?"

"I can't." Mama was literally breathing down my neck. "It isn't possible."

"Anything's possible."

"Not for me."

"I want you to know," he said, "I'm not giving up."

A boy had never said anything like that to me before.

"I mean, unless you want me to," he said.

My tongue knotted.

"Do you want me to give up?"

I found my voice. "No."

"Good."

Did I say goodbye now?

"Did you get yelled at yesterday," Will said, "or did your dad cool off?"

I was supposed to keep talking. "He was fine."

"Kind of intense, isn't he?"

"Kind of." If Mama weren't monitoring every word, I might have found it easier to talk.

Through the receiver came a shriek and a giggle in the background. "Is your family there?"

"That's Carrie. Steve and Amy aren't here yet. Dinner was supposed to be at two, but Mom's keeping everything warm. What about you?"

"People should start arriving at three, but no one's here yet, either."

"It's almost three now."

The clock on Daddy's nightstand confirmed that Mama had fifteen minutes to finish getting ready.

"I'll let you go," Will said. "I hope you have a good holiday and this weather lets up so you can ride on."

He was deliberately saying "on" instead of "out," like it was a joke we shared.

"Thanks. Happy Thanksgiving."

I pressed the off button on the handset, relieved I'd survived the conversation without sounding like a complete social moron but wishing we could have talked longer.

"There!" Mama said. My zipper shot upward. With cold hands on my shoulders, she turned me to face her. "That was a boy. You were flirting."

"I was not."

"I heard some of what he said. He asked you out. Walt who?"

There was no reason not to tell her. She'd tattle to Daddy, trying to ingratiate herself to him, whether she had Will's name right or not, and he'd figure it out.

"Will." I returned the handset to its base. "Not Walt. Will Howard. We have a class together. Daddy was late picking me up yesterday, so Will gave me a lift."

"And your father was okay with that?"

"He didn't know about it until we met him at the overlook. He brought me the rest of the way."

"What else doesn't he know about?" Her wrapper floated behind her as she went into her closet.

"Nothing. Nothing happened."

"It might be nice if you went out with a boy," she said from the closet. "It doesn't have to be a date. A group of you could go out."

I picked up one of the pill bottles. Below the alphabet-soup name of the drug, the label read, *For anxiety*. Must be working. Mama didn't sound anxious. She sounded delusional.

She came to the door of the closet. She had put on a high-necked, long-sleeved black sheath that skimmed her knees. "If you dated a boy your age, it might free up your father to see me in a new light."

I didn't need to set Daddy free. It was the other way around. Besides, her affair wouldn't go away as if it had never happened.

She dropped a pair of tall black heels on the floor and stepped into them, and the frowsy drunk disappeared. She was stunning, tall, impossibly slender. No wonder she'd expected a successful career.

"Well?" she said.

"You look pretty, Mama."

"I wasn't asking for a compliment. Do you want to go out with this boy?"

"I don't think so. He has some problems."

"So do you," she said.

"So do you. What about Mr. Dashwood?"

The veneer she'd slapped on our lives warped and splintered.

She walked over to her dressing table and spritzed on perfume. "Did you tell your father?"

"I didn't, but someone will."

She sat down at the table and pressed her palm to her forehead, scrunching her fingers in her hair. Her eyes were closed, and she was deep-breathing like she was about to go into the arena. "This isn't what I wanted."

The floorboard down the hall creaked. Mama straightened up, smoothed her hair, and began reapplying her lipstick, her face blank as a mannequin's.

Daddy, in soaked jodhpurs, a heavy sweater, and socks, blew into the bedroom. "God, I'm ready for a hot shower." His eyes rested on me. "Darlin', you're a knockout."

Mama had succeeded in buying me a dress he appreciated, but she didn't look happy about it.

"Isn't Mama beautiful?" I said.

For a moment, all three of us looked in the mirror. My mother's imperfections were hidden, and if my father had ever felt anything for her—anything resembling love or even compassion—he'd say yes, she was beautiful.

Mama's pursed lips and half-lowered eyelids might have been caused by his lack of response, or they might have been caused by the way I'd set her up and knocked her down again, even though that hadn't been my intention.

"Roan," she said, "had a phone call from a boy."

I knew she'd tell.

"Oh?" Daddy said.

"Will Howard. I left my sweater in his truck. He'll bring it to school Monday."

Plausible. Yesterday's hostage exchange had been quick.

"All right." Daddy went into the bathroom, turned on the taps in the shower, and raised his voice over the running water. "But you're too young to be getting calls from boys. No more phone calls. Tell him that."

The shower door opened and closed.

I looked at Mama. "Happy?"

"Not since you were born," she said, and strangely, there was no malice in her words, only truth.

SHORTLY AFTER WE went downstairs, the phone began ringing with calls from guests stranded by accidents blocking the interstate, flooded surface roads, and downed trees and light poles. They might have to turn around and go home, but they would make it if they could.

After the third call, Daddy brought the handset from his study into the living room, where a fire crackled in the fireplace and we were playing cards at the coffee table. We were normal. That was the impression guests were supposed to have when they arrived and saw the interrupted game, like we had a family game night or something. It made me melancholy, glimpsing the way we might have been and weren't.

"Uno." Mama placed her next-to-last card in the discard pile. It was a Draw Four card.

I drew the cards. I was accumulating quite a handful.

The phone rang again, and Daddy glanced at the caller ID and then at me.

Oh, no, not Will again.

"Hello." Daddy was still looking at me. "Speaking."

As much as I might—perhaps—like Will, it would be totally controlling of him to ignore what I'd said and go behind my back to talk to my parents.

"May I ask you to hold a moment?" Daddy was being polite. Not Will, then. He wasn't completely drug-addled.

"I need to take this in my study," Daddy said to Mama and me, and he crossed the entrance hall and pulled the heavy rosewood-paneled pocket doors closed.

"It's his turn." Mama placed her single card facedown on the table.

I put my cards down, too. Mama opened the doors of the armoire and turned on the TV. She brought the remote back with her and flipped through the channels.

It was black as night outside. The rain washed in sideways, and water ran down the windowpanes flanking the front door. The covered porch offered no protection.

I got up and stirred the fire and added a small log.

"I should rearrange the place cards, since so many people have all but canceled," Mama said but didn't move.

I joined her on the sofa again as she scrolled through TV channels. On the local stations, the news crawl across the bottom of the screen was full of severe weather warnings, thunderstorms, floods—and some stations showed a map of Virginia flashing red where the weather was especially bad.

Mama sipped her bourbon and paused on a movie where Henry Fonda and Lucille Ball were toasting with champagne. "You like old movies, don't you?"

"I do." I liked black-and-white movies better than color, but I was surprised she knew I liked any movies at all. "Do you?"

"No."

"Then put on something else."

She resumed surfing. "I don't watch TV. I keep it on for company."

She was still surfing when Daddy returned.

"Five-thirty. We've heard from nearly everyone. Obviously it's just the three of us. Roan, have the caterers remove the extra place settings and tell them they can serve."

He looked the same. He sounded the same. But a hot, sharp vibe radiated from him, and I would have obeyed him even if I hadn't been conditioned to it.

The table seemed even more vast and formal with only Daddy's place at the head, Mama's at the foot, and mine forlornly in the middle. We wouldn't be so remote from one another if we removed the extensions, but Daddy was already escorting Mama to her place. I'd never seen him do that.

The candlelight didn't soften the hard line of his mouth. The way he picked up his wineglass made me think he could snap the bowl from the stem with a twitch of his fingers.

Mama pushed her food around on her plate and downed two glasses of wine before the second course. No one was speaking, but the atmosphere was spiraling downward. I wanted the table full of guests. I wanted the card game back, even if we were only playing parts, even if it made me sad.

Albert emerged from the kitchen during the main course. "Is everything to your liking?"

"Excellent, Albert, thank you," Daddy said.

"Wonderful," I added.

Daddy gave Mama a pointed look.

"Lovely," she said.

Albert returned to the kitchen.

"Darlin'," Daddy said, "when you finish, take your dessert up to your room. Your mother and I have something to discuss."

A bite of Gertrude's dressing stuck in my throat. I swallowed it and looked at Mama, who should have been alarmed but just seemed tired. I didn't know who that last caller had been, but I was sure of one thing.

Daddy knew about Mama and Mr. Dashwood.

# - Seven -

THE PECAN PIE and milk on my nightstand looked like the bountiful end to a happy holiday meal.

I sat cross-legged on my bed and strained to hear something through the storm that battered the house, but the human silence welled up the stairway and flowed under my door. When I couldn't sit still another second, I tiptoed down the stairs in my bare feet.

The doors to the study were closed.

". . . unless you want to nullify . . . no question . . ." Daddy spoke so quietly that I only caught disjointed phrases.

Mama raised her voice, babbling.

Daddy interrupted her, but all I understood was the last word. ". . . Dashwood?"

Abruptly I didn't want to know what they were saying. This was between them. Back upstairs, I stood indecisively outside my room. I wanted to talk to someone. I tried to talk myself into calling Chelsea, but I really wanted to talk to Will. I could ask about his brother. Concern for a friend was a good excuse to call.

Was he a friend?

Before I could overthink myself into inaction, I ran down the hall, grabbed the handset from Daddy's nightstand, and ran back to my room. I closed my door and bounced onto my bed, ready to dial.

I didn't know the number. I visualized the logo on the side of Will's pickup. Howard Construction—and in smaller type was another name and a contractor's license number. The name started with an *H*. Henry. I dialed information, and in seconds I had the residential number of Henry Howard. I punched it in.

The telephone rang twice, which was enough time for my courage to waffle, but then a woman answered. "Steve?"

There was such distress in her voice that I nearly hung up.

"No, ma'am. It's Roan Montgomery. May I speak to Will?"

"Hold on." She called Will's name, and then, her voice muffled, added, "Don't stay on the phone too long."

"I won't," Will said. "Hello."

"It's Roan. Is everything all right?"

"Steve and Amy haven't turned up yet. Mom's freaking out."

He sounded strained, too.

"I'm hanging up," I said.

"No, don't. How's everything there?"

Daddy and Mama's marriage was no one else's business. It was barely even mine. Will had a much worse crisis to deal with, but when he prompted me—"Roan?"—I answered.

"You know Sass's cartoon? Well, it's true. Daddy found out, and now he and Mama are having this big fight."

"I'm sorry."

"It's nothing," I said. "They fight a lot."

"It's not nothing. My parents don't fight much, but when they do, it's not nothing."

That made me smile a little.

"I think my mom needs me," he said. "Can I call you tomorrow?"

"I'll call you. Daddy says I'm too young to be getting calls from boys."

"How many boys are calling you?"

"Dozens."

He laughed. "Night."

I clicked off the handset and returned it to my parents' bedroom.

Back in my room, I added a splash of bourbon to my milk and got ready for bed. Maybe Will's brother had pulled over somewhere safe and lightning had struck a cell tower so he didn't have reception.

I downed my milk, rinsed my glass, brushed my teeth, and crawled under the quilts. I intended to keep my lamp on, thinking Daddy or Mama would tell me what was going on, but lightning flared, and with a pop, the lights went out.

A WEIGHT NEAR my hip made the bed dip. Under the covers, I stretched my legs, and Bailey settled down against my thigh. He had his own bed, a big pillow on the floor, but I liked feeling him tucked up against me.

He growled softly, and through the covers his body tensed.

"Down," Daddy said. "Roan, why's the dog on the bed?"

Bailey's growl became an openmouthed snarl, and he lunged.

I jerked awake. The lamplight was blaring, the red numbers on my alarm clock blinked 12:00, Bailey was dead, and Daddy stood by my bed holding a mug.

"Time to wake up, darlin'," he said.

Slowly things started coming together. The electricity had gone out and I'd fallen asleep in the blackness.

"What time is it?" My voice was congested with sleep.

"Ten-thirty."

"A.M. or P.M.?" It was a legitimate question. With the heavy blackout drapes over my window, I couldn't tell morning from night.

"You are the sleepyhead. A.M. Sit up. Have some cocoa."

I should have been at the barn hours ago. Daddy handed me the mug. I was barely awake, but I sipped. He was wearing the same suit he'd worn yesterday. He'd loosened the tie, and stubble darkened his jaw and upper lip. Daddy could get as down and dirty as any stable boy, but I'd never seen him look disheveled when he was dressed up.

Then I remembered.

"Daddy—"

"Drink up, darlin'. Then we'll talk."

He didn't say anything further until I finished the cocoa. Then he took the mug, set it on the nightstand, and sat down on the edge of the bed.

"Roan . . ." He frowned. "I know what happened at school."

My heart stopped.

"It's okay that you didn't tell me."

My heart started again. Not telling him could have been construed as taking Mama's side.

"Linda Dashwood called last night. John told her everything, and when I confronted your mother, she admitted it. We've decided the best thing for everyone, and that means you most of all, is for your mother to move out."

My breath came in shallow rapid inhales and exhales. She was saving herself.

Daddy put his arms around me and hugged me to his chest.

"Nothing's going to change for you. You and I will stay here, and you'll train and go to school, just like always."

Just like always.

"She hasn't left yet, has she?"

"She's packing."

"Already?"

He let me go. "There's no reason to prolong it. We're in agreement for the first time in a long time. She doesn't want to be here, and I don't want her here."

I knew kids could decide which parent they wanted to live with—and I knew with just as much certainty that a future with Mama meant living somewhere else. She wouldn't stay in Sheridan. She hated it here. Going with her took me away from Daddy, from Rosemont and my horses. Leave Jasper and Vigo? Let someone else win on them?

"Your mother doesn't want—" Daddy broke off. "Why don't you get dressed, go down to the farmhouse? Gertrude will make you breakfast."

"I don't want breakfast. Mama doesn't want what?"

"Darlin', I'm sorry." His forehead furrowed. "Your mother's giving me full custody. She doesn't even want visitation."

My ears buzzed like they were full of bees.

"You're not alone," he said. "She doesn't want me, either."

The difference was that he didn't care.

I CURLED UP under the covers. Mama's rejection wounded me, but not fatally. I never missed her when Daddy and I were at a show; I dreaded running into her when I came home from school; meals were always emotional ordeals.

So why did this hurt so much?

Because Mama knew the truth. Ignoring it was bad enough, but abandoning me was worse. How could she leave me all alone with him?

Something bumped against the floor in the hall.

"Got the dolly," said an unfamiliar male voice.

Heavy work boots clomped down the hall.

Movers. That hadn't been Mama's doing. She wasn't that organized. Daddy had been on the phone a long time before dinner last night. He couldn't have had that much to say to Linda Dashwood. He'd decided how everything would be handled, right down to scheduling the movers, before we'd even sat down at the table. He must be paying them a fortune.

I was chilled, so I layered on an undershirt, a turtleneck, and a sweater, even though it was the kind of cold that came from the inside, and the warmest clothing couldn't alleviate it.

Down the hall in Mama and Daddy's room, a man in gray coveralls was emptying a dresser drawer into a big box with MOVING TARGET printed in red on the side. Lingerie and night-gowns spilled into the box. He replaced the empty drawer and pulled out another one.

Mama emerged from the closet in yoga pants, flats, pony-tailed hair, and no makeup. She didn't meet my eyes.

"Mama? What happened?"

The mover tipped the contents of another drawer into the box.

"Didn't your father speak to you? He said he would." She picked up a tall, empty box.

"Yes, but . . ." I couldn't have this conversation in front of the mover.

"I didn't think it would come to this," she said. "I didn't think he'd care."

How could she have been married to him all these years and not know him at all?

"Don't look at me like that. You judge me all the time, both of you."

The mover started thumping the drawers and boxes around, as if he didn't want to hear what was said.

"I'm not judging you." I didn't want him to hear it, either. "Let me help you."

"You can't help me."

I couldn't, not in any way that would truly matter. "I'll help you pack."

She scoffed. "Of course."

I followed her into the closet, where she started yanking dresses from hangers, and I waited for words to come to me—not words that would make her stay, but words that would make her want me.

"I tried," she said. "I wanted to be a good wife, a good mother—"

*Really, Mama?*

"—but neither of you needs me. Neither of you loves me."

"I love you, Mama."

"You never say it."

"I don't like saying it."

She stuffed her dresses into the box. "Then why do you say it to him?"

"Because he says it to me."

She looked at me, her eyes like lasers. "Are you telling me you don't love him?"

"No, I do—"

"End of story." She pulled some blouses from their hangers, which dangled and swung from the rod. "You love him. You chose him. You're thick as thieves, and you expect me to believe he's hurt you? You've played us against each other one too many times. It's over. You win. He's yours."

No wonder I didn't have any words. All the words belonged to Mama.

I felt shaky, sick. "Did you ever even try to stop him?"

"Did you?"

Instantly hot tears seared my eyes, but she would *not* make me cry. It wasn't my job to stop him. It was hers. She was the mother.

She stuffed her blouses into the box. "If you're going to help, help. Get a box from the bedroom."

The room she shared with Daddy had begun to look empty despite the pecan-wood furniture, the art, the heavy brass lamps, the room-sized Persian rug. Those were family pieces. They weren't going anywhere. But the nightstand clutter that irritated Daddy was gone—fashion magazines, hair clips, greeting cards bought and never sent, stray pens, a collection of journals that remained blank.

Also missing: the pill bottles from the top of the dresser. If the mover had packed her scripts and Mama couldn't find them, she'd have a fit, but it was unlikely she'd have left the packing to him. She'd have done it herself first thing.

The mover picked up a silver-framed photograph and flashed the picture toward me: Mama, Daddy, and me on Roxie at a show on Long Island when I was ten. It was the last time she'd seen me ride. "This stay or go?"

On Long Island, Mama's dislike of horses had been irrelevant. The parties and dinners were a chance for her to socialize. In public, she and Daddy gave every outward appearance of happiness. Being Monty Montgomery's wife had its perks in the equestrian world, including lots of attention. He was the sun and she was the moon, reflecting his glory. But the next week, he was out of town, and she'd let me spend the night at Chelsea's. Sass was there, too. She was too old to play with Barbies, she said, which I didn't want to play with, either, but we had until Sass asked me, "What's Ken doing?"

"Kissing Barbie."

Sass frowned. "Boys can't kiss you there."

"They can kiss you anywhere."

Chelsea, who had driven Barbie's convertible off the edge of her desk, left the scene of the accident. "What are you talking about?"

So I told her and Sass what boys and girls could do, and the more Sass insisted it was impossible, the more I insisted it *was* possible, until she ran down the hall to tell Mrs. Yost, who came into Chelsea's room, looked at Ken with his face planted between Barbie's legs, and suggested we play Monopoly.

When Mama picked me up the next morning, she asked me whether I'd had a good time.

"It was okay."

"What did you do?"

"We played Monopoly. I won."

"I'm sure you did. What else?"

"Watched TV."

"What else?"

I knew then I was in trouble. "That's all."

"I talked to Chelsea's mother. Were you girls playing Barbies?"

The deliberate neutrality of her tone put me on guard.

"It was boring."

"Apparently not. What was Ken doing to Barbie?"

"Kissing her."

"Where?"

"I was just playing."

"Where?"

She'd never sounded this way before. She was often sarcastic, often irritated, but stern was Daddy's territory. I was surprised that coming from her, it had the same effect on me, like a combination of a lie detector test and truth serum.

"Down there."

"What makes you think boys kiss girls down there?" Her voice had lost its sternness, which made it easier for me to lie again.

"I've seen it in movies." That was what I'd told Chelsea and Sass.

"What movies?"

"I don't know."

"Roan, I'm going to ask you a question, and you need to answer it honestly. Has a boy kissed you down there?"

"No, ma'am."

"Let me rephrase that. Has anyone kissed you down there?"

"No, ma'am."

She swerved into the overlook and braked so hard that I was slung forward against my seat belt.

"Who was it?" Her voice was almost a growl.

Crying never made Daddy sympathetic to my cause, but it might work on Mama.

She struck the dashboard with her palm. "God*dammit*, tell me who it was."

My tears became genuine. If I told her, he'd find out I hadn't kept our secret. He'd be mad. My horses would be sold.

She grabbed me by my shoulders and shook me. My head snapped back and forth. Fierce pains shot up my neck into my brain. Daddy never touched me in anger.

"Tell me!"

My tears turned into big gulping heaves, and I was about to throw up my breakfast, and my eyes rolled around in my head like marbles.

"Daddy," I gasped.

She released me.

Only my sobbing and snuffling broke the silence. I wiped my nose on the sleeve of my jacket and waited for all the terrible things to happen, starting with Mama right here, right now.

She was breathing funny. "What else has he done?"

I edged closer to my door. "Nothing."

Her fingers clamped on my wrist and she hauled me toward her. "You tell me right now."

She was hurting me, squeezing the bones in my wrist. My hand went numb. I began to talk, at first hoping she'd let go of me, but once I started, I couldn't stop. I told her everything, even though I didn't know the right words for some things. The whole time, Mama kept her eyes closed. She looked like she did when her head hurt and her stomach was iffy.

When I finished, her grip on my wrist relaxed. I took my arm back and rubbed it. The tingle of circulation crept into my hand.

"Mama." My voice was small, clotted with snot and tears. "You won't say anything, will you?"

She opened her eyes. "What?"

"If you say anything to him, he'll sell Roxie and Hank." More tears.

Mama looked blank, as if she didn't know who Roxie and Hank were, or who I was, either. "I don't know what I'll do. But you? You don't say a word to anyone. Not Chelsea, not Sass, and for God's sake not Gertrude or Eddie." She breathed out a shaky sigh. "Stay here."

She got out of the car, not bothering to close the door. Cold mountain air swirled into the car immediately. With the back of my hand, I wiped my cheeks and watched through the windshield as she walked to the safety rail at the edge of the overlook, her shoulders narrow under her wool jacket. I unclipped my seat belt and crawled across the console, stretching to close her door, but as I reached for the door handle, a full-throated scream made me jump.

Mama was screaming with her whole body, doubled over, and the echo bouncing off the granite walls of the gorge made me shiver. She straightened, and I shrank back in my seat and fastened my seat belt without closing her door, afraid of what she'd do to me when she came back. But she did nothing except drive us home and go upstairs.

Over the next two days, we ate silent dinners in the dining room. I had breakfast in the kitchen with Gertrude, who took me to school and picked me up, and I spent as much time as I could with my horses, saving up things I'd need to remember if Daddy sold them: Hank's silken coat, Roxie's ripply mane. At night, I fought myself, wanting to run down the hall and crawl into bed with Mama but knowing she'd send me straight back to my room, so I stayed put, bouncing between the hope and the fear that she *would* say something to Daddy, wishing I'd never told her, dreaming of how life would be if she made him stop.

Then he came home, and of all the things I'd imagined, the one that happened was a huge relief and a bigger betrayal than I realized at the time. Mama kept our secret.

"Kid?" The moving man waggled the photo. "Leave it or pack it?"

"Pack it." I was sure Mama didn't want it, but I wanted her to have it. Every time she looked at it, I wanted her to see the ten-year-old girl who'd told her mother—a mother who'd done nothing.

A scraping sound made me turn. She was pulling a packed box from the closet into the bedroom.

She took an empty box from the collection by the bed. "Are you helping or standing there?"

I got another box and went back in. Daddy's clothes hung on one side, but without Mama's clothes cramming every inch of it, I could almost envision the closet as the nursery it had once been. There were even windows, which had been shuttered.

I knelt and started taking shoes from the bottom row of cubbyholes, black stilettos, strappy bronze sandals, black kid boots, all tall. The extra height was slimming, she said.

"For God's sake." She swooped over my shoulder, pulled shoes from cubbies, and tossed them into the box. "I don't have all day."

"Won't he give you more time?"

"I don't want more time. What don't you understand, Roan? I want *out* of this fucking house, away from your father, and away from you."

One time Eddie had taken me fishing, and I'd watched him gut a fish. That was how I felt, like my guts spilled all over the floor.

"Finish your own packing." I stood up and pushed past her.

"Roan—"

I stalked across the bedroom and down the hall.

I'd cried—when I was ten. I wasn't about to cry now.

In my room I closed the door and leaned against it. No surprise she didn't want me. She hadn't wanted me as a baby, either.

And she accused me of rejecting her.

There was a soft knock.

"Roan? This isn't how I want to leave things."

*Then open the door. You know it doesn't lock. Open it and put your arms around me.*

"I've got to take care of myself," she said, "before I can take care of you."

"I don't need you to take care of me."

I sounded cold, but if she loved me, she'd open the door and hug me no matter what I said.

I looked down at the doorknob. If it moved, her hand was on it. If it turned, she was coming in. If she came in, I would forgive her.

I waited. The movers' heavy work boots went up and down the stairs, up and down the hall. Eventually the house became still.

Mama was gone.

# - Eight -

AFTER SHE LEFT, I wandered through the house. It was remarkably unchanged.

Daddy, at his desk, looked up when I stood in the doorway of his study. "You all right, darlin'?"

"I think so." I wasn't, but that was what he wanted to hear. "Are you?"

"Tired. You'll be okay if I take a nap?"

I nodded. "I'm going to the barn."

I needed to change into riding pants first, so I went upstairs with Daddy. He paused outside my room.

"We'll be okay." He kissed the tip of my nose. If he wasn't tired from his late-night negotiations with Mama, I thought, it would have led to more.

In fleece-lined jodhpurs and riding boots, I walked down to the barn in a cutting wind. The trees were bare, the driveway littered with limbs and mushy brown leaves.

Jasper lay in the straw but lurched to his feet when I pushed open his stall door.

I'd planned to ride indoors, but as I tacked him, I felt more and more like I needed space.

The broad grassy aisle that ran as a buffer between the pastures and the driveway made a mindless place for a walk. The boughs of the oaks dipped and swayed, the sharp black branches scratching the sky like witches' fingers. Jasper whinnied at the broodmares. One of them trumpeted back and thundered toward the fence, keeping us company for a hundred yards or so before wheeling and returning to the herd.

As we neared the birch grove that marked the corner of the driveway, I glimpsed something white through the trunks. I nudged Jasper into the grove.

Will Howard's pickup was on the shoulder of the road. He sat behind the wheel, staring straight ahead. Another internal chill went through me. Was he a stalker?

I tied Jasper to the top rail of the fence, climbed over it, and rapped on the passenger window. Will turned his head. His face was white, his eyes red, his mouth drawn.

I opened the door. "What are you doing here?"

"Nice horse."

"Thanks. What are you doing here?"

"Can you get in?"

I climbed in and closed the door. The truck was freezing. Will started the engine.

"I can't go anywhere. Jasper—"

"Just warming it up." He adjusted the heat. Warm air smelling of ashes blew gently into the cab. "You look cold."

"So do you," I said, embarrassed by my assumption he'd been ready to drive off with me. "Are you okay?"

"Not really." He opened the ashtray, took out a stubby hand-rolled cigarette, and pushed the lighter into the dash. "Mind if I smoke?"

I hated smoking, but it was his truck.

The lighter popped. He held the glowing end to the cigarette and drew in a breath. A sweet tea-like fragrance filled the cab. Not a stalker. A stoner. Figured.

I reached for the door handle.

Will exhaled a cloud of smoke. "Going somewhere?"

"I have better things to do than sit here while you get stoned."

"My brother's dead."

I hadn't even asked about Steve. Mama was right. I did think everything was about me.

He was looking straight ahead again. "All of them. Amy and the kids. Marley was only eight months old. A semitruck crossed the median. The car was ripped apart." His voice was so emotionless that it took me a moment to understand what he'd said.

"My God, Will. Are you—" I was about to ask him if he were all right, but how could he be? Instead I said, "I'm sorry," and the words sounded inadequate, a grain of sand dropped into an ocean, not enough to displace a single drop of water. "I can't imagine."

"Neither can I." He slumped forward in the seat and started to rock back and forth, hugging himself. I inched closer and rubbed between his shoulder blades, his denim jacket soft-coarse under my palm. He stopped rocking and began to sob. He wasn't emotionless. He was in shock. I couldn't bring myself to say something stupid like "It'll be okay."

After a while he wiped his face on his sleeve. I patted his back in a "there, there" gesture and put my hand in my lap.

"Steve was my best friend. I hang out with Rico and Wedge, but Steve got me."

I glanced out the window. Jasper stood unperturbed by the clatter of branches overhead.

"The cops came to the door around six this morning. Mom knew before they ever said a word. I can still hear her: 'Not my son. Not my son.' I'll never forget that as long as I live." He relit the joint. "Carrie's, like, a sponge, *saturated* from crying. And Dad's just dealing. He said he's doing the last thing he can for Steve." His voice got unsteady on the last few words.

"What about you?"

"I've lost my best friend. How would you be?"

I didn't have anything to compare it to. Losing Gertrude? Jasper?

"I drove around and started thinking about giving you a ride the other day, and I wound up here. I've just been sitting here."

"How long?"

He looked at the dashboard clock. "Couple of hours."

"Seriously?"

"Does it bother you?"

I'd never be able to explain it to Daddy if he found out, but I shook my head.

Will tapped some ash into the ashtray. "I saw your mom leaving. You look like her."

"They're splitting up."

"I figured. I saw the moving van, too. So you're staying with him?"

"Yeah. They worked all that out."

"Without asking you?"

He was shrewd for a drug addict.

"It's what I want. Mama won't stay in Sheridan, and my horses are here. Even if she supported my riding, which she doesn't, I couldn't leave Rosemont—my horses, my training."

"You could."

"I don't want to."

That was the simple fact of it. I wanted to stay.

I nodded toward the joint. "Can I try some of that?"

"Don't you have better things to do?"

"Sorry about that."

"If you're sure."

"I'm not," I said, "but what the fuck."

He looked startled. "For a good girl, you have quite a mouth on you."

"Good girl" sounded like a title, the same way "bad boy" did. Maybe we were wrong about each other. He was wrong, anyway.

He lit the joint and gave it to me, his cold fingers brushing mine.

"What do I do?"

"Draw in your breath, but don't inhale all the way into your lungs or you'll cough. Hold it here." He tapped his upper chest.

"Is that how you do it?"

"I'm hard-core. I inhale."

"Then that's what I want to do." Suddenly I wanted more than anything else to be a normal hard-core what-the-fuck pot-smoking teenager. I put the joint to my lips.

"Don't say I didn't warn you," Will said.

The smoke hit my lungs like a kick in the chest. I started coughing.

"Told you," Will said.

"Why," I wheezed, "would anyone do this?"

He said something I couldn't hear over another lung-shredding coughing fit. He took the joint from me.

"You'll see," he repeated when I finally stopped. My chest ached. "Want to try again?"

I glared at him.

"Don't be pissed at me. I told you not to inhale."

That was true.

"Okay." My voice was raspy. "I'll try again. I guess people wouldn't do it if there wasn't something nice about it."

"This time, don't inhale."

He lit the joint again. I drew in the smoke but not too deeply.

He replaced the lighter in the dash. "Tell me when you're ready to exhale. I want to show you something."

I was afraid I'd start to cough again, so after a few seconds I pointed to my chest.

"Ready?"

I nodded.

He leaned toward me. I started to pull back, but he said, "It's all right. I'm going to put my mouth over yours, and then I want you to exhale. It's called shot-gunning. Two hits for the price of one."

Wait, what? I didn't have the makings of a normal hard-core what-the-fuck pot-smoking teenager after all, but whether it was the effects of the pot or the fact that I liked him—and I did like him—I let him place his mouth on mine.

Lightning struck me. His lips were unexpectedly soft. I breathed out, and he breathed in, robbing me of air. Then he was kissing me, his eyes closing, his tongue touching mine, his hands on either side of my face. Only Daddy had kissed me like this.

I lurched back. "What are you doing?"

"Sorry." He didn't sound sorry. "Didn't mean to do that."

"Well, don't do it again." My hand was back on the door handle.

"I won't. You don't have to go."

I didn't want to leave, but I couldn't sit around smoking pot and kissing boys. Maybe other girls could. Not me.

"I have chores. I'm sorry about Steve."

Showing me how to smoke, kissing me, had diverted his attention. My words brought back reality. His face was bleak, stunned, struggling.

"I should go, anyway," he said. "I left the house without my phone. My folks'll be worried. They've got enough—" He took a few seconds to compose himself. "See you around."

"See you." I opened the door and slid out of the cab.

I climbed the fence and untied Jasper. When I was mounted, I looked back at the truck. Will watched me through the window. A freezing rain began to streak down. I turned Jasper toward home and touched my heels to his sides. He leaped forward, and as we cantered up the hill, somewhere behind me Will's truck rumbled into gear.

AFTER I GROOMED Jasper, I got an early start on mucking my stalls, trying to sort out what had happened.

Since Wednesday, I'd had the idea some things might be possible, but as Daddy said, I didn't have time for boys. I especially didn't have time for a boy who heard me say, "My father says I'm too young to be getting calls from boys"—and then showed up at the end of my driveway. Was he high or stupid?

Not stupid. Definitely high. Grieving. Ignorant of how carefully I had to engineer my life.

I doubled down on my cleaning efforts and had just finished when the grooms began trickling in for evening chores.

"I'll take that." Mateo nodded toward my rake. The wheelbarrow was only half-full, so he commandeered it, too.

"Thanks." I unclipped Vigo from the crossties. "Did you have a good Thanksgiving?"

"Yeah. Fernando cooks a killer turkey. You?"

As soon as he asked the question, his face took on a dismayed expression, as if he'd said something wrong. He knew about Mama. That meant everyone knew.

"Fine," I said.

I returned Vigo to his stall.

On the way to the house, I met Daddy. He peered out from under the hood of his rain jacket. "Go take a hot bath. I don't want you getting sick."

In my bathroom mirror, pale pink rimmed my eyes. If Daddy noticed, I'd blame it on crying, but I hadn't shed a tear. It must have been the weed. My mouth was a desert. I gulped a handful of water before I stepped into the shower.

I dressed in sweats and took the back stairs down to the kitchen, where I started reheating leftovers.

So, Will Howard smoked weed. That wasn't a big deal, even if it hadn't done anything for me. That kiss, though, had done plenty. The memory sent a current of energy through me.

I was wrapping dinner rolls in foil when Daddy came in. He'd left his jacket and boots on the screened porch, so he was in rain-spotted jodhpurs and socks, as he had been yesterday. He hadn't shaved, but he looked more rested than he had earlier, straight from the pages of *Horse & Hound*, tousled and masculine, the successful horseman at home. In fact, he'd been profiled in that very article a few years back.

He smiled, and I remembered who he was.

"You're making supper. Good girl."

There it was again. Good girl. Me.

"Leftovers." I put the rolls in the oven.

"I'll be down in ten minutes."

I set the table. The extensions had been removed, so it was back to its normal size, still big enough for twelve. I put the Maker's Mark and a pitcher of water at his place.

He returned in jeans and a polo shirt, his hair damp, and sipped his drink while I served our plates in the kitchen and brought them to the table.

"Good," he said. "You have an appetite."

We ate in silence for a while.

"You know, darlin', in a practical sense, your mother's being gone won't matter."

"I don't want to talk about her." All she'd needed to do was open the door.

"We don't have to, but I want you to know, we're all right. You are. I am. She is."

Almost unwillingly, I said, "She is?" I didn't know how Mama would make it on her own. I reminded myself I didn't care.

He splashed more bourbon into his glass. "She has plenty of money to do whatever she wants."

Money had been the subject of many arguments between my parents. Mama had her own checking account, but Daddy

was the one who fed money into it—never enough according
to her and an insanely generous amount according to him. His
estimate was more trustworthy. Mama's need for money and
things was insatiable.

"Is it enough?" I asked.

"I believe so."

He'd been furious with Mama, so their definitions of *plenty*
and *enough* could be poles apart.

"How much?"

"We had a prenup. It would have been naïve of me if we
hadn't. This farm is mine and yours, not hers."

I couldn't fathom Mama wanting a single square foot of
Rosemont, but she might have tried to take it out of spite. A
prenup made that impossible.

He swirled his drink. "Your mother received a certain sum of
money for each year of marriage, plus a bonus every five years.
It's held in trust because she can't manage that kind of money—
and also because there's a fidelity clause. If she strayed outside
the bounds of marriage, she'd get nothing."

"Then she has nothing."

"She has five hundred thousand for each year we were married, plus a million for every five years, plus something on top
of that. It's still in trust, because she has to comply with certain
conditions. If she doesn't, the money goes away."

I did the math in my head. "You gave Mama eleven million
dollars?"

"More."

She'd cheated, and he'd held up his end of the prenup and
then some?

"Why?" I asked. "What did she give you?"

He smiled. "You."


AFTER SUPPER, HE showed me the prenup and the irrevocable relinquishment of custody, prepared by an attorney, signed by Mama, witnessed by Gertrude and Eddie.

Her signature, a spiky heartbeat of ink, looked more hopeful on the prenup than her hurried sign-off on my bill of sale. I wasn't the only thing she'd sold. A nondisclosure clause prohibited her from discussing the marriage and our family. She'd sold her silence.

Daddy stuck his head in the kitchen while I was washing dishes. "Come on, darlin'. Leave the rest. The video's cued up."

In the living room, he sat on the sofa and patted the seat next to him.

The video was the Middleton cross-country phase.

He didn't critique my ride, since we'd already had that discussion, but we reviewed the performances of the other riders, Daddy pausing frequently to point out a weak takeoff or poor landing or to ask what my competitors were doing wrong. When we came to Jamie's fall, Luna plunged into the water like a stone, and Jamie cartwheeled off, catching a hard blow of hoof to helmet and a battery of hoofs to the chest as Luna scrambled out of the water.

"Frank says he's concussed, but compared to what it could have been . . ."

Jamie was lucky to be alive and likely wouldn't have been were it not for his safety vest and helmet.

Daddy rewound. "He walked the course like the rest of us. That was a ballbuster, but he knew it was coming. Here, watch."

He pressed Play and then Pause. "He's tentative on takeoff." He advanced the video frame by frame. "See how he's sitting, too far forward and too high on her back? It's inevitable that she's going down and he's coming off."

Watching it once had been bad enough. I closed my eyes, and even when I knew we were past the fall, I didn't open them. I couldn't. They were weighted.

Daddy's fingers wound in my hair. My eyes flew open.

The living room was dark. I'd fallen asleep with my cheek on his shoulder.

With his free hand, he raised my chin. His tongue pushed into my mouth, stubble grating my skin. This was not like Will's kiss. Will had kissed some girls, but Daddy knew what he was doing. After a minute he pushed my head downward.

This morning, when he'd told me Mama was leaving, I hadn't wanted to abandon the life I knew, Rosemont and my horses—but this was also the life I knew. I didn't want this, and I did, and I didn't understand why.

There were things I hadn't told Mama, when I was ten or ever: the way I didn't fight or scream, the way my body responded to his, the ease with which he made me come—the fact that I came at all.

There were things I could never tell anyone.

# - Nine -

MONDAY MORNING, SHERIDAN Academy resumed its regular class schedule after a school-wide assembly at which the associate headmaster, Mr. Felton, announced he had replaced Mr. Dashwood, who had resigned because of family concerns.

I imagined a silent collective groan from the student body. Mr. Felton delivered a short lecture on behavior becoming an Academy student. Previous administrations had been lenient. Discipline would now be stern and swift. Chelsea told me later that Sass and Annabelle had been expelled, not suspended; during their suspension, they'd posted photos on Instagram of Sass's cartoon and tagged me in the posts.

"This is why you need a phone." Chelsea whipped hers out and poked at the screen. "I mean, the posts were deleted, but I took some screenshots. Stupid idiots. Look."

#whoremother #horsedaughter #roanmontgomery

No wonder Daddy said social media would distract me. He'd seen the posts, and undoubtedly he'd had something to do with the expulsions. For once, I didn't mind the layer of protection he'd built between me and the world. I was glad Sass and Annabelle were gone, glad Mr. Dashwood was gone. Glad Mama was gone.

The one person I wanted to see didn't come to school that week. Will surfaced in my mind often, and not only because of his kiss. He'd sat in his truck at the base of my driveway for two hours. Why hadn't he gone to see Wedge or Rico? Because they didn't get him? What made him think I did? Likewise, why had I called him instead of Chelsea Thanksgiving night? He wasn't even a friend, just a classmate. He'd move on to another girl when he saw I wasn't interested. I wasn't.

On Friday, the school held a memorial service for his brother. A decade ago, Steve Howard had been captain of a nationally ranked lacrosse team, honor society president, valedictorian, poster child for the school's crème-de-la-crème university-prep image. It hardly seemed possible Will was related to him.

After an abbreviated morning schedule, we reconvened in our homerooms and tramped down to the phys ed building under a glaring white sky.

"You don't think we have to see their bodies, do you?" Chelsea said.

"It's a memorial, not a funeral. They don't have bodies at memorials."

The service had expanded beyond the school to the town and consequently was being held in the gym. Chairs for students and faculty were lined up on the basketball court. Will stood paper-white and gaunt in a receiving line with his parents and his sister, a wisp of a girl, no more than six. He accepted a hug with some manly backslapping from Wedge and a punch to the arm from Rico.

The line inched forward until I stood in front of Mr. Howard, an older version of Will, tall and broad-shouldered and dry-eyed. He shook my hand.

"I'm so sorry," I said.

"Thank you, dear."

Another hand touched the small of my back, and my body knew before my mind did that it was Will's. The layers of heavy winter woolens fell away as if he'd touched skin.

"Dad," he said, "this is my friend Roan."

Friend. Okay.

"Of course." Mr. Howard released my hand and patted my arm.

"Mom," Will said, "this is my friend Roan."

Mrs. Howard was tall and slim, with short streaky blond hair. Her face was composed but strained. "Thank you for coming."

"I'm so sorry," I said.

"And Carrie," Will said.

Will's sister leaned against Mrs. Howard's hip, her ponytail tied with a navy ribbon that matched her dress.

"Carried away," Will added, raising a brief, wan smile on her lips.

"Carrie *Howard*," she said in a tone of long-suffering tolerance.

Will led me a step away from his family.

"How are you?" I asked.

"Okay. Well, sometimes. Other times I don't think I can stand it."

Mrs. Tomich, directing the juniors to their seats, waved me forward with a baton of rolled-up papers.

"I should sit down," I said.

"Can we talk after this?"

"Okay."

"I'll find you."

Chelsea had waited for me, and as we walked to our seats she said, "What did he say to you?"

"Nothing."

Mrs. Tomich handed each of us a program—her baton had been a batch of them—and Chelsea and I took the last two seats in a row.

"I didn't know this many people lived in Sheridan," she whispered.

A hush fell over the gym, and the Howards passed by to take their seats in front. Mr. and Mrs. Howard walked arm in arm. Will followed, holding Carrie's hand. Mr. Felton took the small, portable stage at the far end of the court, turned on the microphone, and said, "We're ready to begin."

A minister led an opening prayer asking for comfort and healing. Harold Moon sang a hymn in his pitch-perfect tenor, accompanied by Mr. Hanlon on the school's Steinway. From all over the gym came sniffing and sometimes gentle laughter as different people told stories about Steve. After several speakers, the minister said a closing prayer, and Mr. Felton invited everyone to visit with the family in the lobby, where the school was providing refreshments.

Chelsea and I got separated in the shuffle to the doors. I saw the back of her head, but several other heads bobbed between us.

A hand took my elbow.

"Let's go out the back way," Will said.

He angled us toward the exit by the girls' locker room. We went down a short flight of stairs, he pushed open the door, and we stepped out into the cold. The door sighed on its pneumatic hinge and closed with a clunk.

"That was a nice service," I said.

"It wasn't as bad as the funeral. Then there was a service at the graveside. I wasn't sure how many more funerals I could take, but it was good to hear people who knew him talk about him. I didn't know half those stories." On his cheeks were faint salty streaks where tears had dried. He took a breath, let it out in a cloud of condensation, and nodded toward the football stadium. "Let's take a walk."

The air was bitter. I put my hands in my pockets, but Will seemed oblivious to the cold.

The gate to the stadium wasn't locked. The school's honor code led to very few places being locked during school hours. Will lifted the latch and let me through. We climbed the concrete steps to the top of the bleachers and looked over the safety railing. A few people had come out of the gym and were making their way to their cars.

"Sorry about the other day," he said. "I didn't mean to kiss you like that."

"How did you mean to kiss me?" I said it as a sort of joke, but it gave him the perfect opportunity to say, "Like this," and kiss me again.

"I didn't mean to kiss you at all," he said.

Instantly my face was hot enough to sear meat. I was an idiot. Pathetic. But he'd asked me on a date and said he wouldn't give up, and I'd thought that kiss had meant something.

"I shouldn't have offered you the weed, either," he said.

How had I grown to like him so much so fast?

Humor might hide my humiliation. "So . . . this blows." I tried to chuckle, but a bray came out instead, and Will didn't even smile.

I turned to start down the steps and stumbled over the shreds of my dignity.

He grabbed my arm to keep me from falling. "Bailing on me again?"

"First you act like you like me, and now you're saying you don't, and, I mean, that's fine, but I don't want to stand around talking about it."

"I do like you."

"Just not *that* way." I looked pointedly at his hand on my upper arm, and he released me, but he said, "No, I *do* like you that way."

The heat began to bleed out of my face. "What?"

"I moved sort of fast the other day. I didn't mean to, but I did, and it freaked you out."

"I got over it."

"Reckon you did." He leaned on his forearms on the safety railing, the wind ruffling his hair. "Seriously, I like you—*that* way—and enough to do this the right way. We ought to hang out, do stuff together."

"I don't have a lot of time for hanging out and doing stuff," I said, still smarting.

"We'll find a way."

I watched people leaving the gym. "Why do you like me, anyway?"

"You fought back."

I frowned, not understanding.

"When Sass drew that cartoon, you fought back. She always whomps on you. I thought you were sort of spineless. Smart, but you didn't have any spark. Then all of a sudden you did, and I thought, maybe there's more to you than I figured. Why do you like me?"

"Who says I do?"

"I think you did," he said steadily.

He was so frank that I wasn't even embarrassed.

"I've gotten into it with Sass before. You just weren't around to see it. But it was nice of you to stand up for me. I thought you were sort of a burnout."

"Reckon I am," he said.

I got more than enough exposure to people and their addictions at home, but I was the one sneaking bourbon. I wasn't better than Will Howard.

He nudged me with his shoulder.

I nudged him back. "Will you be at school Monday?"

"Yeah. I wanted to come back this week, but there was the funeral, and we made some trips to their house, and . . . it's been hard. I keep thinking everything will get back to normal, but what's normal now?" He checked the time on his phone. "It's almost noon. You need to get back. I do, too."

We started down the stairs, so close that our arms bumped now and then.

"How are you managing without your mom?"

"Fine." I sounded too bright, too determined to be fine, but he just said, "Has she contacted you?"

"She doesn't want contact."

"That's got to be hard."

I shrugged. "Mr. Dashwood resigned."

"Rico told me."

We reached the bottom of the stairs.

"What's your cell?" Will said.

"I don't have one."

"Well, you said I can't call your house again, so will you call me this weekend?"

"Why?"

"We really have to work on your social skills. Call me so we can talk. Don't ask me about what. It doesn't matter. Don't you ever call your friends?"

"Sure," I said, as if I had friends I called all the time. "What's your number?"

He told me. "I was wrong for thinking you were spineless. We both lost someone, and you're just handling it. Me, not so much."

"You and Steve were close. Mama and I never got along. She says I'm too much like Daddy."

"You don't seem at all like your father to me."

I didn't respond. In the past week, I'd learned I was more like Daddy than I had known.


AFTER CHORES, LESSONS, and breakfast on Sunday morning, Daddy suggested we ride out.

It was the mildest day we'd had since before Thanksgiving. Without the bitter whipping wind, the air felt almost warm.

Diva fidgeted beneath me in the stable yard while Daddy tightened Byron's girth, eliciting a teeth-baring display of displeasure from his horse. Besides Daddy, only Eddie, Mateo, and a couple of other senior grooms handled Byron. I doubted he was any worse than Diva, but generally I gave him a wide berth.

Daddy mounted Psycho Pony the Elder. "Let's ride up the fire road."

Many fire roads snaked over the farm's nearly three thousand acres, but there was one we often rode on. It rose steeply into the hills and made good conditioning ground for the horses.

We walked the horses down the mile-long back drive to the service road. Daddy leaned down from the saddle to punch in the gate code, and we rode through. As the gate slowly closed behind us, Byron's head flashed toward Diva with the speed of a copperhead striking. She jerked her head out of biting range. Byron's teeth snapped together audibly.

"They need to work off some of this piss and vinegar," Daddy said. "Ready?"

Without waiting for an answer, he gave Byron an invisible cue, and the stallion broke into a canter down the service road. I clicked my tongue to Diva, and we followed.

Byron bucked, putting his head down, lashing out and upward with his back legs, dropping first his right shoulder and then his left, a move virtually guaranteed to unseat a rider. Daddy stuck in the saddle. He could still outride me, dissolving the distinction between horse and rider in a way I'd not yet achieved.

He settled Byron and resumed the canter. "Get a move on, darlin'!"

I urged Diva into an extended canter until we were alongside Byron, who pinned his ears. Diva returned the gesture.

As soon as we turned onto the fire road, Daddy gave Byron a guttural "Yah!" The stallion broke into a gallop. I touched Diva with my heels, and she lunged after them. Within three strides we were beside them, but only for two paces. Then we passed them, bare branches and pine boughs flashing by.

We'd been in a steady gallop for several strides when Diva accelerated. Peripherally I saw Daddy and Byron coming up on our left. They pulled ahead.

I leaned forward. "Go!"

Diva flattened her stride, long legs devouring the ground. I had an impression of Daddy—black hacking jacket, blue-black horse—as we flew past.

The pine tree lying across the road must have come down in the Thanksgiving Day storm. Diva met it as perfectly as if we'd jumped this tree in this spot a hundred times, rising into the air with her forelegs tucked, floating over it, and landing neatly on the other side. I risked a look over my left shoulder and saw Byron sailing over the tree, Daddy laughing.

We raced up the hill. Byron and Daddy kept pace a horse's length behind us but didn't pass us again. Finally, I began to slow Diva, and with one rebellious shake of her head, as if she were saying, "No, this is what I was born to do," she dropped down to a jog. Daddy and Byron drew alongside again. Together we slowed the horses and brought them to a stop.

Byron was huffing and blowing.

Daddy chuckled. "Y'all are too much for a couple of old men. Let's take a break." He swung down and led Byron off the fire road onto a track that ended in a clearing. I dismounted and followed.

The pine needles muffled the clop of the horses' hoofs.

"I'll have someone come up with a chain saw to get that tree off the road," Daddy said. "Well done, by the way."

"You, too."

Daddy kept the woods free of underbrush, but here and there were fallen trees that would be cut for firewood when they'd aged a year or two. He tied Byron to a branch of a fat pine log. The stallion half-heartedly curled his lips back when Diva and I approached, too tired to make a genuine attempt at intimidation. I looped my reins around a branch. Diva could have freed herself, but with Byron nearby, the suggestion of being tied was enough to keep her there. As nasty as they both were, they preferred company to striking off on their own.

Daddy came up behind me and put his arms around me. "We're all right, darlin'." He pressed up against me, as solid as a wall. "Everything we need is right here."


WE RUBBED DOWN the horses and put them away, and I walked up to the house while Daddy took care of paperwork in his office in the training barn.

Upstairs, I pulled off my sweater and checked my back in the bathroom mirror. Blood had beaded and dried where the pine bark had scratched my skin. I hadn't expected it to happen like that, standing up, and on a chilly day in the woods.

When the water in the shower hit the raw places, I winced, but I deserved the pain. A few years ago I had avoided bathing, hoping to make myself so disgusting that he'd leave me alone. It hadn't worked. Now I showered all the time. He could make me give in to him, but he couldn't do anything about the way I felt afterward.

I shut off the taps, toweled dry, and dressed. One o'clock. On Sundays Gertrude served dinner at two, our nod to a normal family tradition when we were home.

I'd wanted to call Will—until now, when I had the opportunity.

I could still feel Daddy inside me, but Will believed I was normal.

With him, I thought, I could be.

Daddy's room, like mine, overlooked the barn. I kept an eye out for him while I picked up the handset, put it down, and picked it up again.

On the third ring, Will answered. "Hello."

"It's Roan."

"I wondered if you'd call." He sounded pleased.

"This is the first chance I've had."

"Yeah? Where's your dad?"

"At the barn." I watched one of the grooms pushing a manure cart.

"What have you been doing this weekend?" Will asked.

As I told him about riding out, the exhilaration of pounding along at thirty miles an hour on horseback, it dawned on me that even if I initially felt awkward and unsure when we talked, Will wound up making it easy.

"They go that fast?"

"Faster. We were going uphill. What did you do?"

"I went for a run, and I tried to work on this backgammon set I'm carving for Dad, but it's not the same. I mean, the work is the same, but I'm not. Christmas is coming too fast. We need more time before we have to act happy. What are you giving your dad?" he added abruptly in an obvious shift of attention from his family to mine.

"Mama always helped me pick out something. I don't suppose . . ." A plan started to form, more of a wish really, but hanging out with Will wouldn't come about organically. We'd have to engineer it. "What if I tell Daddy I want to go shopping one day after school? You can meet me in town, and he can pick me up later. I'm done at one and you don't get out until three, but we'd have an hour or two."

"That's not enough. I'll cut class."

"You can't do that."

"I do it all the time."

"Really?"

"Yeah. I'd have been kicked out a long time ago if Mom and Dad weren't Howard Construction."

I'd had the same thought.

"What day?" he said.

I didn't know when I'd stopped paying attention to the road between the barn and the house, but the floorboard down the hall creaked and adrenaline crackled through me.

"I have to go." I clicked the phone off, put the handset in the base, hoped Will had the good sense not to call me back.

Daddy stopped short in the doorway. "What are you doing in my room?"

If I'd had more than two seconds to think, I might have said something else.

"Waiting for you."

He wanted to believe me. In this moment, I controlled what happened next. If he could use my body, I could, too.

I held his gaze, and he closed the door.

# - Ten -

GETTING DADDY'S PERMISSION to go shopping after school turned out to be easy. I raised the question at Sunday dinner shortly after our encounter in his bedroom, and the next morning he dropped me off at school. "I'll pick you up on the north side of the courthouse at four. Do you have money?"

"My allowance."

He paid me ten dollars a week for doing chores. It wasn't much, because he wanted me to learn the value of money, but since I never went anywhere, I never spent anything. I had this year's entire allowance with me, and part of last year's, too.

Will waited by my locker, collar unbuttoned, tie loosely knotted, shirt untucked, hair shaggy and bed-heady.

"Everything okay at your house?" he asked.

"Yeah. Why?"

"You hung up on me yesterday."

"Daddy was coming."

"Did you get in trouble?"

"No. He said I can go shopping today."

The surprise in his expression made me think I was too eager.

"It's your first day back," I said. "No one will think twice if you leave early."

Lame. Will didn't need me to find an excuse for him.

"Good idea," he said. "I parked behind the gym. Meet me there after lit. I'm guessing we shouldn't walk out together."

He was catching on.

All day I caught glimpses of him—in the hall between classes, heading into the boys' room with Wedge, and finally in lit class, where I had trouble concentrating on Melville because the back of Will's head was fascinating. I'd never noticed all those shades of blond—honey and butter, lemon and wheat, a whole bakery's worth of goodness.

After class, I dawdled at my locker to give him time to leave first. I waited for the second bell and then left via the doors at the end of the hall.

He was already in his truck, but he leaned over and opened the passenger door. I climbed inside to a choking cloud of smoke.

"Ugh."

"What?"

I put my books on the seat between us. "It's smoky."

"Oh." He rolled down his window.

"Are you okay to drive?"

"Why wouldn't I be?"

"Aren't you stoned?"

"Not really. Would you rather walk?"

The smoke was clearing, and he couldn't be any more impaired than Mama had been when she'd taken me shopping, and we were only a few blocks from the square.

"I'll ride with you," I said.

Stoned or not, he was a better driver than Mama. We left the school grounds via a road used mostly by maintenance staff and reached the square without incident.

He parked on the south side of the courthouse, pulled his tie over his head, and tossed it on the dashboard. "Want to start here?" He nodded toward the courthouse.

In the hundred years since the county seat had moved, Sheridan's courthouse had been reincarnated as an antiques mall. The town was in a post-Thanksgiving lull, but the shops glittered with decorations and reeked of pine-scented candles and cinnamon sticks, and in a few weeks, the rental cabins that dotted the mountains would fill up for Christmas.

We stood amid a display of *Virginia Is for Lovers* mugs and burlap bags of extra-large peanuts.

"You really think we'll find something for your dad here?" Will asked.

"No, not here."

We wandered into a larger shop. He picked up a pewter chess figure painted with a Confederate army uniform. "Does he like chess?"

"We have a chess set. A regular one. It's weird, don't you think, a Civil War chess set? You don't see Nazi chess sets."

"I bet somebody makes them." He replaced the Confederate soldier. "Check out the queen. It's Scarlett O'Hara."

I looked at the Union queen. "Who's she?"

"Harriet Beecher Stowe?"

"You're not nearly as . . ." There was no good way to finish that sentence.

Will supplied the rest of it. "Dumb as people think I am? Don't tell. I like to manage expectations."

I bought a set of three tall, fat ivory-colored candles with sturdy wrought iron holders for Gertrude. While the saleswoman wrapped them, Will and I browsed. The shop was like a labyrinth, one room after another of shelves, tables, and display cases crammed with merchandise.

I studied some old books in a glass-fronted case. Daddy liked to read. If there were a rare first edition . . . but these were only old schoolbooks.

"What do you think?" Will, modeling a conquistador's helmet, struck a pose.

"Definitely you."

He pulled it off and ran his hand through his hair. "It weighs a ton. Imagine wearing it in Florida in August—sun on steel." He hung it on the rack he'd taken it from and removed a broad-brimmed picture hat. "Try this." He placed it on my head and pointed toward a gilt-framed mirror.

I grimaced. "Talk about Scarlett O'Hara."

"Not your style? Try this one." He whipped the picture hat off and replaced it with what looked like a top hat, but then I saw the netting.

"It's an old riding habit." I pulled the veil over my face and wrapped the end around my neck.

"That looks cool." He unwound the netting and lifted it from my face. "But I like it better this way."

He was standing right in front of me. I kissed him.

He closed his eyes. I touched the tip of his tongue with mine. He sucked gently on my lower lip. I was melting, right down to my core. I wanted more, and suddenly afraid of how much more, I started to pull back.

He broke the kiss. "I'm not apologizing for that one."

It had been a sweet kiss, but the other sensations flooding through me were anything but sweet.

He removed the hat. The net snagged on my hair and pulled a strand of it across my face. My nerve endings sang as he tucked it behind my ear. He returned the hat to the rack and took my hand.

For a moment, I tried to figure out what to do with my fingers; I hadn't held hands with anyone since I was about six.

Will twined his fingers with mine. "Like this."

A tingle ran all the way from my fingertips up my arm into my shoulder and halfway across my back, but as we walked to the front of the store, I pulled my hand free and picked up a heavy glass paperweight, round and clear and smooth, a kaleidoscope of colored glass trapped inside as bright as hard candy. I bought that for Eddie, and a pair of dangly amethyst earrings for Chelsea.

On the street, Will's hand brushed mine, but I ignored it. In the back rooms, though, lacing our fingers together eventually became less like the world's stupidest thumb-wrestling match. I decided I liked holding hands.

Three gifts down and one to go. What did I give a man who always got what he wanted?

We left another store where I'd rejected half a dozen possibilities. The afternoon had taken on the pale light of early winter. I shivered.

"Let's get something warm," Will said.

We went to Murphy's Coffeehouse, which had once been the corner drugstore. The soda counter was now a coffee bar. A few people sat nursing oversized mugs, and at a table, a man in a knit cap pecked away industriously on a laptop. Christmas music played on the sound system.

"Grab that table," Will said. "I'll order. What would you like?"

"Hot chocolate."

I claimed the table he'd pointed out, a tall table in the back corner with barstools instead of chairs. I put the shopping bags on one stool and took gunslinger's corner so no one could sneak up on me. I gazed out the window at the storefronts twinkling with Christmas lights, the massive Virginia pine glittering with ornaments on the courthouse lawn, Mama's green Jaguar gliding by.

Instantly I was on my feet. She'd come back for me.

Then I saw Mr. Dashwood in the passenger seat.

And then they were gone.

Will joined me, bearing a tray that held two big mugs and two spoons.

I stared out the window. "That was my mother."

"Where?"

"She drove by with Mr. Dashwood."

I turned away from the window and slid onto my barstool. Gunslinger's corner wasn't foolproof. Someone had sneaked up on me after all.

Will set a mug crowned with whipped cream in front of me. "You okay?"

I nodded, rattled but trying to get a grip.

He put a mug of tea on the table and returned the tray to the counter while I collected myself.

When he came back, his face was thoughtful. "When Steve died, you said the most profound thing to me: 'I can't imagine.' That's exactly what I needed someone to say, because that kind of loss is unimaginable, and you weren't pretending it wasn't. I wish I didn't have the opportunity to say it back to you, but I can't imagine how it feels to be abandoned by your mother."

Neither the kiss nor the tingling had shot a bolt that directly to my heart. Daddy had asked if I were all right, if I missed Mama, but he expected a yes and a no, in that order; he wasn't inviting me to tell him how I felt.

I was about to cry. I was an awesome date.

"It's not like I'm a baby."

"Still hurts, doesn't it?"

I liked Will's lack of pretense, too. I wasn't used to that. Even Eddie and Gertrude and I had our pretenses. They pretended my family was normal, and so did I. I realized I'd have to do that with Will, too. People expected normal.

"I don't want to talk about her," I said, and I led her into a stall and closed the door.

"I get that." He dipped the tea bag in his mug a few times.

"So you're a tea drinker," I said after six dips.

"Steve thought it was funny, too." He stirred in some sugar. "It's weird, you know, all of them gone—like someone flipped a switch and a river stopped running. Like a river stopped *being*." He put his spoon on a napkin. "You wouldn't believe how fast Wedge and Rico change the subject whenever I mention him."

"I'm not changing the subject."

"Thanks, but right now, I don't want to talk about things that hurt, either. Tell me about the horse thing."

"You really want to know? Once I get started, you can't shut me up."

"I don't want to shut you up. You ride giant horses. You're really good at it. You go fast. You like to ride on. What else?"

I described the three phases of eventing, avoiding the dizzying detail the sport entailed. Will drank his tea.

"Are you an Olympian?"

"Not yet. But the year after next is an Olympic year. Since I'll be eighteen before the end of the calendar year, I'll be eligible for the eventing team. It can take years to make the team, but I want to do it when I'm seventeen."

"You're serious."

No one else had ever doubted me on that point, not even Mama. "You don't think I can?"

"I absolutely think you can. I've just never known an Olympian."

"Daddy."

"What?"

"He's one of the most decorated Olympic equestrians ever. Three golds, two silvers, and a bronze."

"And he's training you to follow in his footsteps."

"He's a great coach, and he says he'll get me there. I don't know that anyone else could. He wrote *The Book on Eventing*. That's not an expression—it's the title of his book. He's a god in our world, and that's our bible. People would sell their souls to work with him. The other day, when I said I can't leave Rosemont, that's why."

He absorbed that without comment. "Tell me about your horse."

"I have three. Vigo is fearless and a good jumper but a little dim. Diva's psycho."

"Which one did I see?"

"Jasper. Jasper and I can read each other's thoughts."

"I didn't know horses had thoughts."

"They're like us, except more honest."

He asked me about my training schedule, and after I described it, he said, "You really don't have time for boys, do you?"

"Not a lot of boys. Maybe one." I said it to be funny, like when I'd told him dozens of boys were calling me, but it didn't sound like a joke. I reached under the table for his hand and encountered his knee. His leg jerked so hard that it banged my knuckles into the underside of the table. A tiny wave of cocoa slopped over the side of my mug.

"I was going for your hand." I started to pull back.

He put his hand over mine. "Sorry. Did I smash your fingers?"

He had, a little, but I shook my head.

"It didn't seem like you wanted to hold hands in public."

"I don't want Daddy to find out." I glanced around the coffeehouse. No one was paying attention to us, but if they had been, they couldn't have seen our hands under the table.

Will rubbed his thumb across the back of my hand. More tingling. "He keeps you on a short leash, doesn't he?"

"He's afraid I'll be distracted."

"Maybe you could use a distraction," Will said, which was so cheesy that we both laughed—but what was the point of jeopardizing my future for a distraction? And if Will turned out to be more than a distraction, that was an even bigger problem.

No matter how much I liked him, I couldn't do this. I needed to tell him it was impossible, thanks for the cocoa, see you around.

"Does he ever go out of town?" Will said.

"He's teaching in Del Mar in January. He'll be gone three or four days."

"So in January, what if we have a real date?"

The leash pulled taut. Daddy didn't want a boy calling me. He definitely didn't want one kissing me or making me tingle—and it wasn't because he was afraid I'd be distracted.

I *was* distracted, though, by the memory of yesterday morning in the woods, the soft thud when Daddy dropped my helmet on the ground, his weight pressing me up against the cold bark, the painful friction.

"Okay," I said slowly, "but if we're going to see each other, there are conditions."

He laughed.

"I mean it. I train all the time. Nothing can interfere with that."

"We'll work around your schedule."

"And Daddy can't know."

"Obviously. Do you feel bad about going behind his back?"

"Not if I don't get caught."

"What else?"

"That's it, I guess."

"Well, future Olympian Roan Montgomery, I agree to your conditions."

"Future Olympic gold medalist Roan Montgomery," I said. "I'm ambitious."

"I stand corrected."

"What about you? What are your conditions?"

He shrugged. "Reckon I'm not the type of person who goes into a relationship with conditions in mind."

"Yeah, what kind of asshole does that?" I said.

"Someone who's not very trusting," he said. "Or someone who's afraid."

In the half hour that remained before Daddy picked me up, we launched an all-out mission to find his gift.

Will spotted it in minutes in one of the heavily scented shops on the square: an antique trunk a bit larger than a shoebox, its arched lid secured by a heavy lock that opened with an iron skeleton key. Will said it had dovetailed corners and was made of American chestnut, but the real reason it was a perfect gift for Daddy was that he liked to keep his possessions under lock and key.

It was nearly four when we left the store. We retrieved my books from Will's truck, and he carried them to the north side of the courthouse. The sun slanted blindingly between the brick buildings.

"This was good." He shifted the books from his arms to mine. "I'd kiss you again, but I reckon that's out of the question."

"Daddy will be here any minute."

"So . . . see you tomorrow."

"See you."

He started to walk away and then turned. "Ah, what the hell." He kissed me swiftly on the lips.

I took a step back. "You can't—"

"I think about you all the time," he said.

And that was how he left me—standing there breathless, alarmed, and on the verge of falling for him.


IN THE WEEKS before Christmas, I mucked my stalls mornings and evenings and had a lesson every afternoon. Sometimes Daddy and I worked out together, and occasionally we rode out, but the weather had turned glacial.

After evening chores, I started homework. Gertrude served supper at seven, and then I washed dishes and finished my homework. Most nights, after I'd turned off my lamp, Daddy came to my room. He'd been right when he'd said nothing would change for me.

He'd also been wrong. For the first time in my life, I lived to get to school, inventing reasons to go early two or three days a week: I'd made an appointment to talk to Mrs. Kenyon about my term paper, I was on the decorating committee for the Christmas tree the honor society was putting up in the lobby, I'd volunteered to help Ms. Simi catalogue a shipment of library books.

"You don't need to get involved in extracurriculars," Daddy said.

"It's only until training picks up again."

In reality, my extracurricular activity was meeting Will.

The bleachers where we'd gone after Steve's memorial had become our special place because no one used the stadium in winter. Sitting on the top row, huddled together against the cold, we'd kiss, and he'd put his arm around me—and I was getting better at hand-holding. Mostly, though, we talked. There was much I couldn't say, but I knew me. I wanted to know him.

We talked about his brother, conversations that often ended with Will unable to speak. Once, after he'd told me about making custom cabinets for one of the houses his parents had built, planing the wood with finer and finer planes so it didn't have to be sanded, he said, "If I don't go into the business, I'll be the second son to disappoint them."

"Do you mean that?" I slipped my arm through his and put my hand in the pocket of his heavy winter jacket.

"No. Steve was never a disappointment."

"But you are?"

"What do you think?"

His parents probably hadn't been too happy about the failed drug test, but his grades weren't that bad—although he was too smart to be skimming by with a C average.

"You don't ever think about giving up pot or trying to get better grades?"

"Pot's the only reason I'm getting the grades I'm getting."

"So why don't you give it up?"

He hesitated. "I'm not supposed to tell anyone."

I had too many secrets of my own to pry into his, so I waited for him to decide whether to continue.

"When I was ten," he said, "I was diagnosed with ADHD."

That was his secret? Probably half the kids in school had attention deficit hyperactivity disorder.

"The drugs used to treat it gave me migraines. I couldn't eat or sleep. When I was twelve, I said no more. It was a battle, but once they took me off the meds, the headaches mostly went away. But I had to repeat seventh grade because I couldn't do the work. It's frustrating, not being able to absorb what's right in front of you no matter how hard you try."

I hadn't known he'd been held back a year.

"Steve got me into running, which helped. Then a couple of years ago, I was at a party and somebody had a joint . . . and I found out weed helps. It lights up this part of my brain that was always dark before. I can concentrate."

"And your parents know?"

"My parents help me get it."

I stared at him.

"They didn't believe me at first. What's a better story than 'Hey, getting stoned makes me functional'? But the proof's in my grades."

So he wasn't really a stoner—not in the conventional sense.

"Isn't it legal for medical use?"

"Not for this, and not for minors. My parents would be in real trouble if anyone found out they get it for me. Mostly I use edibles, but I buy some smoke from Wedge now and then. The only side effect is people think I'm a burnout."

"Does that bother you?"

"Better than puking all over myself because I've got a migraine."

I suspected that was true. "Do you use anything else?"

He shook his head.

"So why do you say you're a disappointment to your parents?"

"Because I'm not Steve."

He said it as if he'd worked a puzzle and that was the last piece, the one that made the whole picture make sense.

As much pressure as I was under and as twisted as our relationship was, I'd never felt Daddy wanted me to be anyone but me.

"I like who you are," I said.

"I've been thinking the same thing about you. I like who you are."

I melted a little bit inside before I remembered: He liked who he thought I was.

He kissed me, one of those perfect, sweet kisses, chaste but with a promise of heat behind it. He had more respect for my body and my boundaries than Daddy did. What Will offered felt safe.

But for me, safe felt like something was missing.

\*     \*     \*

THAT AFTERNOON I came home from school to find wreaths entwined with blue and silver ribbons on all the windows and doors, garlands winding up the banister, and a big fragrant blue spruce in front of the bay window in the living room. It was decorated with shiny blue and silver ornaments and topped with a shimmery silver starburst.

After supper and dishes, I took a closer look at the tree. The ornaments belonged to the florist whose staff decorated the house in a different theme each year. I fingered a sparkling angel with feathered wings and a pale porcelain face.

The chandelier overhead went out. I stiffened. The lamps at each end of the sofa were extinguished, too, until the room was illuminated only by the tiny white lights on the tree. Daddy folded his arms around me. When he put his lips on my neck, I turned in his arms. Daddy wasn't safe. I felt it in the way his tongue probed my mouth. I wasn't safe, either.

Afterward we lay side by side on the rug, my knees on fire with carpet burns. Good thing it was winter so I could wear tights instead of knee socks to school.

"My God, darlin'," Daddy said, winded. "What's got into you?"

There was no way to answer that.

"Come here." He drew me to him, and I rested my head on his shoulder. Under my cheek his skin was clammy with sweat.

"Now," he said. "Tell Daddy what you want for Christmas."

I closed my eyes. All I could think was *Will*.

## - Eleven -

I NEVER UNDERSTOOD why the exams before Thanksgiving were called midterms when they were held past the middle of the term. Finals, right before Christmas, came up fast. Biology, algebra, and French required little effort. The night before winter break began, I crammed for history and used Daddy's computer to write my lit paper.

As usual on exam days, there was no homeroom. I went first to Mr. Diaz's history class and developed writer's cramp scrawling answers to his essay questions. When the bell rang, I went to lit.

Will and Chelsea were at their desks, presentation folders ready to hand in. Mrs. Kenyon had assigned us a term paper in lieu of an exam, but we had to sit through an introduction to the syllabus for the second semester, which included reading assignments for the break.

Finally, the bell rang. Will and I exchanged a look. We'd have a whole hour and a half in the bleachers before Daddy picked me up, because I hadn't told him classes were on a short schedule.

"Are you going anywhere over Christmas?" Chelsea asked as we walked to our lockers.

"Where would I go?"

"I thought you might visit your mom."

"No," I said.

"Sorry. I shouldn't have brought it up."

Christmas had never made Mama nicer to be around. She bought too many presents, which made me uncomfortable, which led to comments about my lack of gratitude for the privilege I was growing up in, which led to accusations that I looked down on her.

I opened my locker. I'd left Chelsea's present and Will's inside this morning before class. "It's okay. What are you doing?"

"Going to my grandparents' place in Charleston."

I handed her the small gift-wrapped box that held her earrings. "Merry Christmas."

Her eyes lit up, and then her face crumpled. "I didn't get anything for you."

"Doesn't matter."

She tore into the gift wrap and opened the box. "Oh, wow. These are gorgeous."

"Is purple still your favorite color?"

"It is." She hugged me. "Thank you. I'll bring you something from Charleston."

"You don't have to."

"No, I will. Merry Christmas." She embraced me again. "See you next year."

Next year was something I was looking forward to. I'd be a year closer to the Olympics, Daddy would be going to Del Mar, and Will and I would have our date. I'd embarked on a subtle campaign to persuade my father to allow me to stay by myself in the house; if I stayed with Gertrude and Eddie, there would be no date.

It was another clear, cold day, the sky bright and hard. Will waited at the top of the bleachers, a plaid wool blanket spread over the concrete steps, picnic-style, with a plastic bag of Christmas cookies, a Thermos, and two disposable cups.

He gestured grandly. "Merry Christmas."

I joined him on the blanket. "This is great. I'm starving."

While he poured cocoa, I selected a tree-shaped cookie decorated haphazardly with green and red icing.

He held out a cup to me. "Cheers."

We bumped the cups together.

The cookie, buttery and sweet, tasted better than it looked.

"Did your mom make these?" I was trying to resolve the sloppily iced cookie with the stylish, elegant Mrs. Howard.

"She started them. After she mixed up the dough, she broke down crying. But Carrie had been looking forward to it, so I cut them out and baked them, and Carrie decorated them." He must have seen the astonishment on my face. "What? I can't bake cookies?"

"Evidently you can."

He looked away. He didn't want sympathy. In the past month I'd learned a lot about Will and a few things about myself. I wouldn't have expected Mama's departure to leave me vulnerable, but without her, Daddy threatened to engulf me. Will gave me something to hold on to.

I helped myself to a snarling snowman. "I'm trying to imagine Mama baking. The gingerbread man has diet-pill eyes and a tranquilizer smile."

Will came back from the hard, sharp edges of grief. "What do diet-pill eyes look like?"

I assumed a crazed expression, like Norma Desmond in *Sunset Boulevard*.

He laughed. "That's how I felt when I was on all those meds. Maybe your mom's overmedicated."

"You think?" I took his present from the shopping bag. "For you."

"I have something for you, too." He reached under the seats and brought out a box wrapped in metallic Christmas paper. It weighed almost nothing. "Open it."

"You first."

He removed the wrapping paper to reveal a box of polished dark wood. He started to examine the workmanship.

"The gift's inside," I said.

He found the latch at the front of the box and opened it. Inside were individual compartments, each with its own lid. He peered at them and grinned.

It was an array of teas from around the world, thirty different kinds. Daddy hadn't blinked when I'd told him my favorite teacher loved tea. He'd taken me to Murphy's to buy the tea chest for Mrs. Kenyon.

"This is great. I'll think of you every time I drink"—he checked one of the labels—"jasmine ginger dragon tears. Thanks. Your turn."

I untied the ribbon and tore the gift wrap from a flimsy white shirt box. Inside, buried in tissue paper, was a manila envelope. It held a single sheet of heavy textured paper, a pen-and-ink sketch. From the arch of the neck, the curve of the ears, and the soft dark eyes to the powerful haunches and the set of the tail, it was unmistakably Jasper.

"You did this?"

"All by my ownself."

"It's incredible. I had no idea you could draw."

"Drafting and design. It's all angles and curves."

"But you've only seen him once."

"He's all over the internet. So are you. You've never Googled yourself?"

I shook my head. "I love it. Thank you." I tucked the drawing inside my lit book.

After we finished our picnic, we stuffed our trash in the shopping bag. Then I climbed onto his lap, straddling his thighs, and pulled the picnic blanket over our heads. In the cozy darkness, we kissed, and the promise of heat became more than a promise. His erection pressed against me. His hands slid down my back to cup my butt, pulling me closer, and together we found the rhythm. Then he tore his mouth away. "Wait—"

I bit his earlobe.

"Wait—"

"There's no one around."

He put his hands firmly on my hips. "Stop."

I did. "What?"

"This isn't how it should be. Not here. Not now." He kissed me again, his lips soft and sweet and hot.

I rested my forehead against his, aching with the effort of stopping.

"Anyway, we don't have time." Beneath me, he pulled out his phone to check. "It's almost one. What did you tell your father?"

That was an unwelcome non sequitur. "About what?"

"Picking you up."

"I just didn't tell him we were getting out early."

"Yeah, but everybody's gone. I parked behind the gym so he wouldn't see my truck, but all the other cars are gone."

The breath whooshed out of my body the same way it did when I hit the ground in a fall. I had planned this rendezvous so carefully—but not carefully enough.

"Shit." I scrambled off his lap.

"Is it really that big a deal?" Will emerged from the blanket.

"Yes." Why didn't he *get* that?

He scooped up my books and shoved them into my arms. "Hurry."

I ran as if water dragged at my legs. We had an underwater treadmill at the farm, used for exercising horses when they were recovering from leg injuries. This must be how they felt, galloping along, getting nowhere.

I'd barely plopped down on the bench in front of the school when Daddy turned the Land Cruiser through the gates. I was breathing hard. He'd never think I'd been sitting here.

My heart jumping like a rabbit, I opened the passenger door.

"Where is everybody?" he asked. "Why are you out of breath?"

Best defense, good offense. "I've been waiting more than an hour."

"You didn't tell me you were getting out early."

"I told you last night in bed."

He flinched. He didn't hesitate to talk dirty when we were naked or about to be, but context was everything. Casually tossing out the euphemism "in bed" violated our intricate rule system.

"The school was locked by the time I realized you must've forgotten." Assigning fault to him was a ploy I used with care. He couldn't stand being wrong. "I went down to the gym, but the pay phone's broken. Then I thought you might be here, so I ran back. And here you are."

Slightly too play-by-play, but possible. I fought the urge to explain why the school gates were wide open: The custodial staff must still be here, but I hadn't been able to find them.

"If I had a cell phone," I said in the third wave of my offensive, diversion, "I could've called you."

For the first time since I'd made him flinch, he looked at me closely. "Why do you need a cell phone?"

"Most of the time I don't."

"I'll think about it. Guess I wasn't paying attention last night. You must be freezing." He reached over and squeezed my hand. He held it until I pulled free to tuck my hair behind my ear.

Only when we were through town and on the open road toward home did I relax my guard enough to remember Will. I'd left without saying goodbye or Merry Christmas or even looking back. Warmth flushed through me when I remembered the way we'd made out. I couldn't *wait* for January.

PART OF MY master plan to convince Daddy he could trust me to stay by myself involved spending time with him over winter break. If I appeared to like the time we spent together, he wouldn't suspect me of wanting to spend time with someone else. I hung out with him at the barn, taking on extra chores like cleaning the tack room and the feed room. I accompanied him on the evening walk-through. We went out to lunch at the historic tavern on the square, where we weren't the only ones having a father-daughter date. Will's father and little sister were in the corner booth. They didn't notice me, but I observed them. Mr. Howard was indulgent, gentle, sad, but now and then Carrie said something that made her father smile. When they left, they were holding hands, and Carrie was skipping.

On Christmas Eve, Albert and his crew took over the kitchen shortly after breakfast, and that night all the employees and their families came to the farm's annual holiday party, where a hired Santa—a good one, with a real beard—distributed toys to the kids and Daddy slipped envelopes containing bonuses to the employees.

The next morning, there was a pile of presents under the tree. I was afraid Mama had made an appearance via consumer-excess proxy, but all the tags read *Love, Daddy*. He usually bought me one or two nice things, not loads of stuff. He was compensating for Mama's absence. It was weirdly touching, something a normal father would do.

After breakfast, we opened gifts. Mostly I opened them, because I'd only given him the wooden chest, but he seemed pleased by it.

I liked my new hunt jacket, which fitted me as if I'd been measured for it. He gave me a pair of soft black kid gloves to replace my old ones, some boot socks with crazy patterns on them, a book on Olympic equestrians that included an entire chapter on him, a pair of dressy blue paddock boots, and a galloping gold horse pendant studded with diamonds and strung on a gold chain. I held up my hair while he fastened the clasp.

On my birthday, just before New Year's, a heavy snow closed the roads. Daddy canceled the dinner reservations he'd made for us in Leesburg. Gertrude made shrimp étouffée for supper, since crawfish wasn't in season, and Daddy beat me at chess and triumphed in a Scrabble tournament. Then he was through playing games.

As we undressed upstairs, I wondered whether Will still thought about me all the time. Maybe two weeks with no contact was too long for a boy. It was pretty long for a girl, too, but I couldn't stop thinking about him—except when I led him into one of the stalls in my mind and shut the door so he couldn't see, wouldn't know, what I did with Daddy.

SERIOUS TRAINING RESUMED on New Year's Day. I started off the year with a fall when Vigo swerved away from a jump and dumped me off to the side.

Jarred but unhurt, I stood up, spitting out dirt and brushing myself off.

Daddy caught Vigo. "Pay attention to what you're doing."

"Sorry." I accepted the leg up he gave me and trotted back to the beginning of the course.

A few days later, he drove me to school for the start of second semester.

"See you at one."

I got out of the Land Cruiser, hefting my new backpack, a birthday gift from Eddie and Gertrude.

"Oh, and good lesson this morning."

"Thanks." I closed the door and walked sedately into the building.

Will lounged against the wall outside the office. Without a word he straightened and took my arm, hustling me across the lobby and into the alcove that led to the cafeteria. He caught me in a hug and swung me off my feet. "That was the longest two weeks of my life."

"Mine, too."

He looked up at me. "You're a lot heavier than you look."

I punched his shoulder. "It's called a backpack, and it has about twenty pounds of books in it."

He set me down. "When," he said, "is your father's trip?"

TEN DAYS LATER, Daddy dropped me at school on his way to the airport. With negotiation skills worthy of a diplomat, I'd persuaded him to let me stay by myself while he was in Del Mar, but all the way to school I expected him to change his mind.

"Wouldn't you feel safer with Gertrude and Eddie?"

"I'll set the alarm. Besides, Rosemont's like a fortress. I've never been scared to be alone there."

"You've never been alone all night long."

"I might as well have been. Mama was out cold every night."

Daddy looked briefly pained.

"Also," I said, "I need the computer for homework."

"Only homework." He'd check the browser history, and he probably had keystroke software, too. Sometimes I had a passing curiosity about what he-as-me had posted on Instagram and Facebook, but mostly, I wasn't interested in staring at a computer screen any longer than I had to. Besides, Chelsea would show me anything I needed to see. He turned steel-gray eyes on me. "Can I trust you?"

"Of course."

"I'll call you every night," he said, and because I was certain he'd do exactly that, on Friday night, Will came to Rosemont.

\*     \*     \*

DADDY CALLED AT seven, an hour earlier than he'd called last night, as I was about to walk out the door to meet Will at the back gate. He was having drinks and dinner with his students, he said, and might be out late.

"You okay by yourself?"

"I'm fine. I'm going to take a bath and work on my French project."

"Are all the doors are locked? Is the alarm on?"

"Yes, sir."

"Okay. Love you, darlin'."

"Love you, too, Daddy."

If he called back, I'd given myself some cover by saying I was about to take a bath, but not even the best plan was fail-safe. I'd taken every precaution I could imagine except not going through with the date, which was unthinkable. This date was happening.

Frozen snow gleamed on either side of the back driveway, the moon so bright I didn't need a flashlight.

At the gate, I punched in the code. It swung open. I climbed up and sat on the top rail of the fence. Meeting Will here meant I was dressed for the weather, unfortunate since my down jacket made me look like I was inflated, but I was warm.

Headlights strafed the road, and Will's truck pulled into view. I waved him through the gate and closed it behind him.

When I opened the passenger door, the aroma of garlic with an undercurrent of pot greeted me. Will picked up the big flat pizza box on the passenger seat and handed it to me.

"I promised you pizza and a movie." He held up a DVD. The artwork showed Laurence Olivier and Joan Fontaine in sepia tones. In the bleachers, he'd thought my fondness for old movies was quaint, but tonight, he'd turned up with—

"*Rebecca*?" I said, dismayed. "Hitchcock's scary."

"No, I read about him. He didn't do horror. It's a psychological thriller."

"Psychology can be pretty horrifying."

"How can you call yourself a fan of old movies if you don't watch Hitchcock? He's considered one of the masters. I'm broadening your cultural horizons. Work with me."

"Fine. But if I have nightmares, I'm calling you."

"Please do."

He gave a low whistle when the barn came into view. "This is a *barn*?"

"I'd show you around, but Eddie might check on the horses."

I pointed him toward the house. He pulled the truck around to the screened porch, where Eddie and Gertrude would be unlikely to see it even if they came to the house.

In the kitchen, I immediately shed the jacket, hung it on a hook by the door, and checked the phone to see whether anyone had called. All clear.

"Pizza's probably cold," Will said.

"I'll reheat it." Glad to have something to do, I washed my hands, turned on the oven, and arranged the pizza slices on a cookie sheet.

Will took off his jacket and hung it over the back of a chair. He wore jeans and a plaid shirt—untucked, naturally—his hair as messy as ever.

I put the cookie sheet in the oven. "Do you want something to drink? There's Coke, orange juice, milk, mineral water. Tea. Beer?" Bourbon? I should have had a shot before I went down to the gate. I was less worried about Daddy calling or someone coming to the house than I was jittery at finally being alone with Will.

"Coke's fine, but first . . ."

He put his arms around me and kissed me. He tasted minty, or that might have been me. I liked the way our tastes mingled. This I knew, kissing, fitting my body to his.

"You smell good," he murmured.

"So do you."

He stepped back. "And you look nice."

"So do you."

I fixed two Cokes and handed him a glass. "The pizza will take a few minutes. Want to see the house?"

"Sure."

I'd shown him the dining room and living room, and we'd gone into the entrance hall when he said, "Your house is like a museum."

"Wait'll you see the dead-ancestor paintings. It's like an art gallery upstairs." I flipped on the lights in Daddy's study. "And here we have the inner sanctum."

Will went immediately to look at the medals in their glass case under the spotlight. Daddy had known what he was doing when he put them there. They commanded attention. His father's and grandfather's medals, displayed more discreetly in a smaller case to one side of his desk, escaped notice.

Will studied the photos of Daddy in the book. "How many times was he in the Olympics?"

"Three. Some of those are from the Pan Am and World Games."

"He really is a big deal, then."

"He thinks so."

He took in the trophies on the bookshelves. "These are his, too?"

"The impressive ones are. Most of mine are in my room."

"Do I get to see your room?"

I matched his casual tone. "Let's go."

It was strange, seeing my room through his eyes, the double border of ribbons strung near the molding by the ceiling, the shelves of trophies and cups, the photos on the wall over my desk.

He leaned forward to peer at a photograph of four-year-old me, lanky legs straddling a wide Dutch warmblood named Roxie, a blue ribbon affixed to her bridle, my face split in half by a grin.

"That was my very first competition ever."

"And you won. What a surprise." He touched the frame of the photo hanging next to it. "Where's your dog?"

It was the only photo I had of Bailey and me—and Mama. Gertrude had taken it the day Mama had brought him home. We sat on the front steps, his body stuck to mine like he was held there by Velcro, and Mama had her arms around both of us. She knew she'd done well, and something like happiness had transformed her face so much that she was almost unrecognizable. She'd taken Bailey and me into town to the feed store, where she'd helped me pick out a big pillow-like dog bed for him, and a red collar and matching leash, and ceramic bowls with paw prints on them for his food and water.

In one of my forays into magical thinking, I stubbornly hoped the photo would turn Bailey, and maybe even Mama, into something that wasn't painful, but the perfect moment it captured had been eclipsed a few days later when Daddy half dragged him behind the barn while Mama tried to stop him, her bird-claw hands grasping at his arm, and Jamie pleaded,

"Monty, I'll take him. You don't need to do this." Daddy had shaken Mama off, and Jamie had turned to me, the helplessness on his face something I felt all the time.

The gunshot had been hardly more than a puff. I'd been surprised that it didn't make a sharp cracking sound like gunfire in movies.

"We had to put him down." That sounded detached and clinical, something the vet would do, not something Daddy had done with a .22.

"Was he sick?"

"He bit Daddy. So that's my dead dog. Want to see my dead relatives?"

I showed him the portraits. Both my grandfather and great-grandfather had died long before I was born, but their faces were familiar. Daddy looked so much like them that they could have been triplets. They'd been painted with their Olympic horses, Gustavo and Pert, according to the brass nameplates screwed into the bottom of the picture frames, and in the background of my great-grandfather's portrait, our barn was identifiable. The rest of the ancestors were less interesting—no horses.

"We'd better check the pizza," I said.

We picnicked on the floor of the living room, leaning back against the sofa with our legs outstretched while the movie played. I'd turned out the lights so the room would be dark, like a theater, and we ate in the blue light of the television screen. When we finished the pizza, Will put his arm around my shoulders and pulled me closer. I rested my head on his chest. Beneath my ear, his heart beat fast.

We kept watching the movie—which wasn't scary at all.

"Hey, they have portraits, too," Will said when the freaky housekeeper showed the second Mrs. de Winter the painting of the woman in the wide-brimmed hat.

"She's setting her up, isn't she?" I said.

"Watch and see."

I watched, but the movie couldn't distract me from the feeling that every single cell of my body was awake and aroused. Will had to feel it, too. He couldn't be touching me like this without feeling it.

"Does she have a name?" I asked. "Or are we just going with 'you little fool'?"

"No name. That's one of the conventions of the book and the movie."

There was a book? No-name had a dog named Jasper, which was a weird coincidence, and Olivier was condescending and superior, which reminded me of Daddy. I tried to pay attention, and after an eternity, the end credits started rolling.

"What'd you think?" Will asked.

"Well—"

He kissed me with no trace of the restraint he'd always shown before. His tongue moved in my mouth, and the kiss went on for some time. Then he pulled back.

"This is dangerous." His voice was both soft and rough.

"No one's here but us."

"That's why it's dangerous."

"We're just kissing."

My fingers stroked the back of his neck. He kissed me again, and when I felt no misgivings or reluctance in him, I shifted, took the front of his shirt in my fist, and tugged. He didn't resist, his body following mine as I lay back on the floor. He was lighter than Daddy, more angular. I pushed my pelvis against his, and he responded, moving against the most sensitive part of me. Wetness flushed inside me.

I hooked one leg around his waist, and he made a sound of appreciation, but he wasn't the only one who liked the change of position. My climax spread through me like wildfire.

My cry caught in my throat, my fingers gripping his shoulders, little quakes traveling through my whole body.

He lifted his head, and I drew in breath as the beats between my thighs subsided.

"Did you . . ." His eyes searched mine. "Are you all right?"

He was so earnest that I giggled. "Yes."

"Reckon we're not just kissing anymore."

"Reckon not."

The television screen was frozen on the main menu of the DVD. I reached for the remote, pushed the off button. The room went black and silent.

"Let's go upstairs," I said.

"We should talk about this."

"No. No more talking."

In the dark, I led him up the stairs to my room, hands linked. Bare tree branches scratched the windowpane. I knelt in front of him, lifted his shirttail, and started unbuttoning his jeans.

He drew in his breath when I touched him. "You don't have to do this."

"I wouldn't if I didn't want to."

He smelled and tasted different from Daddy, more spice than citrus, but not so different that I didn't know what I was doing. What if he could tell I knew what I was doing? Suddenly he groaned. I swallowed once, then again, and a third time, and a fourth. That was different, too—so much of it. And it had been really fast.

Gently, I disengaged and looked up at him. He held out a hand to me and I stood up. Even in shadow, his expression was dazed.

"You're the first . . . that was the first . . ."

Understanding flashed through me. Will was a virgin.

I gave him a sly smile. "Are you all right?"

He chuckled. "That was amazing. I thought you'd be more shy."

He'd had no reason to think that—I'd been all over him in the bleachers—but I was trying to come up with an explanation for why I wasn't shy when he kissed me. His hands roamed downward and then up again, but now they were under my sweater. I raised my arms, and clumsily he pulled the sweater over my head, static electricity crackling. He moved my bra strap off my shoulder. "You sure?"

"I'm sure." I unbuttoned his shirt, kissed his chest, and led him to bed. He removed his clothes and then mine. I reached behind my back, unhooked my bra, and slipped it off.

He exhaled. "Jesus."

Daddy was the only other person who had seen me completely naked since I was a baby. And I had never seen a naked boy—man—except Daddy.

Under my hands and mouth, Will's skin was smoother and tauter, and the hard runner's muscles in his thighs were leaner. His hands glided over my body, cupping my breasts, sliding over my hip, as if he were sculpting me. He kissed and sucked my nipples gently and then harder as I pushed my breasts against his mouth. That was okay, wasn't it? And was it okay that I opened my legs wider and tilted my hips upward against his hand? Were these learned responses or natural ones?

Will kissed my stomach and then moved lower. "Okay?"

"Yes." This. This was where I could lose myself.

He kissed me gently between my legs, and then, with more concentration, used his tongue until I was swollen and wet and wanted him inside me. If we did this, there was no undoing it. There was no more Daddy's girl. He'd no longer be my one and only.

"Will," I said. "Now."

He crawled up my body, his knees between my thighs. I reached down and touched his penis. It surged in my hand, and I guided him inside me with a moan.

He froze. "I don't want to hurt you."

The feeling of deceit was strong, but I drew his head down to mine and whispered, "It's okay."

I wished he'd been the one to hurt me. I wished I'd never felt any of this before. A few thrusts, a sharp cry, and he was done. If he'd lasted longer, I might have come.

I trailed my fingertips down his spine and back up again.

He kissed my shoulder and cleared his throat. "It'll be better next time."

"It was perfect this time." Good enough, anyway.

"I know the first time for a girl—"

"Will—" Telling him it wasn't my first time would lead to a very dark place, and right now, this was as close to perfect as I had any right to expect. "I'm glad it was you. I always wanted it to be special, and it was."

A hard knot closed my throat. He kissed me, and tears slid from my eyes, but I had them under control before he even noticed—until I sobbed in his mouth.

"Roan?" He withdrew, a loss I wasn't ready for. "What is it?"

"Nothing." My voice sounded like air squeezing out of a balloon. "Sorry."

"Sorry we did this?"

"Oh—no. I'm not sorry about this. I'm just emotional." It was better if I didn't talk.

He held me, one arm circled around me. "It's okay, you know. Cry if you feel like it."

I could have, thinking about everything I'd lost with Daddy, more than I could measure, but my tears dried up. I'd found something with Will, and at the edges of my mind glimmered the thought that it might be beyond measuring, too.

# - Twelve -

NOW THAT WILL knew the way, I gave him the gate code. He came to the house the next two nights. We didn't get as far as my bedroom before we had our clothes off. The kitchen counter, one of the leather chairs in Daddy's study, even the stairs—joyful, passionate, and fun, sex was possible anywhere.

Still, we were careful. The first night, he took the empty pizza box with him so Gertrude wouldn't find it in the trash. The next night, he brought condoms. Condoms had never crossed my mind. Daddy didn't use them; he'd had a vasectomy after I was born.

"Should've had these last night," Will said, "but I didn't know things would go that far."

"Really?"

"Really. Did you?"

"I hoped they would," I said.

He lacked Daddy's expertise, but the learning process had its own rewards. Under the guise of exploration, I showed him what I liked and led both of us to discover what he liked: everything.

Sunday night we faced each other over a cloud of fluffy white lavender-scented bubbles in the big clawfoot tub in my bathroom.

"Why did you stop dating Sass?" I asked. "Was it because she wouldn't . . . you know."

"No. I mean, she wouldn't, but that was kind of okay. We only went out for a couple of months. But the more I got to know her, the less I liked her. She was shallow, you know?"

"Oh, and I'm deep?"

"You are," he said seriously. "She talked about people. You talk about—"

"Horses?" I slid my foot up his thigh.

He laughed. "Life. Ideas. Goals." He caught his breath as I worked my foot underwater. "At first I thought she was fun and cute, but she turned out not to be who I thought she was."

He grabbed my wandering foot at the ankle and yanked me toward him. I slipped under the bubbles with a shriek, water sloshing everywhere, and came up sputtering.

Sex in the bathtub threatened to drown me so we went back to bed.

He had learned to slow down, prolonging his pleasure and mine—and I did find pleasure with Will, although I'd come only that first night when we were both fully clothed. It had happened once; it would happen again. We were still getting used to each other.

We lay breathless in the damp, twisted sheets.

"What do we do now?" he said.

"I've read about a few things we could try."

He laughed. "We'll come back to that, but what I meant was, what do we do now that your father's coming home?"

I'd known what he meant.

"I don't want to think about him," I said.

The silence stuttered between us. I was never eloquent, but maybe that was weird, what I'd said.

"I mean," I said, "I'm going to miss this. That's all."

"Me, too." He propped beside me on one elbow. "Everything's changed since we were at school on Friday. How can I see you and not do this?" He lowered his mouth to my nipple. "Or this." He kissed my stomach. "Or this."

The pleasure was intense, and soon he'd brought me right to the brink of coming, and I held my breath, straining for it.

The phone rang.

Will groaned. "Are you kidding me?"

I reached for the handset. "Sorry."

After last night, when I'd flown down the hall to grab Daddy's call before the phone stopped ringing, I was keeping the handset nearby. He'd already called once tonight, shortly before I'd run the bath. I'd hoped for more distance from him this weekend.

I clicked on the handset. "Hello."

No reply.

"Hello."

Someone sighed.

Gross. I was *not* having phone sex with my father.

"Daddy?"

There was a click and then dead air. I hit the off button.

Will looked up from between my thighs. "Wrong number?"

I pressed Caller ID. Since I'd assumed it was Daddy, I hadn't looked at the screen when I'd answered. *Anonymous.* So, not Daddy. His cell number showed up when he called, as did Gertrude's and Eddie's and the number of the phone in the barn.

"Wrong number with bad timing." I replaced the handset on my nightstand.

Will kissed my thigh. "Doesn't matter. I could do this all night."

"We don't have all night." I stroked his hair. "What if I tell you about that thing I read?"

"What if you show me?"

Some time later we raided the refrigerator and carried the food back to bed.

"I love it that you're so well-read," he said around a mouthful of cold chicken.

He wouldn't love it if he knew I'd never read about what we'd just done. It was a variation Daddy liked now and then. If Sass had turned out to be someone different from the person Will had thought she was, what would he make of me?

As he dressed, I gathered the condom wrappers and put them in the paper bag that held the evening's used condoms.

"When will your father go away again?"

"He only does a couple of clinics a year."

"We'll figure something out," Will said.

He helped me take our dishes downstairs. I handed him the paper bag, the top folded. He put his arms around me. I could have stood like that forever, in a warm, thoroughly fucked, post-sex trance, but after a lingering kiss, he left in a gust of cold air from the porch, and his truck rumbled away.

I washed and dried the dishes. As I put away the platter that had held the chicken, I remembered Gertrude's comment yesterday afternoon when she'd come up to the house to make sure I didn't need anything: "My land, sugar, you're eating enough for two people." Since Friday, she'd been astonished to see the disappearance of a sun-dried tomato torte, a nutty rice pilaf, bunches of grapes, a loaf of homemade olive bread, and an assortment of cheeses. Tomorrow, she would discover that I had apparently eaten an entire fried chicken. Will could pack away mountains of food.

"Your fault," he'd said last night as he scarfed down the last brownie from a batch Gertrude had made in the morning. "You keep making me work up an appetite."

I debated whether to fry more chicken—I'd baked replacement brownies at midnight last night—but the raw chicken was frozen. I decided not to, since no one suspected me of sneaking a boy into the house, but I'd better make sure there was no evidence he'd been here.

I checked the house room by room. Everything was normal except for my bedsheets, a mess of spots and splotches. I'd tidied up each evening after Will left, and I'd made my bed every morning as usual, but I'd have to wash the sheets before Gertrude saw them.

The grandfather clock began to chime, twelve rich, resonant strokes.

Tomorrow, I thought. Monday was laundry day, and Gertrude wouldn't think a thing about it if I started the wash except that I was helpful. Nothing unusual about that.

Before I put on my nightgown, I checked my body front and back. Will hadn't left a mark on me. I looked exactly as I had the last time Daddy had seen me. I didn't feel the same, though.

Sore and tired to the marrow, I snuggled under the quilts and hugged myself, trying to capture the physical memory of being in Will's arms, but in its place was an old familiar void, and into that void I fell asleep.


AT SCHOOL THE next day, I felt the truth of Will's observation: Everything had changed. We'd have been discreet even if the school didn't strictly forbid public displays of affection, but every time I looked at him I felt warm inside, like a chocolate bar that had been left in the sun. Love was making me gooey.

At one, he walked me to the front door of the school, where Gertrude waited outside in her Subaru, reading the newspaper.

"We'll find a way, you know."

He had no idea how hard it would be, but I said, "I'll take your word for it."

My heart wasn't in my lessons, and Eddie, always more lenient than Daddy, let me go early.

"You and Vigo could use some time in the hills."

Vigo was getting bored and stale with only dressage and jumping to occupy him, and I needed some time to make the transition from being with Will to being with Daddy. How great would it be to come home and find a message from him that he'd missed his flight?

Fat chance.

By the time I returned from my ride, dark clouds were crowding out the sunset. I couldn't tell whether they'd bring rain or snow, but the wind cut through my jacket. I rode around the side of the training barn and found Daddy talking to Mateo.

He'd gotten some sun in California. "Hey, darlin'." He gave Vigo a pat. "Rub him down and let's go up to the house. Teo, have someone muck her stalls."

I put away the tack and groomed my horse, but it hadn't been a hard ride. I blanketed Vigo for the night, rolled the stall door closed, and looked in on Jasper. I wanted to join him in his stall, press my body to his and disappear, like a chameleon. Become part of him, invisible and safe.

"All done?" Daddy said.

As we walked up to the house, he told me about the clinic and asked me about school. The wind made my eyes water. I flicked a tear from my cheek. We went in through the kitchen, where Gertrude was making gumbo; it would be ready when we were. I hung up my jacket, the same one I'd worn Friday night.

Since the gumbo was only simmering into further tenderness, Daddy told Gertrude to go home before it started to rain. Thunder had begun to rumble.

"I haven't made the salad."

"We can manage that, can't we, darlin'?"

"Yes, sir."

Gertrude relented and took her coat from its hook.

"Do you want a ride?" Daddy asked.

"You've been traveling all day. I like the walk, and if I get rained on, I'm not made of sugar." She buttoned her coat. "Glad you're back."

When she'd left, Daddy turned off the flame under the gumbo. "Let's go upstairs."

"I have a ton of homework."

"Come on." He reached out to brush back a strand of hair that had come loose from my ponytail.

I pulled my head back. "I don't want to."

"Since when?"

"I never want to."

"Right. Come on."

My heart kicked in my chest. "No."

"You don't want to play this game, darlin'." He reached out again, and when I took a step back he took a bigger step forward, pushing me up against the heavy butcher-block table. He caught my chin and his mouth came down on mine. With both hands on his chest I tried to push him away.

His mouth was all over me, lips on my neck, teeth nipping my earlobe. Damn—I'd gotten that earlobe thing from him. Of course I had. Everything I knew came from him. His hands were everywhere, one hand gripping my hair to keep control of me, the other pulling my shirt up, stretchy sports bra with it, and then diving down the front of my jodhpurs. He pushed a finger inside me and chuckled. Then he pulled my jodhpurs down to my knees, lifted me onto the table, got his own pants down, slammed into me.

He was hairier than Will, more heavily muscled, confident where Will was eager, deft where Will was unpolished, sure of himself, and sure of me. He knew where to touch me, how to touch me, when to be gentle and when—now—to be forceful.

My climax was so strong that I couldn't breathe. It swallowed me whole and went on and on, and somewhere in the middle of it he came, too.

He kissed me. "So much for 'never want to.' I know you better than you know yourself." He pulled out, pulled up his pants, and turned away.

My bra was hitched over my breasts, my jodhpurs hobbling me around my knees, my naked butt on the table. I put myself back together and walked unsteadily down the hall to the guest bath to clean up. *So much for "never want to."*

I *hadn't* wanted to and it had happened, anyway, but that didn't mean nothing had changed. I'd changed. He just didn't know it yet.

*       *       *

THE WEATHER WAS so foul for the remainder of January that I went for days without riding out, and when I did, Daddy accompanied me. I was training hard on all three horses, dressage every morning, jumping every afternoon. Daddy recorded the lessons, and we reviewed the videos after supper.

Because the broodmares were getting ready to drop, I usually did the evening walk-through with him. When I didn't, I paced the floor to keep myself from calling Will. I didn't want Daddy catching me with the phone. Anonymous had called a few times, and the hang-ups were raising his suspicions. He wasn't always in the house when the calls came, so he didn't know how many there really were, but one evening in his study after he'd fielded one, he turned to me.

"Is Will Howard harassing you?"

Hearing him say Will's name stunned me. Neither of us had mentioned Will since Thanksgiving.

I tried to look indifferent. "I don't think so."

"Did you get your sweater?"

What sweater?

The one I'd left in Will's truck. I'd forgotten about it.

"He gave it back. I keep it in my locker."

"We weren't getting calls like this until he called you at Thanksgiving."

"I'll ask him," I said, "and if he's doing it, I'll tell him to stop."

"If he's doing it, you'll tell me. I almost hope he is."

"Why?"

"You're in the public eye, darlin'. You're a potential target. I'd rather deal with some snot-nosed high-school punk than a real threat."

Cyber predators, kidnappers, and the like were Daddy's official reason for curtailing any small freedoms I might otherwise have had. Considering who he was and what we did and how his mind worked, he'd taken a couple of big steps in letting me go Christmas shopping alone and stay by myself at the house. Things like that gave me hope that one day he'd allow me to step into my own life.

I knew Anonymous wasn't Will, and I didn't think it was a threat. I thought it was Mama. After the first few calls, I'd stopped hanging up immediately. Instead, I stayed on the line and strained to hear anything that would tell me she was on the other end. Once I'd said, "Mama?" The call had disconnected instantly. That wasn't much to go on, but the lonely, abandoned part of me saw *Anonymous* and thought *Mama* and wanted the connection, even if it was only the sound of her breathing. If I told Daddy, he'd change the number or get rid of the landline.

By the first week of February, foals were being born. Most of them came late at night, often after midnight, so I rarely was present for a birth, but no matter how many hours Daddy spent at the barn, he always had time for me.

Gradually the days started to warm, and Gertrude's hyacinths and jonquils poked through the earth. On a sunny Saturday before Valentine's Day, Daddy was in his study working on entry forms for the spring shows. He waved me off toward the barn.

"Ride out, darlin'. Have a good time. Wear your helmet."

I was still in riding clothes from my morning lesson, so I went straight to the barn, suppressing the urge to skip. I hadn't ridden out alone in the month since Daddy had returned from California. This presented a rare opportunity.

I called Will from the phone in the office, keeping an eye on the aisle to make sure no one overheard me. "Can you meet me?" I asked without preamble.

"Now?"

"Now. And bring condoms."

He laughed. "I like it when you take charge."

I gave him directions to the fire road, saddled Jasper, and set out at a brisk walk down the back driveway. At the gate, I entered the code, and then we were on the service road. The limbs of the trees were nubbly with buds beginning to unfurl into soft yellow-green leaves. All around us, birds chirped and fussed. The sun was almost directly overhead. It was a perfect day for meeting a boy in the woods.

At the fire road, I practiced half-passes while I waited. For the past month, Will and I hadn't even really talked, much less had physical contact beyond the odd brush of the hand. The school's ban on PDAs was killing me.

I heard his truck. It came around the curve and stopped.

Will rolled down the window. "Where now?"

I pointed toward the wide dirt track of the fire road. "A mile or so in, it forks. Go to the right until it dead-ends."

"I'll follow you."

I took Jasper onto the fire road at a canter. The only sign of the pine that had fallen across the road in November was a stump, weeping resin.

At the fork, I bore right and pulled up in the clearing. I hadn't been here since the day Daddy had fucked me against a tree. *That* tree. The abrasions on my back had been sensitive for days, which had been a comfort in a way, because if it hurt, I wasn't responsible.

Will shut off the engine and got out. I dismounted, removed my helmet, and set it on the hood of the truck.

"Hey, buddy." He held out his fingers to Jasper, who wriggled his lips.

I knotted the reins around the same branch where I'd tied Diva in the fall. "He's trying to manifest carrots."

Will took my face in his hands and kissed me, a slow, succulent, deep kiss. My eyes began to close. His lips moved to my neck.

I undid the top button of his jeans.

He retrieved the condoms from the truck, and from the storage area behind the seat he took a blue sleeping bag. It didn't soften the ridged metal bed of the truck by much, and too little sunlight fell through the pine canopy to ward off the chill, but I was ravenous.

He was, too, unbuttoning my shirt and pulling my bra over my head, gently sucking my nipples while he unbuttoned and unzipped my riding pants. He sat up briefly to pull off my boots and my pants. He grinned at my socks, patterned with horses doing the cancan, but his face sobered as he ran his hands up my thighs. I shut my eyes. He slipped a finger inside me, the same way Daddy did.

My eyes flew open, but I wasn't looking up at a ceiling. Pine needles crosshatched the sky, black against the blue. I wasn't in my room. He wasn't Daddy.

"You okay?"

"Yeah."

"You went all tense."

"I'm fine."

Unconvinced, he withdrew his finger and used his tongue, hot, soft, agile—and inventive. I sighed, the hard ridges digging into my back, my body stretching taut. I reached for his hands. His fingers twined with mine.

*Do you want Daddy to make you feel good, darlin'?* The voice came out of the past—an afternoon when Daddy had blown raspberries on my belly, tickling me, making me giggle. Then he'd pulled aside the crotch of my panties and put his mouth on me.

I wouldn't let Daddy spoil this. When I was with Will, I was pure.

"Come up here," I said.

Will kissed his way up my abdomen, up my torso, lingering on my nipples.

"Kiss me," I said, and he did, a raw, hungry kiss. Then he reached for a condom.

He straightened up long enough to put it on. I opened my legs and closed my eyes again.

*Daddy's penis tore into me, but I didn't make a sound, even though the pain shocked me.* It had shocked me again and again, until one day it hadn't, and he hadn't needed to put his hand over my mouth, and he'd shown me how this could feel as good as everything else we did.

I didn't stand a chance of being normal, and I'd never been pure.

I heard a cry, and I knew it wasn't mine because Daddy had told me to keep quiet or Mama would hear.

Will pulled out and collapsed beside me.

"Sorry," he said.

"For?"

"You didn't seem to be . . . having a good time."

I moved closer to him and rested my head on his shoulder, my hand on his chest. "I always have a good time with you."

We were getting dressed when Will said, "I want to learn more about eventing, so I've been Googling you . . . but any article about you is always about your dad, too. He doesn't seem so bad. You don't think he'd be cool with us?"

"I know he wouldn't. He's . . ." I paused to decide how to complete the sentence. "Strict."

"Is that all?"

Where had that come from? I forced myself to sound casual. "If you ever went to a show, you'd see a hundred other parents and trainers and coaches exactly like him—and he's all three wrapped up in one." I pulled on my boots. "You know, when I was waiting for you, I was thinking that when I ride out alone, I'll call you—if I can—and we can meet here."

He was quiet.

"Unless you'd rather not." That was one of Daddy's negotiation tricks: Take something off the table.

"No, I want to. It's just what you said—you'll call if you can. I can't call you ever, and you can only call me when he isn't around."

Time away from Daddy was hard to come by; riding out without him and meeting Will here would represent a lot of work on my part. I didn't expect his thanks for it, but some understanding would have been nice. Some. Not too much.

"It's the best I can do," I said.

"I know," he said, and he kissed me.


TWO DAYS LATER, on Valentine's Day, I found a small pink gift bag in my locker before homeroom. I dug through tissue paper until I found the present: a cell phone. As I held it in my hand, it began to vibrate. I examined the screen, followed the instructions to slide my finger across it, and put it to my ear.

"I was thinking," Will said, "we've been grabbing what we can—a kiss here, a phone call there. This'll make it easier for us to talk."

I spotted him at the end of the hall, walking toward me, his own phone to his ear.

"Now you can call me whenever it's good for you. It's always good for me, by the way."

I watched him weave through the crowded hall. "You're a genius."

"Very few people recognize that. It's prepaid, so there won't be a bill. I loaded it with a thousand minutes. Let me know when you're low, and I'll refill your account."

"How can I tell I'm low?"

"I'll show you. I set it on vibrate, but I won't call you, so you don't have to worry about it going off when your dad's around. Or you can keep it turned off if you don't trust me." Will stopped in front of me.

"I trust you," I said.

"You can hang up," he said. "I'm right here."

# - Thirteen -

DADDY'S VOICE WAS urgent. "He's coming in too fast."

I tightened the reins and sat slightly against my horse, but Vigo took off too early. His back hoofs knocked the rail, and I heard a hollow plop behind us.

"Keep going," Daddy said in my ear.

We were trying out a new headset. It fitted under my helmet and over my head like a hairband, the receiver snug in my ear, a tiny microphone near my mouth. Daddy wore one, too. It saved him from raising his voice, but hearing him right in my ear was creepy.

Vigo's striding was off as we approached the next fence.

"He's rushing the fence," Daddy said. "Circle away."

Vigo shook his head, annoyed, when I cantered in a big loop instead of taking the fence.

"Bring him over," Daddy said.

I rode to the center of the arena.

"Get off."

Daddy and I changed places.

"You need to force him to take an extra full stride." He leaned down and lengthened the stirrups. "It'll slow him down. Watch."

Vigo took off at exactly the right place for the first fence and then took nine strides into the next one rather than the eight and a half he'd tried with me.

I sighed.

"What was that for?" Daddy said.

Damned headsets.

"Nothing."

He circled the next fence twice before letting Vigo take it. Then he rode toward me.

"I want you to jump one and approach two, but circle when you get there. Take three, circle four. Every other fence. He needs to know you're in charge of when he jumps and what he jumps. Big circles, more oval than round. Get him on a straight line to the fence for three or four strides."

He gave me a leg up. I shortened the stirrups a couple of notches and cantered around the arena.

"Slower," Daddy said. "Keep him relaxed."

None of the fences was taller than two and a half feet, but fences were more interesting than cavalletti, which I'd trained over for the past week. No sense in depleting the horse's energy before a show, Daddy said. Vigo left Wednesday for Greensboro. We'd do a final schooling over bigger fences when Daddy and I got there Thursday, which would be enough to raise Vigo's sights for competition.

We completed the course cleanly.

"That's better." Daddy started toward us. He switched off his headset. I turned mine off, too. "Eddie can rub him down. You tack up Diva."

I sighed again, but inwardly. It was a sun-drenched Sunday morning, and I'd hoped to meet Will at the fire road. Having a cell phone was great. I could call him when I rode out, and on the nights I didn't do the walk-through with Daddy, we talked or texted.

"Like the headset?" Daddy asked.

"I'm getting used to it."

At the barn, Eddie was measuring supplements into buckets for the midday feeding.

"How'd he go?"

"Rushing the jumps," Daddy replied, "but we have a couple of days to work on it. Will you rub him down? We're going to work Diva."

Psycho Pony pinned her ears and eyeballed the lead rope as I opened her stall door, the sclera visible all the way around the iris of each eye, but she stood resigned in the crossties while I groomed and saddled her. Grooming was the start of the horse's workday, but unlike the boys, Diva didn't enjoy the fuss. She wanted to punch in, do her job, and punch out. Fine by me. If we finished early enough, I could still meet Will.

Daddy emerged from the office. "Go ahead and warm her up."

After a twenty-minute warm-up, we met Daddy at the jumps.

We made the opening circle in a slow canter and approached the first fence. Diva easily cleared it, the oxer that followed, and the triple combination after that.

At the fourth fence, she gathered herself to jump, but instead of taking off, she locked her forelegs, and I was airborne. I tried to tuck myself into a ball, fall the way I'd been taught, but my shoulders smacked into the fence, the rails tumbled down with me, and I hit the ground flat on my back.

The impact knocked the breath from me. I'd taken countless falls, and I was always quick to roll to my feet and catch my horse, but when I tried now, my left side stabbed.

Daddy knelt beside me, Fernando hovering next to him. "Lie still. Don't move."

He unclipped the chinstrap of my helmet and eased it off my head. He removed the headset, too, which had skewed across my face.

"You okay?"

I pointed to my rib cage. Daddy prodded, his hands firm and cool under my shirt, sending a tidal wave of nausea through me.

He grimaced. "You might've broken a rib. Fernando, tell Eddie to bring the car."

I couldn't catch my breath.

"Can you sit up?"

I did, with his assistance. My head felt like a cracked eggshell.

"Can you put your head between your knees?"

I drew my legs up, which was bad enough, but leaning over was out of the question.

"Forget it. Sit here, catch your breath." He rubbed my upper back, which increased my urge to throw up.

I found my voice. "Don't touch me. I'm trying not to puke."

He took his hand away.

"Diva?" It would count against me later if I didn't ask.

"She's fine. Mateo's taking her back to the barn."

Eventually, Eddie came with the Land Cruiser. His face was concerned, but he said, "You're young enough to bounce pretty good."

Daddy helped me to my feet, and I broke a clammy sweat, but walking wasn't any worse. He eased me into the passenger seat.

"You with me?"

"Yes, sir."

"You going to pass out?"

"No, sir," I said, and then I did.

*        *        *

X-RAYS REVEALED THE displaced fracture of three left ribs
but no damage to my lung. After a CT scan, the ER doctor,
a stocky man with a shaved head that was sprouting stubble,
added mild concussion to the diagnosis.

"We'll keep her under observation overnight," he told
Daddy, who was leaning against the counter. "She's probably
fine, but we don't take chances with head injuries."

I listened as if "she" and "her" were someone I didn't know.
The back of the gurney was raised like a lounge chair. From the
needle stuck in the crook of my right arm, a plastic tube ran
up to a bag of saline dangling from a chrome stand. Earlier a
nurse had injected a painkiller into the line. The stabbing in my
side wasn't quite so sharp. The anti-nausea patch she'd applied
behind my right ear wasn't working yet, but I looked forward
to that.

The doctor turned back to me. "Let's get you fitted with this
rib belt. Sit up. Nice and tall."

Sitting up wasn't pleasant. He untied the neck of the hospital gown and lowered the top to my waist. I freed my left arm
from the sleeve and held it over my breasts, and he passed one
end of the belt around my torso. Over his shoulder, I glimpsed
Daddy's face. He didn't like the doctor touching me.

"Normally we don't use these because you need to breathe as
deeply as you can, but all three bones are broken all the way in
two. Don't want them moving too much." Dr. Stubblehead—I
almost giggled as the name occurred to me—brought the ends
of the belt together in front and secured them with Velcro
straps. The pressure on my ribs shot through the painkiller.

"Tough girl." He helped me put my arm back through the sleeve of the gown and retied the strings behind my neck. "Mr. Montgomery, questions?"

"No. Thank you, doctor."

"We'll get her in a room soon." He left through the curtain at the end of the cubicle.

"There goes Greensboro." The flint in Daddy's voice cut through the haze. "Columbus, Athens, Ocala. You're out of commission for the next six weeks."

"Well, I'm not happy about it, either." My voice dragged like Mama's did when she was drunk. "I didn't do it on purpose."

"Not on purpose, but where's your head? I told you to give her more leg. Why didn't you do it?"

"I didn't hear you." I struggled to process what he'd said, impaired by the workings of the painkiller.

"You were wearing the headset. I took it off you myself."

"I forgot to turn it on."

"Maybe this is for the best, darlin'. You weren't ready for Greensboro."

The endearment did nothing to disguise his irritation. I'd miss some big shows, and worse, I'd miss six weeks of training.

"I'm sorry." I'd never been sorrier. Unexpected tears welled in my eyes.

He ripped a tissue from the dispenser on the counter. "Don't cry."

It was a command. I blew my nose, which exploded my brain and turned my ribs into razor wire.

The curtain whisked back, and a nurse in cartoon scrubs pushed a wheelchair alongside the gurney. "My name's Patricia. I hear they've reserved the princess suite for you tonight."

A tear leaked out. I crushed it with my knuckle before it reached my cheek, pretending to rub my eye.

Daddy took his phone from the back pocket of his jeans. "No bars. I'll find a signal and call Eddie to tell him you're all right. See you in your room."

I wasn't all right. I was injured and he said it was for the best. Time to be what Dr. Stubblehead had said I was, tough.

Patricia helped me off the gurney and into the wheelchair. She hung the IV bag on a chrome pole sticking up from the back. "Ready to roll?"

She pushed the chair down the hall and onto an elevator, telling me about the hospital and its trauma center and how many broken bones were treated there every year. When the doors opened, she rolled me out into a wide hallway painted with balloons and kites and clouds, all fluffy childhood innocence.

"Welcome to pediatrics," she said.

"I'm not a child."

"You are if you're under eighteen."

The room was a plain hospital room, not that I'd believed in any princess suite. I got in bed. She locked the bedrails in place, clipped a thing like a clothespin to my left index finger, stuck a thermometer in my mouth, and took my blood pressure. When she was done, she typed something into a computer mounted on the wall and then pointed to the buttons inside the bedrail.

"This raises and lowers the bed. This rings the nurses' station. This works the TV and your reading light. I'll get you some water."

Daddy came in while she was setting a big plastic mug of ice water on a tall table that rolled over the bed.

"I'll be back later, but ring if you need anything."

She left the door open. I didn't like being on display for anyone who passed by to gawk at.

Daddy stood at the foot of the bed, impassive. "Gertrude's putting together some clothes for you. Do you want anything in particular?"

"No, sir." As soon as I said it, I had an image of him alone in the house digging through my backpack. He had no reason to, but I couldn't risk him finding my cell. "Oh. My backpack."

"You have a concussion. You don't feel like studying."

"Not right now, but I might later. I don't want to fall behind. I already miss so much school as it is."

"You don't have to worry about that for the next month and a half," he said.

So much for impassive.

Patricia popped in periodically to take my blood pressure and temperature and make sure I wasn't seeing double. She asked me to rate my pain on a scale of one to ten using a chart of ten cartoon faces to quantify the club drumming in my skull and the dagger digging into my side. The first face beamed happily over the caption *Pain free!* The tenth face looked like it was dying of a medieval plague. It was captioned *Unimaginable/unspeakable.*

At first I settled on Six, the disgruntled face labeled *Intense*, but over the course of the afternoon I bumped it up to Seven, *Very intense.*

"Why is it getting worse?" Daddy asked.

"The Dilaudid she had in the ER is out of her system. If it gets too bad, we have standing orders to give her something."

"Darlin', you're the only one who can tell us how much it hurts."

The drug that had blunted my pain had also blunted my thinking. Being less than sharp-witted around Daddy was never a good idea. I closed my eyes against the stripes of daylight coming through the blinds. "I'm okay."

Maybe memories of his own concussions and broken bones kept him quiet, but Daddy didn't lecture me beyond what he'd said in the ER. Everyone came off the horse sooner or later. Some people came off a lot. Jamie, for example. Besides breaking his collarbone before Thanksgiving, he'd broken his femur a couple of years ago. He'd had long layoffs from training, and he'd missed important shows, and he was still a top-notch rider.

A small mouse of a thought scratched at the back of my brain, something about the *way* I'd come off. For sure I hadn't been paying attention. *Where's your head?*

My head was right here on my shoulders, doing its best to burst. Thinking made it worse, so I tried not to.

Around four o'clock, Gertrude and Eddie arrived with an overnight bag, my backpack, and a pint of peach ice cream. Daddy gave Gertrude the single visitor's chair and sat at the foot of the bed, where he rested a hand on my ankle. I'd exchanged my long boot socks for shorter slipper socks in the ER, and through the cheap cotton blanket and the sheet, his hand was warm.

"How do you feel, sugar?"

"Seven," I replied.

Daddy patted my leg and explained the pain chart to Gertrude, but I wasn't very good company, and she and Eddie didn't stay long.

She kissed my forehead lightly. "See you tomorrow, sugar."

"Stay out of trouble," Eddie said.

I gave him a thumbs-up.

"You'll be okay if I leave?" Daddy asked when we were alone.

"I'll be fine." *Leave. Leave, leave, leave.*

He squeezed my toes through the covers. "You scared me when you didn't get right up."

I understood it was an apology—I'd scared him, therefore he'd been pissed off—but I was the one who said, "I'm sorry."

"You didn't mean to." He wiggled one toe at a time, as if we were playing This Little Piggy. "I'd trade places with you if I could, darlin'. Being thrown isn't nearly as bad as watching the person you love not get up."

I was sure he'd trade places with me; it nearly killed him not to compete.

"They'll bring supper around in an hour," Patricia said from the doorway. "They have roasted chicken or tofu scramble."

"Chicken," I said.

"Good call. I'll let them know."

Daddy stood up. "It's almost time for evening chores. I'll see you in the morning. Love you, darlin'." He leaned over. The touch of his lips on top of my head was lost in the drumbeat of pain.

"Love you, too, Daddy."

Once he'd left, the room seemed to expand, to become big enough for me. Even with the open door and Patricia and a nurse's aide in and out all the time, it offered more privacy than I had at home. I studied the phone on the bedside table, but hospitals might work like hotels, giving you an itemized statement when you checked out, complete with any phone numbers you'd dialed.

I pressed the call button.

Patricia came in. "What can I do for you?"

"Will you get my backpack? It's in the closet."

She opened the closet door and picked up the backpack. "Mercy, girl, you won't be carrying this for a while. It weighs a ton." She set it beside me in the bed and then spotted the ice cream. "Peach. Yum. Do you want a spoon?"

"I don't want it."

"There's a fridge at the nurses' station. I'll stick it in the freezer. Ring if you change your mind."

I zipped open the backpack and dug to the bottom for my phone.

"Can you get away?" Will said by way of greeting. His voice wrapped around me, warm, hinting at the Sunday afternoon I'd hoped we'd have.

"I am away. I'm in the hospital."

I heard a sharp intake of breath. "In the hospital? What happened? Are you all right?"

Daddy had said I was.

"Diva threw me. I broke some ribs and hit my head, so they're keeping me overnight."

"Some ribs? Like more than one?"

"Three."

"Jesus," he said. "You sound terrible. Do you feel as bad as you sound?"

Sharp beats of pain kept time with my pulse.

"Pretty much."

"Where's your dad?"

"He just left."

"Is he coming back?"

"Not today."

"Want a visitor?"

It took all my willpower to turn him down. "The nurse keeps coming in. If she said something to Daddy, he'd ask how you knew I was here. Besides, everything hurts, and I feel barfy."

If all else failed, the prospect of seeing me vomit might keep him away.

"I'm sorry," he said. "Do you even feel like talking?"

"I'd rather listen. What have you been doing today?"

Breakfast out with his family, a long run into town and back, homework.

"Then I started watching a Vincent Price marathon, and—hey, do you have the Classic Movie Channel?" He'd set about educating himself on old films. I liked them for escapism, but Will studied them earnestly. "There's an Orson Welles marathon tonight. *The Third Man* starts in an hour. We could watch it together."

I turned on the TV and found the channel, which was airing the end of the Vincent Price marathon, some movie too campy to be scary. "I have it, but you're there and I'm here. How is that watching it together? It's just watching at the same time."

"You're so literal. We'll be on the phone together while the movie's on."

I glanced at my battery icon. I hadn't had a chance to charge my phone last night; Daddy had stayed in my room. "I don't have enough juice for that."

"We can text instead."

A text-and-movie date sounded wholesome compared to what we'd been doing.

"Okay, but I'd better hang up or I won't have the juice for that, either."

"Text me when the movie starts," Will said.

I stuffed my phone under the pillow and spun through the channels, finally returning to the Vincent Price movie. I muted the sound. I didn't feel like thinking any more than I felt like talking, but I couldn't seem to help it. I should have anticipated Diva's refusal. If I'd remembered to turn on the headset, I'd have heard Daddy's warning. I might not have come off. At the least, I could have fallen the right way.

I shifted, seeking a more comfortable position, and experimented with the buttons that raised and lowered the head and foot of the bed. I wound up half sitting, which was better, but the rib belt was hot and confining. I didn't care what Dr. Stubblehead said. I had to get out of it.

The IV was plugged into my right arm, so I folded my left arm into a chicken wing and tried to pull it inside my gown, planning to loosen the Velcro straps, but the maneuver generated a shock of pain that stunned me. Fuzzy-edged patches of brown and gray dappled my vision. Through them, pinpoints of light flew toward me like snow.

I struggled to get free of the sleeve, but I could neither work my arm out nor pull it all the way inside my gown. My armpits prickled with sweat, and my core was hot, like a volcano was inside me. My breath shortened. Then it was gone.

My pulse blurred into a vibration in my temples and wrists and neck, and a weird, heaving wheeze was coming out of me—sound but not air—and it got louder and louder.

From the corner of my eye I saw color and movement.

"What's happening here?" Patricia sounded part soothing, part perky.

The head of the bed elevated more. She pressed her palm firmly against my breastbone, which made me feel even more trapped.

"Breathe out. You're hyperventilating."

Out? I needed more air, not less.

"Don't breathe from your chest. Use your abdomen. Exhale. Come on. You can do it."

The razor wire had wrapped itself around my torso again. I couldn't exhale or inhale. I could only wheeze.

"Cup your hands over your nose and mouth. Breathe through your fingers. You're okay."

I clutched at her hand. "I can't breathe." My voice sounded shot full of holes.

"You're breathing right now."

She was crushing the air out of me. I tried to pull her hand away from my chest, but she had the advantages of weight and leverage and not being injured and not freaking out.

"I'm going to cover your mouth," she said.

"No—"

She clamped a latex-gloved hand over the bottom half of my face.

"Breathe through my fingers. Come on."

I was going to die with the smell of latex in my nostrils. It smelled like condoms.

I sobbed once, and then I was getting air, sweet, cool anti-septic air. The tension began to bleed from my muscles.

Patricia made eye contact. "Okay?"

I nodded. She released me but remained ready to pounce and smother-crush me if I started wheezing again.

A few seconds passed. My breathing was shaky, but otherwise normal. My heart jumped like it was bouncing on a trampoline, my head thudded, razor wire was cutting me in half.

"Anything like this ever happen before?" she said.

"No." I could hardly think because I hurt so much.

She eased my left arm out of the sleeve that trapped it, clipped the clothespin monitor to my finger again, took my blood pressure. "Want to tell me what got you so upset?"

"The belt's too tight."

"Leave that belt alone." She listened to my heart, took my temperature, flashed her penlight in my eyes. Then she lowered the head of the bed a few inches. "Rest for a minute. I'll be right back."

I closed my eyes. Soft-soled shoes squeaked out of the room.

What the hell had happened?

She was gone more like ten minutes, but she returned eventually with a hypodermic needle.

"What's that?"

"Sedative."

She inserted the needle into the stub that hung off the IV, and slowly the liquid disappeared from the syringe.

The bed began to rock gently, like a boat. There was no motion sickness, only soft waves lapping at the mattress, flowing through the bedrails, washing over me, but I could breathe underwater. I could even sleep.


I WOKE IN the early morning, my room lit gray through the blinds. The bed was in dry dock. My body was filled with rocks, jagged and heavy. My eyeballs had been peeled. My head pounded.

I'd slept with the TV on, as I sometimes did in hotels. The sound was off, but the old newsreel on the screen showed Orson Welles.

Orson Welles . . . *The Third Man*. Will. I felt under the pillow for my phone. Still there, but the battery had drained.

My backpack was in the visitor's chair. Sometime in the night I'd been untethered from the IV, so I was free to get up. I inched down to the end of the bed, past the bedrail, and put my legs over the side. Carefully, I stood up. I was steady on my feet, and hungry.

I stashed my phone in my backpack and made my way to the bathroom.

When I came out, a breakfast tray waited on the rolling table over the bed. Chewing made my head hurt, but the scrambled eggs were soft, so I swallowed them in tiny bites and sipped orange juice from a plastic cup.

Patricia breezed in as I finished the juice. "Good morning. How do you feel?"

"Better. Thanks."

I looked past her to the woman who'd followed her into the room.

"This is Mrs. Adams." Patricia started checking my vital signs. "She works at the hospital. I thought you two might like to talk."

A halo of thick, pretty white curls framed Mrs. Adams's face. She carried a manila folder, but from her black pantsuit, I knew she wasn't a doctor or nurse.

"Nice to meet you, Roan."

I took the business card she offered me. Beth Adams, LCSW. What was LCSW?

Patricia typed her notes into the computer. "Looking good. I'll leave you two to talk."

I disliked her again. I'd started to like her last night when she'd been nice, but now she'd betrayed me. If Mrs. Adams and I were supposed to talk, I had an idea what her job was, even if I didn't know what the letters stood for. I put her card on my tray.

She sat down in the visitor's chair. "Roan, Patricia told me your father brought you to the ER yesterday with a concussion and some broken ribs." She consulted a printed form in her folder. "Can you tell me how that happened?"

I nodded toward the folder. "Don't those papers tell you?"

She scanned the form. "It says you were injured in a riding accident, Roan, but it doesn't say how exactly."

Talking about that was harmless. "My horse refused a jump, and I came off."

"Was your father there, Roan?"

The way she kept saying my name made me think she was trying to maneuver me into being comfortable with her.

"Yes. We were in a lesson."

"Anyone else around?"

"The jump crew, Mateo and Fernando."

"They witnessed the accident?"

Witnessed? With a shock, I realized she was fishing for evidence Daddy had hurt me. No one had ever suspected him of that.

With another shock, I realized I could tell the truth.

She was all but inviting me to spill my secret. I longed to tell her. I saw myself riding, competing, winning, all without Daddy there ready to claim the credit and tell me what to do next. I didn't know where he'd go—prison, maybe. It was a satisfying fantasy, my father in prison stripes and maybe chains.

The problem was, he was inseparable from the horses, the farm, and my future. If I told Mrs. Adams or anyone else, Daddy wasn't the only one who'd be punished. I'd be ripped out of my own life. Leaving Rosemont and Jasper and Vigo would kill me.

The desire to tell the truth evaporated.

"Roan?"

"Sorry. I was thinking maybe Kevin was there, but it was Mateo."

She made a note on the form. "Where was your mother, Roan?"

"My parents are divorced. My father has custody."

"Full custody?"

"Mama and I don't get along."

Mistake. Her eyes became more alert. "How so?"

I stalled for time. "Are you a doctor?"

"I'm a social worker." She spoke as if she hadn't tried to lure me into destroying my whole life. "Patricia said you had a panic attack last night."

Didn't I have the latitude anywhere to *feel* without having to explain and cover up?

"'Attack' is a little extreme."

"She said you hyperventilated."

"The rib belt made me feel like I couldn't breathe. I panicked, but it wasn't an attack." I shook my head, discrediting Patricia and her wild imagination.

Mrs. Adams made another note. "Roan, Patricia overheard your father in the ER. She said he was harsh with you."

If Patricia's only concern was that Daddy had been harsh, I was home free.

"He wasn't happy with me."

"Because . . ."

"I can't ride for six weeks."

"It's important to him that you ride?"

"It's important to me."

There was a beat of silence. The pieces weren't falling into place for Mrs. Adams, which meant I had some damage control to do.

"When she overheard him," I said, "he was speaking as my coach, and my coach is annoyed. My father, on the other hand, apologized later." Close enough, anyway.

"Do you see him as different people?"

I laughed. "No, but he wears a lot of different hats."

"Why did he apologize, Roan?"

"For coming down on me so hard. And for God's sake, would you please stop saying my name?"

She wrote something down.

"What're you writing?"

*"Patient is irritable."* Her glasses had slipped down her nose, and she contorted her face to scoot them back into place. She looked clownish, but I didn't laugh. She wasn't funny. She was smart and astute. She could ruin everything.

"Look, I'm sorry." I didn't sound sorry. I tried to soften my tone. "I don't feel well. Daddy apologized, but he went easier on me than a lot of other trainers would have."

"Is it only the two of you in the house? Do you see your mother?"

"No. I mean, yes, it's only the two of us, and no, I don't see Mama."

"Why don't you get along?"

She'd already asked that. I couldn't not answer a second time.

"Where do I start?" I had never told anyone, not even Will, how hateful Mama was. Daddy and Gertrude had seen her in all her rabid glory, but we never talked about it.

"Start wherever you like. Tell me anything that comes to mind."

"She doesn't like horses. I train five or six hours a day. She's never understood why I'd want to do that. She has an eating disorder, and I know that's an illness, but she used to criticize me because I'm heavier than she thinks I should be. She's an alcoholic. She abuses prescription drugs. She blames me for everything."

It felt good to say awful, true things about Mama.

"What does she blame you for?"

"Her failed modeling career. Her isolation. I don't have time for mother-daughter shopping trips or pedicures or stuff like that."

"What do you have time for?"

At last, an opportunity to make myself sound normal. I could claim I had pizza and slumber parties with friends—but I wasn't normal, and even if I didn't tell the truth about everything, the first tenet of lying was to be as honest as possible.

"I don't have spare time."

"No friends, no dating, nothing?"

"You don't get gold medals for having a social life."

"Tell me about riding. Do you feel a lot of pressure to win?"

"Pressure comes with the sport."

"Does your father pressure you to win?"

"No one wants to lose, right?"

That sounded glib, like I was deliberately playing a game with her, only this was no game.

"I don't lose too often." Better arrogant than glib. "I have goals. I'm focused, I'm determined, and I work hard. What's wrong with that?" Arrogant *and* defensive. Great.

"Nothing. Is there anything we haven't discussed that you'd like to talk about?"

It was my last chance. Tell her now, and put an end to the lies.

Tell her now, and put an end to everything I wanted.

"Not a thing," I said.

She closed her folder and stood up. "I enjoyed our talk. Would you like to talk again sometime?"

"Nope."

She started to say something, but Daddy rounded the doorway. His face registered mild surprise and nothing more at seeing a stranger in my room.

"Hello," he said.

"Good morning." She extended her hand. "I'm Beth Adams."

Daddy shook her hand. "Monty Montgomery."

"Mrs. Adams is a social worker," I said.

He smiled benignly. "How you feeling, darlin'?"

"Better."

"Good." He picked up Mrs. Adams's business card and examined it. "Any particular reason for your visit?" He struck exactly the right tone: casual, curious, somewhat amused.

I sensed something, as if the patron saint of deception had whispered it in my ear: Mrs. Adams had been on the verge of leaving, but now that Daddy was here, she wanted to observe our interaction. She wanted to see what I'd say to him. What I wouldn't say.

"Daddy, did Patricia tell you what happened last night?"

"I haven't seen her. What happened?"

I told him, downplaying it, as I had for Mrs. Adams. Obviously Patricia had exaggerated.

Daddy displayed concern about the hyperventilation—"My God, darlin', are you all right?"—and when Patricia came in he asked all the right questions, and during their conversation, Mrs. Adams slipped away.

How about that, I thought. Daddy and I had passed the normal test, as administered by a licensed mental health professional.

# - Fourteen -

THE HOSPITAL RELEASED me in the late morning. A sallow light shone on the new leaves on the oaks lining the driveway, and the air smelled like rain. In the pasture, the foals stuck close to their mothers. The babies were all legs, the mothers all belly, the fate of the broodmare.

Daddy was quiet. He had to be thinking about Mrs. Adams. I was. In fact, we might have been thinking the same thing: I'd had an opportunity to tell someone, and I hadn't.

He stopped in front of the house. "Let's get you to bed."

I got out of the car in stages. The rib bone was connected to every other bone and muscle and nerve and joint in my body.

From the entrance hall, I caught the smell of browning onions; Gertrude was in the kitchen. I followed Daddy upstairs. He set my duffel and backpack by my desk and turned back the covers on the bed. I crawled in. The extra pillows Gertrude had propped against the headboard were like clouds, the sheets smooth and cool.

Daddy pulled the covers up to the middle of my chest. "Okay?"

"Yes, sir."

"You're bruised." He stroked the blue smudge the needle had left on the inside of my elbow. "We need to talk about what happened." He sat down by my hip. "It's not like you to lose focus in the middle of a lesson. Is there a bigger problem?"

"It was only a lapse."

"Darlin', you can't have a lapse when you're on the back of a fifteen-hundred-pound animal."

Obviously I could.

"And a panic attack? That's not like you, either."

All I wanted was to close my eyes and be quiet. "I felt claustrophobic."

"Since when are you claustrophobic?"

"I'm not. It's this thing." I indicated my torso and by extension the rib belt. "I freaked. Anyway, it wasn't a panic attack. The nurse made it into a bigger deal than it was."

"However you think you came across, she was concerned enough to give you a shot of Ativan. You can't allow it to happen again. What if it happens at a show?"

I understood the layers of meaning behind the question. First, someone who went around having panic attacks would appear psychologically vulnerable. My competitors would see me as weak, and weakness could be exploited. Second, since I wasn't known for being weak or vulnerable, people might start asking questions.

"If you have a breakdown in public," Daddy said, "the sponsors won't like it."

Third, the sponsors. Had to keep them happy.

I registered the first part of what he'd said.

"It wasn't a breakdown."

"What do you want to call it?"

"A misunderstanding."

"Fine. But that misunderstanding is the reason a social worker was in your room this morning."

Fourth, the social worker. Someone who went beyond asking questions. Someone who could analyze the answers. I didn't want that any more than he did.

"It won't happen again."

"Good." He started to stand up, and then, with the same casual amusement he'd used with Mrs. Adams, he said, "What did she ask, anyway?"

He wasn't the only one with power.

"A lot of questions about you."

"Me?" He sounded baffled but not uneasy, not worried—not the reaction I'd wanted.

"Patricia overheard you in the ER. She thought you were harsh."

He briefly considered that idea. "I didn't say anything harsh."

"It might have been your tone," I suggested.

"I wasn't harsh."

"However you think you came across," I said evenly, "she was concerned enough to call a social worker."

That got his attention. It had never occurred to him that someone might see through the act. It had never occurred to me, either. We were pretty good at it.

"Exactly what did she ask?"

"Whether it's only the two of us now that Mama's gone. If it's important to you that I ride. If you pressure me to win."

He looked unimpressed. I wasn't too impressed myself. The questions seemed less insightful than they had earlier.

"She asked if I'd like to talk to her again sometime." I wanted him to ask me how I'd answered, to think, if only for an instant, I might have said yes.

He didn't.

"Don't you want to know what I said?"

"You said no. It wouldn't serve you well to have said yes. You have too much to lose." He stood up. "Get some rest."

I listened to him go down the stairs. If I'd ever had any power, I'd given it away when I'd decided not to tell the truth.

My brain was approximately the size of a basketball; it even felt like someone was dribbling inside my skull. Sounded like it, too. My head hurt worse than my side until I started to get up, and then my ribs screeched back into first place. I went to my window, anyway. After a moment, Daddy came into view, walking toward the barn.

I retrieved my phone and squatted in front of my closet. On the back wall was an ancient electrical outlet; it was a stupid place for an outlet, and its safety was questionable, but I plugged in my phone and put it in my boot.

Stretching to reach the outlet left me hurting, but the doctor who'd discharged me said aspirin should be sufficient for pain relief. I swallowed two tablets from the bottle in my medicine cabinet and washed them down with water cupped in my hand.

"Sugar?" Gertrude stood in the doorway of my room, a tray in her hands. "Want some soup and cornbread?"

She waited while I got back in bed and propped myself up.

"Thanks for the extra pillows."

She set the tray on my lap. "It wasn't me. Your daddy must've done it."

Fuck. Even as a father, he got it right some of the time.

I took a cautious spoonful of black bean soup, which was topped with crispy brown onions. The smokiness of paprika and chipotle cleared my sinuses.

She glanced toward the window. "It's going to pour. Good day to stay in bed. How about I unpack for you?"

She kept me company as she put yesterday's riding clothes in the hamper, my boots in the closet—nowhere near the old boots that held my contraband—and the empty duffel on the overhead shelf.

She gestured toward my backpack. "What about your books?"

"Leave them in there." I didn't want her to get in the habit of looking in my backpack.

"Want anything else?"

"No, thanks."

She came back to my bedside and smoothed my hair back, a Daddy gesture. A Will gesture, too.

My leg jerked, and the tray tilted precariously. I grabbed it. Good thing my bowl was empty.

"Nothing wrong with your reflexes." Gertrude picked up the tray. "I'll check on you later."

Alone again, I pushed Daddy's extra pillows onto the floor. Daylight lanced through my eyelids, but the cool breeze bathed my face. The rib belt was as stiff and binding as it had been yesterday, but I wasn't losing my shit over it today. The belt hadn't triggered my panic. It hadn't helped, but the trigger had been something else: the memory of being touched by both of them, Daddy and Will.

THUNDER GRUMBLED. RAIN pattered on the roof and then intensified. My room was dark.

Daddy's voice came to me under the sound of the rain. "You awake, darlin'?"

I flinched. Pain spiked through me.

"Figured sleep would do you more good than supper, but I'll bring you a plate if you're hungry."

There was a chance I could have slept through what he'd said, so I didn't reply.

He lifted the edge of the covers and carefully folded himself around me, tucking his legs behind mine.

He drew in his breath, inhaling me, and wrapped my hair around his fingers, massaging my scalp lightly. The sound was loud, like static, but I could still, maybe, have been asleep.

He squirmed closer and pushed his erection against my buttocks. When I was little, he'd hold me on his lap while he put on my socks and shoes, his erection pressing against me like this, except now he rubbed against me. This wasn't so bad. All I had to do was lie here. I might as well have been an inanimate object. A piece of furniture.

The rain fell harder. A sound filled my mouth. It could have been a scream or a sob; I'd never know which because I stayed silent. This was what I did. I *managed* this.

With a soft groan, he finished. Warmth and wetness seeped through the back of my sweatpants.

His breath was heavy with bourbon. "Didn't mean for that to happen."

He'd been rubbing his dick against me. What had he thought would happen?

He kissed the back of my head. "Go to sleep. I'll see you in the morning."

He got up as carefully as he'd lain down. The door closed behind him.

I'd chosen this. It served me well.

# - Fifteen -

I WATCHED THE clock until daybreak, when I finally let myself get up. My ribs still felt like knives, but my headache had faded into a low, steady drone, the all-over soreness had diminished, and I had no nausea. I was healing already. Maybe it wouldn't take six weeks for the bones to knit. That would make Daddy happy. Me, too.

I unfastened the Velcro and peeled off the rib belt. The elastic had left impressions in my skin—but by the time I finished showering, my ribs cried out for the belt. I dried off and cinched myself back into it, tightening the straps until I saw stars.

The leaves of the trees outside my window dripped from last night's rain, but the sky had cleared. It was cool, so I dressed in jeans and a hoodie. Then I picked up my sweatpants from the floor. I'd taken them off last night and let them lie where they fell. Now I shook them out and checked the back. The semen stain was barely noticeable, but I turned them inside-out before I put them in the hamper so Gertrude wouldn't see it.

Daddy was at the dining room table, his newspaper folded into quarters. He put it down when I came in. "Look who's up and about. How do you feel, darlin'?"

"Better. Sore."

"You should take it easy today. Sit down. I'll fix your plate."

He served my plate from the chafing dishes on the sideboard and set it in front of me with a glass of orange juice. This was familiar, acting like nothing had happened the night before. I started on my eggs.

"I spoke to Vic this morning. He's coming out Sunday to interview you. They want to document your recovery—show how a winner copes with a setback. They'll film every Sunday and cut clips into their coverage of Athens and Ocala. Then the whole thing will air during Bluegrass."

The Bluegrass International Cup, held in Louisville the first weekend in May, would be my first two-star ever. If I hadn't broken my ribs, I'd have had three other two-stars under my belt by then.

"We'll run through some questions and answers before they come," Daddy said. "This Sunday will be the big interview, but they'll ask a few questions each week, and as you start working out they'll get footage of that."

I envisioned the mini-documentary Daddy had in mind, an athlete profile that would show my grit.

"Sounds good," I said.

"And I posted on your social media channels last night."

His rationale was unspoken but understood. The only sensible thing to do was take advantage of my injury. Posts allegedly written by me the day after sustaining three broken ribs and a concussion would illustrate my toughness.

"As for the horses," he said, "I'm keeping them in training. I'll work them myself."

It was bad enough that I was losing training time. The horses couldn't lose it, too.

"I can observe," I said. "It'll be like auditing a clinic."

He raised his eyebrows in surprise, which was a little insulting. I reminded myself to stay on his good side. "It's better than nothing."

"All right. Do you feel up to it this morning?"

I didn't feel up to much of anything, but I didn't want to stay cooped up in the house, and my ribs and head would hurt no matter where I was.

We walked down to the barn together. The asphalt gleamed in the early-morning sun. The earth smelled damp, the wet grass like freshly cut watermelon, the horses . . . like home.

"There she is," Eddie said. "You feeling better?"

"Loads. I won't be riding for a while, though."

"Or mucking," Mateo said as he led Vigo from his stall. "Which I know you'll miss."

While I was injured, Daddy didn't want me interacting with the horses too closely in case they spooked and knocked into me. I hung back as he tacked Jasper. Childishly, I was jealous.

I got more jealous watching him work my horse. His cues were invisible, his hands light, his seat elegant, and Jasper elevated his own game in response. *Traitor*, I thought.

Next Daddy rode Diva, who would never dream of throwing him. I shouldn't have come off Sunday. I should have been paying attention. When I could ride again, I'd work harder. Meanwhile, I'd focus on Daddy's flawless form.

I did, until my pain inched up and the aluminum bleachers became intolerable.

"I'm going back to the house," I called.

Daddy nodded, acknowledging my departure without interrupting Diva's piaffe. She was demonstrating perfect impulsion and suspension. She and Daddy both looked exactly like the elite athletes they were.

I went into the house through the screened porch off the kitchen, where Gertrude was watering the potted herbs she used for cooking. She took one look at me and told me to go to bed.

Upstairs, I took more aspirin, changed into an oversized T-shirt, and got in bed. Under the sheet, I stretched my legs into the cool depths of the bedclothes.

Gertrude brought my lunch on a tray again.

I sat up. "I can eat at the table."

"Don't push yourself." She nodded toward the tray. "I'll come back for this."

After lunch, I made the strange discovery that lying on my left side, the injured side, alleviated the pain a bit. I was more comfortable than I'd been in a while, and exhaustion dragged at me, pulling me under.

"Sugar?" Gertrude called softly. "Wake up."

I started awake.

"Someone's here to see you."

I struggled to sit up, pushing my hair back from my face. "Who is it?"

She stepped aside, and Will Howard appeared in my doorway.

Panic rose in me like vomit. "What are you doing here?"

"You have homework." He indicated the books and notebooks tucked under his arm. "And I brought you these." He held out a bunch of radiant yellow daffodils.

"Aren't those pretty?" Gertrude prompted me.

What was he *thinking*, coming here?

She gave me a look that said, *Say thank you*, but manners were the last thing I was worried about.

"Let me have them, sugar," she said to Will. "I'll put them in water."

"Can I come in?" he asked when she'd left.

"You have to leave before Daddy sees you."

"Too late. He saw me on the way in."

If I were ever going to hyperventilate again, this would have been the moment.

Will came in without an invitation, snagged my desk chair, pulled it close, and sat down. "He was down by the barn. I waved. He waved back." He put my lit and history books and notebooks on the bed, withdrew a folded sheet of paper from the pocket of his blazer, and handed it to me.

In Will's round, fat handwriting were my assignments for the rest of the week.

"I called the hospital," he said, "but they told me you weren't there."

"I haven't had a chance to text you." That wasn't true. Why hadn't I texted him?

It didn't matter right now.

"You need to leave."

He smiled, which irritated me. "Nice to see you, too."

"I mean it. You shouldn't have come."

"Somebody had to bring your books. Why not me?"

"You're not just somebody."

"Glad to hear it."

"That's not what I meant. He'll know something's up."

"You could be wrong about him."

"I'm not," I snapped.

The brightness in his eyes dimmed. Gertrude returned bearing a vase, the daffodils erupting like sunshine over the top. She set it on the nightstand.

"I took some brownies out of the oven a while ago. They're almost cool enough to cut."

Will didn't take his eyes from mine. "I won't be staying that long. But thanks."

She looked at me. "Sugar?"

"No, thanks."

When we were alone again, Will said, "I thought you'd be happy I figured out a way to see you."

"I didn't want you to come to the hospital. What made you think I'd want you to come here?"

He flushed.

"I'm sorry, but I'm not happy. Neither is he. I'm missing a bunch of shows and weeks of training."

"You had an accident." He looked at me closely. "He's blaming you for it, isn't he?"

"He's right. I wasn't paying attention. I was thinking about—"

There it was. Right before I'd come off my horse, the only thing I'd wanted was to be finished with the day's lessons so I could meet Will. Meeting him had been more important than riding.

Exactly as Daddy had predicted, a boy had been a distraction.

I remembered how he'd looked on Jasper. I'd never be the rider he was if I didn't make another choice, here and now.

Shocks shot out from my spine, stinging me like wasps from within. "We talked about this. Remember? Nothing can interfere with my training. Sunday . . . I was thinking about getting through the lesson so I could be with you."

"And that's my fault?"

"No, but I don't have room to fuck up."

His face took on that stony expression I'd seen whenever he stopped himself from crying about Steve. "Are you breaking up with me?"

My pulse beat in my temples, my ribs. "Yes."

He stared. "What the hell, Roan? After everything we've done, I can't . . . I know I shouldn't have come here, but . . . no, fuck that." He stood up. "I'm not the problem. I can't figure out this thing with your dad. There's something wrong with him, or with you, or fuck, I don't know, both of you."

This was for the best, I thought, before he got any closer, before he figured it out, before I gave in to the urge to blurt out the truth to him, like I wanted to do right now.

I remembered the elasticity of Jasper's back, how engaged and balanced he'd been, the calm connection he'd had with Daddy.

Did I really want a boyfriend who knew the truth about me, in which case he wouldn't be my boyfriend for long, because what boy would want a girl who was fucking her father? Or did I want to be the rider Daddy was?

My throat tightened. "This isn't about him. It's about riding and training and—"

"Keep telling yourself that." Will turned to leave and nearly smacked straight into Daddy.

The room vibrated as if they'd hit head-on. Suspicion flooded Daddy's face. Will's muscles tensed as if he were about to take a swing at a man who had two inches and thirty pounds on him.

"Will," I said sharply.

Both of them looked at me.

"Will," I repeated, "you remember my father. Daddy, Will brought my homework assignments."

Daddy obviously didn't believe me, but the ordinary words, spoken in an ordinary tone, diffused the tension. His expression smoothed into blandness. He put out his hand. "Of course. Will Howard from lit class. Good of you to come all the way out here."

Will waited a beat too long before briefly shaking Daddy's hand.

"No trouble. I was just leaving."

"Thanks," I said.

"No problem." He shot me a dark look.

It was an awkward parting, no "see you at school," no goodbye. Will simply left. He was through playing along. I should feel nothing but relief. He was unpredictable and careless. He'd known better than to come here. Yes, this was for the best.

*Keep telling yourself that.*

"What was he doing here?" Daddy said.

I held out the sheet of notebook paper with my assignments on it.

He scanned it. "I could've emailed your teachers for this."

I patted the books beside me. "I needed these, too." I tucked the paper inside my lit book.

"Did you ask him to do this?"

"No, sir."

"So why him? Why not another one of your classmates?"

"I don't know," I said.

Daddy touched the edge of a daffodil. "And these?"

Will could opt out, but I was committed to playing along. "They're from the class." Any girl could get flowers from a boy.

I had other flowers in my future—namely, those bouquets riders received when medals were hung around their necks.

"You still want me to believe he isn't the one calling the house all the time?"

I tried to make a dismissive face. "I asked him. He said no."

"You expected him to tell the truth?"

I'd played Daddy's game all my life. The playbook was proven and effective.

"It doesn't matter. I don't care about him. Change the number. I don't care. Everybody who needs to call you has your cell. Why do we even need a landline? I don't ever use it. Get rid of it."

"Maybe I will."

I fake-yawned and scooched down in the bed. "Will you wake me for supper? I want to eat with you at the table."

I closed my eyes. He left, but I knew he wasn't satisfied with my answers. Neither was I. Through my relief, I was starting to hurt—but one day, I'd look back and believe sacrificing Will and even parts of myself had been worth it. Will wasn't the love of my life. The love of my life was in the training barn. That's what I had to focus on. Jasper, and riding, and my future.

Not some boy who didn't understand the rules.

# - Sixteen -

SHORTLY BEFORE SIX, I started getting ready for supper. I couldn't be inert and dull-witted at the table. Daddy wouldn't be. He'd had time to think about walking in on Will and me. He'd be on the hunt.

I dressed in clean jeans and a fresh polo shirt and went to my closet for my sneakers. My phone was still plugged in. I'd come to think of it as a lifeline, but my life didn't depend on Will, and my future damned sure didn't.

The person it did depend on was coming up the stairs.

I sat on the edge of my bed to put on my sneakers.

Daddy paused in the doorway, his hair windblown, the smell of horse strong. I missed being grubby and horse-scented.

"You're awake already," he said.

"I had a good nap." I hadn't slept, but I didn't want him to think I'd been lying awake feeling . . . what? Sad. Heavy. Alone. "How'd the afternoon go?"

"Everyone got a good workout, including me. I'm feeling it."

"Good. I mean, I'm glad everyone had a good workout."

"All that riding is a lot on top of everything else," he said. "Rosemont doesn't run itself."

"How can I help?"

He blinked. Score one for me. I'd prove my devotion to him and my career.

"You could show me how to use the bookkeeping program. I can write the checks and print them for you to sign."

His eyes narrowed as he parsed my suggestion. I knew what he was thinking. How much of my offer stemmed from the desire to help, and how much stemmed from the desire to draw attention away from Will's visit?

I laced my sneakers as if I weren't keyed in to every fucking nuance of his thought process. "I need to learn it sooner or later. Or maybe I can do something for Eddie that would free him up to help you."

"I'll see." He meant it literally, that he could see, with his still-narrowed eyes, what I was up to. "I'm hitting the shower."

In the kitchen, Gertrude hummed along with the zydeco streaming from her phone. She took a casserole dish from the oven. Molten cheese bubbled up through cracks in a breadcrumb crust. On the range, something sizzled at high heat in a cast-iron skillet.

"Supper smells awesome."

"Catfish." She closed the oven door with her hip. "And mac and cheese. You look like you feel better."

I opened the silverware drawer. "I do."

She smiled. "Nothing like flowers to brighten someone's day."

I paused in gathering forks and knives. "They were from the class."

"Never said they weren't." She bumped open the swinging door and disappeared into the dining room with the macaroni and cheese.

The bourbon was on the table and supper was on the sideboard when Daddy came downstairs, his hair damp.

He sat down and started making his drink. "I was thinking about your offer. What if you start writing your own blog posts?"

I hated to write, but I couldn't argue with him. I'd offered to help.

"Okay."

His eyebrows went up. I added being too agreeable to the list of things I couldn't be if I didn't want to tip him off.

"We'll draw up a schedule for the posts. I'm thinking twice a week. I'll help you with content."

"Twice a week?" My dismay was real.

"You can't pick and choose the jobs you want to do. It all has to be done."

Score two for me, sort of. I'd have to come up with two posts a week, but I'd steered him back into thinking I wasn't trying to ingratiate myself with him. I almost asked if I would be allowed to post on Facebook and Instagram, too, but I knew the answer. No way was he letting me loose on social media.

Gertrude set his plate in front of him.

"What is this?" he asked.

"Blackened catfish, but I went light on the cayenne."

He gave her a dubious look. She wasn't the best judge of heat. I'd seen her eat raw jalapeños straight from the garden.

"Try it." She took my plate and turned back to the sideboard.

Daddy sampled the fish, and his face relaxed. "Excellent. Thank you."

Steam rose from the food on my plate as she put it back on the table. "That was a nice boy who came to see you this afternoon."

My face went so hot it had to be glowing red. Unfortunately, as I'd learned in biology, flushing was an involuntary response.

"He didn't come to see me. He brought my books."

Daddy's eyes were on me, but he directed his words at Gertrude. "Nice? He struck me as rude."

"Maybe you made him nervous," she said. "Meeting the father?"

The heat flooded down my neck. "He's met Daddy before. He wasn't nervous. He's a jerk. May I have the pepper, please?"

Daddy set the salt cellar and pepper grinder by my plate. "It *was* nice of him to bring her books."

"It was only school stuff," I said.

"And flowers," Daddy reminded me. "Don't forget about those."

He wouldn't.

"They were from the class," Gertrude said.

"So I've been told. Still, he went out of his way. We should thank him."

I ground pepper on my macaroni. "I did thank him."

"What if we invite him over for supper?" Daddy said.

The flush spread to my entire body. "He'll think we're freaks."

"Friday, Gertrude?"

"That'll be fine." She pushed through the swinging door into the kitchen.

"He doesn't want to have supper with us," I said to Daddy.

"Then he can say no. We'll call him this evening and find out."

"I'll ask him at school tomorrow."

"You're staying home the rest of the week. Sitting in the bleachers was too much for you this morning. You're not ready to sit three times that long at a desk. And thanks to Will, you can keep up with your schoolwork."

He only wanted to keep me away from Will until he had a chance to assess the relationship firsthand, but there was no relationship to assess. We'd broken up. Anyway, Will would say no.

After we ate, we went into the study. Daddy sat behind his desk, picked up the handset, and held it out to me. I caught myself before I started to dial.

"I need the phone book."

He put it on the desk between us and leaned back in his chair while I looked up the Howards' number as if I didn't know it by heart. I punched it in.

Mrs. Howard answered. "Hello."

"Hi, Mrs. Howard? This is Roan Montgomery." Saying my last name seemed stilted. I'd talked to her a couple of times. She knew who I was. "May I speak to Will, please?"

"Of course. How do you feel? He said you were hurt."

"I'm fine. I'll be back at school next week." Like a lone rider venturing into the wilderness, if I told someone when to expect me back, I'd have to turn up then. Daddy couldn't hold me captive indefinitely.

"I'll get Will. Glad you're feeling better."

"Thank you, Mrs. Howard." I looked down at the rosewood desk, warm with the patina of age and use.

"Put it on speaker," Daddy said.

I couldn't not do it. I pressed the button. People could usually tell when they were on speaker because the sound was tinny, but I'd have to let Will know right away so I could head off any romantic pleas to get me back.

Daddy and I waited in silence.

"What?" Will's voice was clipped.

Scratch the romantic pleas—but his anger could be telling in its own way.

"Can you hear me okay? You're on speaker."

"Yeah." Still clipped. "Why am I on speaker?"

"My father's here with me. We thought you might like to come to supper Friday." I had no problem sounding cool myself, but my face was approximately the temperature of a geyser.

"Okay," Will said. "What time?"

Okay? He was supposed to say no. I'd make him change his mind before Friday. I'd tell him I didn't want him here. That had been pretty effective this afternoon.

Daddy was expressionless, but his brain was like a computer. Software was always running in the background.

"Five." He spoke loudly enough for Will to hear him.

Supper was always at seven. What were we going to do for two hours?

"I'll be there," Will said.

Like hell.

"See you then." I clicked off the phone and gave the handset back to Daddy. He replaced it in the base.

"I'm tired and my side hurts," I said. "May I go to my room now?"

"Go ahead. I'll be up later to check on you."

Upstairs, I swallowed some aspirin and changed into my nightgown. Then I paced and kept watch from my window, waiting for Daddy to leave the house. An hour passed before he went down to the barn.

I took my cell from the closet.

Will answered after the second ring. "Hello."

He never answered that way.

"It's me," I said.

"Just you?"

"Yes. You can't come to supper."

"How'd I get invited in the first place?" He'd dropped his shortness of tone.

I was too annoyed to modulate mine. "How do you think? You showed up here, and he's all over it."

"What do you mean?"

"The dinner invitation wasn't my idea. He wants to see how we are when we're together."

"So what's he going to see?"

"Nothing, because you're not going to be here."

"You don't think I can pull it off."

"I don't care whether you can pull it off. I don't want you here."

"Since your father invited me, I don't think you can disinvite me."

Anger made my voice unsteady. "Don't do this. I'm telling you I don't want you here. If you show up, anyway . . . I guess that tells me who you really are."

"I guess it does," he said.

The call dropped. Depending on weather and where I was—reception was good by the closet, better near the bed, and nonexistent in the bathroom—service could be sketchy. When I called him back, I went straight to voicemail. He could have been trying to call me at the same time, but there was no beep telling me I had an incoming call, only the beep that came after "It's Will. Leave a message."

The call hadn't dropped. He'd hung up on me and turned off his phone.

"Don't come," I said. "Call the house Friday morning and say you're sick. Unless you want to make my life a whole lot harder, stay away."

I turned off my phone, put it back in the boot, and got in bed, where my heart beat so hard it hurt. Will's visit reflected badly on me, but it had caused me to regain my senses. All he'd done was make my life harder. I'd never needed a boyfriend. I hadn't wanted one. I hadn't known how to hold hands, much less date. I'd known how to fuck him, and I'd done it because like every other rebellious teenager in the world, I'd wanted to defy a parent.

Something about that line of reasoning felt wrong, but I squelched the feeling.

Daddy was right when he said normal was another way of being average. Ordinary.

I wasn't average or ordinary, and I knew it.

In my mind, I tore off the pages of a calendar one by one, all the way back to November, when Will had first noticed me. Mentally, I set fire to the pages, and winter, when my hormones had run away with me, turned to ash. Now it was spring, and I was back in control.

THE NEXT AFTERNOON, after some resistance—who even blogged anymore?—I labored through the first post I'd written in ages. I titled it "When Accidents Happen." In it, I accepted responsibility for not giving my full attention to my lesson, and I gave Daddy credit for anticipating that I needed to give Diva more leg. *Next time Monty Montgomery tells me to do something*, I concluded, *I'll do it!*

At supper, Daddy read it with a skeptical eye. "It doesn't sound like you."

"But I wrote it."

"I'll fix it when I post it."

I looked down at my plate. "How can you sound more like me than I do?"

"Practice. The image we put out to the public is to protect you. People think they know you, but what they really know is your persona—funny, a good student, a good athlete."

"But I am a good student and a good athlete. Or are you saying I'm not?"

"No, the real you goes into it, but what you present publicly is a façade. Speaking of which, we should run through some interview questions."

He started to drill me immediately: Tell me about the accident. What are you doing to stay on top of your game? How have things changed for you since your mother left?

"Why would Vic ask about Mama?"

"Because I think he should."

"You're telling him what to ask?"

"I've made a few suggestions."

"I don't want to talk about her."

"Adversity is an opportunity to show strength."

Like my broken ribs, Mama's abandonment was something we could use, although the opportunity hadn't presented itself until now.

He reached for his water goblet. "What about boys?"

He was trying to throw me with that one.

"What about them?"

"Anyone special?" He adopted Vic's come-on-you-can-tell-me tone. Now and then Vic got a rider to say something embarrassing or overly personal. People like that probably didn't have a façade.

"There has to be someone." He'd nailed Vic's technique.

"Why? Are you jealous?"

It was only a smart-ass remark, but once I'd said it, it took on a different meaning.

His face became stone. "You're suggesting Vic's attracted to you. That's inappropriate."

Both of us knew I hadn't meant Vic.

"I was trying to be funny."

"That wasn't."

"I'm sorry." There was enough regret in my voice for him to give me a short nod.

Since he had all the answers, I appealed to his ego. "What should I say? And what should I say about Mama?"

"I'll work with you on that, but you need to think about what you want to convey."

The chances Mama would see the interview were slim, but if word got back to her, I wanted to make sure she understood how I felt.

"That I'm tough," I said. "I don't need her."

"Think resilient instead of tough. And don't say you don't need her. It's too hostile. We'll work on it."

For the rest of the meal, we made small talk, and then I went to my room. He'd get over the jealousy remark, and by not continuing to apologize, I was giving him room to save face, allowing him to buy into it being a snappy comeback gone wrong. Daddy the Invincible was jealous of a boy he'd called a "snot-nosed high-school punk."

I scanned the pages of my lit book and forced myself to make notes, because otherwise I reached the end of each page without retaining the information, but I kept seeing Will in

Mrs. Kenyon's classroom, sitting one row over and one chair ahead, his head bent over his book.

Daddy tapped on my door and stuck his head in. "Want to do the walk-through?"

I was tired and various parts of my body reminded me I was injured, but I said, "Sure."

My side twanged, so while he walked through all the barns, I hung out with my horses.

"It was my fault," I said to Diva, dropping chunks of carrot in her bucket and withdrawing my hand before she could bite it. "You did what I told you to do."

She nosed around in her bucket and ate some carrot, her ears so flat against her head that she looked earless. Still chewing, she slithered into the recesses of her stall.

Two doors down, Jasper pressed his muzzle against the bars of his stall door and breathed on me. I reached through the bars and stroked his ears while he ate. "I'll try harder."

Back at the house, Daddy and I went upstairs together.

He paused in the doorway of my room and looked at my desk. "Keeping up with your homework?"

"Yes, sir."

His eyes roamed around my room and landed on the daffodils on my nightstand. I should have thrown them out.

His hand went to the back of my neck. His fingers slid the elastic from my ponytail and wound through my hair, loosening it. Then he held the elastic out to me.

I started to take it, but he pulled it out of reach. I had a hundred ponytail holders in my bathroom so there was no need to reach for it—except he wanted me to, so I did, which brought my mouth within an inch of his.

"Don't stay up too late." He pressed the elastic into my hand and kissed my forehead. "Love you, darlin'."

He turned and went down the hall.

The feeling that I'd been subtly humiliated kept me standing there for a moment. One of these days, I'd be the one who walked away.

I considered texting Will, but what would I say? *Don't come. Do come, but play by Daddy's rules, if you can figure out what they are. I wish I hadn't broken up with you.*

That last sentence was reason enough not to text him. I ignored the ache swelling inside me and resolved to focus on being who Daddy and I wanted me to be.

# - Seventeen -

I GOT THROUGH Thursday and most of Friday by doing homework, drafting another blog post, practicing for the interview, auditing lessons, and making notes about where I needed to improve. All day Friday, I felt alternately feverish and chilled from nerves.

In the afternoon, Daddy finished working Diva. I climbed down from the bleachers to accompany them to the barn.

"Go change, darlin'. Your guest will be here in an hour."

My jeans and T-shirt were clean, mostly. Earlier Vigo had blown a big horsey raspberry as I'd passed by him in the cross-ties, spraying me with grass-colored saliva, but my shirt was only slightly spattered. "What's wrong with this?"

"Go change."

"Into what?"

"Something more appropriate for company. Do you want me to pick it out for you?"

His agitation caught me off guard. He'd been masking it well the past few days.

"I'll find something," I said.

Changing clothes wouldn't be enough. Even though I wasn't riding or grooming, I'd picked up the horse smell. I showered and washed my hair and strapped myself back into the rib belt. My ribs made it impossible to keep my arms up long enough to use the blow-dryer, so I towel-dried my hair and braided it while it was still damp. It was a fat, lopsided braid, but it was off my face and out of the way.

I'd been trying to demonstrate that Will wasn't worth dressing up for, but Daddy, keen on my being appropriate these days, would find meaning in whatever I wore. I chose gray linen pants and a gray-green cotton sweater Mama had brought home from one of her shopping marathons. I took the scissors from my desk drawer and snipped off the tags, slipped on a pair of ballet flats I'd never worn, either, and looked at myself in the mirror. Modest. Drab.

With luck, the whole evening would be drab. Daddy would see nothing, and Will would . . . I had no idea what Will would see or say or do. I imagined whispering in his ear, *The reason I can't keep seeing you is that I can't keep fucking both of you.*

In my mind, I saw his horror and disgust. He wouldn't understand. No one would. In many ways, I didn't understand, either, so why should I expect anyone else to? I'd chosen cooperation and obedience, and I had to live with everything that meant, including keeping the secret. I would *not* allow my carefully constructed life to fall apart. The only people who needed to know were Daddy and me.

The grandfather clock in the hall chimed five o'clock, and I turned away from the mirror.

In the study, Daddy was checking his email. He'd showered and changed, too.

"That's better." He paused. "Your hair looks pretty."

Saying I hadn't been trying to look pretty would be like clipping a precariously balanced rail. I didn't want any rails coming down tonight.

"Thanks." I sat in one of the leather chairs and paged through the current issue of *Classic Equine*. Daddy clicked through his inbox, sometimes typing a reply before moving on to the next message.

I turned the page and spotted an ad for barn blueprints. "What if I write about that toy barn I had when I was a kid?"

"Why?"

"A lot of kids play with them. I could write about always having this dream, and how a dream turned into goals."

"You have advantages other kids don't. The finest horses money can buy. Me."

"Even a kid with a backyard pony can work on being a better rider. Not everyone wants to go to the Olympics."

"I'm not sold. Keep trying."

"You said you'd help me with content."

"I'm helping you by telling you to keep trying."

*What if I write about what you do to me?*

Will's engine grumbled in the distance. My stomach dove toward my knees, and Daddy's ears all but swiveled toward the open window. I folded down a page corner to mark an article on hoof care.

"What if I did a how-to video? How to groom a horse."

"Too elementary."

I looked back down at the magazine.

"I believe your guest is here," Daddy said.

"You keep calling him that. He's not my guest. He's yours."

The engine stopped outside the window. The door to the truck opened and closed, and I heard—we heard—someone coming up the front steps.

The doorbell rang.

"Answer the door, darlin'."

In the few steps it took me to get to the door, I thought, *You'll get through this*, but one look at Will and I had my doubts.

His eyes hadn't become bluer in the past four days; I'd forgotten how blue they were to begin with. I remembered well, however, how flinty they'd been when he'd left on Tuesday. The flint was gone. I'd worried that if he didn't look angry, he'd look wounded, but his expression was composed.

My irritation with him ebbed, but in its place was the emotional rawness I'd buried all week—and now wasn't the time to feel it, either, much less show it. I had to keep control of everything tonight, starting with myself.

"Hi," he said.

How could he sound the same?

"Hi." I sounded the same, too. Maybe that part wasn't so hard. "Come in."

"How do you feel?"

"Better, thanks." I closed the door, my back to him. Wow. Heartache was an actual physical thing. "This way." I led him through the wide double doors into the study.

Daddy was typing. "Be right with you, darlin'."

Will stopped at the medal case, as if he'd never seen Daddy's medals before. He leaned over to examine them, and his hair fell forward. He wore khaki pants and a blue oxford shirt. I almost made a comment about his shirt being tucked in, but conversation needed to be impersonal and polite, like he was a stranger.

He straightened and caught me watching him. "Are these what I think they are?"

"Depends on what you think they are." Good. Flippant.

"Olympic medals."

"Then yes."

"Among others." Daddy clicked the mouse with finality, stood up, and came around the desk. "These"—he tapped the glass, indicating the cluster of medals displayed in the center—"are the Olympic medals."

Will eyed the cups and trophies on the shelves. "How many of these do you have?"

"A few. Some are my father's and grandfather's. Some are hers." He indicated me with a tilt of his head. "Thanks for coming, Will. I always like to get to know Roan's friends."

He'd had approximately zero interest in getting to know Roan's friends until now, not that there were many to know.

"Thanks for inviting me," Will said.

They shook hands.

"Thought you might enjoy a tour of the farm before supper. You up to a walk, darlin'?"

"Yes, sir." I'd crawl, if I had to, to keep them from spending time alone with each other.

With Will on his right and me on his left, Daddy launched into tour-guide mode, pointing out different parts of the farm as we made our way toward the barn.

We approached the field where the yearlings were turned out.

"You'll have seen this year's foals on your way in. These are last year's." He vaulted lightly over the fence, showing off.

Even the youngest foals knew and trusted Daddy; he imprinted on them as soon as they were born. The yearlings trotted up to him eagerly. Will and I waited outside the pasture as he moved among the horses, rubbing an ear here, scratching a shoulder there. A bay nudged his arm. "Hi, Sadie." He stroked her neck and began telling Will how she'd colicked and lost her foal the night before Thanksgiving. "If I remember correctly, that's the day you gave Roan a lift."

"That's right," Will said.

I braced myself.

"When Sadie recovered, I put her with this group. This mare here, Marvel"—Daddy nodded toward another bay—"is her mother, and that dark colt with the star is her brother Buddy. Marvel took care of Sadie, which was what I'd hoped would happen, but the bond between Sadie and Buddy surprised me. You'd see that in a band of wild horses, but not on a breeding farm."

"Do you think they knew they were siblings?" Will asked.

"Could be. I've been around these animals since before I could walk, and I'll still never know everything about them."

He distributed some farewell pats and rejoined us outside the fence.

"Will you breed Sadie again?" Will said.

"Already have. All these mares are in foal. By the time the babies drop, the yearlings will be two-year-olds and ready for sale. Since we only breed any given mare every other year, we keep the mothers and foals together for two years. I have a real resistance to treating horses like they're on a production line."

I could find fault with Daddy for a lot of things, but the way he bred and trained horses wasn't one of them, and it was good, I guessed, that he and Will were talking.

At the barn, the grooms had begun their evening chores, mucking, bringing horses in from the pastures and paddocks, and tending to any small ailments. The horses pinned their ears and showed their teeth. Diva pawed at the bottom of her stall door in a steady, deafening rhythm that made everyone cringe.

"Feeding time," Daddy said over the banging.

Eddie poked his head out of the office. "Evening, boss."

"Eddie," Daddy said, "this is Roan's friend Will. Eddie's my assistant."

"Nice to know you." Eddie smiled broadly and pumped Will's hand.

Daddy's eyes took on a shrewd vigilance; Gertrude had told Eddie about Will.

I pressed my hand to my side. "Ow."

All eyes turned to me.

"You all right?" Daddy asked.

"Little uncomfortable." My ribs didn't hurt worse than they had all day, but the interruption served its purpose: diverting attention from Eddie's overly warm welcome of Will. "I'm okay."

"Hey, boss," Eddie said, "you got a minute? I have some questions about the new supplements."

"Darlin', why don't you show Will your horses?"

Will followed me down the aisle to Diva's stall. She stopped pawing at her door long enough to rake her teeth against the bars, making the metal ring.

"Jesus." He took a step back.

"This is Diva," I said.

"The one who threw you?"

I felt Daddy watching us, even though he stood with Eddie outside the office.

"Yeah. Moving on."

We stopped in front of Jasper's stall. He came immediately to the door and pressed his muzzle against the bars.

"This is Jasper," I said. "Sorry, no treats. Dinner's on the way."

"He's huge," Will said, playing along with the charade that this was the first time he'd seen him.

I introduced him to Vigo, whom he'd seen before, too. I'd ridden him to one of our meetings on the fire road.

He studied Vigo through the bars. "You okay?" he said quietly.

"Why wouldn't I be?"

Diva's banging made it impossible for anyone except Will to hear me, but I was annoyed he'd asked. A boy who hardly knew me wouldn't have asked that, not in the way Will had.

He shook his head, as if he shouldn't need to explain why I might not be okay, as if breaking up with him should have devastated me.

"You said you could pull this off," I reminded him.

"I can." He looked past me and smiled.

"Let's get away from this racket," Daddy said from behind me. Chills rippled through me. "I'll show you the breeding stallions."

His expression was pure tour guide, but he put a firm hand at the small of my back and kept it there even when Will and I fell into step on either side of him.

On the wide pea-graveled paths that separated the stallions' paddocks, he continued his patter. "Each stud has his own enclosure. They're close enough to see each other and feel like they're in a herd, but they'd fight if they had a chance. They do, in the wild. The dominant stallion even chases off his male offspring when they're two or three years old. It avoids inbreeding. Nature's smart."

The gravel crunched under our feet.

"What about the female offspring?" Will said.

"He doesn't breed with them. They'll breed to one of the subservient stallions."

"Would horses like this know not to do it?"

"No," Daddy began, but Mateo approached us leading Noble, who was tossing his head and rattling the stud chain, and we went temporarily single-file to allow them to pass. "These animals haven't been in a feral environment for generations. They don't have the same relationships they form in a band. Given the chance, any one of them would mount his own daughter."

*Mount his own daughter* branded itself in my brain.

We came to Byron's paddock.

"Most of the stallions tend to be hard to handle," Daddy said. "All power and testosterone."

Byron plunged up and down the fence line, bucking and snorting.

"This is Byron, the last of the horses I competed on. The others are dead now."

"You rode this thing?"

I couldn't see Will, on Daddy's other side, but he sounded impressed.

"All the way to half a dozen gold medals. I still ride him a couple of times a week. Keeps both of us in shape."

Byron shied at a figment of his imagination and bolted around the paddock.

Will leaned forward so he could see me. "He looks like the one who threw you."

"She's his daughter," I said.

"Like father, like daughter," Will observed.

"That's a good point, Will," Daddy said. "They're both destined for greatness, Diva and Roan, if they want it enough."

That last part was intended for me.

"It's all I've ever wanted," I said.

If Will were stung by my response, he hid it. "So, one day you'll have your own case full of gold medals and more trophies than you can count?"

"If she works hard," Daddy said.

"Well . . . doesn't she?"

That wasn't exactly confrontational, but in the pause, I knew Daddy was wondering why a boy I professed to barely know had given any thought to how hard I worked.

"I mean," Will said, "she's on this special schedule at school—"

That one might be okay. Plenty of kids resented my schedule.

"—and I watched some videos, and she wins a lot."

Whether he meant to or not, he sounded like he was defending me. Daddy would wonder about that, too.

I kept my eyes on Byron, bucking on the far side of his paddock.

"What videos?" Daddy asked.

"I searched Montgomery eventing. Hundreds of videos came up. I only watched a few, but I saw you ride in the Olympics. Not this horse, though. It was red."

"Brandy," Daddy said. "She broke her neck during the cross-country at Pan Am three years later. What did you think of the videos?"

"They blew me away."

"Did you see any difference between Roan's riding and mine?"

Will hesitated. "I don't know enough about riding to have noticed."

Daddy forgave his ignorance with a fair degree of tolerance. "If she's going to carry on the legacy, she needs to work harder. Be better. Stronger. She can be good, or she can be the best. Up to her." He took Byron's halter from the hook on the fence. "Let's bring him in."

He went into the paddock.

*The legacy?* Will mouthed.

I shrugged and watched Psycho Pony the Elder gallop up to Daddy and skid to a stop, clods of earth flying up. Daddy rubbed the thick, muscular neck, passed the headstrap of the halter behind Byron's ears, and slipped the noseband over his muzzle. "Darlin', get the gate."

He was showing off again, demonstrating that he was more than a match for all that equine power and testosterone. I swung open the gate, and Will and I stood well back while he led Byron out. The stallion danced around, pulling on the lead rope. Daddy jiggled the stud chain to distract him.

I closed the gate, and we followed at a distance, out of kicking range, but not necessarily out of earshot. Just as well. If I talked to Will, I'd be forced to think about what I'd given up. I had to focus on what I was gaining. We were approaching the magical, peaceful hour that came after lessons, after grooming and cleaning, after feeding, which made it easier to see my future. The boy walking beside me made it harder. Breaking up with him had been the right thing to do. I ordered myself to feel better about it.

Byron minced sideways for a few steps, flinging his head high, and I sensed more than saw the lag in Will's gait.

I broke my silence. "Don't worry. Daddy's got him."

"It's like he speaks Horse."

"It's his first language."

Daddy led Byron into his stall and removed the halter. The stallion pushed his head into his bucket of grain. Daddy joined us in the aisle and rolled the door closed.

"It's incredible," Will said, "the control you have over a horse like that."

"It comes from knowing the animal." Daddy hung the halter and lead rope on the hook on the stall door. "Want to see more?"

"You bet."

Pain pulsed in my side like the world's worst stitch.

In the breeding shed, Daddy explained that there were no live covers because of the risk of injury to both the stallion and the mare. He pointed out the tease stall, where the presence of an in-heat mare was used to arouse the stallion.

"The scent is enough to let him know he's in a sexual situation," Daddy said.

*Sexual situation* hung in the cool, tranquil air.

"Stallions have different preferences when it comes to collecting semen," he continued. "This is the breeding mount. We apply some of the estrus mare's urine to the mount, and between that and the tease stall, most of the stallions are more than ready to mount it. The AV handler usually stands about here."

"What's an AV?" Will asked, even as I mentally begged him not to.

"Artificial vagina." Daddy took a few steps to a cupboard, opened the cabinet door, removed a long plastic cylinder, and tossed it underhanded to Will. "AV."

Will held it as if it were made of thorns.

"There are various models, but they all work the same way. The handler stimulates the stallion's penis and deflects it into the AV right before he—"

"Okay," I interrupted. "That's enough."

"What is it, darlin'?" Daddy's eyes glinted.

"We get it." I returned the AV to the cabinet. "Can we move on?"

"I'll leave it up to your guest."

Will's face remained neutral. "What do you do after you collect the semen?"

Daddy led us into the lab, and his patter became less about sex and more about equipment. Ultrasounds, microscopes, and sperm counters were all nice and scientific. It was like being in biology class, except for a mercifully brief description of how the mares were inseminated.

The tour ended in the dressage arena, where Daddy explained what the mirrors and letters were for and Will asked an occasional question, but the pain in my side had increased so much that I could barely follow the conversation.

When at last we started back to the house, I trailed behind them.

Will looked over his shoulder. "You okay back there?"

*Don't ask about me.*

"My side hurts."

They waited for me to catch up.

Daddy put the back of his hand on my cheek. "You're warm. Take some aspirin when we get to the house." He stroked my cheek and then gave it a pat.

The walk to the house wasn't long, but it was uphill, and I was breathless when we reached the front porch. I went straight upstairs, gulped down a couple of aspirin, and returned to the study, where Daddy was making a bourbon while Will looked through a copy of *The Book on Eventing* and drank something fizzy from a tall, icy glass.

"Gertrude brought you a ginger ale." Daddy indicated an identical glass on a cocktail napkin on his desk, next to a platter of homemade cheese straws and bite-sized appetizers made with radishes and sugar-snap peas.

I sat down in the chair beside Will's.

He closed the book. "Such an interesting career you've had. What was your favorite part?"

"I've enjoyed all of it. Riding, writing, even modeling." Daddy pretended to fasten an imaginary cuff link. "This was my signature pose, for what it's worth."

Will smiled.

"What I love most is what I'm doing now. Training horses, you get to know them in ways even their riders don't. And coaching, you get to know your students in ways they don't know themselves. You see their potential. And their flaws."

A lot of riders called themselves Daddy's students, but they'd only taken clinics with him. He'd coached two riders full-time, Jamie and me, and he wasn't coaching Jamie anymore. The potential and flaws were mine.

"I heard you say I speak Horse," Daddy said. "She does, too. She was born with talent." He reached for a cheese straw. "Problem is, most people who are born with it never accomplish anything because they think talent's enough. Have a cheese straw. Gertrude's an incredible cook."

Will took one and looked at me. "Do you think talent's enough?"

"I know it isn't."

"The dedication and discipline it takes to get where she wants to go," Daddy said, "are as rare as talent."

We sat there, three cheese-straw-munching fools. Well, Daddy was no fool. And Will wasn't, either. I'd been the fool, believing I could have everything I wanted.

At last, Gertrude called us to the table.

"What do you think of the farm?" Daddy asked Will as we took our seats.

"It's amazing. I didn't know about the training and breeding. I just thought you rode horses."

"I've been fortunate to do quite a bit of that, too. So has Roan."

"You can still outride me," I said to Daddy.

"For now," Will said.

"You make another good point, Will. Her whole career is ahead of her if she doesn't muck it up."

Gertrude had prepared the kind of meal she used to make when Mama was here, a variety of colors, flavors, and textures to tempt the palate, overcompensating for the simple meals Daddy and I preferred.

She set a dish of butter on the table. "Did you enjoy seeing the farm?"

"Very much," Will said. "There's a lot more to it than I realized."

"Sugar, you feeling all right?"

I forced a smile. "I'm fine."

She looked doubtful but didn't press me. When she returned to the kitchen, Daddy said to Will, "You made quite an impression on Gertrude the other day."

Will spread his napkin in his lap. "All I did was drop off some books."

"And those pretty flowers," Daddy said.

"I told you, they were from the class," I said before Will could comment. That was what I should have texted him, a warning that the flowers were from the class. I stared at him, trying to communicate telepathically.

"Chelsea's idea," he said. "The yearbook staff did their daffodil fundraiser this week."

"Tell me about your family," Daddy said. "Your parents own a construction company?"

Will wasn't the only one who'd done his research.

"Mom's the architect and Dad's the builder. They specialize in green building. I help during summers and school holidays."

"Is this what you want to do for a living—go into the building trades?" He sounded incredibly class-conscious, not his usual style.

"I might. I'm not sure."

"You have time," Daddy replied. "No reason someone your age should commit to anything."

I almost spat out a mouthful of asparagus. He'd mapped out my future when I was a zygote.

"Do you have any brothers or sisters?"

"A sister. She's six." Will hesitated. "I had a brother. He died a few months ago."

That brought Daddy up short. "I'm sorry. It must be hard for your family."

"I've been trying to take his place in some ways, you know, spending time with my parents, doing stuff with Carrie. It's too bad she won't have the same big brother I had."

I looked across the table at him, unexpectedly moved. His eyes met mine. I looked away immediately, the exchange as brief as a heartbeat, but in the pause that followed, I knew Daddy had seen it.

"I'm sure your parents appreciate what you're doing." If the note of sympathy in his voice rang true, it was because he knew how to hide his emotions better than Will and I did. My nerves began to gin up that feverish feeling again.

"Who are you reading for the literary naturalism essay?" I asked.

"Steinbeck. You?"

"Stephen Crane."

"Mrs. Kenyon said anyone who writes on Crane won't be graded higher than a B. Don't reckon you'd like that with your GPA."

My grades were like my short schedule, perhaps something he shouldn't have noticed but not uncommon knowledge. Still, this was an opportunity to prove to Daddy there was nothing between Will and me.

"You might have told me when you brought my homework." I hadn't started researching much less writing the essay, but Will and Daddy didn't know that.

"She only told us yesterday."

"You could've called." Too late I remembered that associating phone calls with Will was a bad idea around Daddy.

"You said calling was against the rules," Will said.

One of those full-body flushes bloomed inside me.

Will looked from me to Daddy and back at me. "After Thanksgiving you told me not to call you again, right?"

I had told him that. Daddy had directed me to. I couldn't get in trouble for doing something he'd told me to do.

"I'm curious," Daddy said. "Have you been doing it, anyway? Calling the house?"

His tone was pleasant, his eyes lit by what could have been amusement, but his I-was-young-once conspiratorial demeanor was a trap.

Will never called the house, never even called my cell. "No, sir."

"The thing is, Will, we keep getting these hang-ups. We don't know where they're coming from because whoever it is blocks Caller ID. The only thing that shows up is *Anonymous*. Are you Anonymous?"

"Like I said, it's not me. I'm pretty sure the only time I've called was Thanksgiving."

"Pretty sure," Daddy said, "or sure? Be precise."

A second had never seemed so long.

"I'm sure I've called precisely once," Will said. "How's that?"

Daddy's squint made the wrinkles radiating toward his temples look like smile lines, but they weren't.

Will's smile wasn't real, either.

"Good," Daddy said, "because if you were calling, I'd tell you Roan's too young for boys."

"That's between the two of you, but if I wanted to date a girl, I'd just ask her out."

Gertrude swept in to clear the plates. "How was everything?"

"One of the most amazing meals I've ever had," Will said. "Thank you."

"Thank you, sugar. I hope you saved room for dessert."

Daddy declined dessert in favor of another bourbon. Gertrude returned from the kitchen with coffee for him—good, he'd had a lot of bourbon—and small pyramids of gelato for Will and me.

I ate a spoonful of ice cream and surreptitiously watched Will take a bite.

"Are you in the honor society, Will?" Daddy asked.

"Afraid not."

"What are your grades like?"

"Cs mostly."

"Well, that's average." He sounded as if he were reassuring Will that there was nothing wrong with being average. "Roan spends quite a bit of time on schoolwork. Hard work pays off."

Will didn't offer any explanation for his grades. As much as I wanted to jump to his defense, I couldn't.

"I believe in being prepared," Daddy said, "whether it's homework or a show or an interview." He regarded me with that trademark look, a combination of pride and indulgence, the look I always returned with a gaze that said, *I'm Daddy's girl, the luckiest girl in the world.*

I produced the gaze.

Will studied his dessert.

"Did Roan tell you about the interview she's doing with SNN?"

"Sports News Network?" Will said. "Cool."

"No big deal," I said.

"Sounds like a big deal to me."

Daddy gave me a stern look. "It is a big deal, Will."

The way he kept calling Will by name reminded me of Mrs. Adams repeating my name. Daddy was trying to soften him up, and Will didn't know how to be cagey, not like I did.

The combination of nerves and listening to Daddy spin the SNN interview into something bigger than it was and eating too much rich food made my stomach hurt. I put my spoon down, and after another bite, Will did, too.

He appeared to be listening attentively, but as soon as Daddy paused in his monologue, he said, "I'm sorry, but my head is killing me. I need to get home."

"Put your tongue in the roof of your mouth," Daddy said. "Best cure for an ice-cream headache."

"It isn't the ice cream. It's a migraine. I noticed when we got back to the house that you both had these shiny auras. That's how they start." He placed his napkin on the table. "I have to get home before it gets worse. I might still be able to take something and head it off."

Did he really feel a migraine coming on, or did he just want to leave?

"Do you need someone to drive you?" Daddy asked.

"I'm okay to drive."

"We'll walk you out."

We followed Will into the entrance hall. Daddy put his arm around my shoulders.

"Thanks for having me over and for the tour."

"Our pleasure." Daddy pulled me close and pressed his lips on top of my own pounding head. I dropped my eyes, but not before an odd expression crossed Will's face.

"See you Monday." His voice was hesitant, and in it I heard, *Look at me.*

I didn't. "Yeah."

We waited in the doorway while Will went down the steps and got in his truck. He started the engine, and it idled for several seconds. I wished he'd get out and bound up the steps and punch Daddy in the throat.

He shifted into gear and drove down the hill.

"Has anything happened?" Daddy asked.

"Sir?"

He spoke slowly and distinctly. "Has anything happened between you and Will?"

I raised my eyes to his and kept my voice level. "Of course not."

"He knows a lot about you."

I didn't blink. "He watched some videos."

"Darlin', I can tell when I'm being lied to. I could tell with your mother, and I can tell with you."

"I'm not lying." I started to go inside, but he caught my upper arm and kissed me, hard. His hubris took my breath away, but as always, he was invincible. No housekeeper appeared in the entrance hall to catch us. No boy in a white truck rode to my rescue.

He broke the kiss. "You have feelings for him."

"I don't."

Daddy followed me inside. "He brought you flowers."

"From the class."

He trailed me up the stairs like he had my scent. "What class?"

"The junior class. He was the delivery boy. That's all."

I went into my room, but when I started to close the door, he pushed his way inside.

"Have you had sex with that boy?"

"Jesus, Daddy. Of course not."

He closed the door.

"Gertrude's downstairs."

"Not the first time," he said, but he hesitated. All that bourbon had left him less sharp than usual.

"Go to bed," I said.

"You're in love with that boy."

"No, sir, I'm not." I didn't dare blink.

"Don't lie!" he roared, and he so seldom yelled that I couldn't help cringing.

My mistake. I'd shown weakness, and he pressed his advantage, my ribs be damned, the pain be damned, *me* be damned.

He didn't bother to undress himself or me all the way. I still wore my sweater and the rib belt and he was still in his polo shirt when he thrust into me so hard that my vision went gray except for a blizzard of twinkle lights.

I'd made my choice, and this was the consequence, and it must have been acceptable or I'd have chosen differently, and now, with Will gone, I needed to convince the calculating, angry, drunken man glaring down at me that I'd chosen him. I hated him, his hairy forearms braced on either side of my head, his hot breath, his citrus smell, but I'd chosen him.

His steady thrusting drew whimpers from me. He wasn't concerned with the cause, pleasure or pain or abject misery. He was getting what he wanted.

After a while, he withdrew and turned on his back. I turned on my left side, seeking relief, and as soon as I did, his body spooned around mine, and he pulled the elastic from my braid, his fingers loosening the plait. His nose rooted through my hair, and he kissed the back of my neck.

*Come back, Will. Come back. Come upstairs. Find me like this.*

As awful as that would be, whatever the consequences, this— this *thing*, whatever it was Daddy and I did—would be over.

# - Eighteen -

"FLIP THEM OVER when you see bubbles," Gertrude said.

What were the globs of pancake batter on the griddle going to do, boil? But she was busy juicing oranges, so I watched for bubbles. Sure enough, air bubbles began to pock the surface, bursting and making pinprick holes in the batter. I leveraged the turner under each pancake and flipped it, leaving thin smears of batter that hardened immediately.

The sound of the juicer drilled into my brain. My headache had been constant since my fall. I wondered if Will had been able to stop his migraine before it took a stronger hold—if he'd even had one.

"Did you have a good time last night?" Gertrude asked.

"It was okay."

She paused, half a hollowed-out orange in her hand. "Sugar, you're allowed to have a good time. You can like a boy."

"I don't like him. And I have a good time."

She halved another orange with a *thock* of the knife. "All you do is ride horses and go to school. When do you have fun?"

"Riding's fun." I lifted the edge of a pancake and tried to see under it. "Are these done?"

"Yeah. Put them on the plate under the warmer and pour some more batter on the griddle."

The juicer whirred intermittently. I stacked pancakes on the waiting plate and ladled out more batter. It ran together to form a giant four-leaf clover. Good luck.

She poured the juice into a chilled pitcher. "You don't ride for fun. You ride to win."

"Winning's fun."

"You aren't that thick, sugar. You don't want to hear what I'm saying."

I sighed. "What are you saying?"

She assumed a firm expression. "You need to not work so hard all the time. You need to be a teenager and have fun for the sake of having fun."

"Tell that to Daddy," I muttered and then added quickly, "No, don't. Please."

"I've worked for your daddy for thirty years. I know when to say something and when not to."

"I don't think you do."

The firmness of her expression replaced by offense, she turned away and put the orange peels in the trash.

I didn't have so many allies that I could afford to lose one. Besides, Gertrude was the last person I'd ever want to hurt.

"I'm sorry. I didn't mean that the way it came out."

A scorched smell rose from the griddle, and she shouldered me aside, taking the turner and flipping the cloverleaf.

"Please don't be upset. It's just . . . that 'meeting the father' thing last night. Daddy doesn't want me to have any distractions."

"I know what your daddy wants."

The same words I'd just uttered popped into my mind again: *I don't think you do.*

She put the overdone cloverleaf on the warming plate. "He wants you all to himself."

I stared at her.

She poured batter into evenly sized puddles on the griddle. "He didn't want to share you with your mother. He doesn't want to share you with friends. And he sure doesn't want to share you with a boyfriend. That was evident last night."

Unspoken words crowded against the back of my teeth, my standard defense of Daddy, most recently delivered to Mrs. Adams: I trained all the time. I didn't have time for friends.

Gertrude smiled gently. "It isn't my place to interfere. Eddie reminds me of that every time I want to say something."

Eddie and Gertrude talked about us—and to the degree that she'd expressed opinions about Daddy's parenting? I didn't have time to digest that little tidbit before she continued.

"You know you can talk to me, right, sugar? About anything."

I wasn't about to volunteer any information, but I wouldn't demean her offer by playing dumb, either.

"I know," I said.

She nodded and turned away from me, conversation over.

I filled a stoneware mug with coffee and took it outside to the front porch. Gertrude didn't know about Daddy and me, I thought. She was just inviting me to open up to her, the same way Mrs. Adams had.

I sampled the coffee, which tasted like dirt and skunk. I set it aside and leaned against one of the big white columns. The oak trees formed a soaring green arbor that ran the length of the driveway. The vast lawn was manicured into placidity. The pastures where the horses grazed were comparatively wild, and beyond them, the wooded hills wilder. Rosemont was the perfect prison. It held me more securely than any cell.

My jailor came into view, striding up the hill. As he neared the porch, I picked up the mug and held it out to him.

"What's this?" he asked.

"Poison."

Another wise-ass answer gone wrong.

I backpedaled. "I don't know how you drink it like that."

He took the cup from me, peered at the coffee, and sipped. "Tastes fine to me." He sat down beside me on the step. "What are you doing out here?"

"Gertrude's making breakfast. I was in the way."

He took another drink of coffee. "How do you feel?"

The delicacy of his tone told me it was not an ordinary inquiry but a morning-after question.

"That hurt last night," I said.

He lifted his chin in acknowledgment. "We should hold off until your ribs heal." He studied his coffee. "Darlin' . . . I need to know you take this seriously—all of it. I meant what I said to that boy. You have the potential for greatness. I won't watch you throw it away."

He usually delivered that line as part of a lecture, complete with the assurance that if I wanted to be ordinary, he could make it happen. Today he sounded concerned, which was undoubtedly genuine, but also a means of manipulating me. I didn't exactly fall for it, but I preferred it to his harshness.

"I'll push you right to the edge sometimes," he said, "but I'll make you the best. You have to want this life, though. It isn't a hobby. If you lose focus, if you lose your head over some boy, especially a boy like that . . ."

*A boy who was kind and compassionate and funny. A boy who made me feel okay.*

With each pulse of my headache, I could have sworn my eyes bulged out of my skull, cartoon-style. "I want it." I paused. "I'll do whatever it takes."

"That means you ride, you go to school, you smile for the cameras, you do what I tell you to do."

"Yes, sir."

"You don't lose your head over Will Howard." His mouth quirked when he said Will's name, an involuntary tic.

"I'm not losing my head over anyone."

His eyes bored into mine. Before Will, he'd never doubted me. I'd done this to myself.

The front door opened behind us. "There you are," Gertrude said. "Hope you're hungry. Roan made pancakes."

Daddy stood up. "Really?"

"I messed some up." I could get up and down on my own, but to reinforce the idea that I didn't mind his touch, I took the hand he held out.

In the dining room, I helped myself to a short stack of Gertrude's perfectly round, perfectly golden pancakes. As I sat down, I glanced across the table at Will's chair. I hoped he *had* been lying about getting a migraine, because if migraines felt anything like concussions, I wouldn't wish this on anyone.

I reached for the maple syrup.

"Tomorrow's going to be demanding," Daddy said. "You're shooting all day. Oh, and Vic and Laura are staying for supper."

I'd accepted I'd spend a full day filming; I wasn't prepared for guests staying into the evening, but I assumed a cooperative expression. Daddy needed to know I was up to the job.

"I want you fresh tomorrow. The point of this is to show people you're strong, not weak. I don't want you at the barn today."

"It doesn't take much strength to watch you ride," I said, though watching Daddy ride my horses was hard. It reminded me I wasn't good enough for them.

"Take a nap. Do your homework, write a post, review your answers for tomorrow—not so much that you sound scripted, though. I want you to sound unrehearsed."

That would be a challenge. We'd been running lines since Monday.

He opened the newspaper Gertrude had left beside his plate, removed the sports section, and folded it into quarters. Fucking Vic, I thought. No, that wasn't fair. The interview wasn't Vic's fault. Daddy could have scheduled it in another week—except, being Daddy, he couldn't. I had to prove to everyone right fucking now that I was still the prodigy roaring toward a place on the U.S. team. Unstoppable.

Gertrude moved in and out of the room, refilling Daddy's mug, removing the serving dishes, giving me a wink, which I returned with a wink of my own, though I didn't feel much like it. Her insight about last night had been sobering. She disappeared into the kitchen.

"What was that for?" Daddy was looking over the top of the newspaper.

"What was what for?"

"That winking business with Gertrude."

"I don't know. Sometimes we wink."

He refolded the sports section into its original size and reassembled the newspaper. Mama used to leave sections of the paper scattered all over the house, which drove him crazy.

Gertrude returned to take away our dishes. "What would you like to serve tomorrow night?"

"What about the tenderloin you mentioned?"

"The lamb?"

"Yes, that'll be fine."

Lamb. For me.

"Pick out something nice to wear tomorrow," Daddy said as he stood up. "Something practical for walking. They want B roll of you showing Vic around." He turned to go and then turned back. "How about your navy polo shirt and a pair of those cuffed riding pants with the paddock boots I gave you for Christmas? Blue looks good on camera."

He knew exactly how he wanted me to be in this interview: fresh, unrehearsed, and in blue. At least I got to pick out my own socks and underwear.

"Cool," I said.

"Good. Well, I'm off to the barn. See you at lunchtime. Rest up."

Then and there, I learned I didn't have to see him ride my horses to feel bad about it. Knowing he was riding them was enough to hollow out my midsection.

I hoped the physical act of opening my lit book would give me the momentum to find another writer for my essay. I'd chosen Crane because I only had to read a short story and do some superficial research and I'd be done. I needed to pick someone else today, because Vic would be here all day tomorrow and the outline was due Monday.

Opening my book gave me no momentum whatsoever—but even if I settled for a B, I'd still pull an A for the course.

Good enough.

I took my notebook downstairs, booted up Daddy's computer, which I had blanket permission to use for homework, and outlined Crane's short life. His death at twenty-eight was a bonus, since I didn't have decades to cover, but he'd packed a lot into those years: a career, travel, affairs, scandal, adventure. I focused on the wreck of the *Commodore* and the short story he'd written afterward, "The Open Boat." No wonder Mrs. Kenyon wouldn't grade essays on Crane higher than a B. This was too easy. I finished the outline and printed it.

Homework done, I returned to my room, pulled out the clothes Daddy wanted me to wear tomorrow, and hung them on the closet door.

I considered writing a blog post, but he hadn't liked the ideas I'd pitched yesterday. After tomorrow, I could write about the interview. I'd approach it humbly—*Gosh, this was so much fun!*—but it would promote the mini-doc. He'd like that.

What else had he suggested? Oh, yes, a nap, because he wanted me fresh. Broken bones, a headache, and heartache probably ruled out freshness. Besides, the last time I'd napped, I'd woken to find Gertrude showing Will into my room.

*See you Monday.* I'd wanted to hear something else in the words, but that was all he'd said, and that was all he'd meant, and Monday and every day after that were going to suck. Seeing him at school would be awful.

I took my phone from the closet. His phone, actually. I'd give it back Monday. No point in keeping it. I turned it on to check for missed calls, voicemails, texts. Nothing.

Some consolation was in order. I uncapped the bourbon and took a long pull on the bottle. Warmth and sweetness spread through my sinuses and down my throat and outward from my center.

I reread Will's last text. It was from Sunday night, when we'd planned to watch *The Third Man* and instead I'd been having a meltdown or a breakdown or a panic attack or whatever that had been. *Guess your battery died. It's OK. Some other time. Sweet drug-induced dreams to you.* Winking smiley face.

I scrolled back further. *I'm thinking you're not there.*

*Recognize Ashley Wilkes?*

*You there?*

*Got your popcorn?*

*P.S. I will lick every inch of you.*

I'd scrolled back to last Friday, when Daddy had been doing his walk-through. The previous message was also Will's: *Yes to fire road. Good night.*

The one before that came from me: *Gotta go. Let's try to meet on the fire road Sunday.*

I stashed the phone and the bourbon back in the boot and went into the bathroom to brush my teeth.

"As a matter of fact, Vic," I told the mirror, "yeah, I do take a drink now and then." I shook my head. "No, I wouldn't say it's the *most* surprising thing about me. Funny you should ask."

AT SUPPER, DADDY recapped today's training sessions and told me Jamie was in first place at Greensboro. Better Jamie than Bree or Michael, but whoever won, I decided to send a congratulatory note. That was the sporting thing to do, even if it didn't come from the heart.

After supper, I washed the dishes while Gertrude prepped for tomorrow, the two of us working in slightly uncomfortable silence. At least, I was uncomfortable. I didn't know about her. But I was glad when I finished drying the dishes and put them away.

I stopped by the study to say good night to Daddy, who stood behind his desk, sorting papers.

"Night. Oh, darlin'—were you researching Stephen Crane today?"

Did he check the computer *every* time I'd been alone in the house?

"Was that okay?"

"It's fine, but why were you researching Crane?" He tapped the papers into a tidy stack.

He hadn't paid as much attention to my conversation with Will as I'd thought.

"I have to write an essay on literary naturalism. Crane's considered the first American naturalist." A fact I'd learned today.

He gave me a tolerant look. "I'm aware. I didn't forget about the essay, but Will Howard said a B's the best grade you can make if you write about him. Why would you want a B?"

"I don't *want* a B—"

"You do if you go in knowing that's what you're going to make. Is that what you want to settle for?"

Once I felt better, I'd work harder on my own path to success—good grades, good rider, good girl—but I said, "If you're leaving it up to me, I'm fine with it. If you want me to write on someone else, tell me now, because it'll take me all night."

He put the papers in a folder. "I want *you* to want to write on someone else, but it's your call."

It was an unsatisfying way to end the conversation, but I'd already said good night. I turned to leave.

"Odd, Will Howard mentioning your GPA."

"Everyone knows about my GPA."

"Hm."

I turned back to him. "Nothing's there, Daddy." If he started obsessing over Will—and maybe he already was—all my compliance simply wouldn't matter.

He didn't look at me.

The only way I knew to distract him was to initiate sex, but tonight the idea turned my stomach. Being compliant was bad enough, but instigating sex made me complicit. I wouldn't do it again, I thought—and realized with surprise that I'd created a boundary. Daddy might not know it was there, but I did.

"Good night, Daddy."

He nodded shortly, and without a "Good night, darlin', love you," I didn't have to say I loved him, too.

# - Nineteen -

IN THE SPACE between registering the earthy aroma of cocoa and Daddy's fingers playing with my hair, I indulged in the illusion I'd had a safe hot-chocolate childhood.

"Morning, darlin'. Time to shine." He set the mug on my nightstand and turned on the lamp. "Nervous?" He wore jodhpurs, boots, and a polo shirt, and he smelled of soap and shaving cream. He was The Face, the Olympian, everything he'd always been and more.

"No, sir."

"Good." He handed me the mug. "Just be yourself."

He meant I was to present my persona. My self was someone who'd settle for a B and drink bourbon from a boot and fuck a boy in the back of a pickup truck.

"The crew will be here at seven. Do your own makeup. They'll touch it up if they need to. What are you doing with your hair?"

I didn't think I could hold up my arms long enough to braid it again. "Ponytail."

"That'll work. Gertrude's busy, so get your own breakfast. See you downstairs." He paused by the closet for a final look at the clothes hanging on the door. "Wear a thong so you don't spoil the line of your leg."

My self decided to treat me to a splash of bourbon in my cocoa. I should dump the booze soon in the name of compliance—or wow, maybe not. Cocoa and bourbon should be a thing.

Since I was on the floor by the closet, anyway, I checked my phone. Will's continued silence added to the weight in my chest.

I showered and washed my hair, but when I reached for the conditioner, the bottle was empty, which didn't bode well for a smooth, sleek ponytail.

Twisting to dry off and again to pass the rib belt around my torso made sweat bead on my upper lip, my forehead, even my scalp. I opened the door to allow steam to escape and cinched the straps. Pain. Stars. And my hair was hopelessly snarled. The wide-toothed comb I always used to work out tangles got stuck. In frustration, I yanked at it, which trapped it more securely.

The bathroom walls shrank toward me. I was hot, light-headed—corkscrewing down into that panicked place I'd landed a week ago.

I gripped the edge of the bathroom counter. This shivering hot-cold mess wasn't me. I was strong and decisive and determined.

"Then be those things." My voice was thin as gauze, but the room stopped shrinking.

That was a start. *Now breathe.* Ow—ribs, lungs, not okay. *Breathe, anyway.*

Gradually, the room opened up, my runaway heart slowed, and the light-headedness lessened.

*Get the comb out of your hair.*

I worked at it until sweat rolled down my face, collected on my chin, and dripped onto my chest. The bathroom walls started to close in again.

Panting, I stepped into my room. The breeze coming down from the mountains and through my window was cool. I examined the tangle in the mirror on the back of the bedroom door. Once I got the comb out, I'd still have to unsnarl my hair and subdue it into a ponytail—a task so impossible that when I spotted the scissors I'd left on my desk Friday evening, I picked them up and sheared off the tangle, comb and all.

In my hand, the comb was embedded in an enormous wad of hair. In the mirror, the hair remaining on my head was profoundly asymmetrical. I grasped a snarl on the other side and cut again. That did nothing for the asymmetry, but the feel of the hair separating from its roots was satisfying. My side seared, but I cut again and again, not stopping until I was unfamiliar to myself.

The hair that remained was short and ragged, as though I'd shorn it with a weed whip.

I removed the rib belt and took another shower to wash away sweat and loose hair. Then I toweled off and ran my hands over my hair. It had already dried in spikes and jagged edges and cowlicks.

Daddy wouldn't like this.

But I did. I was a stranger to myself.

With steady hands, I applied makeup and cleaned up my former hair from the floor, discarding it in my wastebasket. I strapped myself into the rib belt again and dressed, starting with the thong.

SNN ARRIVED AT seven sharp. Gertrude let the crew in, which meant Daddy was still at the barn. From upstairs, I listened to her offer them coffee or tea.

"Coffee, please," a woman said immediately, followed by a small chorus of agreement.

Voices came in clearly as people carried equipment inside and faded when they went outside to fetch another load. Through a screen of tree branches, I watched the light move across the pastures and the woods. I caught snatches of the crew's conversation about rearranging furniture, followed by grunts and thumps.

Gertrude delivered coffee and received the fervent thanks of the desperate.

A minute later, Daddy was walking up from the barn, warm smile already in place.

I checked my backside in the mirror before I went downstairs. He'd been right about the thong—no panty lines—but I suspected he wouldn't notice.

His study had been transformed into a studio. Cords ran everywhere, lights and reflectors top-heavy on tall, spindly stands. Two cameras fed into monitors. The leather chairs had been moved to the cozy backdrop of the fireplace, where a small fire burned the chill off the room and provided warm ambient light.

Four SNN staffers, none familiar to me, stood drinking coffee and eating tiny muffins from a tray Gertrude had put on Daddy's desk. Gertrude was chatting with one of them, a man in a plaid shirt.

"Hi," I said in a voice as warm as Daddy's smile. "I'm Roan."

Everyone turned toward me, including Gertrude, who gasped. I stuck out my hand to the closest person.

She shook it. "Jasmine. PA. Production assistant."

"Nice to meet you." I shook hands with the rest of the crew: Priya, director of photography; Ruby, sound recordist; Owen, camera operator and plaid shirt enthusiast. Everyone's expression was polite, glazed. My hair was making an impression.

"Sugar—" Gertrude cut herself off as the front door opened and closed.

"Good morning." Daddy, still smiling, walked into the study and nearly extended his hand to me before he realized who I was. His smile became ice. He closed his fingers on my wrist. "Excuse us, please."

He steered me out of the room and down the hall and shoved me into the first room we came to, a bathroom. He shut the door.

"What have you done? What the *fuck* have you done?" With rough hands, he turned my head this way and that, as if he might find more hair. "What were you thinking? You've butchered yourself." He released my head with a push. "I signed contracts saying you wouldn't do this."

"You said I wouldn't cut my hair?" No one besides Daddy cared whether my hair was long. He'd wind his fingers through it to tug my head back for a kiss or to control the rhythm with which I sucked his cock.

"Your endorsement contracts have an appearance clause. Unfuckingbelievable. Goddammit, Roan."

I hadn't known about any appearance clauses, but they wouldn't have mattered.

"It's my hair."

"We signed *contracts*," he said again, so I repeated myself, too.

"It's my hair."

From his expression, I halfway expected him to deny that it was.

"You are unfuckingbe—"

Someone tapped softly on the door. "Can I come in?" Gertrude whispered.

"We aren't through," he said to me. He opened the door a crack.

Gertrude squeezed through. "We can hear you."

There was no judgment in her voice, but Daddy's lips thinned into a slit. He never showed his temper to Gertrude, much less anyone else, and technically the SNN crew members were media. I entertained a brief fantasy in which a puff piece became actual journalism.

"How much did you hear?"

"Enough."

He turned an accusing eye on me, but I hadn't made him raise his voice. He'd done that on his own.

Gertrude put her fingertips under my chin and turned my head back and forth, up and down, far more gently than Daddy had. "I'll run home and see if I have anything that'll help."

He nodded. "Thanks."

She left, quiet but urgent, on board with the idea that my haircut constituted an emergency.

Daddy pointed at me. "You are a product." He'd lowered his voice. "A brand. We signed those contracts based on your image. This isn't it."

"It is now."

He gave me a warning look.

I tried to soften what I'd said. "The sponsors might like it."

"Like it? Have you seen it?" He squished my face between his thumb and fingers and turned my head toward the mirror.

I'd seen how I looked. I was more interested in how he looked. As clearly as if he were writing a formula on a whiteboard, he was working out how he'd smooth over both the haircut and his reaction. Should he be charming or apologetic, or should he go with worried father?

"Those companies only care if I win," I said through puckered fish lips.

He released me. "Why doesn't Jamie Benedict have any endorsement contracts?"

"How should I know?"

"Picture him."

Jamie was a prince on horseback, but with his pockmarked face and crooked teeth the color of candlelight, no one pressured him to model. No, he got to concentrate on riding.

"So what if the endorsements go away?" I said. "We don't need the money."

Daddy's face was incredulous. "It's not about income. It's about exposure for the sport. Endorsements up your value as a candidate for the team. How do you not get this?"

I'd never thought of that. Money wasn't Daddy's bottom line. He was about winning. Goals. Career.

I was about those things, too, now. "Can't you talk to the sponsors?"

"I'll have to, but there's a roomful of people down the hall I need to talk to first. And before I do, we need to decide what you'll tell Vic."

He'd scripted everything else. He might as well script this, too.

"What do you want me to say?"

"You cut your hair," he said slowly, putting together the answer as he went, "because long hair is a lot of work. The less time you spend on your hair, the more time you can spend on your horse. Say it."

I recited the lines.

"All right. That's good enough for Vic. Not for me. What the fuck were you thinking?"

"It was tangled. I couldn't get the comb through it."

"You expect me to believe that? There's got to be more to it."

The phantom sensation of his fingers in my hair made my skin ripple, like a horsefly had landed on me.

I whispered my answer. "Wind your fingers in this."

He went very still. "What did you say?"

"I said, 'Wind your fingers in this.'" This time the words lilted on my tongue.

His face turned hard and white as a glacier. Without another word, he left the bathroom, closing the door behind him.


I SAT ON the toilet lid and waited for Gertrude, unable to decide what was more exhilarating—the haircut, the reactions I was getting, or the experience of making my voice heard, if only to Daddy. Chopping off my hair was one big "fuck you" he couldn't do anything about. It wasn't like he could glue it back on.

I wanted to scream an actual "fuck you" to him, but one live mic of that would end my career regardless of how much good I did the sport. I'd backed him down. That was enough. More than enough. It was everything.

The bathroom door opened. Gertrude came in and hoisted a tackle box onto the vanity.

"Are we sticking fishhooks in my face as a distraction?"

"Wouldn't help, sugar." She popped open the lid, revealing an array of products, hairpins, barrettes, and small scissors with pointed blades.

I looked doubtfully from the tools to her smooth ash-blond bob. "Do you use all this?"

"Not every day. But I know what to do with it." She draped a towel around my shoulders and went to work, gelling and scrunching and trimming. "Why did you do it?"

I tested my interview answer. "Long hair is too much work. The less time I spend on my hair, the more time I can spend on my horse."

She snipped in silence for several minutes. I hoped my answer would be more convincing in the interview.

"Guess it'll grow," she said.

I had no intention of growing it out, but I didn't want to argue with her.

She stopped snipping. "I would've taken you to a salon."

I hadn't had time to make an appointment, because cutting my hair hadn't been a conscious decision. As soon as I saw my scissors, I had to do it—immediately. It was that simple and that complicated.

She rubbed something called hair putty on her fingertips, applied it to my hair, and stood back. "Take a look."

She'd rearranged what was left of my hair and glued it down using nearly every product in her tackle box. The cowlicks had been subdued. No scalp showed. Objectively, "no bald spots" was about the best that could be said for it. Subjectively, my gapped-up haircut was beautiful. I'd lost my hair and found my power.

"Thanks," I said. "I like it."

She looked doubtful. "Oh, sugar." She removed the towel cape, careful not to get hair on my shirt, and mustered a smile for me. "You'd better go. I'll see you at lunchtime."

Vic and Laura had arrived while I'd been in the bathroom. Vic was listening to Daddy, who had opted for worried father, but not *too* worried because that would concern the sponsors. Since the haircut couldn't be kept secret, it had to be managed.

"I lost it." He projected exactly the right amount of rue. "It's not like me. I apologized, but I was rough on her. Solo parenting is the hardest thing I've ever done."

"Nobody could do any better," Vic said.

"If this is the worst thing she does, you're lucky," Laura said. "When my daughter was her age, she was sneaking out of the house to meet her boyfriend."

*Jesus, Laura, don't help.*

"Good morning," I said.

"Wow." Laura gave me a bright smile. "That is quite a change."

Vic had known me longer. "What were you thinking, kid?"

Daddy chuckled weakly. "See what I mean?"

Nothing about the look he gave me was weak, but I matched it. I'd met him on his own turf and shown him I wasn't weak, either.

I laughed. "Like I told Daddy, long hair's a lot of work. The less time I spend on my hair, the more time I can spend on my horse."

"Can you give me the same answer in the interview and sound like it's the first time I asked?"

I could forget about real journalism.

Ruby clipped a tiny microphone to my shirt. Jasmine put me in the chair nearest the fireplace, tucked tissues around my collar, and dabbed foundation on my nose. Priya tilted a round white reflector toward me, took a light reading, and adjusted the reflector. Jasmine removed the tissues from my collar and stepped out of frame.

"Quiet," Laura said. "Let's get room tone."

The room fell silent except for the snap of the fire. On the monitor that was turned my way, I saw a girl I didn't know. To her left, firelight flickered.

"Good," Laura said. "Vic?"

Vic picked his way through cables and equipment and settled into the chair opposite mine. "Your hair shocked me so much I didn't ask about your ribs," he said as Ruby miked him. He was already wearing foundation. He wore it at shows, too, always camera-ready.

"I'm better every day," I said. "How have you been?"

"Can't complain, and no one would care if I did." He looked down at the blue notepaper clipped to the outside of his leather portfolio.

Daddy stationed himself beside the monitor that faced me. I smiled sweetly. He smiled, too, giving off an affectionate "Darlin', what am I going to do with you?" vibe for the benefit of the crew.

Onscreen, everything looked perfect.

"Everyone ready?" Laura said. "Owen?"

"Rolling."

The red light on the camera beside the monitor glowed.

"When you're ready, Vic," Laura said.

"Three, two, one." Vic's voice took on a concerned tone. "Tell me how you broke your ribs."

So the Haircut That Shook the World wasn't the lead.

It came up about fifteen minutes in.

"I've known you all your life," Vic said, "and since you were little, you've had long hair, so I have to ask, what's with the haircut?"

I replicated the laugh that had preceded my answer the first time he'd asked. "Long hair's a lot of work. I wanted something easier to take care of. The less time I spend on my hair, the more time I can spend on my horse."

Beside the monitor, Daddy wore a faint smile, a single father bewildered and out of his depth with his teenage daughter. We were practically a Disney movie. All that was missing was a horse that acted like a dog and a pretty veterinarian who'd steal his heart and love me like I was her own.

"I can't say Daddy's too thrilled," I added, lending authenticity to his single-dad act.

"You want in on this, Monty?" Vic asked.

Daddy held up one hand, shaking his head.

Vic moved on to Sheridan Academy's rigorous academics, which led to a brief discussion of my grades. Then he said, "High school's a whole different world. You're always the youngest rider when you compete, but at school you're with people your own age. Do you find it easy to be in both worlds? And just between us"—there was a low laugh from the crew—"are you dating anyone?"

Daddy had made him ask, but I was prepared. "If I don't have time to blow-dry my hair, I don't have time for dating. As for being in two worlds, I'm on a short schedule at school, so I'm in and out—go to class, come home, and ride. School is school—but riding is my life."

Daddy hadn't scripted that answer. I was being honest.

"Tell me," Vic said, "about your mother."

I arranged my expression into something neutral, reserved. I'd practiced in the mirror, and I could see myself in the monitor. "There's really nothing to tell." I'd practiced that cool tone, too, channeling Grace Kelly in *To Catch a*

*Thief.* Hitchcock didn't scare me anymore. "My parents are divorced. My mother moved away. My life is here."

We broke for lunch at noon. In the dining room, we served ourselves from the sideboard, where Gertrude had laid out bread, cold cuts, cheeses, and condiments. I assembled a big, thick sandwich.

Daddy took his plate to the head of the table, but Laura had taken my seat, so I found myself in Mama's old spot, slightly removed from the conversation. I'd never sat here before. I squinted to blur out Vic and the crew and tried to see the table as Mama had, Daddy at a distance and me between them, the same way we'd been as a family.

Daddy never even looked my way. I took a reading on his mood: still furious over the haircut but pleased with my performance. I'd come across as spontaneous and authentic. More important, we'd presented that indivisible bond we were known for.

At one, lights, cameras, crew, and Daddy followed Vic and me to the barn. Owen shot B roll along the way. Our mics were off and we were being shot from the back mostly, but Laura had said to be animated.

I gestured toward the pastures and the arenas. "You've seen it all before."

Vic turned his head toward me and laughed. In the footage, we'd appear to be having a delightful conversation. They'd slap on some voice-over, maybe Vic talking about the generations Rosemont had been in the family.

"Good job," Laura said when we got to the barn.

Eddie had a moment's astonished reaction to my hair, which fortunately was not captured on camera.

"What the hell?" he said under his breath.

"Not you, too."

"Whatever, girl."

He greeted everyone, introduced himself, and helped Owen get the shots Priya and Laura wanted, leading my horses out one by one to a knoll above the memorial garden, where I stood close to them while Eddie held the lead rope and Vic and I chatted about each horse.

Jasper was first, giving a shrill whinny when he spotted me, performing for the cameras like a true Montgomery. I laughed, and Vic chuckled on cue.

"Jasper's your newest horse, but you had an unprecedented season on him last year. How would you describe the development of your partnership?"

I stood in the curve of Jasper's neck and felt the heat from his body. I'd missed touching him. If the camera weren't on us, I'd have leaned against his shoulder and closed my eyes and just breathed him in.

He nosed my hand for the carrot stick I'd swiped from the tray at lunchtime. I held it out, palm flat, and he skimmed it up.

"The way we've grown together has been amazing. It isn't only under saddle. I've bonded more closely with him than I've ever bonded with another horse."

Daddy caught my eye.

"But a rider's only as good as her team," I said. "Eddie and Mateo and everyone else who works at Rosemont are a huge part of my success. I never forget that."

Vic asked Eddie a few questions, but even after three decades as Daddy's groom and then his assistant, Eddie remained uncomfortable on camera. He offered up a couple of halting answers.

"Should we bring Vigo out next?" I patted Jasper goodbye, and Eddie, looking relieved, led him back into the barn.

Vigo posed like the equine royalty he was, and then Diva was up. Eddie led her out on a short lead rope, but one hind hoof flashed backward, fast as a lightning strike, and she'd have made contact with Ruby if she hadn't misjudged the distance, a rare miss.

Her behavior led naturally to a conversation about her temperament. I described the special accommodation she required at shows. Vic knew about that, but the audience might not.

"You're both Olympic prospects, both descended from Olympians," he said. "Look into the future. Is she the one who gets you there?"

"If I'm lucky enough to make the team, which would be a dream come true . . ." I hesitated so I'd sound as if I regretted what I said next. "I don't see it happening on Diva."

Daddy looked interested, as if my opinion were news to him but worth taking into consideration.

"Why is that?" Vic asked.

I nodded at Eddie, and he led her away.

"She's an incredible athlete, but mind-set's as important for the horse as it is for the rider."

Daddy couldn't argue with that.

"Who do you think it'll be?"

"Horses come and go. I might have another horse this year, next year."

"You're being coy."

"Okay, okay," I said as if I were giving in, but I wanted everyone to know my answer. "When I visualize riding in the Games, I'm on Jasper."

We shot all afternoon. There were more questions, and Laura wanted additional B roll. She invited Daddy to join us on camera. We retraced the route of Friday evening's tour, walked up and down the driveway under the oaks, and sat on the front steps like we hung out there all the time. Much of the footage featured Daddy and me alone together. Vic's voice-over was writing itself: "Montgomery is not only coach and father but also mother to his sixteen-year-old daughter." Gag.

At sunset, the crew packed up the van and everyone left except Vic and Laura. In his study, Daddy poured drinks for the three of them. I excused myself and went upstairs to take some aspirin and chisel the makeup off my face. Walking and talking and smiling had worn me out, but the heavy-as-rocks feeling was lighter—and then I checked my phone and found a text from Will: *We need to talk.*

I TRIED TO follow the conversation at dinner and failed.

"You poor thing, we wore you out," Laura said.

Daddy noticed my lack of participation and appetite for the first time. "Go to bed, darlin'. Tomorrow's a school day."

"See you next week," Vic said as I stood up. "Great job today."

"Thanks. Good night."

What good would talking do? I thought as I went upstairs. Nothing had changed since Will and I had broken up.

That wasn't true. Just today, *I'd* changed. I'd put Daddy in his place.

In my room, I looked at my phone to see if Will had responded to the message I'd sent before supper: *Can't tonight.*

He had. *In person. I'll be in the bleachers before homeroom tomorrow.*

I texted back *OK.* Then I turned off the phone, hid it, and got ready for bed. I'd have to find a reason to go to school early, which would make Daddy suspicious. I shouldn't have weed-whacked my hair. No, the haircut was good. It was giving me courage. I'd think of something.

I was drowsing when I heard voices from downstairs. Vic and Laura were leaving. I peered at my clock. Just after midnight.

Distantly, I heard Daddy set the alarm, his tread on the stairs, my door opening.

I squeezed my eyes shut.

"Gertrude will take you to school tomorrow." His voice was flat. "I'm riding out on Jasper."

Why didn't he ride out on his own horse?

*Grow up.* Jasper would be in excellent hands—better hands than mine. Lighter. Quieter. And I could lie to Gertrude more easily about going to school early.

"Thanks." I made my voice sound sleepy, but I opened my eyes.

The doorway was empty.

Down the hall, the floorboard creaked.

He'd left my door open. After he closed his own door, I got up and shut mine again, the latch clicking softly.

I stood there, uncertain, unsettled, and then I dragged my desk chair to the door and wedged the back under the doorknob.

# - Twenty -

GERTRUDE HAD PUT the tackle box in my bathroom, so Monday morning after my shower I examined the contents, but my hair was already dry, untouched and randomly spiky. Gutsy.

In the kitchen, I told Gertrude we needed to leave early because I had some teacher conferences before homeroom.

"But your breakfast—"

"I'll eat in the car."

I smeared peanut butter on toast and retrieved my backpack from the dining room. I carried it in both arms, not letting on how severely the weight tweaked my ribs, or she'd insist on carrying it into the building, where she might find out I wasn't meeting my teachers.

"Do you have everything?" she asked as we got in the station wagon. "Books, homework?"

Daddy never asked. Mama never had, either.

"I do. Do you know who won Greensboro? I want to send a note." I'd already drafted it in my mind. I could have written it and filled in the name later—it was that generic—but I hadn't wanted to take the time this morning.

"Eddie didn't say. That's nice of you, though."

Not really. I wanted to remind the competition that my injuries wouldn't keep me down for long.

At the end of the driveway, she looked left and right before pulling onto the road. "How do you think the interview went yesterday?"

"Fine."

"I've never seen your daddy so upset—and right before you had to go on camera." She slowed to take a curve. "How'd you do that? Everyone heard him blow up at you, and even though he was sorry—he apologized to all of us—"

*Not me*, I thought.

"—he was still furious, and you went out there and put on this performance like he hadn't yelled at you."

"I'm a pro," I said lightly.

"You're a kid." Straight vertical lines creased between her eyebrows, like the number 11 had been etched there.

"It's fine. He was worried about the sponsors, but he'll make it right with them."

"You always say everything's fine."

"It is."

"If it ever *isn't*," she said slowly, "do you promise you'll tell me?"

I gave my answer no thought at all. "Of course." *Not.*

"Are you picking me up, too?" I asked when we stopped in front of the school.

"I'll check with your daddy. And, sugar—"

I slid out of the car and bent down to look back at her.

She smiled a little, but the 11 was still there. "Have a good day."

"You, too," I said, and suddenly my eyes and nose stung like I was going to cry. Gertrude cared about me, not about my performance in the arena, in front of a camera, or in the classroom.

I gave a little cough. "See you later."

The school smell hit me when I went inside, books and toner and industrial floor wax. I put my backpack in my locker. Voices and laughter came from the faculty lounge down the hall, but students wouldn't start arriving for another half hour.

I went out the front door. Student parking was empty.

Will didn't owe me a conversation, and since we were already broken up, I didn't see how things could get any worse even if he'd changed his mind about talking, but when I reached the stadium and found him waiting for me at the top of the bleachers, all the assurances I'd given myself that I was fine without him and that the hell of the past week had to be the worst of it—all of that vanished.

I climbed the steps, wondering whether we'd hug when I got to the top. I ached to feel the strength of his arms—or maybe my ribs just hurt. I didn't need his strength. I was strong myself.

His eyes widened as I climbed the last four steps. "When did you cut your hair?"

"Yesterday."

"Wow. It's hot."

He shouldn't be saying that.

"How's your headache?" I asked.

"How'd you know I have one?"

I hadn't—I'd been referring to his excuse for leaving Friday night—but I said, "I know you pretty well. How bad is it?"

"Worse over the weekend than it is now."

He didn't mean anything by that—for example, that seeing me with my hot haircut was so wonderful that his headache had spontaneously disappeared.

"Let's sit down," he said.

Back in the winter, we'd huddled together side by side, partly for warmth but partly because even through woolen clothes, the feel of his thigh pressed against mine or my arm looped through his had been intimate. Today we left several inches between us.

Will observed the space without comment. "How are you feeling?"

"Okay."

"How's your father?"

Daddy asked about him sometimes, too, just to see my reaction. I wondered if that was what Will was doing now.

"Okay," I said.

"Does he always drink like he did Friday night?"

"Sometimes."

"Normally how much? Like, on a typical night?"

"I don't keep count." I always had a general impression of how much Daddy consumed, but I measured it by his mood.

"Does he have a problem?" Will asked.

I laughed, a sharp Bailey-bark that was louder than I intended. "No, he's perfect."

"I mean, is he an alcoholic?"

No one had ever suggested that. He had a reputation as a hard drinker but one who could hold his liquor, never obnoxious or indiscreet or unkind—in public. I turned over the word *alcoholic* in my mind. "Probably."

"You never mentioned it. You told me about your mom, but all you ever say about your dad is he's strict."

"He is."

"I noticed. But he's more than that."

I didn't like where this was going. "What's your point?"

"What kind of drunk is he?"

At one time, I would have said, *It mellows him out*, but he'd been noticeably irritable Friday night.

"Roan, I'm trying to ask if he hurts you."

He spoke carefully, almost reluctantly, but the fine hairs on my arms stood up.

"No, that's ridiculous. He loves me. You don't hurt someone you love."

Will's smile was wry.

I had hurt him, but it couldn't be helped. "Is that all you wanted to talk about? Daddy's drinking?"

"Not all."

Here it came—the plea to get me back.

He sat forward, his elbows on his knees, his hands clasped. "I want you to know I get it. You. Your father."

My brain automatically generated a denial—"No, you misunderstood—but I couldn't get the words out, and Will was talking again.

"When I saw what Rosemont is, I finally got who you are and who you have the potential to be and what you have to do to get there. I'm in the way."

"What?" I said faintly.

"I thought about this over the weekend. You know how you had conditions for our relationship? I have conditions for our breakup." He turned his head toward me and gave me a crooked smile. "No weirdness at school. We don't ignore each other. You keep the phone. Call or text anytime you want."

He didn't know anything.

I gave a weak laugh. "We won't even notice we're broken up."

"I'll notice." Pain cut through his steadiness. "But it won't be like it was last week. I won't turn off my phone. If I don't answer, leave a voicemail and let me know if it's okay to call you back."

"Why are you being so nice?"

He paused. "Because there's nothing you could do, nothing you could say, that would ever change the way I feel about you."

The rhythm of his words was like a heartbeat.

"And how is that?"

"I love you," he said quietly.

Daddy and I told each other that all the time, and it didn't mean anything. But it sounded different when Will said it. It felt different. It felt like I'd lost something valuable.

"Like you said," he added, "you don't hurt someone you love. I get that you don't have room for a boyfriend, but maybe you could use a friend."

Friendship shouldn't make me weepy. I rolled my eyes skyward. "I probably could."

And just like that, we were in the friend zone.

AFTER CLASS, WILL walked me to the door. Beyond the portico, rain drizzled down.

"See you tomorrow." He held out my backpack.

I took it, careful not to touch his hand. "See you."

The day had been hard, but he was putting genuine effort into being friends. I would, too. Most anything worthwhile, Daddy said, was hard.

I waited under the portico, and mercifully, Gertrude was on time.

"How was your first day back, sugar?"

"Long. How was your day?"

Gertrude had worked in the garden until the rain started. We were having osso buco tonight. Daddy wanted me at the barn right away.

In the house, I threw my uniform across the foot of my bed, pulled on jeans and paddock boots, and snagged an apple on my way to the barn. Diva and Vigo whinnied hopefully, so I bit off chunks and dropped them in their buckets, but I saved most of it for Jasper.

He wasn't in his stall, so I walked out to the paddocks. Empty.

Back in the barn, I left the apple in his bucket and headed to the covered arena. Daddy was probably working him. They must not have ridden out after all.

In the arena, Jasper was under saddle and executing a flawless counter canter—but Daddy stood with another man outside the fence, their backs to me, both of them watching whoever the hell was riding my horse.

I stopped short.

The tall, lanky rider was a prince on horseback. Jamie Benedict. Which meant the man standing next to Daddy was Frank Falconetti.

# - Twenty-one -

"WHAT'S GOING ON?"

Frank turned. "Hey, kid. Whoa—that's some look you've got going."

I wasn't sure whether he referred to my hair or my expression. Why was Jamie riding my horse?

Smiling, Frank turned back to the rail.

Daddy pushed his hands into the pockets of his jacket. "Nice," he called to Jamie, who had transitioned into an extended trot.

Heavy-legged, feet like cinder blocks, I joined them at the rail.

"Daddy?" I cleared my throat. "What's going on?"

He rolled his head to the right, cracking his neck. "I told Frank about our conversation. About this being your decision."

"I know how attached you are to him," Frank said.

Daddy rolled his head to the left, making more popping sounds. "She knows better than to get attached."

He'd done it. He'd sold Jasper back to Frank.

My world tilted so sharply that I staggered, but their eyes were on Jamie and Jasper, *my* horse—who, well trained as he was, performed perfectly under yet another skilled rider who wasn't me. The scene in front of me was sharp, glassy. The smells told me it was real, horse and leather and sweat—mine.

Eventually Jamie reined in by the gate. "What a treat to ride him again. I can't thank you enough."

"You're doing us a favor by taking him off our hands," Daddy said.

Jasper wasn't a burden. He was my best horse, and together we were magic. Weren't we?

"Hey, Roan," Jamie said. "Cool haircut."

"Fuck you," I muttered under my breath, but the words could have been "thank you," and they were lost, anyway, because Frank said over me, "Shall we load him up?"

Jamie hopped off, transforming from swan prince into awkward duck as soon as his boots touched the ground. "Hell, yeah."

Daddy swung open the gate. "Let's get him ready for the road."

Jasper stretched his head toward me, but Daddy took the reins behind the chin strap. "Watch out, darlin'."

I took a step back. Daddy and Jasper led the way to the barn, Jamie and Frank following, me bringing up the rear, my throat aching all the way into my ears, my head filled with woodpeckers drilling into my skull. I couldn't let them know he'd done this without me. They were the competition. But how could Jamie think I'd agreed to this?

Unable to watch but incapable of not watching, I sat on the knoll above the memorial garden, my arms hugging my knees. The wet grass soaked the seat of my jeans, while in the training barn crossties, Daddy unsaddled Jasper.

"Cut on the overheads," he said.

Jamie went to the switch by the door and turned on the lights. Now I wouldn't miss a single thing about Jasper's last moments at Rosemont. Daddy began to rub him down.

From the doorway, Jamie's eyes lit on me. He approached me, curious but not apologetic. "Hey, you're okay with this, aren't you?"

"What do you fucking think?" My vocal cords were as taut as violin strings, but I made sure not to speak too loudly so Daddy wouldn't hear me.

He glanced back toward the barn. "Monty said—"

"What? What did he say?"

"Nothing except he doesn't have time to ride all three horses and keep up with the farm. All I have to do is ride. Frank does everything else." He paused. "Michael's been riding more. Did you see any of the footage from Greensboro?"

"No." I hoped Michael had won and Jamie Benedict Arnold had come in dead last.

"He killed it."

If he were waiting for a reaction, he could wait forever.

"Anyway," he said, "Frank wasn't going to say no to taking Jasper back, and of course I want to ride him. I'm not a fool."

Not a fool and not my friend. Daddy always said this was a business, one that had the potential to break your heart. Obviously Jamie and Frank and Daddy were all business, while here I sat in the cold and the wet, heart effectively broken.

"He said it was your decision," Jamie added.

"I won't always have broken ribs. I'll be riding again in a month." Well, five weeks.

"Yeah. How are you feeling?"

I shook my head. *Don't pretend you care.*

Daddy swaddled Jasper's legs in padded wraps.

"I'll take good care of him." Jamie started back to the barn.

I exhaled sharply. Friendship had its limits, and I'd hit mine, but he *would* take care of Jasper.

"He likes ear rubs," I said.

He smiled, as if I'd caved in. "I think I'm the one who told you that."

Daddy threw a light blanket over Jasper and strapped a poll cap to his head.

"Come say goodbye, darlin'," he called.

My jaw clenched so tightly that I was in danger of cracking my molars. I climbed to my feet. Frank had snapped a lead line onto Jasper's halter, and Daddy was unclipping him from the crossties.

If I could speak, I'd have whispered to Jasper: *You're mine. Kick and bite and buck every chance you get, so you'll come back to me.* But Jasper was no Diva. He was perfect. Wordlessly I caressed his ears, put my forehead against his, and then stood back while Frank walked my horse down the aisle, turned left, and led him out of sight.

"I'd better run and open the trailer," Jamie said. "Thanks again, Monty. Roan . . ."

I glared at him.

"See you," he said.

He jogged down the aisle and disappeared.

Daddy leaned over and picked up Jasper's grooming kit and took it into the tack room. He should have given it to Frank.

Rain began to fall hard.

He'd sold my horse.

I didn't care what deal they'd struck. I couldn't let this happen.

I started down the aisle at a walk, then broke into a trot that jarred my ribs and forced me back into a speed-walk, my hand pressed to my side. I turned left, toward the covered arena, and then right, shortcutting to the parking area for the farm's fleet of trailers and work trucks. Cold rain pelted the top of my head.

The taillights of Frank's trailer glowed through the rain. Jasper always had been easy to load. Jamie was in the passenger seat, and Frank was pulling onto the back driveway, the asphalt as glossy as black glass. The diesel engine growled as he accelerated.

I waved my arms over my head and gasped as pain lanced through my left side, but I kept flailing my right arm as I speed-walked after the truck. "Frank! Stop! Frank!"

The lights shrank into distant red blurs and vanished altogether as the trailer went down the hill toward the back gate.

I bent over and braced my hands on my knees. The rain was so loud that I could no longer hear the engine, only the downpour and the wheeze of air in and out of my lungs.

"Stand up," Daddy said.

Ready for a fight, I pushed myself upright. His lips stretched into a cold smile. Rain ran down the back of my neck, and the chills under my clothes penetrated my muscles.

"I know what you're doing," I said.

"I should hope so." This wasn't the stunned, distant Daddy who'd told me to sleep in because he was riding out. This was Daddy with a plan. "The question is, do you know what *you're* doing?"

That brought me up short. Chopping off my hair and acing that interview had felt right, like I was figuring out how to live with myself and with Daddy, but now he was punishing me. He hadn't just sold Jasper. He'd toppled me right off my high horse.

On the other hand . . . he'd lost his leverage.

I laughed.

"Something funny?"

"You. Now that you've sold him, what do you have to hold over me? Nothing."

He popped the collar of his jacket against the rain. "I didn't sell him. Yet. Frank would jump at the chance to keep him, and you saw what a good fit he is for Jamie." He reached out and tugged a wisp of my hair. "How much do you want him back? Enough to stop challenging me? Figure out what you want, darlin'. It's your choice."

Once again—still—always. He had me where he wanted me.

AT SUPPER, HE told me Jamie had won Greensboro.

I should have known he wouldn't finish dead last. At least I didn't have to hate him or Frank anymore. They hadn't stolen my horse. So far as they knew, the situation was exactly as Daddy said: He didn't have time to ride all three horses.

If I wanted Jasper back, I had to rise to the occasion. "How'd Michael do? Jamie said he's been training more."

"Close second. Want to watch after supper? SNN has the highlights online."

That subtle example of Daddy's power had been lost on me until now: Vic was SNN's lead correspondent for eventing, but he'd interviewed me instead of covering Greensboro.

"Can we watch while we eat?" I asked.

Daddy accepted my enthusiasm as his due.

We ate at his desk, his computer monitor angled so both of us could watch. Jamie had won on his Oldenburg, Deo Volente, turning in a strong performance on the dressage test. He rode like a centaur, an opinion delivered by Vic's substitute, Odette Thibodeaux, a onetime Olympian and lesser god of eventing. Daddy didn't own the sport.

He owned me, though, so I made appropriate assenting noises as he critiqued Jamie and Michael and Sophie, who'd placed third. Initially I was faking it. Then Odette began to create a narrative around the rivalry between Jamie and Michael. When her cohost mentioned my name, Odette dismissed me. "The story here is these two riders. You can see the intensity and drive each of them has."

I'd missed one show, and I'd become irrelevant.

The video wrapped up a three-day show in thirty minutes.

"I want to send Jamie a note," I said.

Daddy looked at me.

"To say congratulations."

He opened one of his desk drawers and gave me a thick white note card blind-engraved with the word *Rosemont*.

I scrawled out the note I'd written in my head last night:

*Dear Jamie,*

*Congratulations on winning Greensboro. I'll have a lot of catching up to do when I'm riding again, but don't worry—I'm coming for you. Haha.*

I drew a smiley face.

Now for the part I hadn't written last night. My fingers stiffened around the pen, and the act of writing felt unnatural.

*Take care of my horse. Remember to rub his ears, and tell him he'll come home soon. Sincerely, Roan.*

I pushed the card across the desk to Daddy.

He scanned it. "Sincerely? You don't sound sincere."

"Oh, I'm sincere."

"In your congratulations."

"Well, I'm not sincere about everything."

Despite his own reputation as the embodiment of sporting conduct and his irritation with me, his lips twitched. Even the slightest genuine smile from him looked nothing like the cold, lipless smile he'd given me in the rain.

"I'll mail it tomorrow." He stuck the card in a matching envelope and was addressing it when the phone rang. He glanced at Caller ID and hit the speaker button. "I made it clear you're not to call this number again."

Anonymous. The menace in Daddy's voice compressed my heart, making it small and tight.

*It's Mama*, I mouthed.

"What?" Daddy said.

"Mama," I said.

Instantly there was a click from the handset and then a dial tone. That was it. She'd never call again.

Daddy pushed the off button. "What makes you think it's your mother?"

"I just . . . wanted it to be."

He leaned forward and folded his arms on his desk. "Every one of your mother's actions was a choice. When she chose to cheat on me, she chose to leave both of us." He paused. "You understand, don't you, that when you chose to cut your hair, you chose to give Jasper to Frank."

"Here you are," Gertrude sang out, and the artificial cheer in her voice told me she'd overheard. "How was supper? May I bring you anything else?"

Daddy complimented her on the meal. I couldn't remember what we'd eaten.

I helped her clear, taking the serving dishes into the kitchen.

"Sugar," she began.

"Don't," I said. "Just don't."

She touched my shoulder while I ran hot water into the sink. I was so accustomed to deflecting attention from Daddy and me that—as always—a defense of him came to my lips, but I'd chew off my tongue before I stood up for him or Mama ever again. I patted Gertrude's hand and smiled at her over my shoulder. Maintaining a façade was easier when people weren't kind.

I went upstairs as soon as I'd brought in the last dirty dish and texted Will. *Daddy sent Jasper away.*

*What? Why?*

*He's punishing me.*

*For what?*

*My hair*, I replied, but that was only part of it. Daddy was punishing me because of what he suspected about Will and me.

Anger curled up in my tight, constricted heart. I held on to it. I had to. If I ever released it, it would obliterate everything.

# - Twenty-two -

I ROSE EARLY the next morning and churned out two posts, one about the SNN interview and another about Jasper's transition to Frank's barn. I acknowledged Frank and Jamie's expertise and generosity in working with him while I recovered—and though it rankled me to do it, I included a paragraph about how hard Daddy worked and the enormous responsibility he bore in running Rosemont. I said I was watching videos of the competition, and I lifted a line from the note I'd written to Jamie: I was coming for them, haha, smiley face. *Love and hugs, Roan.*

Every time Vic interviewed me, I regurgitated the same information, reframing it so it sounded fresh. I never wavered in saying Jasper would come back to Rosemont. Sunday after Sunday, I put it out there like I was wishing on a star. By the third interview, I was working out for the camera, executing lunges, squats, planks, and stretches while Daddy coached me through them. My ribs still hurt, but not unbearably. At Daddy's suggestion, I took aspirin to school in my backpack, but I'd ditched the rib belt.

Between Sundays, I audited his training of Vigo and Diva. In the evenings, I screened videos with him and asked questions and made notes. I *was* coming for the competition, and there was no haha, smiley face about it.

At school, Will was kind, but the friend zone was hard and empty and sad.

I didn't want to dwell on my sadness, but one Sunday night, when I was worn out from yet another day of being upbeat and positive for Vic and his crew, I texted Will: *Ever think about us?*

Several minutes passed before he replied. *Always.*

*Miss us?*

*Yes.*

*Me, too.*

I resolved not to ask questions like that again.

Gradually the pain in my side went away. One Friday after school, Daddy took me to the doctor's office, where X-rays showed the bones had knitted.

On the ride home, he said we'd restart my training the next day.

"We don't have time to ease back into a routine, darlin'. Bluegrass is two weeks away."

"When is Jasper coming back?"

"What makes you so sure he is?"

I couldn't have been more breathless if he'd gut-punched me. "Why wouldn't he? I've done everything you've asked."

"We'll see. Anyway, you're riding Diva at Bluegrass."

That had been decided months ago, but I wasn't thinking about Bluegrass. What more did I have to do to get Jasper back?

I knew the answer to that.

My lamp was off and the clock had struck eleven-thirty when the doorknob turned.

He drew back the bedclothes.

His mouth was hot and wet on my ear. "How much is Jasper worth to you?"

It was no big deal. I'd always done it. It was what I did.

I imagined myself floating up to the ceiling, where I hid in the shadows and looked down at the people on the bed. A pale, naked body—mine—opened to a man who shouldn't be doing what he was doing. Neither should I, but I didn't know how to stop. And I desperately wanted to.

BEING ON A horse had always come naturally, but the next day, when Daddy gave me a leg up and I settled into the dressage saddle, everything was strange. Vigo's neck seemed too long, his head oddly set at the end of it. The reins were dead in my hands instead of a living connection to the horse's mouth.

I gave him too much leg and he lurched forward in a trot. I bounced to the left before I caught my balance.

"Deepen your seat," Daddy said into the headset.

I was a sack of potatoes, flopping all over Vigo's back as I warmed him up at the trot and the canter. My muscles were weak. My balance was shit.

After forty-five endless minutes, Daddy walked over to us and patted Vigo's shoulder. "You have some work to do."

The dressage lesson on Diva yielded no better results. The afternoon's jumping lesson on her was dismal. Daddy normally liked to end a training session on a high note, stopping when the horse and I had executed something particularly well, but today there had been no high notes.

I summed it up in a text to Will that night: *I'm back on the horse and I suck.*

*You're riding again?*

*Yes, and I suck.*

*You've been training since you were two. You can't have forgotten everything you know.*

He was either confident in my abilities or dismissing my concern. I wasn't sure which, but it annoyed me.

Not long after I'd put my phone away, Daddy tapped on my door. "Come downstairs. I want to show you something."

In the living room, he sat down on the sofa, the remote control in his hand, and patted the seat next to him. Just what I wanted to do, cuddle with him and review training videos.

After my performance today, I didn't dare whine. I sat down.

"Do you remember your fifteenth birthday?"

"That's the day I got Jasper."

"Watch."

He pointed the remote at the television and clicked a button. The red-and-white-striped metal walls of Frank's indoor arena snapped into focus. I trotted onscreen riding Jasper. I hadn't known Daddy had recorded us.

Jasper had put on muscle in the time I'd had him. His neck was thicker, his rump rounder and more defined, his shoulders heavier. He'd retained that floaty gait, though, hoofs skimming the ground, long legs moving in graceful cadence, big body appearing lighter than air.

"He looks good," Daddy said on the video.

"She looks good on him," Frank said.

Jasper's trot was so silken that I'd barely moved in the saddle.

"Canter," Daddy called.

Effortless.

"Figure eights."

Through figure eights and lead changes and side passes, Jasper was perfection, and on his back, I was perfection, too.

"Take him over some jumps."

Jasper took wing over each of the jumps in the middle of the arena, landing softly, his legs and shoulders absorbing the shock like springs. After the last jump, I called, "I feel like I've ridden him every day of my life."

Daddy paused the video. "You and that horse bonded the very first time you rode him. I understand the connection between you. You think I've never felt that?"

I wasn't sure what Daddy felt.

"Today, you were trying too hard. That day, you weren't trying at all. It came as naturally as breathing. That's what I want to see from you. I want to see it on Vigo and Diva. When I do, we'll talk about bringing Jasper back." He stood up. "If I were you, I'd watch this until I felt it."

I listened to him go up the stairs, my eyes on the TV. Then I pressed the button and started from the beginning.

EVEN AN ACTUAL sack of potatoes would have improved under Daddy's intensive instruction. My balance returned, and the view looked familiar, and I watched the video of Jasper so obsessively that I knew every flick of his tail and twitch of his ears. After I'd watched it countless times, Daddy said, "Enough. If it were going to do any good, it would have done it by now."

I tried harder.

At school I talked to Will, but at night I fell into bed without texting him, drained from A.M. and P.M. chores, lessons, homework, and walk-throughs. My head swam with training videos, Daddy's narration, instructions he'd given me in lessons.

On the Sunday before Bluegrass—the first Sunday Vic and his crew hadn't come to Rosemont—Diva was favoring her off foreleg. After an ultrasound, Glenn diagnosed a strain injury. He prescribed hydrotherapy and bute to reduce inflammation and advised putting her on stall rest.

"Nothing serious," he said, "but you won't be riding her next weekend."

I'd trained hard on Vigo, too, and was prepared to compete on him.

At breakfast the next morning, Daddy told me Jasper was coming home.

He expected gratitude, but if I collapsed with the deep-down relief I truly felt or threw my arms around his neck, he'd accuse me of being dramatic. I smiled broadly, which wasn't too hard to do under the circumstances. "Thank you, Daddy."

He smiled, too. "I have more news."

*Jasper was coming home.* I couldn't wait to tell Will.

"I gave it some thought," Daddy continued, "and you'll ride Jasper this weekend."

"Bluegrass is this weekend," I reminded him.

"That's where you'll ride him."

I stared. "I haven't ridden him in two months."

"Perfect ending to your comeback story. You're not only back, you're back on Jasper. Think of the optics. Or Frank could keep him. Your choice."

Putting me on a horse I hadn't been training on was an unnecessary risk, but I understood why he was doing it: to show me he controlled who I rode and when I rode—and to a large degree, whether I won or lost. He wasn't wrong about the optics, and no way was Frank keeping my horse.

I had no real choice, but when Daddy presented me with the appearance of one, I needed to opt for the decision he wanted me to make.

"Well, then," I said, "looks like Jasper's going to Bluegrass."

# - Twenty-three -

THE THURSDAY BEFORE Bluegrass began, Louisville buzzed with energy, traffic, and people. Derby celebrations had been under way for two weeks, and Churchill Downs commanded almost everyone's attention, but the race those young Thoroughbreds ran on Saturday would be won or lost in two minutes. Eventing horses were seasoned warriors, competing full tilt for three days.

Daddy and I had left Rosemont at four A.M. When we reached Bluegrass Show Park shortly after two, we went straight to the barn. Jasper greeted me with an ear-splitting whinny that caused everyone, even me, to wince.

"He settled right in," Eddie said, and while he and Mateo caught up with Daddy, I went into Jasper's stall, wrapped my arms around his neck, and breathed in. He'd been waiting for me when I got home from school Tuesday. I'd ridden him in back-to-back dressage and jumping lessons, and we'd clicked as though our training had never been interrupted. Daddy hadn't said so, but he'd been impressed. I could tell.

Beyond that, Jasper and I hadn't had any time together, because Eddie and Mateo had trailered him to Louisville yesterday. I stuck my thumbs in his ears and rubbed the outside with my fingers, and he stretched his neck out farther and farther.

I laughed. "Giraffe."

His eyes gleamed. Unlike Diva and Vigo, Jasper had a sense of humor.

"Let's go, darlin'." Daddy was watching us through the bars in the stall door. "Orientation."

I half listened to the show officials and lifted my hand in a wave as they welcomed me back. There was a smattering of applause from the other riders. Daddy beamed as if he were responsible for my bones knitting.

Jamie caught my eye from across the room, but I didn't have a chance to speak to him until we were filing out the door.

"Are we good?" he asked.

"Yes. Thank you." I refrained from explaining my reaction the day he and Frank had taken Jasper. "Have a good show."

"You, too."

Daddy took my elbow.

After the official walk of the cross-country course, we returned to the barn, where Mateo had readied Jasper for the jog. He passed the vet check, and then I was on his back again. It felt like coming home.

"Just ride him around the park, darlin'."

I'd thought we'd use this time for another lesson.

Daddy smiled. "You've earned it. Be back in an hour."

Cruising around the park was the next best thing to riding out—relaxing, unstructured time, a chance to reconnect with Jasper outside the ring. Some of my competitors were riding around the park, too, while others rode in warm-up arenas and open fields. I kept to the paths, cushioned with pine needles that smelled of turpentine.

The park covered hundreds of acres, meticulously landscaped to mimic nature at its most beautiful. We skirted artificial lakes and fields of dark blue-green grass, and a peace settled into me. I didn't have everything I wanted, but I was where I wanted to be.

"Good luck," Will had said last night. "You've got this."

We never talked about anything in depth anymore. Sometimes the things that went unspoken pushed up from underneath what we did say, and we'd both go silent.

At sunset, Daddy and I left the park to check into the hotel and get ready for a private supper he'd scheduled with Confections Cosmetics, whose marketing staff thought I might be the new face of their teen skin-care line. I wasn't particularly looking forward to the evening, but I'd resolved to do my best to land the deal.

The hotel parking lot was mobbed. Daddy went inside while I waited in the Land Cruiser and visualized tomorrow's dressage test. I felt even better about it than I had on Tuesday. Daddy had made the right choice, letting me ride around the park instead of putting me in a lesson.

He returned and got in with a sigh. "We have to share a room."

"What?" The word escaped before I could translate it into the customary "Sir?"

"They oversold the rooms. It's either share a room or find a different hotel—and it's Derby weekend."

Fuck. *Fuck.* I'd counted on having my own space here.

He moved the Land Cruiser into a narrow parking space. I carried the garment bag and my backpack while he brought the heavier luggage.

Our room was large and bright, with an antique maple dresser, a matching desk—and one four-poster king-sized bed. My gut plummeted.

"The desk clerk said there were two beds." Daddy crossed the room to the telephone. "I'll see if they have a cot. You get ready."

I hung up the garment bag and went into the bathroom, locking the door behind me and pressing my ear to it.

"So nowhere in this hotel is there a foldout bed? May I speak to a manager?"

I turned on the taps in the shower. *Don't let it throw you.* It wasn't ideal, but we'd spent whole nights together before.

When I emerged from the bathroom wearing one of the hotel's robes, Daddy said, "There's nothing. We'll have to manage."

While he showered, I put on the red dress Mama had bought me for Thanksgiving. The dinner yawned before me like a chasm. I should be getting some rest tonight, not spending hours at some stupid restaurant with people I didn't know trying to convince them to like me.

I applied makeup in the bathroom while he dressed in the bedroom, awkward roommates not speaking until both of us were ready.

"That dress looks better and better on you."

The frank appreciation in his expression made me feel dirty. I crossed my arms. "I hate it."

"Then why are you wearing it?"

"You asked me to."

"I didn't know you hated it." He put his wallet in the inner breast pocket of his jacket. "You should have said something. I'll take you to Leesburg next week. You can get something you like."

"I don't want you to take me to Leesburg." I was deliberately provoking him the same way Mama used to.

"Then Gertrude can take you."

"Gertrude won't drive in traffic."

"Then I'll drive, and I'll wait in the car, and you and Gertrude can shop without me. What the hell is your problem?"

*I'm half-naked and you like it. I don't want to have dinner with these people. I have to sleep with you tonight. I can't do this.*

"Nothing."

He blew out a short, exasperated breath and then said in a carefully modulated voice, "I'll chalk this up to nerves. You look beautiful. Let's go."

On the drive, he reminded me we were interviewing the Confections people as much as they were interviewing us. He'd handle business. I was to put on my public persona: Be modest, be charming, be confident, but don't be cocky.

"And don't sulk."

I slouched in my seat.

The restaurant was his kind of place, clubby, all dark wood and leather. We arrived before our hosts and were shown to a round table in the middle of the room, a see-and-be-seen location. Daddy ordered a bourbon for himself, a sparkling water for me.

Our hosts, a woman with silver hair styled in a severe pageboy and a young man with shaggy blond hair, arrived before the drinks did. She made the introductions—Elise, vice president of marketing, and Tanner, director of marketing. But Tanner's real job, the one he was uniquely suited for, was to make me miss Will with breathtaking intensity.

He sat to my left, and if I didn't look at him directly, he could have been Will. Peripherally, his hair looked exactly like Will's. I had an almost uncontrollable urge to reach over and run my fingers through it. I wondered if he'd kiss like Will.

No point in thinking about that. I'd gotten my horse back by the skin of my teeth.

He and Elise had read *The Book on Eventing*, and they asked informed questions. Before the waiter even took our order, they'd fallen under the sway of Daddy's passion and expertise. He feigned self-deprecation so well that I almost forgot who he was.

Tanner sampled the wine and nodded to the waiter, who started to pour a glass for me.

"No—" I began.

"She's sixteen," Daddy said.

"Oh. I'm sorry, sir."

I met Daddy's eyes as the waiter moved on to the other glasses. I was pretty sure he'd never ask me to wear this stupid dress again.

"You asked how we came up with the name Confections," Tanner said to Daddy. "We wanted something sweet, and in making the products we've used derivatives from plants that are commonly associated with confections—cocoa, vanilla, nuts, coconut, honey, sugar."

"Honey's not a plant," I said.

He chuckled. "I like that. You're unfiltered."

Right.

"We want everything to be appropriate for our market, not only the products but also the way they're represented. That's why it's important to choose a spokesperson who's a genuine role model."

Elise nodded. "We know a lot more about you than we did when your name came up at our marketing meeting nine weeks ago."

"The Clox ads are genius," Tanner said.

"I just did what they told me to." Namely, that had involved wearing two dozen sports watches on each arm while spread-eagled in the doorway of a specially constructed stall in a studio in Chicago, which hardly seemed like genius.

"Not everyone has such a compelling relationship with the camera. You come by it honestly, though," he said, acknowledging Daddy. "We saw some of your work."

Daddy gave an affable wave. "That was a long time ago."

Over the main course, the conversation turned to Bluegrass. While Daddy answered Elise's questions, I focused on my lamb chops and wished Will were at the table instead of Tanner.

"You'd rather be riding than sitting here, wouldn't you?" Tanner asked.

It was better to look at him directly. Straight on, he resembled Will less.

"I'd always rather be riding," I said.

"Do you enjoy modeling?"

"I'd rather be riding."

He laughed—not Will's laugh.

Daddy lifted one eyebrow a fraction of a centimeter, an almost invisible warning, but he'd said this was like an interview, and I'd been asked a question. I couldn't sit in silence.

I sipped my fizzy water. "Where will Confections be sold?"

"We'll have no trouble getting into boutiques, but we're in negotiations with a couple of department stores. We hope an association with the right spokesperson will get us there."

"Wouldn't you be better off with a real celebrity?"

"Celebrities aren't as real as you might think. Some people have a lot of style but not much substance to back it up.

We want both. You've actually achieved something. But it doesn't hurt that you have two successful campaigns to your credit—or that your skin is incredible."

"Soap and water."

"There's that refreshing quality again."

Daddy's conversation with Elise had tapered off. "Where do you plan on running the campaign?"

Tanner nodded toward Elise. "This is in your ballpark."

She rattled off a list of magazines. "We're launching in September, so we'll shoot in late June, primarily in New York, but we also plan on some location shooting. Everyone says your farm is very picturesque."

That should have been Daddy's opening to talk about Rosemont, but he said only, "It is."

"With your permission, we'll send over samples of the entire line. If Roan likes the products, all we have to do is draw up a contract that meets with your approval, Monty."

She and Tanner looked pleased. I was surprised Daddy didn't. I'd all but nailed the contract, another win for him and his clever management of my career.

"That'll be fine." He took a business card from the inner pocket of his jacket and handed it to Elise. "I'm sorry to cut the evening short, but we've had a long day, and we have an early morning. Thank you." He was already standing up, holding the back of my chair.

I'd wanted dessert, but I stood up. "Good night." I shook Elise's hand. "Thank you." I started to extend my hand to Tanner, but Daddy took my arm and turned me around with a genial but firm "Good night" to our hosts.

We'd barely made it outside before he said, "I won't have this."

"Sir?"

"You. Coming on to that man. I won't have it."

I gaped. "What are you talking about?"

He marched me through the parking lot and opened the passenger door of the Land Cruiser, slamming it behind me. The sound jolted through me. In the side mirror, I watched as he stalked around the back of the car.

He started the engine and reversed out of the space. We lurched forward with a shift in gear as abrupt as his change in mood, the streetlights casting shadows across his face.

"That man is at least thirty years old. I won't have this, Roan."

"How was I coming on to him?"

"You know how. The way you looked at him. Crossing your legs. Letting your hem ride up your thigh."

I didn't remember crossing my legs.

He wasn't through. "'I'd rather be riding.'"

"What was wrong with that? We were just talking."

"Like Will Howard was just giving you a ride home from school. Like he just brought you flowers. Like he kept calling the house until I got rid of the landline."

"You said it was an interview. We were feeling each other out."

"You acted like a goddamned tease."

Anger rushed through me. "That's not true."

"Shut up. Not another word."

I passed the rest of the drive back to the hotel chewing the inside of my cheek.

In the lobby, he handed me the key to the room. "Go on up. I need a nightcap."

Yeah, me, too. The minibar tempted me, but I changed into my nightgown, washed my face, brushed my teeth. Then I got in bed, as near the edge as I could be without falling off, switched off the lamp, and pulled the covers up to my chin.

I hadn't done anything wrong. So what if I'd thought of running my fingers through Tanner's hair and kissing him? Thoughts weren't actions, Tanner wasn't Will, and Daddy wasn't normal. Neither was I. If I were, I'd be figuring out how to defuse him instead of missing Will so acutely that I could all but feel myself pushing my fingers into his thick blond hair, kissing him, fitting my body against his and having his cock harden instantly. My nipples grazed the inside of my nightgown.

The click of the electronic lock sent a shock through me. The door opened and closed. The dead bolt locked.

My pulse thumped.

Daddy's zipper slid down, and hangers scraped on the rod of the closet. In the bathroom, water ran, and he brushed his teeth.

He got into bed, irritation sparking off him.

Tangible physical tension stretched across the king-sized expanse between us. I felt like I was going to erupt out of my skin.

I didn't want this; I didn't want *him*. When he reached for me, I squeezed my eyes shut and lay still, willing my physical body to be as stoic and leaden as my thoughts and emotions. He fumbled with my nightgown, my underwear. I didn't help him, but I didn't have to. He rose over me and drove his cock into me. All I had to do, I thought, was lie here and take it like I had countless times before.

That was all I did, and still an orgasm rose in me like a tide. I tried to stop it, but it rolled through me in waves, and it was too much for him, and he came, too.

I looked up at him. His anger was gone. He'd fucked it out of his system—but if I'd hoped that would work for me, it hadn't.

He rolled on his side and curled his body around mine.

*What are you doing?* The voice was so real that for an instant I thought someone had spoken aloud.

*I don't know*, I thought. *I don't know.*

# - Twenty-four -

WE ARRIVED AT the show park before dawn. Daddy went to the barn, and I went to the trailer and poured myself half a cup of coffee. While I drank it, Bluegrass woke up, horses and people silhouetted against the pink-and-gold sunrise as they walked along the paths, voices and the occasional nicker punctuating the quiet.

It was horse-show business as usual. Daddy had risen early, dressed, and gone downstairs to wait for me in the lobby. As soon as he left, I locked myself in the bathroom with my phone and brought up Will's number. He'd said I could call anytime. It was easier to text, but even then, not so easy. How did I get from here to there?

*Good morning.*

Innocent.

Delete.

*I've never said it before, and it doesn't seem fair to say it now, but I want you to know I love you.*

I stared at the message for a minute before I turned off my phone without sending it. Messing with his emotions, making him sad or giving him hope we could be boyfriend and girlfriend again, wouldn't make me feel better about last night. Mentally I led Will into a stall in my mind. I had a dressage test to ride.

I had drawn a good position in the order of go, thirty-eight, so I would ride near the end. As Daddy and I sat in the stands and watched my competition, I tried to put last night out of my mind, listening as he commented on the other riders' flaws and strengths.

At one, I went to the trailer and suited up, my reflection cool and confident. Look like a winner, feel like a winner. I practiced a winning smile. Too many teeth.

Eddie and Mateo had spent all morning polishing Jasper to an almost otherworldly luster. I fed him a sugar cube while Daddy snapped photos with his cell, documentation of my comeback, assuming it wasn't disastrous. It wouldn't be, I thought.

Jasper pawed the ground.

"He's ready to rock and roll," Eddie said.

"Me, too," I said.

We walked over the grounds to the practice arena, Jasper strutting along in what Eddie called his parade walk. I put on my white kid gloves and flexed my fingers. Daddy gave me a leg up and straightened the tails of my jacket.

With a clean cloth, Mateo buffed my boots and dusted Jasper's legs and hoofs.

Daddy looked up at me. "Take a deep breath and let it out."

I did.

"Again. . . . One more. . . . Good. You're ready. Jasper's ready. You'll ride a great test."

We'd been warming up for half an hour and had practiced some movements from the test when I heard applause. The previous rider, a young woman from England, exited the competition arena and dismounted.

Eight minutes between competitors. Jasper and I were up. I kept him in a slow trot. My dress helmet and jacket drank in the heat. Sweat filmed on my face, trickled down my back.

After a time, the announcer's voice came over the loud-speaker. "That was Prima, owned and ridden by Alexia Morse of the United Kingdom, with a score of 48.2. Next is number thirty-eight, Emerald Jazz Dancer, owned by Rosemont Farms and ridden by Roan Montgomery."

The bell chimed.

"Knock 'em dead, darlin'," Daddy said, but I was already leaving him behind.

Jasper entered the arena in a controlled canter. As always, the rest of the world went out of focus until the only things I could see clearly were my horse's neck and ears and the expanse of arena. We halted at I, a good, solid halt. I saluted the judges, and we went directly from the halt into a collected trot, tracking right at C. Maintaining the trot, we moved laterally from M to B, Jasper's left foreleg crossing over his right.

He was supple, collected, rhythmic, willing to do everything I asked of him as we executed changes of gait and direction, but there was more to his performance than any of this alone or even all of it together. I wasn't a rider on his back. Our minds and hearts and muscles had coalesced so completely that I was part of him.

We moved down the centerline in a collected canter and halted at X. I bowed my head in salute to the judges. Thunderous applause broke the spell.

I leaned over and hugged Jasper. Laughter rippled through the stands.

Daddy met us as we exited. "God*damn*, that was gorgeous."

I dismounted and hugged Jasper again. His eyes were bright. He knew he'd done well.

Mateo led him away. I removed my helmet. Daddy helped me take off my number, and I unbuttoned my shadbelly and shrugged out of it. Eddie bundled everything together and waited with us to hear the results.

"That was Emerald Jazz Dancer, owned by Rosemont Farms and ridden by Roan Montgomery, coming back from a training injury with our best score of the day, a near-perfect 37.9."

The stands erupted again. Daddy hugged me. Cameras clicked and whirred.

He released me. "Proud of you, darlin'."

It was a rush, all of it, the ride, the applause, his praise, the attentions of the photographer from *Classic Equine* and then Owen, the SNN camera operator, and fans, too, shooting us with their cell phones, capturing our closeness, Daddy's pride.

"Let's go see how that horse of yours is doing," he said.

That horse of *mine*—not Frank's.

Jasper looked fresh. Mateo had already hosed him off and was scraping excess water from him. My sweat-soaked shirt clung to me.

"Go change." Daddy handed me the key to the trailer. "Meet me back here. We'll have lunch."

In the trailer, I took a sponge bath and dressed in the jeans and polo shirt I'd worn to the show park. If I'd had my phone, I'd have texted Will now—not the message I'd written earlier, but something simple, like *Dressage test went great*. He was cutting class to watch the live stream, so he might know. He might know I loved him, too.

Lunch was messy Kentucky brown sandwiches purchased from one of the park vendors and eaten in the makeshift tack room, the four of us sitting on hay bales, everyone good-humored and joking. I slipped into Jasper's stall with carrots and ear rubs. "Thank you," I whispered. I kissed him between his eyes.

The rankings were in by midafternoon. A rider from Brazil was in third, Jamie was in second, and I was in first. Michael who? Odette shouldn't have written me off.

We gave interviews to Vic and writers from *Eventing Today* and *Classic Equine*. On our way to walk the cross-country course again, we accepted congratulations from competitors and strangers alike.

On most cross-country courses, the last few fences were relatively easy, but here, two jumps from the end was a pool hidden by a hedge, and after the final fence, the run-in to the finish was slightly uphill. Grueling.

Daddy studied the water jump. "It's a lot to ask of a horse this late in the course. Pacing will be important."

Back at the barn, he went into the tack room to talk to Eddie, and I visited Jasper for one more ear rub. I pressed my cheek to his neck, his tangy scent prolonging my illusion that I was happy, except it was more than an illusion. I loved this part of my life.

My high dissipated in the car.

"Since tomorrow's another long day," Daddy said, "what if we order room service?"

Today he'd been who I wanted him to be all the time, but he'd change when we got back to the room. I tried to feel better about last night by remembering that I hadn't actively participated, much less instigated anything, but I felt no less shame, no less complicity. Was I *letting* this happen? How could I stop him? He had all the power.

I looked at the room-service menu first and showered while he placed the order. I put on my nightgown and a hotel robe and wiped steam from the mirror. On the outside, I finally recognized my new short-haired self, but I was having trouble with the inside.

When I went back into the bedroom, Daddy was on the bed, propped on pillows and reading the paper.

He folded it. "If room service comes, add the tip and sign for it."

He took fast showers. I made sure my phone was at the bottom of my backpack, then pulled out my biology notebook. I was reviewing my notes when Daddy came out of the bathroom wearing a robe and rubbing his hair with a towel.

He came over to me and stroked my hair. "That was an outstanding ride, darlin'."

Again I felt a glow at his words—his words, not his touch. If I could keep the conversation focused on riding, tonight might be okay.

"You got me here," I said.

"I appreciate that, but you were the one on the horse." He tousled my hair.

*Quit touching it. Quit touching me.*

A knock came at the door, and he went to answer it. A waiter wheeled in a cart.

Lunch had been late and the sandwich rich, so I wasn't hungry, but I'd have even less appetite tomorrow until after I rode, so I'd ordered a poached chicken breast and milk. The cart also held a steak, a bowl of strawberries, and a bottle of Veuve Clicquot in an ice bucket.

I sat in the desk chair, Daddy on the bed, the cart between us like a table. The cork sighed as he eased it out of the bottle. He filled one flute for himself and barely wetted the bottom of a second flute, which he handed to me.

He raised his glass. "I didn't think you had it in you."

I didn't much want to toast to his lack of confidence in me, but I touched my glass to his.

He watched me. "Do you like it?"

"It's good."

"Some more, then." He poured a trickle down the side of my glass, no more than a sip.

"Why didn't you think I had it in me?"

"You said it yourself. You haven't had any training time to speak of on Jasper."

"So why am I riding him?"

"I wanted to see if you have what it takes."

"And do I?"

"We'll find out."

He ate his steak, and I drank my milk and ate some chicken and strawberries. Then he pushed the cart aside and held out his hand. His nails were perfectly buffed.

*I can't do this anymore.*

"Excuse me." I rose and went into the bathroom and closed the door and locked it.

The doorknob rattled. "You all right, darlin'?"

"I drank too much. I'm going to be sick." If he thought I was drunk enough to throw up, he might leave me alone, but I'd barely had a taste of champagne, so I'd have to make myself puke. I leaned over the toilet and stuck my fingers down my throat, gagging and bringing up the contents of my stomach.

"Jesus, darlin', you didn't have any alcohol to speak of."

"I guess I'm sensitive to it." I flushed the toilet. "I need to lie down."

The odor of vomit might put him off, but I couldn't stand the aftertaste, so I brushed my teeth and then sat on the edge of the bathtub. The sound of him moving around in the other room raked across my nerves. My skin felt sunburned. If we weren't in the same bed, it would reduce the chances of sex. I could sleep on the floor. Or he could. He wouldn't, although in similar circumstances any other coach would so his rider would be rested the next day.

There were no similar circumstances. There wasn't another coach at this event who wanted to undermine his rider. He demanded success but had set me up for failure by putting me on Jasper, but that had backfired, because Jasper and I were magic. Or was he just pushing me to be the best?

He was at the door again. "I got some aspirin from your backpack. Open up. You don't want a hangover."

People didn't even take aspirin to prevent a hangover any—
*My backpack.*

I leaped to my feet and pawed at the doorknob, finally getting the door open. Daddy stood there, aspirin in hand, but my eyes snapped past him to my backpack on the bed, unzipped, books spilling out.

My phone wasn't among the books—he hadn't found it— and I pulled my gaze back to him, but he'd already turned his head to see what I'd been looking at.

He glanced back at me with a suspicious eye, walked over to the bed, and dumped everything out onto the immaculate white comforter. My phone tumbled out, and my bladder spasmed in a sudden urge to urinate.

His face deadly, he turned on the phone and swiped his finger across the screen. I'd never bothered to lock it with a password, but even if I had, he'd have forced me to tell him what it was.

He tapped the screen and scrolled. "You were right, darlin'. Will Howard wasn't calling the house." He tapped again. "'I want you to know I love you.'" He grimaced. "You love him."

My tongue stuck to the roof of my mouth. I peeled it free. "I didn't send it."

He scrolled and read, his face becoming more and more closed. "Oh, look at this. He's going to lick every inch of you."

My face burned. At first, I'd deleted our texts, but then I'd found so much pleasure in rereading them that I'd kept them.

"You have no right to read those." My voice cracked.

He scrolled. "You've met him at the fire road. Our fire road?"

*Our* fire road, where he'd fucked me against a tree, not caring that the bark scraped my back bloody.

"Tell me you had enough sense not to send him naked selfies, or they'll be all over the internet."

Despite the heat of some of our texts, Will and I had never discussed naked pictures.

"He wouldn't do that."

He glanced at me. "But you would."

"You're disgusting." I started for the door, not knowing where I'd go, just knowing I couldn't stay here.

Daddy was on me before I'd taken a full stride, his fingers like iron around my wrist. "How old is he?"

The question was such a non sequitur that I answered. "Seventeen."

"Not eighteen? If he is, that's statutory rape. I swear to God I'll have him arrested, and you better believe he'll spend time in jail. You think he'll have any kind of life after that? He'll be a sex offender. That follows a man forever."

The threat turned my blood to ice water. But Will *wasn't* eighteen—and I was known among my competitors for having solid ice in my veins, nothing watery about it.

I looked at the fingers around my wrist. "You want to talk about who's a sex offender?"

"What happens between us is private."

"What happens between us is wrong." I wrenched free. "We're done. You touch me again, you kiss me or try to fuck me or hurt me in any way, you lay a finger on Will, you so much as threaten to get rid of Jasper, and I'll tell everyone, starting with your good friend Vic."

For a moment, I had him where I wanted him—dumbfounded.

Then he advanced on me. "You lying, cheating whore—you stupid *cunt*—you're just like your mother."

He'd never spoken to me like that before; I'd never even heard him say those things to Mama. But what struck me wasn't being called names. It was the word *cheating*. In what world was it possible for a daughter to cheat on her father?

"You're disgusting." I tried to push past him, but he caught me in a python's embrace, pinning me, my back to his front. His arms crushed the air from my lungs.

"Is that why you came last night—because I'm disgusting?"

I threw my head back and connected with his nose. With a grunt he released me, but I stumbled. He grabbed me again and spun me around to face him.

Anger roiled inside me like magma. I launched myself at him. He sidestepped, picked me up under one arm, threw me on the bed. I started to bounce up, but he was already over me. I jammed my knee upward and caught his thigh. I swiped at his eyes with my fingernails, but he pulled his head back, and I clawed his neck. Furrows of skin rolled up under my nails, which broke to the quick.

He slapped me, his hand cracking against my cheek. His strength was stunning. My jaw felt unhinged, my eyes loose in their sockets.

For an instant I saw remorse on his face. Then his mouth crushed mine. My teeth cut the inside of my lips. I tasted blood.

With one hand he held my wrists against my chest. He lifted his hips. With his free hand he opened the thick hotel robe and pulled up my nightgown.

"Stop," I hissed, knowing he wouldn't.

I turned my head to the side and tried to bite his arm. I kicked until it seemed wiser to clamp my legs together, but he pushed his knee between my thighs, pulled down my panties, and forced his way inside me.

The friction of flesh on unlubricated flesh seared and tore, and in the violence of his assault my aching bladder let go. Pee ran hot between my legs, saturating the covers under me, and the fight left me.

He held me down with no effort, his fingers so tight around my wrists that my hands throbbed from lack of circulation. His face was suffused with blood, and he went from scarlet to nearly purple when he came.

I lay in piss and cum.

After a long time, he went soft.

"If I let you go"—he sounded odd, as if he had a cold—"no scratching, no biting, no hitting, no kicking, no screaming. None of it. Agreed?"

I nodded shortly. He released my wrists and rolled off me, and I filled my lungs. I'd lied—I was going to scream—but when I tried, only a whimper came out. I staggered up, hobbled by my panties. My nightgown and robe were wet. The gown stuck to the back of my legs. I tottered into the bathroom and pushed the door shut.

I got out of the wet clothes and ran water in the sink but didn't wait for it to warm before I held a washcloth under it. I squeezed out the excess and pressed the cloth between my legs. The pressure hurt, but the cold was soothing. When I took it away, it was stained with blood and pale yellow pee and the shine of semen. I rinsed the washcloth and wiped myself down and touched the raised red handprint on my cheek.

The door opened. I was so dazed I'd neglected to lock it.

"Get in the shower."

Indecision kept me standing still. I wanted to wash him off me, out of me. But right now, I could prove what he'd done, and he'd be arrested, and the future he'd predicted for Will would become his future instead. He'd go to prison once I told the police all the things we'd done.

He turned on the water. From four impressive parallel scratches, blood trickled down his neck, down his shoulder, into his chest hair.

"Get in."

I reached for the doorknob. He caught my wrist, pulled me to him, scooped me up, and set me on my feet under the stream of water, all in one smooth move, a clip from a dance number in an old black-and-white film.

He got in, too, and started to wash me, his fingers thorough and invasive. The soap burned like acid. Not for the first time, I saw us together as if I floated above. The dirty old man stuck his soapy fingers inside the bleeding girl. I held on to stoicism as if it would save me.

"You need to know something. You're mine. If you don't want Will Howard to get hurt, stay away from him. A word to the wise, darlin'. Don't threaten me. And don't underestimate me."

It was a mistake I'd never make again.


THE NEXT MORNING we sat in the stands and watched the first riders set off on the cross-country course. He wore a rain jacket zipped up to his neck, which covered the scratches. I'd broken four nails so short that my fingertips hurt. My eyes were puffy, the inside of my eyelids lined with sandpaper. My lower lip felt tender.

None of that matched the pain between my legs. I wasn't bleeding, but physically and mentally, I was in no condition to compete. When I'd told him this morning I needed to withdraw, he'd said, "You want to keep your horse?"

I told myself last night wasn't any different from any other time, but even thinking that way set me on fire with shame. Whether he was gentle or rough, whether I was complicit or not, I finally understood that what he did was always a form of violence. He'd been hurting me forever.

Something was different, though. The man who'd raped me last night was no longer Daddy. Whatever had tethered me to that childish name for him had been severed.

A light rain began to fall midmorning, and the horses thundering over the turf dug a muddy path. Horse after horse fell at the second water jump. All of them scrambled to their feet unhurt, but every time a horse went down, I flashed on what it would be like to take a fall. My rioting mind didn't need that particular image taking hold.

I stood up.

My father broke off his conversation with Frank, who was sitting on his other side. "Where are you going?"

"To the barn."

"I'll go with you. Later, Frank."

"Good luck, kid." Frank winked at me.

What would it be like to train with him? I liked him, so long as he wasn't trying to get Jasper back. He was hard on his riders, but I'd bet he'd never raped anybody.

My father escorted me through throngs of riders, trainers, grooms, spectators. I imagined telling all these people what he'd done. I imagined telling even one of them.

"How long do you plan to keep me under surveillance?" I asked.

"You violated my trust. You have to regain it." He was too close, crowding me.

"What about the ways you've violated me?"

"Not the time. We'll discuss this later."

*This*, I knew, was my behavior, not his.

Eddie was sitting on a hay bale under the shed row, buffing Jasper's bridle.

I could tell Eddie. He'd never invited me to open up to him the way Gertrude had, but we'd had some good conversations in the past, and I trusted him—but assuming he believed me, what did I expect him to do, go to the police? I could do that myself, if I were willing to lose everything.

My father pulled up a canvas folding chair beside him. "Getting muddy out there."

I retreated into Jasper's stall and rested my forehead in the wide, flat space between his eyes. Rain dripped off the roof. He dropped his head lower, pushing it gently into my torso. I gave him what he wanted, an ear massage.

He watched curiously as I stretched in an effort to work some elasticity into my muscles. It wasn't the strangest thing he'd ever seen me do. He'd seen Will and me in the back of the pickup.

A giant hand squeezed my heart.

*Don't think about it.*

I bent over, touching my forehead to my knees, palms flat in the straw. Blood rushed to my head and made my lower lip hurt.

Outside the stall, my father and Eddie chatted amicably. Mateo joined them with coffee from the trailer.

I couldn't work out the soreness everywhere, but after a while the only remaining discomfort was in my private parts. I couldn't fix that, but I could compartmentalize it. Jasper deserved my best effort, and he'd compensate for my shortcomings. Together, Jasper and I were magic, and we always had been.

"Almost time to warm up," my father said.

I left the stall and held out my hand for the key to the trailer.

He gave me a look that told me I'd never have another moment alone in this lifetime. "I'll walk with you."

We walked to the trailer, where he waited outside the miniature bathroom while I changed into jodhpurs and a black polo shirt, in which I neither looked nor felt like a winner. It was damply chilly in the trailer, but the rain was letting up.

He rapped on the door. "Let's go."

My chest protector, gloves, helmet, and armband were back at the barn. Mateo had saddled Jasper, who looked magnificent.

We warmed up in a practice arena and took some easy fences, and I started to think I was fit enough not only to ride but also—maybe—to hold on to my lead.

Eddie walked with us to the starting box. I listened to my father's instructions and tried to compartmentalize the coach and trainer from the man and father.

"You know the course. No one's blazed through it, but there are some decent times. Keep a steady pace. Save something for the end."

Two riders were ahead of us when we got to the box. The horses were sent onto the course two minutes apart, so I had four minutes before I rode. Jasper nickered and pulled at the reins as each of them left.

My father turned on his heel and walked away without a "Knock 'em dead, darlin'," his customary send-off.

Eddie looked after him, puzzled, and then up at me. "Everything all right?"

Not the time, as my father had said.

"Fine."

"Well, you're the one to beat."

"You mean it's mine to lose."

He frowned and smiled at the same time. "I mean you're going to win this thing. I feel it in my bones."

Eddie always had been my number-one fan.

"More guts than brains, right?" I said.

"You're not completely deficient in smarts."

I couldn't help smiling. It amazed me that I could.

I collected the reins and nudged Jasper into the box and watched the rider ahead of me take the third jump, a simple rolltop. The hills and valleys of the course hid the remaining obstacles, but I knew what lay ahead. Bluegrass was heavy on novelty jumps. Spectators liked them, they looked interesting on camera, and they tested a horse's courage in a way natural obstacles seldom did. On the trail, no one in their right mind would jump anything resembling the novelty jumps.

Beneath me, Jasper was taut with anticipation.

"Ten seconds," the timekeeper said. He began the countdown.

When he reached zero, we broke from the box.

The first fence was a split-rail vertical, and Jasper took off in an explosion of speed and power that almost left me behind.

*Shit.* I was riding a rocket.

As we galloped uphill, the terrain checked his speed a bit, but when he flew over the stone wall and the rolltop, I still hadn't caught up to him. Across level ground to the first water jump, I tried to settle him. He jumped two giant wooden duck decoys, splashing down into the lake after each one. Then we shot over the third duck and onto the bank, and once again we were in sync.

The rain had subsided into a warm mist. The air was filled with the scents of damp earth and grass and pungent horse. My pelvis hurt but pain didn't matter right now. Neither did my father. What mattered was riding this course.

We jumped a ditch, a hedge, an elaborately haphazard pile of whiskey barrels.

I checked my watch. We were about a third of the way through the course, with a time of two minutes, fifteen seconds, slightly ahead of our target time, but we had some hills coming up.

We galloped through the woods and jumped from the broad shady path down a two-meter drop onto open ground. The landing jarred me so badly that I cried out. What would viewers make of that? It was a spectacular obstacle, certain to be on camera.

We pounded up a low hill, taking an in-and-out and a broad Swedish oxer along the way. The incline brought Jasper down to a more sensible pace. At the top, the terrain leveled out again. We took a brick wall, the terraced jump, a pair of wishing wells, an oversized coal cart, a fence under an arch of girders. Jasper never hesitated. He soared over the Churchill Downs jump, and as we approached the second water jump, where so many horses had fallen, his energy and enthusiasm showed no signs of flagging. A stride from the hedge, he gathered himself for the effort.

He pushed off, launching us over the hedge and landing in the water, then leaping over the brush pile onto the grassy bank on the far side. We raced toward the next-to-last jump, a skinny with a narrow face. Jasper sailed over it. Twelve strides later we took off over the final obstacle, a rustic split-rail fence, clearing it by more than a foot. My horse could fly.

His front hoofs struck the ground. An audible double snap traveled through his legs and into my body, and he pitched forward. I somersaulted over his head, my right shoulder hitting the wet grass. The blow knocked the wind from me, and everything hurt more than it should have, but I had enough momentum to roll to my feet.

A few yards away, Jasper heaved on his side, raising his head and rocking his big body back and forth, trying to get his forelegs under him. Then Mateo was lying across his neck to immobilize him and Eddie was squatting next to my father, who was on his knees, removing the protective boots from Jasper's forelegs, revealing jagged, bloody bone protruding between the knee and the ankle of both legs.

My father sat back on his heels. "Ah, God."

"No." That despairing little cry came from me.

He got to his feet and intercepted me, his hands on my shoulders. "Darlin', no."

He couldn't hold on to me in public the way he did in private. I threw off his hands and staggered over to my horse and dropped to my knees beside him. His eyes were glassy, the irises rimmed by white. His nostrils flared as he huffed out short, irregular breaths. Sweat poured from his body, not the healthy sweat of physical effort, but thin watery rivers of it, a response to pain and shock.

"I'm here." I took off my glove and put my hand on his muzzle. "I'm right here."

He trembled and exhaled with a sound of pure agony that went right through me.

Two large vans, equine ambulances, had pulled up at right angles. I recognized one of the course veterinarians. The air wouldn't go all the way to the bottom of my lungs.

My father spoke to the vet. I didn't hear what he said. I didn't need to. The compound fracture of two legs wasn't a survivable injury. My broken horse couldn't be fixed.

I began to rub his ears. "I'm here."

He made that horrible sound again. Mateo, crooning a steady "Easy, boy. Easy, boy," met my eyes.

My father squatted beside me. "Darlin', you don't have to do this."

The knot in my throat was strangling me. "I'm not leaving."

Eddie put a hand on Mateo's shoulder. Mateo closed his eyes but never stopped saying, "Easy, boy. Easy, boy." Eddie's cheeks were wet.

I doubled over and whispered in Jasper's ear. "You're the best horse, Jasper. There'll never be another one like you."

The vet probed Jasper's neck to find the jugular vein.

My father put his arm around me. My right shoulder hurt, but I didn't move, except to keep massaging Jasper's ears. "Don't be afraid. You're magic."

The vet inserted a needle into Jasper's neck and drew up some blood to make certain it was in the vein. Dark red blood swirled into the clear pink poison. Slowly, the vet pressed the plunger, and the contents of the syringe fed into Jasper's vein.

His rapid breathing slowed, he released a lungful of air, and he didn't inhale again. His eyes were open, but the life had gone out of them. *A kind eye.*

The vet withdrew the needle, held a stethoscope to Jasper's side, and listened. After a moment, he said, "He's gone. I'm sorry."

I stopped rubbing his ears. I wanted to curl up in the curve of Jasper's neck and stay with him. I turned my head toward my father, who stood up and helped me to my feet.

Screens had been set up to block the accident from spectators' eyes. Red and blue lights flashed. Another ambulance, this one for humans, waited for me. Two paramedics approached us, snapping on latex gloves.

"Let's get you checked out." My father walked me to the ambulance and climbed into the back behind me, followed by one of the medics. The other one closed the doors. Through the windows, I saw the slides and pulleys that would be used to load

Jasper's body into one of the vans. I felt him galloping, flying over fences, landing without missing a stride. *Snap-snap.*

Everything got smaller as the ambulance pulled away. It was close in there, warm. My father started to unzip his jacket and then stopped. The scratches on his neck remained hidden.

The paramedic unbuckled my helmet and removed it. He set it on the gurney beside me, unfastened the straps of the body protector, pulled it over my head.

"What will they do with him?" I asked my father.

"We'll take him home."

"All of him?" Rosemont traditionally buried a horse's head, heart, and hoofs, which had never seemed gruesome before, but I'd never contemplated Jasper's dismemberment before.

"Sure. All of him." My father pulled his phone from the pocket of his jacket.

I hugged myself.

The paramedic put a hand on my shoulder. "What hurts?"

"Ed," my father said, "bring home the whole body."

I put my hands over my ears and squeezed my eyes shut.

"Did you hit your head?" The paramedic felt my skull for lumps or dents, and had me follow the tip of his finger with my eyes, and shined a penlight into them. He made me windmill my arm backward and forward, but I hadn't broken any bones. All the ways I hurt were always invisible. I was fine. I'd be sore. That was all.

My father signed a release declining transport to a hospital, and the paramedics gave us a ride to the parking lot.

My father tossed the body protector and crash hat in the backseat of the Land Cruiser and opened the passenger door for me. He was in auto mode, too.

This was unreal. It hadn't happened. I was asleep, and I'd wake up, and Jasper would be alive—and my father wouldn't have raped me last night, and since I was making things up, we'd just be a normal father and daughter.

It was real. It had happened.

He got behind the wheel. "It's after five, and we still have to check out of the hotel. We won't get home until four in the morning."

I didn't care about our itinerary.

He started the car. "We'll stay the night."

Then I cared. Staying another night meant sharing the bed.

"I want to go home."

He hit the steering wheel with the flat of his hand, a violent gesture that startled me. "We're staying. It's not safe to make the drive."

It hadn't been safe for me to ride, either. Jasper was dead because he'd made me.

I huddled close to my window. Traffic was heavy, horns blaring. Louisville was one huge post-Derby celebration. Restaurant parking lots were full, and the people going in were laughing, as if they'd all backed the winner.

My father's phone rang. He pressed a button on the steering wheel to dismiss the call. "Vic."

In our hotel room, the red light on the telephone was blinking. While he checked messages, I crawled onto the bed and lay down on my right side, pushing my shoulder into the mattress and making it hurt more. The comforter on the bed smelled starchy and clean. Housekeeping had made the soiled bedding and bathrobe disappear.

Through my eyelids the room went dark.

He touched my ankle. My body jerked painfully.

"I'm taking your boots off."

I neither resisted nor helped. Gently, he removed both boots.

"Now your watch and your armband." Bugs scurried under my skin when his fingers brushed my wrist and upper arm. "I haven't forgotten anything you've done, but let's set it aside right now."

I hadn't forgotten anything he'd done, either. I wouldn't set it aside.

He sat on the bed behind me. "Come on, darlin'. Let it out."

Tears clotted my throat, but I would *not* give him the opportunity to touch me on the pretext of comforting me. I'd choke to death before I let myself cry.

He sighed. "I'll get you some aspirin."

Through a narrow gap in the blackout curtains, sunset became dusk. I thought of Eddie and Mateo taking Jasper home.

My father went in and out of the bathroom—pee, flush, wash hands, brush teeth. His wallet thumped on the dresser, his belt buckle clinked, his clothing landed somewhere as he stripped. He got in bed. I lay on my side, far away from him. If he touched me now, I wouldn't stop fighting until one of us was dead.

Who was I kidding? I'd fought last night. He was a thousand times stronger than I was.

He didn't touch me. His breathing grew slower. Dusk turned to night, but night wasn't dark here the way it was at home, where the only light pollution came from motion-detector lights at the barn. A barn blazing with light at night inevitably meant bad news. A horse had colicked or was injured or was having trouble delivering a foal. If the barns weren't yet lit, they would be in a few hours. By now everyone would know Jasper was dead. Will would know, too, if he'd watched the live feed. There would be endless replays and analysis.

Bluegrass was over for me. I no longer needed to compartmentalize. I could think about everything that had happened here, except I couldn't bear to.

But I felt every moment of it. I felt it in my bones.

# - Twenty-five -

WE LEFT LOUISVILLE when the morning was still dark.

I had slept, physiologically incapable of keeping my eyes open. In my dreams he'd assaulted me again and again, and Jasper kept dying, and I'd think I was awake only to find myself in another version of the nightmare, none of which was as bad as real life.

I'd slept in yesterday's cross-country clothes, but this morning I'd put on jeans and a nylon jacket, which I tried to disappear inside, turtle-like, as the last stars faded and the morning turned gray and sunrise began to bloom. Daybreak brought mile after mile of interstate bordered by rest stops and oversized gas stations and low hills. The land was gentler in Kentucky than it was at home, but the hills were such a bright green that the color hurt my eyes.

After a couple of hours, we exited the interstate and pulled into a fast-food drive-through. A stomach-turning eggy smell wafted from the window.

"What do you want?" he asked.

"Coffee." My voice was grainy from disuse.

"And?"

I was silent.

He turned to the window. "Two coffees and two breakfast burgers."

"Breakfast burgers" sounded experimental on his tongue.

"Eat," he said as we drove back onto the frontage road.

I dug into the grease-splotched bag and found two tiny cartons of half-and-half. I took the lid off my cup and considered dumping the contents on his crotch.

With a sound of exasperation he retrieved the bag and put it in his lap, shielding himself from the emasculating coffee burn I imagined. I added the half-and-half to my coffee. It sank to the bottom.

He drove one-handed while he fished out a burger for himself, unwrapped it, and bit into it. Maybe he'd choke to death. Or contract food poisoning.

He swallowed. "Not bad. You should eat."

He was alive and showing no ill effects from the breakfast burger when we crossed into West Virginia. I wasn't accustomed to drinking that much coffee. My stomach felt like it had been eaten away. Caffeine pumped through my veins and made my heart race.

"I've given some thought to this situation with Will Howard," he said. "Whatever you feel for him, it isn't love. You're infatuated. I understand that. An older boy pays attention to you, it's flattering. But he only wants one thing from you."

"The same thing you want?"

"I would never take a chance with your future. Can you say the same for him? Can you tell me you used protection every single time? I know how a teenage boy thinks. Condoms aren't high on his list."

They'd been high on Will's list. Except for the first night, we'd used them without fail.

"You've taken more chances with my future than Will and I ever have," I said. "It wasn't safe for me to ride yesterday, and you made me, and now Jasper's dead, and it's your fault."

"You were the one on the horse."

When he'd said it after the dressage phase, he'd been giving me credit for a strong performance; now he meant I'd ridden Jasper to his death.

Whether the outcome was good or bad, I was responsible for the way I'd ridden, but I said, "I asked you to let me withdraw."

"There was no reason to."

"You *raped* me."

"How was Friday night different from any other night?"

Yesterday I'd tried—so hard—to convince myself it wasn't. I'd wanted everything to be the same; *I'd* wanted to be the same. I'd wanted to compartmentalize what had happened and focus on riding and winning and a straight road to Olympic glory.

"It was different because I told you no," I said. "I told you not to touch me or kiss me or fuck me."

"Or you'd tell everyone?" He sounded as if he'd laid a trap for me that I'd walked right into. "If you were ever going to tell anyone, you'd have told the social worker at the hospital. You didn't say a thing. You never do, because you know what'll happen as soon as you breathe a word to anyone."

I'd thought about the scenario he began to describe, but as he spoke, I could see it coming to pass.

"I'll hire the best lawyers money can buy, even if I have to sell Rosemont to pay for them. And your name might be kept out of the media, but mine won't. Everyone will know who you are."

He could have stopped there.

"The police will take you to the hospital for a rape kit. Some strange doctor will examine you—put a speculum in you, take swabs, make photos. And those photos aren't private. People will see them—police, attorneys, the judge, jurors, even the goddamned bailiffs."

I was as humiliated as if a whole courtroom of people were looking at the photos right now.

"After that, the police will start asking questions, and when they're through with you, my lawyers will just be getting started. When did it begin? How often does it happen? Did you ever tell anyone? Why not?"

"I told Mama."

"Your own mother didn't believe you, darlin', or she'd have confronted me."

The revelation was like being thrown—fleeting weightlessness, and then gravity slamming you into the ground. All these years I'd assumed Mama had tried to make him stop. Her lack of success hadn't surprised me—but my question the day after Thanksgiving had been on the mark. She hadn't tried. She wasn't in my life anymore and she'd still found a way to hurt me.

"She knew the truth," I said.

"No one wants to hear the truth. *You* don't even want to hear it, and you sure as hell don't want to tell it. You want people to know you like it? You want Will Howard to know? Think hard, darlin'. If I go down, you do, too." He paused. "I always win."

West Virginia went by in a nauseating blur. At one time the mountains must have looked like the landscape around Sheridan, but they'd been decapitated by mining. The spaces where the peaks should have been reminded me of myself. Stripped of some essential part.

We reached Rosemont in the early afternoon. From the driveway, I saw Jasper's grave, a mound of fresh rust-colored earth on one of the hills overlooking the farm. Burying his entire body had required a massive grave. My father had picked the spot, the hill Jasper and I had ridden up countless times. From its crest, Rosemont was my toy farm, and everything was perfect.

Now it didn't even look perfect. The grave was like a canker, and underneath the soil, Jasper was rotting.

My father braked in front of the house but didn't turn off the engine. "Do you want to walk up to his grave?"

Seeing it at a distance was like a body blow. I wasn't ready to see it up close. Tears glazed my eyes. I tilted my head back to keep them from spilling over. "No."

We rolled slowly past the house. I assumed he was driving around back to the garage, but he kept going down the hill to the barn.

"Jasper's death is tragic," he said, "and it's a huge loss, but you will *not* turn it into a disaster. Arlington is in two weeks, and we're going to be there. I'm not letting you sabotage your career. You have to toughen up. Understand?"

I understood that I hated him.

"Understand?"

"Yes."

The pall over the farm went beyond the quiet of the afternoon lull in chores, but in the barn, Diva was tied in the wash rack, and Mateo was running water from the hose over her right foreleg. He pulled more hose from the reel. She lurched back against the crossties, her hoofs clattering on the concrete.

"Easy," Mateo said. Then he saw us. "Hey, boss. Roan."

"She worse?" my father said.

"Some heat in the leg." Mateo bent the hose in half to cut off the stream of water while my father ran his hand down Diva's leg. She blew a long rattling snort through her nostrils.

Across the aisle, Jasper's door gaped open. His stall had been swept clean.

"We kept her out of the turnout this morning," Mateo said. "I've been giving her thirty minutes of hydrotherapy every two hours. It's cooler each time. Should we call Glenn?"

My father straightened. "Not if it's getting better. Why isn't somebody else doing this? You and Eddie drove all night."

"Eddie drove. He said it kept his mind off . . . it's better if I stay busy." Mateo looked at me. "You all right?"

I started to nod but my head bobbled. "How about you?"

"Not great. He was special. Oh, I have something for you." He reached in the pocket of his jeans and pulled out a thick coil of something black and shiny—a length of hair cut from Jasper's tail.

"Thank you." My voice broke as I put the coil of hair in my own pocket.

"Someone else will clean your stalls tonight," my father said to Mateo. "Get some rest."

We drove back to the house, parked in the garage, took our bags in through the screened back porch—and there was Gertrude in the kitchen, holding out her arms.

I dropped my garment bag and backpack and embraced her. She rubbed her hand up and down my back.

"I'm sorry, sugar." She would have let go, but I clung to her. "I know how torn up you must be. Those horses are like family to you."

"You're like family, too."

"Eddie okay?" my father said.

"He took a sleeping pill and went to bed. I thought I'd see what I could do up here. There's ham in the fridge. How about sandwiches?" She spoke over my shoulder. I had to let go of her now, but I didn't.

"We can make our own sandwiches," he said. "Go home. Take care of Eddie. He needs you more than we do today."

I wasn't so sure about that.

"All right. I am worried about him. Sugar . . ."

Reluctantly, I let go.

She laid her hand against my cheek. "I'll be back in the morning. That's spinach lasagna thawing on the counter, and—"

"Go." My father smiled. "We won't starve."

"Tell Eddie I'll come see him later," I said.

"Now, darlin'," my father said, "he needs to decompress. You'll see him tomorrow."

He followed me upstairs.

"I'm warning you, don't drag Eddie and Gertrude into this. It'd be a shame if they lost their jobs."

He'd made Bailey and Jasper and Will disappear. Mama, too, for whatever that was worth. Gertrude and Eddie would be easy to get rid of. All he had to do was fire them. Then I really would be all alone. Why hadn't I ever talked to Gertrude? If she knew the truth, she'd never have left me alone with him. She'd have done something, and I wouldn't be here now.

In my room, I dropped my bags on the bed. He left my duffel and his suitcase on the floor, took my arm, and led me down the hall to his room, where he closed and locked the door.

Sickening chills made me start to shake like I had a fever as he walked all the way around me.

"Who else?" he said from somewhere behind me.

"Who else what?"

"Mateo? You fuck Mateo?"

I turned toward him, openmouthed. "Have you lost your mind?"

I stepped back in time to avoid the full force of his backhand, but because I was off balance, it knocked me to my knees. I tried to curl into a ball to protect myself, but he hauled me to my feet, his face distorted.

"You made it a point to thank Mateo and Eddie in your first interview with Vic—but did you thank me?" He pushed his face into mine, breathing me in, and I screamed loudly, wordlessly, shredding the tissue in my throat. He put a hand at my neck, his thumb and index finger lifting up on my jawbone, the flat of his palm pushing against my throat and choking off the sound. He backed me toward the bed. I grabbed his fingers and tried to pull them from my neck, but he squeezed tighter. If he didn't let go of me, I was going to puke or pass out. He shoved me back on the bed. I coughed, gasping for breath.

I hadn't recovered when he got on the bed with me, and though I had no air, I fought, because even if he choked me to death, anything was better than this.

He spooned around me, clamping my arms down, holding both of my legs down with one of his. Both of us were breathing hard. His bedroom had been closed up for three days and was stifling, but the chills and trembling wouldn't stop.

"All I have to do," he whispered, his breath hot, "is loosen the hold that boy has on you, and everything can be the way it was before."

"Nothing will be the way it was." My voice shook, strained from screaming or being choked or both.

He didn't seem to have heard me. Through the long, hot afternoon, he kept me wrapped in the cocoon of his arms, murmuring in my ear from time to time. He had plans for me. My infatuation with Will had nearly ruined them, but we could make this work again.

Under my clothes, drops of sweat rolled across my skin. I was slowly suffocating—struggling to breathe in his constrictor's embrace, my throat so sore that it hurt to swallow. My jeans were too tight and cutting into my crotch. Unlike last night, he slept, but he woke at the slightest movement. I couldn't ease my way free of him, and I couldn't fight him.

The afternoon lasted a lifetime, but finally evening came on, and the house began to cool.

"Time for chores," he said.

I didn't see how I was supposed to go to the barn and muck stalls and act like everything was ordinary, but at least at the barn I wouldn't be alone with my father.

"I need a shower." Speech hurt, too.

He let me up. I went into his bathroom and closed the door, and the thin slab of wood between us was more distance than I'd had from him all day. He could walk in any second, but I felt the scum of sweat all over me, and I wanted out of these jeans. They were damp and hard to pull off because they stuck to my legs, but I undressed and stepped into his shower.

For the longest time, I let the water needle my skin. It stung my nipples, which had bled Friday night, and down below, I'd been turned inside out. I washed gingerly, wrapped a towel around myself, and reluctantly opened the bathroom door.

He followed me to my room. If he went for me now, I was at my most vulnerable, but he only waited while I took clean clothes from my dresser into my bathroom. Still, I leaned against my bathroom door while I dressed so he couldn't open it and come in. I put on a T-shirt and my oldest, softest jeans, which didn't cut into me the way the sweaty jeans had.

Some of the grooms were already mucking when we reached the barn. Even though Mateo and Eddie and I had mostly been responsible for Jasper, everyone had liked him, and they were somber as they offered their condolences.

Fernando looked at me with sympathy. "You don't look so good."

I was sure I didn't.

"Is hurting you here?" He touched his chest.

Diva began to bang on her stall door.

"Bring her out," my father said, "before she undoes all that hydrotherapy."

*Do you see him as different people?*

He *was* different people, and I was beginning to see myself as different people, too. Even more than I hated him, I hated who I was when I was with him.

As I led Diva from her stall, I could feel through the lead rope that she still favored her right foreleg.

My father frowned. "Hold her." He felt her leg. "It's not that bad. Run water over it. We'll call Glenn in the morning."

I tied her in the wash rack and uncoiled the hose. She rolled her eyes.

"Easy," I said. My throat burned. "Easy . . . easy."

I turned the hose on her lower leg, allowing water to cascade from the knee down and keeping one hand on her shoulder so I'd have some warning if she freaked.

Across the aisle, Jasper's empty stall haunted me. He should have had a long, celebrated career and a good long life right here at Rosemont. Unbelievably, my world would go on without him. I'd ride. I'd compete. I'd win. I'd maintain the persona. And my father and I . . . that would continue, too, unless I found a way out.

A tear ran down my cheek. I wiped my face with the back of my hand, inadvertently moving the hose. Diva flattened her ears and bared her teeth.

"Sorry. Easy."

When the half hour was up, I dried her leg with a hand towel and led her into her stall. She was moving normally.

Her head flashed toward me. I pulled back and avoided an all-out sinking of teeth into flesh but caught a hard pinch on my upper arm. I took off her halter and got out the door without further injury. She began to eat delicately from her grain bucket.

There was no justice in a world in which Diva lived and Jasper died.

She gave the stall door a token kick, as if she knew what I was thinking. I hung her halter and lead rope on the door.

"We'll check her again when we do the walk-through," my father said.

Working alongside the grooms, we cleaned stalls and brought in and fed the stallions, the yearlings, the mares.

It was nearly seven when we started back to the house.

"Tomorrow I have some jobs for you around the barn, and then I want you on Vigo. We'll work mostly over cavalletti, but I need to see you're not afraid of real jumping, so we'll go through a round of jumps, too."

I didn't expect to change his mind about keeping me home tomorrow, but I said, "Finals are next week."

"About school, darlin' . . . you're not going back. You'll take your finals with a proctor. Starting this summer, you'll attend classes online. I won't let you throw away your future because of Will Howard. I'm not letting you out of my sight."

"What?" I said faintly.

"You heard me."

I stopped in my tracks. "You can't do that."

"Just you watch." He took my arm above the elbow and propelled me toward the house, letting go only when we were inside. Then he waited while I washed my hands and put the lasagna in the oven.

"Upstairs," he said, and I nearly pissed myself again when he went into my room.

He picked up his bag from the floor. "Unpack." He brushed past me, his footsteps receding down the hall.

*The back stairs.* I could take them down to the kitchen, leave through the back door, call Will from the barn—

No, *really* leave. Take one of the farm's work trucks. The keys would be above the visor, and I'd been driving since I was twelve.

I opened my desk drawer, removed the envelope I kept my allowance in, stuck it down the back of my jeans, and pulled my shirt down to cover it. What else?

The duffel. It was already packed.

The floorboard creaked. He was coming back.

I unzipped the bag, took out a handful of socks, and began to cram them into a dresser drawer.

He closed the door.

Every part of me hurt.

"No." I turned around. "I can't."

He wasn't there.

A distinctive mechanical click came from the door.

I dropped the rest of the socks and jiggled the doorknob. It turned, but the door didn't budge. Sixteen years I'd slept in this room, and I'd had no idea a key existed.

He didn't need to guard me day and night. He could just lock me up.

I retrieved a hairpin from the bathroom and wiggled it around in the keyhole, turning it until blisters started to form on my fingertips. The door remained locked.

I'd been trained to stay cool and make shrewd decisions at forty miles an hour on the back of a prey animal that was all instinct and muscle. I needed to apply the same cool shrewdness now. I wouldn't always be locked in this room.

From downstairs came a flurry of beeps from the alarm system, many more than were needed to set it. He was changing the code. If I did find a way out of my room, I couldn't leave the house without triggering the system's deafening whoops and sirens.

He'd made sure of it: I wasn't going anywhere.


I PUT MY allowance back in my desk and sat down.

Tomorrow Gertrude would be here. Eddie would be at the barn. Things would begin to normalize, but what passed for normal between my father and me had at last become unbearable.

I could get myself out of this. I'd be exposed and have to give up everything I wanted, but I could end this. What would happen to the horses, the employees? To me? I was scared, but I was more scared when I thought about what I'd become if I didn't end it.

After a long time, he unlocked the door. "Supper."

He had showered and changed. He now wore a polo shirt that revealed the scabbed-over scratches on his neck.

We sat at the kitchen table, a first. Even when we were on our own, we ate in the dining room.

I separated the layers of my lasagna.

"I drafted a statement about the accident," he said. "I'll post it to your blog and share it on social media."

His take on Jasper's death, passed off as something I'd written, would evoke sadness and reflection, creating a sense of closure for fans and the media, and undoubtedly looking toward a future I no longer had, because at the first opportunity, I was going to shoot it down.

"You might pretend to take an interest."

"I do enough pretending."

He looked amused. He knew I couldn't hurt him without hurting myself, too. He didn't know I was now willing to do that.

Well, not willing. But I was going to.

I was.

After supper, I cleared the table and washed the dishes.

"Might as well do the walk-through," he said when I was finished. "It's nearly nine."

He punched in the new code to disarm the alarm, his fingers a blur on the keypad.

Outside, crickets and tree frogs chirped. My resolve to tell made me ache.

The motion-detector lights at the barn snapped on. Moths materialized from nowhere, and bats wheeled in the air, catching them. In the training barn, Daddy turned on the lights in the aisle. Vigo nickered hopefully. The horses were accustomed to routine, so he didn't seriously expect to be fed at this hour, but hope sprang eternal in the equine stomach.

My father peered through the bars of Vigo's stall. Vigo snuffled against them.

"Good boy," my father said, and we moved on to Diva.

She stood in the back of her stall, her head hanging low. She wasn't bearing weight on her injured leg.

He clicked his tongue. She didn't bare her teeth or flatten her ears.

He pushed open the door and went in.

Diva gave him a half-hearted glare.

"Easy, mare." He ran one hand down her leg and held his other hand back toward me. "Give me her halter."

I removed it from the hook on the door. Diva rolled her eyes at me.

Out of nothing but instinct, I whipped the lead rope toward her just as my father glanced back at me. A microsecond of understanding crossed his face, and then Diva did what she always did when confronted by a longe line or a hose or a lead rope that was too long.

She exploded.

# - Twenty-six -

SHE SPUN AWAY from me, her big, muscular butt slamming my father against the wall. His head hit the solid wood partition between stalls with a thud. He staggered forward, but before he could regain his balance, she reared. Her front hoofs struck the back of his head, dropping him to his knees. She pivoted and kicked him, both back feet connecting with his upper body, lifting him off the ground and sending him back into the wall. His arms unnaturally straight and limp by his sides, he toppled forward into the thick straw bedding.

Diva quivered, her eyes rimmed with white. I backed away, and she bolted out the door, favoring her off foreleg but moving fast.

Vigo milled and whinnied.

My father lay on his stomach with his face turned toward me, his eyes half-open. Blood spread over the straw.

I dropped the halter and lead line, went into the stall, squatted, and pressed my fingers against his neck. No pulse. My fingers came away slick and red.

I saw the outline of his cell phone in the back pocket of his jeans and plucked it out, my hands trembling as I tapped the keys.

"Nine-one-one. What's your emergency?"

"My father's hurt. He's unconscious and he's bleeding."

"Is he responsive?"

"No."

"Is he breathing?"

I felt the inside of his wrist and his neck and again couldn't find the pulse. I bent close to his head. The metallic odor of blood coated my nostrils. He exhaled faintly. The shaking in my hands got worse.

"He's breathing." My voice shook, too.

"Can you stop the bleeding?"

Still holding the phone, I ran into the tack room and grabbed a stack of clean towels from the shelf. Back in Diva's stall, I pressed a towel to my father's head. Red soaked through the pristine white terry cloth.

"An ambulance is on the way," the dispatcher said.

"You have the address?"

"Rosemont Farms?"

"Yes, but we're in the barn, not at the house. If they follow the driveway, they'll come to the barn. All the lights are on."

Keys clicked as she entered that information into a computer.

"Can you tell me what happened?"

"An accident." The lie rolled off my tongue as if it really had been an accident. "One of the horses trampled him. I want to call our neighbor."

"Call me back as soon as you've done that."

I disconnected and called Eddie and Gertrude's house.

"Yeah, boss?"

"It's Roan. We're at the barn. Daddy's hurt. It's bad. They're sending an ambulance."

"On my way," Eddie said.

"Eddie—Diva's loose."

"Got it," he said.

I was supposed to call the dispatcher back, but I didn't. I removed the blood-saturated towel from my father's head and replaced it with a clean one.

A truck pulled up outside. The door opened and closed. Someone ran down the aisle. Eddie appeared in the doorway.

"Let me see." He knelt beside us. I took my hands away from the towel. He checked underneath it and put it back. "Monty," he said loudly. I'd never heard him call my father anything other than "boss." "Can you hear me? *Monty*. Get more towels."

I brought an armload of clean towels from the tack room and followed his instructions, rolling them and placing them around my father's head for stability.

"Is he still breathing?"

He checked my father's carotid artery. "Yeah. Get a blanket. He's getting cold."

"Is he dying?"

"He's going into shock. Get the blanket. Move."

The horses' heavy winter blankets had been laundered months ago and hung covered in plastic at the back of the tack room. I tugged two of them from their hangers. We spread them over him and Eddie tucked them close. "What happened?"

I'd better get used to answering that.

"He was checking Diva's leg and asked me for her halter." I had to take responsibility without implicating myself. "I fumbled with the lead rope."

Eddie nodded.

I tested the waters. "I should have been more careful."

"Don't blame yourself. It could have been any of us." He changed the bloody towel on my father's head. "What was he thinking, tending to her in her stall?"

Only a fool or my father—no fool but arrogant—would have tried that with Diva, but he'd have been all right if I hadn't spooked her.

I shivered. "It wasn't his fault."

"Here, apply pressure."

I took over pressing the towel to my father's head. Eddie stood up.

"Where are you going?"

"You could use a blanket, too." He disappeared into the aisle and a moment later was draping a blanket over my shoulders. He lifted the edge of the towel.

"Bleeding's slowing down."

"Is he bleeding out?"

"Head wounds bleed like a stuck pig, but he's not bleeding out. The pressure is stanching the flow."

I pulled my horse blanket close. "What's taking them so long?"

"When did you call?"

"Right before I called you."

"They'll be here anytime. Gertrude went down to the gate to meet them."

"Diva's running around out there loose. I think she's really hurt." Was it okay to voice concern about Diva after what she'd just done?

"Teo will call Glenn."

"Mateo?"

"Yeah. I'm going to the hospital with you."

His tone was deliberately casual, which meant Eddie didn't think doctors were going to patch my father up and keep him overnight and release him in the morning. Eddie thought he was dying, and he didn't want me to be alone in a hospital waiting room when that happened.

"Okay." I tried to sound casual, too. "Thanks."

It was little more than twenty-four hours since Eddie and I had faced each other over Jasper's body at Bluegrass, and I'd shown more concern for Jasper than I was showing for my father. I used the corner of a clean towel to wipe some blood from his cheek. "You'll be okay."

In the distance, a siren whined.

"See?" Eddie said. "They're here."

Vigo shuffled in his stall. The siren became unbearably louder. Red and blue lights strobed over the interior of the barn. The siren went silent.

Eddie stepped out of the stall into the aisle. "In here!"

I stood up and backed away as two paramedics appeared in the doorway. They'd brought a gurney, which they left in the aisle. One of them knelt by my father.

"What happened?"

"He was trampled by a horse."

"You his daughter?"

"Yes."

"Don't go anywhere. We'll need some information from you."

"Let's step outside, sugar, give them room to work." Gertrude must have ridden in the ambulance. She led me out of the stall, and we watched through the bars. One paramedic retrieved supplies from the gurney while the other examined my father. They fastened a rigid cervical collar around his neck. The collar was standard. Yesterday after Jasper had gone down, I'd been up and walking, but if I hadn't been, spinal injury would have been presumed until it was ruled out.

They angled the gurney into the stall and lowered it to the ground, pulling the bloody straw away from one side of my father's body. Then they placed a spine board on the cleared floor. That was standard, too. Carefully, they rolled him onto his back on the board.

His skin was the color of putty, and his eyes had closed all the way. He looked like a dead man.

Gertrude hugged me hard with one arm.

The paramedics strapped him to the board, clamped an oxygen mask over his face, inserted a needle into his arm, started a saline IV. Then they lifted the backboard onto the gurney and secured it.

One of them glanced my way as they wheeled him out of the stall. "Come with us."

"We'll be right behind you," Gertrude assured me.

Outside, the back doors of the ambulance stood open. The interior looked cold, sterile. They pushed the gurney in. One of the paramedics climbed in after it. I started to follow.

The other paramedic put a hand on my arm.

"Ride up front with me."

I did, but I turned in my seat and watched the one in the back cut open my father's shirt.

"How old is he?" the driver asked as we set off. Strange—the siren wasn't nearly as loud inside the ambulance as it was outside.

"Fifty-eight."

"Allergies?"

"No."

"Medications?"

"No."

"Any health problems?"

"No."

The paramedic in the back relayed that information into a radio, along with a dispassionate inventory of my father's injuries and symptoms: blunt-force trauma and lacerations to the head and torso, swelling and firmness of the abdomen, possible spinal injury. The patient was in shock and tachycardic. Blood pressure was sixty over forty—half-normal. As she spoke, she continued working, shaving spots in my father's chest hair and attaching electrodes to the bare skin.

"Shit," the driver said.

On the side of the driveway, inches from the hood of the ambulance, Diva flung her head up, eyes wild, and pivoted, more or less cantering on three legs with Fernando jogging after her. Then we were past them.

"That the horse that did the damage?"

"Yes."

"How'd it happen? Horse go berserk?"

*What happened? How did it happen? Did you do this?*

"She spooked."

We drove past the house. Even with the lights on, it looked abandoned.

"What's your name?" the driver asked.

"Roan."

"I'm Darius. You called nine-one-one? You did a good job. You kept your cool."

I hadn't been cool when I'd lashed out at Diva with the lead rope. I'd been cold.

"Is he going to die?"

"We're doing everything we can to see that he doesn't."

When we reached the gate we slowed to make the turn onto the road, but then we drove toward town and the hospital fast. Really fast.

I looked in the back. My father's head had been bandaged. The electrodes on his chest led to a monitor, but I couldn't see the screen or hear any beeps over the sound of the siren.

On the outskirts of town, Darius radioed the hospital we'd be arriving in five minutes, but we pulled up in less time than that. He and his partner rolled my father through the automatic doors of the ambulance entrance.

I followed them in time to see the gurney being rolled away by a bunch of people in scrubs and the paramedic who'd been in the back of the ambulance. Darius, standing in front of a counter staffed by a receptionist, waved me over.

"Roan, this is Anna. She needs you to answer some questions."

I looked toward the heavy pneumatic doors that had closed behind the gurney.

Anna followed my gaze. "We need to stay out of the way while the doctors work on him. You can help by giving us some information."

Darius and I both had paperwork to complete. He led me around the desk to an empty waiting room, where we sat side by side filling out forms on matching clipboards. My father's medical history was easy enough: He was never sick. He was invincible.

Except now, suddenly, he wasn't.

I wrote in his given name, which no one ever used, and then my own name as his emergency contact, followed by Eddie and Gertrude. Did he have a medical power of attorney? An advance directive? I checked *Don't know.*

The automatic glass doors opened. Gertrude rushed in, saw me doing paperwork, and took the chair on my other side.

"Eddie's parking the truck. What's happening?"

"I don't know. They took him in the back. Do you know who his doctor is?" I referred to the form. "His primary care physician?"

"Hendricks."

I wrote it in.

Darius took our clipboards to the receptionist, then went down the hall and through the doors to the ER.

Eddie hurried in just as Gertrude had, but now that my father was in the care of doctors, we could only wait. He sat down across from us.

"Have they told you anything?"

"Not yet."

After twenty minutes or so, both paramedics emerged from the back with the empty gurney, their faces unreadable.

"What's happening back there?" I asked.

"He's alive," Darius said.

"What does that mean? A heartbeat? Brain waves?"

If Diva had bashed his skull in, his heart could keep beating but his brain could be scrambled.

"He's in great physical condition, and that's in his favor," Darius said. "You acted quickly. You did everything right. Good luck, folks."

They left, and briefly, I felt abandoned.

I rested my head on Gertrude's shoulder.

A cell phone rang. Eddie reached into the pocket of his jeans and looked at the screen. "Yeah, Teo."

Faintly, I heard Mateo's voice.

"Call me back after Glenn sees her," Eddie said.

Mateo said something.

"Not yet." Eddie glanced at me. "Yeah, I will." He returned the phone to his pocket. "They caught Diva. She's pretty lame. Glenn's on his way."

I sat up. "Whatever he needs to do, I want to save her."

Eddie gave me a hard-to-read look.

"I'm not losing two horses in two days." I knew who was to blame for this, and it wasn't Diva.

"You want to clean up, sugar?" Gertrude said.

In the women's room down the hall, I scrubbed the blood from my skin and under my nails, but my shirt and jeans needed more attention than I could give them in a restroom.

When I came out, Eddie and Gertrude were talking quietly in the waiting room. Anna wasn't at her desk. Around the corner were the pneumatic doors that led to the ER. *Authorized Personnel Only*, warned a sign on one of the doors. I pushed the bar and slipped through as the doors parted.

He was the only patient, so no one had bothered to close the curtains around his cubicle. The half-dozen people working over him looked identical in papery pale yellow masks and gowns. They spoke in calm, competent voices, not barking orders like doctors in movies.

A tube ran down his throat. He was receiving an IV. The cervical collar and the bandage on his head had been removed, his thick hair had been shaved, and a halo immobilizer had been screwed into his skull. His scalp was bloody. His chest was purple and blue, and his abdomen was bloated. The rest of his clothes had been cut away. Urine drained into a bag hung low on the side of the gurney. It wasn't yellow but reddish brown—blood.

"What's she doing in here?" a woman said.

Half a dozen people looked my way.

"I'm his daughter."

"Out. We'll talk to you later."

In the waiting room, Eddie and Gertrude looked up as I approached. They'd only worry more if I told them what I'd seen. I didn't know what any of it meant except it was bad, and we all knew that much.

"I'm going outside for a minute," I said.

The night air was several degrees warmer than the hospital. I stood a few feet from the ER entrance and used my father's cell to call Will.

He didn't answer. The sound of his voice on the outgoing message nearly undid me, but I sounded fairly steady when I left my own message. "It's Roan. I'm calling from Daddy's phone." Forty-eight hours since I'd stopped thinking of him as "Daddy," the name felt strange on my lips. "Call me back at this number. We're at the hospital in Sheridan. He's been hurt . . . and he may not make it."

The breeze picked up, and my eyes teared. Crying might not be a bad thing. It might reassure Eddie and Gertrude that I felt something. I did, but I wasn't sure what.

The phone rang, and Will's number came up on the screen.

"Will?"

"I'm on my way. Are you all right?"

"I wasn't hurt. Diva trampled him. It was like she was trying to kill him."

More like I was trying to kill him.

On the other side of the smoked glass windows, Eddie was on his phone, too.

"We'll talk when you get here," I said.

I hung up and went back inside.

"Have him call me when he gets the results," Eddie said, "and be careful. Just because she's injured doesn't mean she won't strike out. . . . Nothing yet. . . . I will."

He disconnected.

"What?" I said.

"It's either a stress fracture or a torn suspensory ligament. They're taking her to Glenn's for X-rays and an ultrasound."

At least for now, Diva wasn't getting a needle in the neck.

"Okay. Thanks. And thank you both for being here."

"Where else would we be?" Gertrude said.

Eddie's leg jiggled. "Wish they'd tell us something."

I couldn't sit still, either. I paced and watched the double doors, but the next person to come into the ER wasn't a doctor or a nurse. It was Will.

I walked straight into his arms and buried my face against his neck as if we'd never broken up.

"You're okay?" he said.

"She didn't touch me."

"And you weren't hurt yesterday?"

"My shoulder's bruised. That's all." In fact, sharp pains radiated from my shoulder down my arm and across my back because he was holding me so tightly, but when he released me, I wanted nothing more than for him to hold me like that again.

He took a step back and looked at my shirt.

"Not my blood," I said.

"Glad you're here, Will." Gertrude stood up. "There's a vending machine somewhere. Coffee or hot chocolate?"

I looked at her numbly. It was the simplest of decisions.

"Eddie," she said, "give me a hand. Let's see what we find."

As they walked away, Will and I sat down on a padded bench.

"I was watching yesterday," he said. "You sure you're all right?"

"Yeah." My physical injuries were minor compared to the emotional gutting I'd undergone in the past two days. Minor compared to my father's injuries, too. Mine weren't life-threatening.

"What happened with your father?"

It could take a lifetime to answer that, but I said, "He was in the stall with Diva. He asked me for her halter, and I fumbled when I was handing it to him. She freaked."

He rubbed his thumb over the back of my hand. "It's not your fault."

There was no reason he had to know the truth—except that I deserved to tell it.

"When Gertrude and Eddie get back," I said, "let's go outside."

He nodded, and I leaned against him.

A man in scrubs and a yellow gown approached us, his mask pulled below his chin. He looked familiar, but I didn't know why.

"You're the daughter."

"Yes."

He looked Will over and was no more impressed with him than he was with me. Then I recognized him. Dr. Stubblehead. He'd been nicer when I'd been a patient. "I'm Dr. Campbell. Do you have an adult with you?"

"They went to find coffee." I thought about why he'd want an adult present, and cold overtook me, spreading from my core to my limbs.

"I suppose I can give you the update. He's suffered massive multiple traumas. There's bleeding in his brain and abdomen. The surgeon's scrubbing up."

I heard the dull thud of my father's skull hitting the wall, saw Diva's hoofs connecting with the back of his head. I began to shake inside. "Can I see him?"

"He's already in pre-op."

The shaking spread to the outside. "Don't let him die."

"The priority is to stop the bleeding and control the swelling in his brain, but there's also a fracture of the C4 vertebra, which has compromised the spinal cord."

I'd known several riders who'd sustained spinal cord injuries. The C4 was in the neck.

"Is the cord severed?" My voice was shaky, too.

"Yes."

With that one word, he took away every physical thing that made my father who he was. If he survived, he'd be a quadriplegic.

"Someone will talk to you when we know more," the doctor said, "but it's going to be a long night." He walked down the corridor toward the ER.

Will squeezed my hand. "You know this hospital is a really good trauma center, right?"

The shaking was out of control and I was cold inside and out by the time Gertrude and Eddie returned, each of them carrying two paper cups.

"What is it?" Gertrude asked immediately.

"The doctor came to talk to us." I started to repeat what he'd said, but I didn't get beyond "They've taken him to surgery" before my teeth started clacking together.

Will told them the rest. The emotions that preceded grief—apprehension, dismay—came over their faces.

"Here." Gertrude held out a paper cup. "Drink this."

I took it, hunching over it like it was a tiny campfire. The hot chocolate warmed my fingers through the cup.

"Do you want to call your mother?" She handed the other cup to Will.

"No." My hot chocolate was sloshing right to the edge of my cup.

Will took it from me. "What if we go outside and warm up? You're freezing."

"Go on," Gertrude said. "We'll come get you if there's any news."

Even in the warm air, I couldn't stop shaking.

"Let's get in the truck before you get hypothermia," Will said.

"Gertrude and Eddie won't know where we are."

"We're right here." He nodded toward his truck, in a parking place near the entrance. "We'll watch the door." He set the cups on the roof and took his keys from the pocket of his jeans.

He opened the door for me and I climbed in. He gave me one of the cups and I drained the hot chocolate, nearly tasteless and so hot that it scorched my tongue, but when he held out the other cup and said, "Here," I gulped it down the same way.

He opened the driver's door, retrieved the sleeping bag from behind the seat, and untied the cords. Then he got in the cab, turned sideways on the seat, and held out an arm in invitation. I leaned back against him. His legs were on either side of me, and as soon as he'd spread the sleeping bag over us, he put his arms around me. It was like being in a Will recliner. Plus, I had a good view of the glass doors that led to the waiting room.

"You're still shaking," he said. "Do you want the heater?"

"No. This is good."

Blue-white floodlights illuminated the exterior of the hospital, spilling into the truck like starlight. He rubbed my arms briskly, warming me, until the shaking stopped.

"Better?"

I nodded.

"I'm sorry about Jasper," he said. "I didn't realize until yesterday how risky eventing is."

It was the only sport in the world that required participants to wear their medical information on their sleeves, but no riders had died on that course yesterday. Only Jasper.

"I shouldn't have been riding this weekend. Jasper's dead because I did."

"A lot of horses went down. They're saying the course was dangerous."

"The course wasn't the problem."

"Okay." His tone was the same one I used with an agitated horse: *Okay. All right. Easy.*

Neither lying nor telling the truth was easy. I always did what I believed would keep me safe: obey my father, make him happy, make him feel good. Keep our secrets.

I took a deep breath, held it, and exhaled slowly. "Will . . . Jasper isn't the only bad thing that happened in Louisville. Daddy found out about us. He found my phone, and he read our texts."

"What did he do?" he asked slowly.

Say it. Don't say it.

Say it.

"He raped me."

Will exhaled sharply but didn't let go of me, didn't recoil. He was holding me too hard again, compressing my shoulder, breathing like he'd been running.

"It's gone on a long time," I said.

"How long?"

"I was six the first time, but he did other things before that."

His heart thumped against my back.

"Carrie's six. I . . ."

When he didn't go on, I sat up and turned toward him. He glanced down at his chest, where I'd been leaning, as if he'd spilled the rest of his words there.

"Will, if you can't hear it—"

"I can hear it." His face twisted. "I want to fucking kill him, but if you could go through it, I can hear it. Why didn't you tell me?"

I searched for an answer that had some dignity. "It was private."

That was what my father had said, but he wasn't wrong. My humiliation and shame were mine—to hold on to, to let go of . . . I didn't know yet. I only knew Will didn't have the power to make me feel better about the ugly, jagged truth that had kept me silent all these years: *It didn't always feel like abuse. Most of the time, it felt good. Most of the time, I liked it.*

"Do you need a doctor?" he asked.

I shook my head. I didn't require a doctor, or a police report, or a social worker. The physical abrasions and tears would heal naturally. I'd find a way to deal with the rest.

He held out his arms, and I let myself be drawn back into the Will recliner.

"I'm sorry. I'm sorry he did that to you. I'm sorry I never asked you about it."

"You didn't have any reason to."

He sighed. "No, I did. I could *feel* something wasn't right, but I kept finding ways not to know. I should've asked you outright."

"I'd have lied. I lied to almost everyone."

"Almost? You told someone?"

"My mother."

His shock traveled through him and into me. "Why didn't she stop it?"

"She didn't love me enough."

Another ugly, jagged truth. Mama's feelings about me weren't any more complicated than that.

Will pressed his lips to the top of my head.

"There's more," I said.

"I can hear it."

I smiled a little, but I took my time before I went on. "This afternoon"—instantly I was back in my father's closed-up, overheated room—"he said I wasn't going back to school, not even to take exams. He locked me in my room. My world was shrinking down to him and me." I was shaking again. "Tonight, during the walk-through, when he went into Diva's stall, I didn't fumble with that halter. I snapped the rope at her like a whip."

It sounded cold-blooded when I said it out loud, but killing or crippling my father hadn't been what I'd had in mind. I'd had *nothing* in mind. Something quicker and more primal than thought had been at work. The instinct to survive.

"I'm glad you did it." Will's voice was low, savage. "I wish Diva had killed him."

"If he dies, what happens to the farm? What happens to me?"

He scoffed. "You think he'd jeopardize the legacy?"

As soon as he said it, I understood my father would have arranged for whatever it took to protect his precious legacy. The legacy was the thing he loved, not me.

I knew that wasn't true, just like what would happen to me wasn't the only reason I didn't want him to die. But I wasn't ready to think about that yet.

EVENTUALLY, HIS ARMS clasped around me, Will dozed off.

I nearly did, too, but out of nowhere my body bristled with the memory of my father holding me down. Panic and fear stabbed through me like quills shooting out of my skin.

I breathed my way through it and eventually came back to myself and Will's arms, not my father's, and the cell phone lodged against my hip bone.

My phone had been small, easy to stash. This one was too big to fit comfortably in the front pocket of my jeans. I pulled it out and checked the time. 1:40 A.M.

I brought up the home screen. Dozens of icons popped up. For all those icons, my father used only a fraction of his phone's features. He made calls and texted and made pictures.

I tapped *Gallery*.

Thumbnails of Jasper and me populated the screen. They'd been made before and during the dressage phase on Friday. I enlarged the first image, Jasper and me leaving the arena, a mid-stride shot that showed his muscles in remarkable detail. My heart hurt.

I swiped through the photos. Jasper's final dressage test played out one image at a time in reverse chronological order. Then came pictures of me feeding him sugar cubes, signing autographs, talking to Eddie outside the barn at home, grooming Vigo, saddling Diva, in flight over jumps, pushing a manure cart, walking down the driveway with Vic.

Except for the sugar-cube photos, I hadn't been aware my father was photographing me. The pictures were luminous, some so beautifully lit and rich in depth that they looked like paintings, an incredible achievement considering they'd been made with a phone. I was mystified by his failure to share every one of them online, and then, although there was nothing obscene or in poor taste, an unsettling intimacy began to emerge. I was seeing myself through his eyes.

I came to a series of burst shots made at several frames per second, creating a slow stop-action movie that I envisioned him watching repeatedly. I was showing Will my horses. I knew exactly where my father had been standing—outside the feed room with Eddie—so he'd shot the images at a distance. Motes of hay dust starred the lens. In the rich, buttery light, how Will and I felt about each other was plain.

For weeks, my father had known I was lying to him.

A knock came at the passenger window of the truck, and I nearly levitated, fumbling with the phone as if I'd been caught stealing. Will started awake.

"Jesus," I said. "It's Gertrude." Our breath had condensed on the windows, but I recognized her general outline. I opened the passenger door.

Her eyes were watery. My stomach plummeted.

"A nurse just told us surgery's going well, but he'll be in there several more hours. You should go home."

"Home?" I repeated, stupefied by the scare she'd given me.

"Yes, home. We'll be here. Come back in the morning—real morning, when the sun's up. Will, can you take her home?"

"Yes, ma'am, if that's what she wants."

I hesitated. "All right. But you'll call me if there's news?"

"Of course. Safe home now."

The employee apartments and the farmhouse were dark, as was the barn, but the house was still lit. My father had never been casual about who had access to the house. None of the employees would have trespassed, even to turn out the lights.

Will stopped in front of the porch but made no move to get out.

"Will you stay?" I said.

He turned off the engine.

Inside, I switched off the porch light. Mirrored in the glass of one of the windows flanking the door, I looked like a character from a slasher flick.

"I need to clean up."

"I'll fix you some tea."

Upstairs, I started filling the tub. I returned to my bedroom, left my father's cell on my nightstand, gathered clean clothes, and retrieved the bourbon from my boot. I took a big swallow on the way back to the bathroom. It burned my throat. I set the bottle on the floor by the tub.

The blood on my shirt had soaked through to my skin. I peeled it off. No way was all that blood coming out. I'd throw it away tomorrow. For now, I dropped it in the hamper.

When the tub was full, I lowered myself into it, sucking in air as hot water hit torn flesh.

I took another drink of bourbon, pressed my fingertips into my eyes until agony became merely pain, and took a good look at myself. My shoulder was bruised from hitting the ground when Jasper went down. My breasts and hips bore marks from my father's fingers.

I wanted to get really, really drunk.

No, I didn't. I'd never be like Mama, weak and out of control.

But that didn't stop me from taking one more drink before I washed myself clean.

I dressed in a fresh T-shirt and sweats, picked up my bottle, and opened the door to the bedroom. Will had turned back the covers. A tray on my nightstand held buttered toast and a big mug of tea.

He straddled the seat of my desk chair, his chin resting on folded arms. His eyes went to the bottle.

"I'm not drunk."

He shrugged. "You've got a right to be."

I offered him the bottle. He took it and drank but remained in the chair while I sat on the edge of my bed and bit into the toast.

"Aren't you eating?"

"Not hungry." He capped the bottle and set it on my desk. "Just sleepy."

I hesitated. "Why don't you lie down with me?"

He didn't answer immediately. "You finished there?"

"Yes. I'm not really hungry, either."

He moved the tray to my desk and turned off the overhead light. My bathroom light was still on, and in semidarkness, he pushed off his sneakers.

"Don't get undressed." My voice was rocky.

"Just my shoes."

Both of us got under the covers, lying stiffly apart.

I could continue to allow my father to control me, or I could take control.

I moved closer to Will. He put his arm around me. Tentatively, I rested my head on his shoulder.

"Okay?" he said.

"I will be," I said, with more assurance than I felt.

# - Twenty-seven -

I WOKE UP in my usual state of denial—everything bad that had happened had been a dream—and then I became aware of arms around me. My body jerked to attention. Not a dream.

Also, not my father but a boy who loved me. His breath tickled the top of my head.

The piercing computerized beeps of the cell phone made me lurch for my nightstand.

"Eddie?"

"He made it through surgery."

I pushed back the covers. "I'll be right there."

"Take your time. He'll be in recovery a couple of hours."

Will made more toast and tea while I took a shower, but neither of us had any more appetite now than we'd had a few hours ago. Before we left the kitchen, he removed my fleece jacket from one of the hooks by the door. "Here."

"It's going to be ninety today," I said.

"Not in the hospital."

We had a stop to make first. Will turned the truck between the stacked white limestone walls at the base of his driveway. We followed its meandering path through the woods, crossed a bridge over a stream, and rounded a curve, and the house came into view, a series of staggered white cubes three stories high with floor-to-ceiling windows of black glass.

"Holy cow."

Will chuckled. "Yeah, it's unexpected, isn't it?"

We followed the driveway around the side of the house, pulled up outside the garage, and entered through a door to the kitchen, where his parents and sister were finishing their oatmeal at a granite-topped island.

"How's your father, dear?" Mrs. Howard asked as Will bent to peck her forehead with a kiss.

"Out of surgery," I said. "That's all I know."

"Tea or coffee?" Mr. Howard asked.

"Coffee. Thank you."

Will went upstairs, and I took a seat at the island.

Carrie, in her nightgown, her hair hanging over half her face, gazed at me with her visible eye. "Will talks about you a *lot*. Can I come see your horses?"

"When things settle down," Mrs. Howard said. "Roan's father was in an accident last night."

Carrie went still. "A car accident?"

Will's parents exchanged a look as Mr. Howard set a mug of coffee in front of me.

I added cream from a miniature pitcher. "He was hurt by one of the horses."

"Is he going to die?"

"I don't know," I said.

Mr. Howard held out his hand to his daughter. "Let's get dressed for school."

"I'm tired. I think I should stay home."

"Uh-huh. Let's go."

He picked her up, and she looped her arms around his neck, resigned to a school day.

"Anytime she hears the word 'accident,'" Mrs. Howard said, "she thinks someone's died."

Will came back wearing his school uniform, his tie unknotted, his hair damp.

"You're going to school?" Mrs. Howard said.

He nodded toward me. "She insisted."

The expression that streaked across his mother's face was too quick to read, but she said to me, "So you'll be all by yourself at the hospital?"

"Gertrude and Eddie have been there all night."

"I'll move some appointments around. That way, you won't be alone all day, and you"—she looked at Will—"won't worry."

Protest surfaced like a reflex, but I squelched it. I could use some support.


EDDIE AND GERTRUDE slouched in chairs in the ICU waiting room on the third floor. Gertrude's eyes were closed. A small collection of vending machine coffee cups was arranged in bowling-pin formation on the end table beside Eddie.

"Good timing," he said.

Gertrude sat up, stretching.

"They're moving him to a room. The critical care intensivist"—Eddie enunciated the words carefully—"is supposed to come talk to us."

"The what?"

"ICU doctor. That's what they call them now."

"Good to know."

He gave me a half smile.

We waited. I tried to visualize a good outcome. Maybe my father would be the world's healthiest, happiest quadriplegic. He was strong and athletic, so he had a shot at healthiest. There was no chance he'd be happy.

A petite woman in a physician's white coat approached.

"You're Mr. Montgomery's family? I'm Dr. Lopez. I'd like to talk to you about what's happening."

I absorbed the litany of damage done and repairs made. My father lay in a medically induced coma. A shunt drained the fluid leaking from his swollen brain. A ventilator breathed for him because the drugs used to keep him comatose relaxed his diaphragm muscles, which were also compromised by the spinal injury. The surgeon had removed his spleen and one-quarter of his liver. Because of internal bleeding, he'd received several liters of blood.

I couldn't form a single intelligent question. Gertrude and Eddie were silent, too.

"You can sit with him," Dr. Lopez said, "talk to him if you like, but he won't be responsive. Be prepared. He looks rough."

She led us down the hall to a nurses' station surrounded by glass-walled patient rooms. In turn, a nurse showed us to a room where a bald man with sunken eyes lay in a bed on the other side of the glass.

The ground started to drop out from under me, but this wasn't my father.

"This is the wrong room."

"No, sugar," Gertrude said. "It isn't."

\* \* \*

GERTRUDE AND EDDIE were ragged with stress and lack of sleep, but they were reluctant to leave until I convinced them Mrs. Howard planned to spend the morning with me.

When they left, I was as alone with my father as I could be in a glass-walled room.

I sat in a visitor's chair and looked down at my lap and listened to the horribly human sound of the ventilator, each inhale a gasp, each exhale a forceful puff.

I ventured a glance toward the bed. He was largely hidden behind a cluster of monitors and machines. A blanket covered him from mid-chest down. His shoulders were bare. His arms lay peacefully at his sides.

Chills had risen on my own arms. I pulled my fleece collar more tightly around my neck.

I wondered if he were cold.

Not that I cared.

With a mighty eye roll, I sidled between the monitors and among the hoses and tubes to touch his shoulder. Warm. Did he have a fever? I couldn't decipher all the numbers on the monitors, but I worked out blood pressure, oxygenation, heartbeat, pulse . . . and temperature, 100.2. But he was in ICU, and nurses were watching him.

My eyes followed the brace that led from his shoulders to the halo immobilizer. Sutures sprouted from his scalp. His face was swollen and misshapen, his eyes so blackened that they looked like empty sockets. A tube secured with gauze and tape jutted from his mouth and fed via hose to the ventilator. I lifted the edge of the blanket. Thick dressings covered the surgical incisions. Black and purple bruises splashed across his torso like paint.

I put the blanket back in place. Then I tugged it up to his shoulders.

"Knock knock," Mrs. Howard said from the open door. She held a large paper cup from Murphy's Coffeehouse. "Will said . . ." Her eyes moved past me. "Oh, my dear."

I extricated myself from the machines and hoses. "Thank you for coming."

She held out the cup. "Will mentioned you like hot chocolate." She pulled her chair close to mine, and we sat down. "What are the doctors saying about your dad?"

I relayed what Dr. Lopez had told us.

"We'll do whatever we can to help. You helped Will so much after Steve died." She smiled slightly. "Carrie wasn't kidding. He talks about you all the time."

Funny to think of Will telling his family about me when I'd have chewed my tongue off rather than mention him to my father.

Mrs. Howard stayed until late morning, when she had to leave for a meeting she hadn't been able to cancel. We were strangers, really, but she was kind and easy to be with, like Will. I wondered what it would have been like to grow up in the Howard family instead of mine, but it was a fantasy I couldn't sustain—I didn't have enough experience with warm and loving parents—so instead I began to think about who I should notify of my father's accident.

I searched the contacts list on his cell for Vic and sent a text: *It's Roan. Daddy's in ICU.*

He called immediately.

Vic knew horses were living creatures who sometimes spooked, and he knew Diva, so he absorbed the *how* of the accident without question. He was more concerned about my father's condition and prognosis, but after I told him, there was silence. I checked the screen to see if the call had dropped. Then I heard a sob.

Stonily, I listened to Vic cry for my father. When he stopped, he offered to write a statement on my behalf about both accidents, my father's and Jasper's, for release on the SNN website.

Instantly I was resistant. No one would speak for me ever again.

"I'd appreciate your posting it," I said, "but I'll write it."

"Okay, but your phone will blow up as soon as it's up. Do you want to refer people to me?"

I hesitated, but he'd only be a conduit for information. He wouldn't be speaking for me, not the way my father had.

"Yes, thanks. I'll send something over."

After we hung up, I dictated a text. I aimed to keep the statement short and simple, but when I reviewed it, I'd only covered the facts. There was no warmth to it. I added, *Jasper was one of a kind. So is my father.*

One of a kind, yes. One kind of man, no. Everyone saw him differently. Only I saw all the pieces of him.

*We would appreciate your good wishes. I'll update Vic Embry on my father and Diva as more information is available. Please contact him with any questions.*

*Perfect*, Vic replied by return text.

Probably not, but at least the words were mine—no *Love and hugs.*

Vic sent me a link to the post on the SNN website, and shortly afterward, my father's phone began beeping with calls and plinking with texts. Not everyone followed instructions. I dismissed most of the calls, but I talked to Frank and texted with Jamie for nearly an hour. Then I searched for information about induced comas, traumatic brain injury, and C4 paralysis. I read about specialty hospitals and rehab facilities and imagined my father slowly turning to dust in a room off a dim, echoing hallway.

Will wished Diva had killed him, and were my father conscious, he'd consider death a kindness. But I didn't foresee myself kicking the ventilator plug out of the wall, even as an act of mercy.

AFTER SCHOOL, WILL saw my father for the first time since he'd had dinner at Rosemont.

His face was set and hard when he came into the room, but at the sight of my father, his anger and hatred gave way to shock.

"Jesus. He doesn't look . . ."

"Alive?" I suggested.

He shook his head. "Human."

In the late afternoon, we drove to Will's house, where he went inside to talk to his parents while I waited in the truck with the windows down, listening to the stream bubbling under the bridge that crossed their driveway.

He returned shortly with a duffel bag, which he tossed in the back of the truck.

"Any resistance?" I asked.

"Nothing significant. You know how parents are." He stopped. We had different frames of reference for how parents were. "They're in there reassuring each other that the circumstances are special."

We stopped next at the farmhouse, where Gertrude fed us an early supper of chicken and dumplings while we discussed a schedule for the next few days. She and Eddie would take turns sitting with my father during the day. I'd walk to the hospital after class and relieve whoever was there.

Eddie poured himself a pint glass of Guinness. "What about Arlington?"

I shook my head, saying no to both Arlington and more dumplings. "I'm going to withdraw. I'll shoot for Bromont."

"And training?"

"Frank offered to help."

He nodded.

"But I'd rather train with you. You know as much as Frank. You know as much as my father."

Eddie studied his glass. Below the caramel-colored foam, the Guinness looked like creosote. "When do you want to start?"

"Tomorrow."

"Why don't you wait until exams are over?" Gertrude suggested.

I shook my head. "I've already missed three shows, and Bluegrass . . ." Bluegrass had been a disaster in all regards. "Arlington will make five. I can't lose any more ground if I'm going to have a shot at three-stars next year." Three-star competitions were prime hunting ground for the U.S. team. I looked at Eddie. "We may need to add some winter shows. And I'll need another horse."

"One thing at a time," Eddie said. "I'll see you at the barn at six tomorrow morning, ready to ride."

Gertrude wasn't as clueless about my ambition as Mama had been. She might not understand why I was so driven, but she accepted that I was. "Tomorrow morning's going to come early. Go get your things, sugar. I made up the guest room for you."

"Thanks, but I'm staying at the house."

"By yourself?" She started to shake her head. "I don't . . ." Her eyes landed on Will, and the head shaking stopped. "Oh. Not by yourself."

She appealed to Eddie, but he held up his hands in immediate surrender.

She turned her version of a stern expression on me. "Can I talk to you?" Without waiting for an answer, she stepped outside on the porch. I followed her. The sunset was graying into dusk.

"You know your daddy wouldn't want Will spending the night."

"It isn't his decision."

"Sugar, please don't put me in this position."

"It isn't your decision, either," I said gently. "We can argue about it, but it won't change anything."

Her thoughts were as plain as if they'd been printed on her face: What had happened to the obedient girl who'd never defy her father?

She broke eye contact. "Do you have condoms?"

Will kept a supply in his glove compartment. We wouldn't need them, but there was no way Gertrude would believe that, so I nodded.

"I detected some resistance," Will said when we left.

I glanced at him. "Nothing significant."

It was early for bed, but we'd been functioning on only a few hours of sleep, so we went upstairs to my room. I snagged last night's T-shirt and sweatpants from my unmade bed and went into my bathroom to change.

When I emerged, he'd changed into a T-shirt and sweats, too.

"Bathroom's all yours," I said. "And I hope you don't have the wrong idea."

"About what?"

"Sex. It's not . . . on the menu."

"Didn't think it was. Can I use your toothpaste?"

I got under the covers, reassured, and when he joined me, I didn't hesitate to move close to him and rest my cheek on his shoulder. His arms went around me.

The chirping of tree frogs and crickets through the open window drowned out the memory of the ventilator—gasp, puff—and the faint scent of horse replaced the antiseptic hospital odor, and, finally warm, I sank into sleep.

The floorboard in the hall creaked, and my father said my name.

I convulsed with fear, my whole body taut, my skin crackling, my pulse crashing like cymbals in my ears—but there were no footsteps in the hall. I heard only the gentle sound of Will's breathing next to me.

TWO DAYS LATER, a basket of Confections skin-care products arrived with a note conveying thoughts and prayers from Elise and Tanner but reminding me we were working with a time constraint. If I wanted to proceed with the contract, was there a guardian who could sign it?

The next morning after my dressage lesson, I asked Eddie, "Do you know whether I have a legal guardian?"

"You have two. Gertrude and me. You didn't know?"

My first thought was *That son of a bitch*. He'd played me when he'd threatened to fire them. He'd never intended to get rid of them; it was just a threat to keep me in line. But my second thought was more momentous: Their guardianship meant that even if my father died, I could stay at Rosemont. The farm and the horses wouldn't be sold. My third thought was a more muted relief: It wasn't Mama. The custody agreement had been irrevocable. *All sales are final.*

"Didn't he tell you?" Eddie said.

"I'm sure he did. I just forgot."

As if.

I told Eddie about the Confections offer. "He'd have signed the contract at Bluegrass if they'd put it in front of him." Or, value to the team be damned, he might have been too pissed by my perceived flirtation with Tanner. I squeezed a spongeful of water over Vigo's head. He snorted, splattering me with water and slobber.

"What do you want to do?" Eddie asked.

Every athlete out there wanted to be the face of something— sneakers, cameras, sports drinks. I wasn't philosophically opposed to selling lotion, but since Eddie had asked, I told him.

"All I've ever wanted to do is ride . . . but Daddy says endorsements add value to me as a prospect."

He started coiling up the hose in the wash rack. "He's right."

My father had managed my career capably. Rejecting good advice simply because it came from him would be self-defeating.

"Okay," I said. "I'll do it."

Diva came home that afternoon, her off foreleg wrapped from knee to hoof in a thickly padded gel cast. Glenn had ordered months of stall rest for her, which promised to be miserable for everyone.

He stood outside her stall with me after she was settled. "A tear in the suspensory ligament could be career-ending, and even if it isn't, knowing this mare? She'll reinjure that leg. You may have to put her down after all."

"I can if I have to, but I want to give her a chance."

"Fair enough."

After he left, I searched Diva's eyes for a glint of acknowledgment. We shared a secret. We'd saved each other.

She pulled one of her ugliest faces, ears flat, nostrils flared, teeth bared. She looked like an alien.

At least she was consistent.


I STUDIED FOR finals out of habit, but my longing for the semester to end swarmed through my brain like a cloud of gnats. Will studied more than I did, his concentration aided by weed, but the edible candies his parents supplied tasted strange and made me dull. We hid them in the same riding boot where I stowed my bourbon. Self-medicating with a secret stash didn't bode well for my determination not to be like my mother, but I wasn't drinking at all—much—and I only ate half a candy sometimes to help me sleep.

Every day, Vic forwarded get-well emails from fans. Former competitors reminisced about my father's generosity when he won and grace on the rare occasions he lost. Students from his clinics sent messages describing how he'd transformed their riding, their relationships with their horses, their lives.

Mine, too.

He had a lot of visitors—Will's parents, Mrs. Kenyon, Frank, Jamie, Mateo, everyone who worked at Rosemont. A few times, Chelsea came with Will and sat with me. She didn't try to fill the silence like she usually did. I appreciated the lack of chatter.

I had enough of it inside my head. It got louder during the quiet hours I spent alone with my father, and something in its tenor prompted me to return to the images on his phone again and again, until I understood.

It was repugnant and self-centered, and it had led him—and me—to do terrible things, but the man who'd made these photos loved his daughter.

It was hard to understand. Harder to accept.

NIGHT BROUGHT MY best and worst times.

The best was the walk-through, when the immaculate barns and happy horses—plus Diva—gave me a sense of peace. But even my best time wasn't perfect. The walk-through connected me not just to my father but also to what was *good* in him, which wasn't the high-minded connection it might have seemed. The good in him had kept me off balance and made me believe things could be different.

I tried to find my own good. I tried to love the girl who'd been complicit, to hold her softly, and to find peace with the hard truth about myself: I'd rather be complicit than be a victim. What my father and I had done had been abhorrent, and though I knew he was to blame, I wouldn't render myself powerless by embracing victimhood or even survivorship. My father had done everything he could to take away my power, and he hadn't succeeded. I wasn't about to give it away. What came after survival? There had to be something else.

My absolute worst time was when the nightmares came. The floorboard creaked, Jasper fell away beneath me, my neck was broken. Sometimes my twitching and whimpering woke Will, who woke me. We'd go downstairs and find an old movie and watch Bette Davis or Humphrey Bogart until both of us fell asleep on the sofa, or we'd stay in bed, whispering together like someone might overhear us. The movies were a distraction and some of what we whispered was ugly and dark, but the distraction and the darkness alike broadened and deepened what was between us.

"You know, it's a different world for girls now," Will said one night out of nowhere. I could tell he'd been working up the courage to say something.

"Oh?" I said cautiously.

"A lot of athletes have spoken out, girls who were abused by coaches, team doctors, judges. It's not a secret women have to keep to their graves. It has nothing to do with them, what happened to them."

"Yeah," I said.

"You ever think about doing that? Coming forward about what your father did?"

"I'll think about it," I said, but I wouldn't. I'd spent a lot of hours alone in the hospital room with my father, and now that I had free access to the internet, I'd conducted a lot of searches. The athletes who'd spoken out as part of Me Too had done so not only to seek justice for themselves but also to protect others who might be hurt by the same abusers. My father wasn't a threat to anyone anymore, and I was the only person he'd hurt. He'd never been interested in other girls, only me. Maybe I should start my own movement: Only Me. I'd found my own path to justice, and the only person I needed to protect was myself.

THE DAY AFTER school ended, Will began working for his parents. He picked me up at the hospital at five, texting me from downstairs rather than coming up. When I joined him in the truck, he was grimy with concrete dust and sweat.

The hours I had spent at school I now spent shadowing Eddie, learning as much as I could from him. After lunch, he or Gertrude gave me a lift to the hospital, often staying with me an hour or two.

"He'd be proud of you," Eddie said one afternoon. "Picking up and carrying on. I mean, he *will* be proud, when he wakes up."

"If he wakes up."

Eddie grunted. "You're like him. You insist on seeing the worst. That's how both of you come at everything, always taking the ballbuster head-on. Have some hope."

"*Hope* leads to disappointment. I *hoped* he wouldn't kill Bailey."

"Bailey?" Eddie frowned, puzzled. "He couldn't keep a dog with that temperament, and he couldn't give him away. It was a liability issue."

The gap between what other people knew and what I knew was unbridgeable. I couldn't blame Eddie for what he didn't know. Gertrude might have been uneasy about some of the things she'd overheard and seen—her intuition had been accurate—but

Eddie had witnessed Daddy's professionalism and affection for me day after day at the barn and at shows, and those things had been genuine, too.

There was a rap on the doorframe.

"We have some good news," Dr. Lopez said.

SCANS PERFORMED THAT morning revealed that the swelling in my father's brain was subsiding; the neurologist would begin lowering the high doses of barbiturates and opioids keeping him unconscious.

For days, I detected no difference, but the doctors said he had definitive sleep-wake cycles. Then the changes became obvious. He'd frown or grimace, and compared to the stillness of the coma, it was impossible for me not to interpret it as emotion or pain rather than muscle contraction. Once, when a nursing assistant dropped a tray of metal instruments right outside his room, his eyes opened, but his gaze was vacant, and his eyes drifted shut again.

That night, I had a new nightmare. Police officers and attorneys pelted me with accusations. I tried to defend myself by telling them what he'd done, but my voice was air.

I woke up freezing and sweating and shaking, but for once I hadn't woken Will. I contorted my way out from under his arm and went downstairs. I took a fresh bottle of bourbon from the liquor cabinet into the study and curled up in the chair behind the desk.

I took a shot. Option one: Full consciousness. My father would wake up, know things, communicate. There was virtually no chance he'd remember the accident, but if he did, if he told,

I had my own story to tell. My voice wasn't just air. Nor would it ever be again.

*Here's to Me Too*, I thought. *Or Only Me.* Whatever, it merited its own shot.

Option two, shot three: Minimal consciousness. Breathe on his own, open his eyes, and sometimes have the ability to recognize objects or commands, the equivalent of a dog with middling intelligence.

Option three, shot four: Persistent vegetative state. Breathe on his own, open his eyes, but lack any cognitive function.

Option four, shot five: Death. That looked less and less likely—and it wasn't even what I wanted.

I'd told Will what had happened between my father and me was private, and I'd meant that. I didn't need the whole world to know what he'd done. I only needed my father to know. I needed him to live with full knowledge of who he'd been, what he'd lost, and who he was now. I needed him to be shattered by the same fear and pain and despair that had shattered me.

WEANING HIM FROM the ventilator was the next milestone. Dr. Lopez and an ICU nurse stood by when the respiratory therapist disconnected it for the first time. I hovered near the foot of the bed, holding my own breath.

My father's diaphragm expanded, allowing his lungs to fill with air. He could breathe on his own.

His time off the ventilator was increased every day, and in less than a week the tube that ran down his throat was removed and the ventilator was rolled away.

Free of the machine, he began to look more like himself. His hair was growing back. The surgical staples had been removed; without them, the scars looked vulnerable. He'd lost muscle tone and weight, but every day he showed improvement. He opened his eyes again, and then often. He didn't focus on anyone or anything, but he could track the general direction of movement and sound.

One afternoon, his eyes rested on me. They'd lit on me before in passing, but this was different.

"Daddy?"

He smiled, not a reflexive grimace, but a gentle curving of his mouth. Then he croaked, "Hey, darlin'."

THE FIRST THING he understood was that he was paralyzed. Dr. Lopez broke the news to him with practiced sympathy. He tried to bear it with stoicism, clinging to the pride that had always run through him like blood, but in this new existence he'd woken up to, pride failed him, and he cried.

Not once had I seen my father cry. I thought I would throw up. I swallowed the hot spit flooding my mouth and pulled some tissues from the box on the table beside the bed and blotted his tears.

"It's going to be okay, Daddy."

Where had that come from?

He sobbed harder. I struggled to hang on to the curried chicken salad I'd had for lunch.

"Can't—can't—"

The monitors beeped so rapidly that the sounds harmonized in a long, high-pitched whine.

Dr. Lopez administered a sedative. It took effect almost immediately, and my father's sobs dwindled into small, broken sounds.

"Advances are made every day in spinal cord regeneration research," Dr. Lopez said.

My father's eyes were already heavy-lidded, but he looked up at me with an expression of defeat and fear and cynicism. Only the cynicism was familiar. He'd never benefit from today's research, and he knew it.

Over the next few days, a combination of drugs and depression kept him quiet. He roused enough to greet Gertrude and Eddie by name, but in a hoarse, halting voice, he requested no other visitors. His speech was punctuated by breaths in unnatural places and long pauses while he searched for words, failed to find them, and frequently lost his train of thought.

Doctors and therapists gave him simple commands: Close your eyes, stick out your tongue, look at me. They asked questions meant to evaluate his mental state and administered tests of memory and organization. He took little interest in his performance, at times not even acknowledging the person attempting to interact with him.

I sat on the periphery of the busyness generated by medical personnel circulating in and out of his room. Now and then he gave me the same fleeting but oddly sweet smile he'd given me when he'd first regained consciousness, but mostly I caught him watching me with a sad, baffled expression.

Diva had literally bashed his head in. He'd nearly died. He couldn't possibly remember what I'd done.

THE SPEECH PATHOLOGISTS worked with him every day. One of them was Harold Moon's sister, Kelly.

"Do you remember what happened?" she asked him one day.

"Yes." His eyes shifted to me. "Hurt."

A chill slid from my tailbone to the top of my head.

"Do you remember how you were hurt?" Kelly asked.

"Hurt. Why . . ." He squeezed his eyes shut and wrinkled his nose, casting about for a word that eluded him.

"You were hurt by one of the horses," I said. "Do you remember?"

"I hurt."

"Does he hurt now?" I whispered to Kelly. The neurologist had said the nerves branching out from his spinal cord were going haywire. He couldn't feel external stimuli, but he could feel nerve pain.

"Are you in pain?" she asked.

"No." He scowled and looked directly at me. "Why are you here?"

It was the most complex sentence he'd uttered since he'd been awake—and it revealed complex thought.

I answered with caution. "Of course I'm going to be here, Daddy."

A single tear ran down his cheek. "Why, darlin'?" Then he began crying so hard that he started to gag.

"Can you speak?" Kelly asked.

He kept gagging. It sounded like he was gargling with mucus. Kelly rang for the nurse and began pushing on his chest to help him expel the phlegm.

First one nurse came and then another, who paged Dr. Lopez. With all the people and equipment, there was no room for me. I waited outside the glass and watched while they tried to prevent my father from choking to death.

Once again, he was sedated.

Kelly joined me. "It must be hard to see him like this. But he'll get better."

"He's a quadriplegic. That's not changing."

"His outlook will improve, his speech, even his memory."

"His memory?"

"Speech and memory can improve with time and practice."

His memory was already better. That was why he looked at me with so much sadness and confusion and wondered why I was here.

I should have kicked that plug out of the wall when I had the chance.

"I THINK HE remembers," I told Will that evening when he turned off the shower.

The shower curtain whisked back, and he stuck his head out of the bathroom, his hair dripping. "What?"

"I think he remembers what I did."

"Between the accident and the coma, he's pretty fucked up."

"He knows something. I can tell from the way he looks at me. Today he asked why I was there. Why would he ask that?"

Will was quiet for a moment. Then, his face grim and reluctant and determined, he said, "What if I go with you tomorrow?"

Will could barely tolerate being in the room when my father had been comatose. He'd deliberately stayed away since my father had regained consciousness.

"It's up to you," he said, "but I think we should find out what we're up against."

"Okay," I said slowly. "But if I'm right and—"

My father's cell phone beeped rapidly. I didn't recognize the number, and Vic was still taking most of the calls, but I answered. "This is Roan."

"This is your mother," said Mama.


SHE MET WILL and me in the lobby of the hospital the next afternoon, tall and slim in high heels and a wraparound dress. She'd clearly been spending more on antiaging treatments. She was almost unrecognizable, her face as smooth as a mask. Her hair was still long, still glossy black. Life without my father and me suited her.

She moved to embrace me.

I could have used that hug the day after Thanksgiving, but I didn't want it anymore. I remained stiffly by Will's side, holding his hand, and Mama dropped her arms. She flushed. "You must be Will."

"I must be," he replied.

"Is there somewhere the two of us can talk?" she asked me.

"I thought you were here to see Daddy."

"I'll see him, but I want to talk to you first. Will, if you'll give us some privacy—"

I gripped his hand. "No. He's part of this, too."

The three of us sat in a small grouping of chairs, Mama across from Will and me.

"Are you still riding?"

"Are you still drinking?"

"As a matter of fact," she said, "I'm forty-two days sober."

"How's John Dashwood?"

"Learning to windsurf."

I envisioned him braced on the board, holding the sail steady, toupee flapping in the breeze. He'd been worth coming back for. I hadn't.

It was my turn to say something, but my jaw was locked. She'd called me. She'd come to Sheridan. She could do the talking.

"The hospital wouldn't give me any information. How is he?"

"Paralyzed. Get to the point, Mama. What do you want?"

I hadn't let go of Will's hand. I could feel his discomfort, but also his resoluteness. He wasn't going to bail on me, no matter how uncomfortable this conversation became.

"I called so many times to hear your voice," she said, "but you always hung up. Then the landline stopped working. I didn't want to call your father's cell, but since he's so badly injured, I didn't think he'd be using it."

My heart took up all the space in my chest. I'd been right. Mama was Anonymous.

"You hung up, too," I said. "Why didn't you say anything?"

"I wasn't ready. But . . . I want to tell you I'm sorry."

"For what?"

"The day I left, all I could think about was getting away. I was too beaten down to care who or what I left behind."

She was apologizing for not caring. How could I forgive that?

"When I said I had to take care of myself, I didn't know whether I could. It's the hardest thing I've ever done."

"Eleven million dollars must have made it easier," I said.

She pressed her plump, sculpted lips together. Fillers had reshaped her mouth. "You're not going to give me a chance, are you?"

I hated the part of myself that would have taken her back in a heartbeat just so I'd have a mother. But Mama had never been the mother I needed; she never would be. The only thing I'd ever needed from her was protection from my father, and now I'd taken care of that myself.

"Let's go see Daddy," I said, "and get this over with."

In his room, my father was sleeping.

There wasn't nearly as much equipment in his room as there had been initially, but he still wore the halo, still had a catheter.

"Oh, my God."

The horror in Mama's voice was only an initial reaction brought on by shock. She raised her chin and her voice. "You fucking bastard. You deserve this."

"And what do you deserve, Mama? You never stopped it. You never protected me."

She hadn't come back to Sheridan to see me. She'd come back to gloat at my father's condition, and I wouldn't let her do it.

She managed to narrow her eyes. "Unreal. You're still choosing him."

I shook my head. "I'm choosing myself."


AFTER SHE LEFT—and there were no hugs, no *I love you*s or *Come see me*s—Will and I waited for my father to wake.

After a while, he said quietly, "We can do this another day. It was a lot, seeing your mother."

"No, you were right yesterday. I need to get in front of this."

Eventually, my father stirred—not a movement of his body, of course, but his eyebrows drew down, his forehead creased, and he opened his eyes.

"Hi, Daddy," I said.

He glanced toward my voice. "Hey, darlin'."

He sounded strained, but I went on. "How do you feel?"

"Pins and needles." The words were fairly clear. *Pins and*—raspy inhale—*needles.* The feeling was nerve-related. The neurologist said it might fade, or it might always be present.

I stood up, took the two steps to the bedrail. "I've brought a visitor." I glanced at Will, who joined me by the bed.

My father's expression grew wary. "Will Howard . . . from lit class."

That was how I'd introduced Will to him. Uneasiness crawled around inside me. "Do you remember anything else about him?"

"Supper."

I took Will's hand. "Right. He came to supper. He's my boyfriend. Did you know that?"

Tears filmed my father's eyes. "Hurt."

He could have meant anything, but I had a feeling he was referring to what he'd seen between Will and me in the barn—what I'd seen in the photos.

I steeled myself. "We told you Diva hurt you. Do you remember it?"

He struggled to hook words together. "You hurt."

Will tightened his hold on my hand.

My mouth was dry. "What do you mean?"

My father rolled his eyes to prevent tears spilling over. Had he learned that from me? His mouth turned downward. "I hurt *you.*"

My face prickled. "What?"

"I did bad things. Why are you here . . . after I did bad things?"

He was saying something else, which I couldn't understand. I was already pulling my hand free of Will's.

"Jesus," Will said. "He's asking you to forgive him."

"Please," my father said, as if Will hadn't correctly relayed the message.

How many times had I said "please" to him? Please don't. Please do. How hard had I worked my whole life to please him in every conceivable way?

I turned and walked away.


WILL CAUGHT UP with me by the elevator. "You all right?"

I punched the button again and held up my hand, indicating that I couldn't talk.

"I'll take you home," he said.

In his truck, I leaned my head against the doorframe and listened to the tires sing on the road. My emotions were colliding, but I held on, visualizing my fingers clawing into the earth, afraid the grief would swallow me.

But I could hold on only so long. At home, I went upstairs and curled up on my bed in crash position, protecting my heart and covering my head with my arms, but my grip slipped, and the tears came hard for the mother who didn't love me, for Bailey and Jasper, for the things I'd done and lost, the choices I'd made and never had.

Will spooned around me, holding me.

When I finally stopped crying, I felt like I'd been bled. I was clenched into such a tight ball that my muscles were stiff when I uncurled.

"Sorry. I don't know where all that came from."

Will gave a short laugh. "If anyone ever had reason to cry—" He kissed the back of my neck, a gentle, nuzzling kiss.

I turned on my back. He kissed my cheeks, my eyes, my mouth. His lips tasted salty from my tears. After four or five kisses, I became aware of a current beneath the gentleness, not only in him but in me, too.

He wiped my cheeks with his thumbs. "Okay?"

"Okay what?"

"Are you okay?"

"Yeah. I thought you meant is this okay." I glanced down. He was practically on top of me.

He didn't move. "Is it?"

"Yes." I took his face in my hands and kissed him.

# - Epilogue -

I REINED IN at the crest of the hill. Vigo mouthed the bit. He was always ready to give more, but it had been a hard season. We'd qualified for three-star next year. My career was on track. All of us—Vigo, my team, and I—had earned a rest.

Below me, Jasper's grave had grassed over. So had the one next to it. Diva, who had fought to the end, had deserved to be buried whole, too. In the summer, Will had laid sod on the graves to cover the barren mounds of earth. The grass, tall, waving in the breeze, looked like it might have grown wild.

Below the graves, the oak trees lining the driveway were brilliant with copper and crimson. The fall nights brought frost, but the days were blue-sky perfection, warm with a crisp edge.

My father sat in the sun that slanted under the roof of the front porch. On the footrests of his wheelchair, his feet skewed inward. I was sure that behind his sunglasses, his eyes were on me. He liked to watch me ride and offer notes on my form or observations about Vigo or Pocket, the gelding I'd bought from Frank. There was much he didn't remember about riding and horses, but I pretended what he said was relevant.

"Why are you good to me?" he'd asked once after he came home from months in rehab.

I wasn't, particularly. I chose not to hate him, but I also chose not to forgive him. He'd done something unforgiveable, but I was safe now, and I couldn't bring myself to be cruel.

"You're not who you were," I said.

He knew that, because he knew who he'd been. He knew what he'd lost. Above all, he knew what he'd done. That knowledge had broken him. There were no words that would take away his pain, and even if there had been, I wouldn't have said them.

It would have been easier, tidier, if things were all good, all bad, all one way or another. But they weren't. They never had been.

My whole life, he'd watched me. Coached me. Controlled me. Violated me. Made me his trophy. And now, his punishment was to continue to watch me: Watch me be free. Watch me be in love. Watch me hold the reins. Watch me make my own legacy. Watch me—and never have me again.

# - Acknowledgments -

AS NOBEL LAUREATE Orhan Pamuk said, writing is spending time alone in a room. While that's true, *Dark Horses* wouldn't have made the transition from manuscript to book if I'd been left strictly on my own.

Many thanks to the members of my critique group, No Coast Writers, who heard every word of *Dark Horses* in first-draft form and offered invaluable feedback: Mary-George (Bunny) Eggborn, Martha Grossman, Janet Majerus, Emily Mell, Kyra Ryan Ochoa, Penny Simi, Brian Tacang, and Susan Washburn. Thank you with sugar on top to Penny and Susan, whose backgrounds in psychology enabled me to validate my characters' motivations and actions. And thanks again to Penny and Janet, who talked me off the writerly ledge more than once. Thank you to Lauren Bjorkman and Eileen Wiard, who as newcomers to NCW beta-read the millionth draft.

Thank you to my former agent, Emma Sweeney of Emma Sweeney Agency, who saw the potential in my story, understood why I wrote it the way I wrote it, and supported me through numerous revisions.

My thanks also to my current agent, Margaret Sutherland Brown of Folio Literary Management. Margaret's keen editorial sensibilities helped me polish the story until it shone.

Alison Callahan of Simon & Schuster's Scout Books/Gallery Press imprints, you are my dream editor. Thank you for sharing my vision for this book and for taking a chance on me. My thanks, too, to Alison's assistant, Maggie Loughran. You rock.

Thank you to Layne Dylla, eventing groom extraordinaire, who vetted the eventing sections of the manuscript. Any errors that might have crept in are solely mine.

Thank you to Dr. Bessie Babits, DVM, with whom I discussed Diva.

Thank you to A. J. Calhoun, the critical care tech who advised me on how Monty's injuries would be treated.

My deepest thanks to Nancy Glasgow and the late John Glasgow for their generous support. Equally generous are my mother-in-law, Gloria E. Aragón, and sister-in-law, Cecilia Aragón. Thank you.

It's hard to find words that can adequately express my appreciation of and love for my husband, Frederick Aragón, who supported me in every way possible and always had time to listen to me hash out a problematic scene or character. You're more than a husband. You're a creative force, a fierce advocate, my forever partner, and my soft place to land.

And finally, my thanks to you, the reader. I wrote *Dark Horses* for myself, yes, but I also wrote it for you. Thank you for your time and attention. I hope you found the journey worthwhile.